T0383018

Praise for Kennedy Ryan

"Kennedy Ryan pours her whole soul into everything she writes, and it makes for books that are heart-searing, sensual, and life-affirming. We are lucky to be living in a world where she writes."

—Emily Henry, #1 *New York Times* bestselling author

"Few authors can write romance like Kennedy Ryan."

—J. L. Armentrout, #1 *New York Times* bestselling author

"Kennedy Ryan has a fan for life."

—Ali Hazelwood, *New York Times* bestselling author

"Ryan is a powerhouse of a writer."   —*USA Today*

"Kennedy Ryan is a true artist."

—Helen Hoang, *New York Times* bestselling author

"Ryan is a fantastic storyteller and superb writer."

—NPR

"Kennedy writes these gripping, touching, romantic, transporting books every single time."

—Denise Williams, author of *How to Fail at Flirting*

"The queen of hard-hitting romance books."

—Culturess

"Ryan always manages to ring her heavy stories with an aura of hope and a propulsive narrative that makes them impossible to put down."

—Entertainment Weekly

"Every time I think Kennedy Ryan can't possibly raise the bar any further, she proves me wrong in the most delightful way possible."

—Katee Robert, *New York Times* bestselling author

"Ryan creates characters who are deeply relatable, so compelling and lushly drawn that they feel like old friends."

—*BookPage*

UNTIL

I'm

YOURS

ALSO BY KENNEDY RYAN

THE BENNETTS

When You Are Mine

Loving You Always

Be Mine Forever

SKYLAND

Before I Let Go

This Could Be Us

ALL THE KING'S MEN

The Kingmaker

The Rebel King

Queen Move

HOOPS

Long Shot

Block Shot

Hook Shot

SOUL

My Soul to Keep

Down to My Soul

Refrain

GRIP

Flow

Grip

Still

STANDALONE

Reel

UNTIL

I'm

YOURS

KENNEDY RYAN

FOREVER

New York   Boston

This book is a work of fiction. Names, characters, places, and incidents are the product of the author's imagination or are used fictitiously. Any resemblance to actual events, locales, or persons, living or dead, is coincidental.

Copyright © 2016 by Kennedy Ryan

Cover design by Daniela Medina. Cover image by Shutterstock.

Cover copyright © 2024 by Hachette Book Group, Inc.

Hachette Book Group supports the right to free expression and the value of copyright. The purpose of copyright is to encourage writers and artists to produce the creative works that enrich our culture.

The scanning, uploading, and distribution of this book without permission is a theft of the author's intellectual property. If you would like permission to use material from the book (other than for review purposes), please contact permissions@hbgusa.com. Thank you for your support of the author's rights.

Forever

Hachette Book Group

1290 Avenue of the Americas, New York, NY 10104

read-forever.com

@readforeverpub

Originally published as an ebook and print on demand in February 2016

First trade paperback edition: May 2024

Forever is an imprint of Grand Central Publishing. The Forever name and logo are registered trademarks of Hachette Book Group, Inc.

The publisher is not responsible for websites (or their content) that are not owned by the publisher.

The Hachette Speakers Bureau provides a wide range of authors for speaking events. To find out more, go to www.hachettespeakersbureau.com or email HachetteSpeakers@hbgusa.com.

Forever books may be purchased in bulk for business, educational, or promotional use. For information, please contact your local bookseller or the Hachette Book Group Special Markets Department at special.markets@hbgusa.com.

Library of Congress Control Number: 2016286602

ISBNs: 9781538766934 (trade paperback), 9781455593293 (ebook)

Printed in the United States of America

LSC-C

Printing 2, 2024

Dedicated to all the girls who fight and survive.

Author's Note

I hope you enjoy *Until I'm Yours*, which tells the story of Sofie and Trevor, the sinner and the saint. The bad girl and the good guy who barrel through preconceived notions to find the heart of each other. We first met Sofie in *When You Are Mine*. To some she may seem irredeemable, but you'd be surprised what's going on in a person's mind and heart. I hope you'll give our bad girl a chance. :-)

To help safeguard your mental health, I just wanted to let you know there is discussion of sexual assault (in the past and not detailed or graphic).

Please read with care, and thank you for taking this journey with me!

UNTIL
I'm
YOURS

FIRST SIGHT

Trevor

The Big Apple. The city that never sleeps. If you can make it there, you can make it anywhere.

Blah, blah, blah, blah.

"How long are we here again?" I glance out the cab window and up at the flock of billboards flying overhead in the Times Square airspace, a confetti skyline swirled with Technicolor and kinetic lights.

"Three months, give or take," my assistant, Henrietta, says, not looking up from her phone.

I already miss my house in Atlanta. Despite the many miles I log flying all over the world, I'm a Southern boy at heart. A city like Atlanta makes an excellent home base for me. A world-class city with the charm and sensibility of a much smaller town. When I'm in New York, I feel on edge, like the Big Apple is taking a bite out of *me*. It's not an easy place to negotiate. It's a city bursting with possibility and creativity, but it requires a certain amount of armor. Feeling that way for three months…

"We're lucky to have your sister's place while we're here." Harold, my business partner and best friend of fifteen years, looks at our schedule on his iPad. "We have so many meetings at the UN this month. All the companies interested in buying us out are here in New York. We have several galas in the city over the next few weeks. Makes sense not to keep going back and forth, and just make this our base for a little bit."

"Yeah, at least we'll be staying in Brooklyn." I lean an elbow on the base of the cab window, considering the changing digital billboards while we're stopped at a traffic light. "Downtown gives me a seizu—"

The word freezes on my tongue when one advertisement in particular catches my attention. Or, I should say, the model does. Her name is nowhere on the ad, but it doesn't need to be. Sofie Baston's been one of the most recognizable faces in the world for more than a decade.

She's naked. Even though she's stretched out flat on her stomach with her chin propped on her hands, breasts pressed to the floor, she's obviously naked. Her hair, famously silver and gold, is ruthlessly scraped back, exposing the flawless bone structure of her face. It's rare to see someone like her wearing no makeup at all, but her face is completely bare. Matter of fact, the product she's promoting is called BARE.

BARE: Skin care so good you'll have nothing to hide.

She's naked, no cosmetics at all, and yet her eyes make a lie of that tagline. She's utterly exposed, and though her green eyes are the clearest I've ever seen, they yield nothing.

"You were saying?" Harold wears a knowing grin, glancing from my face to the billboard before it swipes to the next product being advertised. "I hope you'll be less obvious when we meet her in person tonight, Bishop."

"Tonight?" I frown. "What are you talking about?"

"That's Ernest Baston's daughter," Henrietta pipes in, eyes still fastened to her phone. Sometimes I think she has eyes in the back of her head under that ponytail. "She'll be at the Bennett charity dinner tonight. They're at your table, if I'm not mistaken."

I look back at the billboard even though a different image has taken its place. I still see her as vividly as when she stared back at me with those guarded green eyes.

Even when we're several blocks away and have started discussing our upcoming trip to Cambodia, I'm still wondering how a girl naked on the side of a building managed to hide in broad daylight and show nothing at all.

CHAPTER ONE

Sofie

Sofie, over here!"

"One more shot, Sof."

"Could we get one of you by yourself?"

My date moves a few feet ahead, leaving me to stand alone, a lightning rod in the storm of flashing bulbs and the chaos of shouts and snapping shutters. A carnival of exhibitionism, and me the main attraction. Red carpets and runways. There's no place like home.

I stop and strike a pose. Body in profile. Face front. Breasts up. Hips forward. Knee bent. Head high. Like a horse, I could fall asleep standing this way. A very well-bred, expensive horse, and I dare anyone to bet against me.

"Who are you wearing tonight, Sof?"

God, who did I settle on? Several of my favorite designers sent dresses over, and for the life of me…I glance down at the clover green shantung sheathing the long line of my body as if the designer's name might be emblazoned there. Cardinal rule of red carpet—never forget who you're wearing.

"Elie Saab." I lift the hem of the dress mere inches to reveal the glittering glory of my shoes. "Giuseppe's."

I nod my head once and offer a smile before moving down the carpet to join my date.

Michael "Rip" Ripley. Last year's MVP, former Heisman winner and my future ex-boyfriend. This may be the last night we'll share the spotlight. He won't see it coming, but it needs to come.

Actually, so do I. Maybe it won't hurt to wait just one more night before I cut him loose. He is brilliant below the belt. He has this thing he does with his fingers and his tongue while managing to look right into your eyes. Part creepy, part perfection. He *is* a quarterback, so I guess excellent hand-eye coordination should be expected.

"You think there will be more press inside?" That eager light in Rip's eyes reminds me why it *has* to be quits. Probably tonight. Sadly, not even one more visit below stairs.

He wants all of this more than he wants me. I get it. I grew up in a world of calculation, and the most calculating player of them all stares back at me from the mirror every morning. I look her right in the eyes with no regrets, but this—all of this—doesn't feed me. I suspect Rip has quickly become addicted to the spotlight, to the attention. He *needs* it, and I'm allergic to needy. I feel a breakout coming on like a dreaded pimple knotting below the surface of our brief and very public relationship.

We've been going out for less than a month, and he's already shipping us. Looking for ways to combine our names.

"There may be some press inside," I finally respond to his question. "But the worst of it's over."

"Worst?" Rip frowns, a quick bend of his dark blond brows. "This is what you do, Sof. I thought you loved it."

"Yeah, well, I've been doing it half my life. It gets old."

"Not for me. Not yet." He flashes his Colgate smile—literally, he just signed the contract today—and takes my hand. "I'm just getting started."

And I'm ready to stop. Oh, there will still be red carpets at fund-raisers like these, and endorsements and the occasional show, but I've been modeling since I was eighteen years old. In fifteen years I've scored every major cover. Worn all the elite designers. Been through every Fashion Week on repeat year after year. The catwalk is littered with kittens, girls still in high school. It's a girl's game, one that requires constant vigilance. Too much vigilance for something I find means less to me than it ever has before.

My mind wanders to the meeting scheduled with my team tomorrow to strategize the next phase of my career. My first natural smile of the night moves my mouth from the plastic facsimile I offered the cameras to the closest thing to real I'll show in public. My plans for this next stage of my life are completely my own, and they excite me. Maybe I'm jaded, but it takes more and more to excite me these days. That's probably why I've kept Mr. Hand-Eye around for the last month.

Once inside Cipriani, I glance around one of New York's most elegant ballrooms, its Greek revival columns studded with muted lights. Floral arrangements of gold, cream, and rose serve as elaborate centerpieces for each table. The seventy-foot Wedgewood ceiling hovers over the scene like an elegantly painted sky.

"I know I should know." Rip bends his head, the warm breath of his words at my ear. "But what is this event for again? They kind of all run together after a while."

"Uncle Martin is honoring some entrepreneurs for their philanthropic efforts. An excuse for rich people to dress up and eat and have their pictures taken."

"Martin Bennett isn't actually your uncle, though, right?"

"No, but he's my father's closest friend. Daddy was a huge part of building Bennett Enterprises, and he's Uncle Martin's right hand." Yet another natural smile touches my lips. A tiny shrug lifts my bare shoulders. "His son, Walsh, and I grew up very close. Our families took vacations together. We went to the same schools here in New York. We were...well, it was nice."

"You and Walsh ever..." Rip lifts and lowers his eyebrows suggestively.

So there are still some people who don't know every detail of my life that's been blared in tabloids and proclaimed on TMZ as gospel truth. I can't decide if I'm pleased or insulted by Rip's ignorance of my past with Walsh.

"Yeah, we dated a few years back." A bitter pill lodges in my throat, but I force myself to swallow it and say the next words. "That was, of course, before he married his wife, Kerris."

Rip glances at the card the hostess handed us when we entered, and scans the room until his eyes rest on a table near the stage. He points the card in that direction.

"Isn't that them at our table?"

What did I do to deserve this? Who am I kidding? I've done a lot more to deserve much worse, but it seems like a particularly cruel punishment to seat me with Walsh and Kerris Bennett. I spent half my life certain that Walsh and I would marry, that we'd be the envy of all our friends and pretty much the civilized world. Instead, envy pinches *my* heart. They had twins not even two years ago, and Kerris's petite frame shows a small baby bump. She's pregnant again. Already? What are they, rabbits? It's obscene to be that fertile.

And obscene to be that happy.

As I watch, Walsh presses his hand to Kerris's back, seating her and dropping a kiss on her dark hair. Their eyes lock for an extra second, something passing between them that makes me feel like a Peeping Tom. Something that walls out everyone around them for those few moments.

It doesn't hurt anymore, seeing them together, but a whole night of it could drive me to drunkenness and disorderly conduct, two offenses I've avoided for more than a year. There should be a token for that, like a sobriety coin or something. Though my sins have been anything but anonymous. I'm a pap's field day. I know it, but can't make myself care what they report. Most of it's true, and all the fucks I had to give ran out years ago.

I can't figure why I'd be at their table. My mother chairs this event. She wouldn't torture me this way. Mother wouldn't, but Daddy...

Speak and he shall appear. My father materializes in front of me, dapper, distinguished, and as handsome as the day my poor mother married him. The fairness of his hair swallows up the gray, and he looks not much older than in the wedding pictures I've seen from thirty-three years ago. The lines fanning out from the green eyes so like mine only deepen and add maturity to his appeal. Those eyes stare back at me with something very close to...tolerance. That's about all Daddy has left for me these days.

You can't live the way I have, as publicly as I have (refer back to the fucks I ran out of years ago), and expect to remain Daddy's little girl.

Yet I'd do anything for him. He knows it and exploits that weakness at every turn, and I see a turn coming. He glances speculatively between Rip and me.

"Hi, Daddy." I loop my elbow through Rip's. "Rip, this is Ernest Baston, my father. Daddy, you know Rip, right? He plays for the Jets."

"Yes, of course. That was some pass on Sunday." My father reaches for Rip's hand and gives it a friendly shake before dismissing him with the look he reserves for people who can do nothing for him. "I could use your help tonight, Sofie. There's a big fish here we need to reel in."

This isn't the first time he's required my help persuading someone his company would be much better off under the Bennett Enterprises umbrella. I glance down at my cleavage, which is on display, making sure the girls are ready to earn their keep. When your father recruits your sixteen-year-old charms to persuade grown men, you get used to feeling like a commodity. No different from using my legs to sell shoes or my blond hair to sell shampoo. Only the payoff is Daddy's approval. Much harder to come by than any check I've ever cashed.

"Your mother has seated Walsh at your table to help," Daddy continues, his voice low as he grasps my elbow and walks me slowly toward the table, leaving Rip to trail behind just out of earshot. "So Walsh will be in one ear and you'll be in the other."

Great. Not only do I have to watch my former lover and oldest friend's wedded bliss with another woman, but I get to bathe in some old man's drool all night while I convince him he really should be happy when our mammoth conglomerate gobbles up his life's work. And if I start losing him, I'll just point to my chest and say, "And did I mention my breasts?"

"So who is this big fish I'm wiggling on the hook for?" I slow my steps, forcing my father to do the same.

Daddy's lips tighten with distaste at my candor. He has no problem doing distasteful things, but he doesn't like me talking about them. Or maybe he just doesn't like to talk about the distasteful things I do, even when I do them for him.

"Trevor Bishop." Daddy narrows his eyes like he's sighting a target. "Thirty-five years old. He and his business partner are based in Atlanta, but are here in New York for a few months exploring options to expand, taking meetings, doing events like this one."

Well, at least I can knock old off the list. He's not much older than I am.

"So what's his deal?"

"His 'deal' is that he and his college buddy started a business to start businesses, and it's exploded. They focus on developing nations. They've started businesses in Haiti, Kenya, and Cambodia. They're really concerned about training the people in these areas and empowering them economically. It's actually quite brilliant, and good of them."

"If it's so good of them, why can't we just leave them to it?"

"Because, *honey*"—Daddy dips the word in condescension—"they're making money hand over fist, and that bottom line would be even better under Bennett leadership."

"Better because it would be a Bennett holding and you'd get to benefit from it?"

"Me?" Daddy elevates just one brow. "Don't you mean *we*? This is your future, too, young lady. When you're done with this modeling nonsense, there's a place for you at the table."

He says this to manipulate me. He uses my love against me, and I allow it. Daddy probably thinks the only place at the table for me is under it, blowing some client who needs persuading. Not that he's ever actually asked me to sleep with anyone to acquire a company. Even he wouldn't prostitute his own daughter.

I guess. Who knows how badly he wants this fish.

I look at the table where Walsh and Kerris just sat down. Walsh stands back up to greet two men approaching the table. One is the kind of man you'd see and struggle to recall exactly what he looked like five minutes later. He is beige and insipid like oatmeal. His mouse-brown hair is receding. His glasses barely hang on the tip of his nose. He seems fit enough, maybe five ten. That's all I have the attention span for before I have to look away.

The other man—well, the other man you'd never forget. If his friend is beige, this man is a vivid swath of color. His tuxedo—Tom Ford, if my eye is right, and my eye is unfailing—lays against him like a lover. He wears it with a white, open-collared silk shirt instead of a bow tie, and I approve. He is what some would call strapping. Not many men can look down on me, but he could. I'm five eleven barefoot. He must be a good six five, with a broad chest and a tapered waist. The flawlessly tailored pants pull just a little at the muscled line of his thigh. There is a craggy symmetry to his features. A rough balance of high, sharp cheekbones, slashing dark brows, and wide sensual mouth. The almost hawkish nose and square chin make something arresting of a face that could have stopped at handsome. The contrast of his tanned skin and burned cinnamon hair draw my eyes and won't let go.

Ah, a ginger. I've never had a redhead before. I'm a ginger virgin. He could pop that cherry anytime he likes.

"Did you hear me, Sofie?" Impatience tightens Daddy's lips.

"Sorry, Daddy. No. You were saying something about this Trevor Bishop."

"That's him at the table with Walsh. He's the taller one, and his partner is the shorter one with glasses."

"You want me to charm *him*?"

The prospect of flirting with this beautiful beast of a man makes me tingle. It will be like taming a lion with no whip or chair. A bare-handed taunting and tempting with only my considerable female wiles to subdue all that hulking maleness. Deliciously dangerous, and I'm completely up for the challenge.

"Not charm, just…be nice to him. Talk up Bennett when you have an opening." Daddy's mouth goes stern and his eyes turn hard. "I'm trusting you with this, Sofie. Do not embarrass me with this man. He's not like these other men you…entertain."

He casts a glance over his shoulder at Rip, who is looking around the ballroom like he's at Willy Wonka's Chocolate Factory. I just don't get famous people who don't realize *they're* famous. This is now your natural habitat.

"Don't worry, Daddy. I promise not to embarrass you with my wanton ways."

I keep my tone light, but I know my past exploits prompted his warning.

"I'm not worried. You could lure flies away from shit when you set your mind to it."

"What a pleasant image, Daddy. I'll hold it close."

"Do." He brings us to a complete stop, offering my elbow back to Rip with an absent smile. "It was good meeting you, Rip. Keep up the good work this season."

"Sure thing, Mr. Baston." Rip offers the white-toothed smile he's taking all the way to the bank. "Nice to meet you, too."

Daddy nods before returning his eyes to me.

"Remember what I said, Sofie. I need to go check on a surprise guest."

"Surprise?" My interest piques. Daddy does great surprises. "No hints?"

"You'll find out with everyone else, sweetheart."

Of course. Why would I be special?

"You ready?" I ask Rip as my father walks off to tend to his surprise guest.

"Definitely."

Rip kisses my hair, and I can't help but remember the kiss Walsh gave Kerris a few minutes ago. I'm not sure anyone will ever kiss me that way. Not the kiss itself, the practice of lips touching hair, but what lay behind it. I can't put my finger on it, but I'm sure no one has ever touched me that way. No one has ever felt for me what Walsh feels for that woman. I can see it in the simplest contact they share. Whatever they have, I don't think I ever believed in it, and I certainly don't expect it for myself.

We reach the table, and I see my place card to the left of Trevor Bishop's, with Walsh on his right, like Daddy said it would be. At least he seated my date on my other side. Kerris is, of course, on Walsh's other side. There has never been any love lost between that girl and me. She stole what was always supposed to be mine. Walsh and I made sense. She and Walsh defy the laws of social logic, her being a nobody and all, but somehow here they are, obviously besotted with each other and…working.

"Sof, Aunt Billi told me you just got back from Dubai." Walsh walks around the table and kisses my cheek.

"Yep." I lean in to the friendly greeting, knowing friendly is as far as we'll ever go now. "It was a quick shoot."

Somehow we've remained friends despite the disastrous affair a few years back, a desperate attempt on my part when Kerris married Walsh's best friend, Cam. I've been conductor for enough train wrecks to recognize one, and that was some fucked-up shit. Now Cam is married to Walsh's cousin Jo, and Walsh is married to Kerris. A game of musical beds I wish I could have gotten in on.

Come to think of it, with my turn at Walsh, I guess I kind of did.

Walsh has stayed true through everyone telling him what a bitch I am, and let's face it, they're right. He even forgave my insulting treatment of his wife. I mean, we don't talk every day or anything, but he could have used his influence with the Walsh Foundation to take something from me that means a lot. I have served as the foundation's celebrity ambassador for years. If I haven't done anything else right, I have that. Walsh knows how much it means to me, and didn't take it away as retaliation for the bad blood between Kerris and me. For that, and for a hundred other kindnesses he has shown me since we were in preschool, I'll strain to be civil to his sweet wife.

"Sweet" is not a compliment, by the way. Kerris's smile alone gives me a cavity.

"Good to see you, Walsh. Hi, Kerris." I slide my glance to his wife. She returns my nod, wearing a guarded look on her face. Smart girl.

I'll try for my best behavior, but I'm a bitch on a leash that slips from time to time. Best be prepared for anything.

"Sofie, let me introduce you to our guests." Walsh gestures to Mr. Oatmeal. "This is Harold Smith, co-founder of Deutimus Corp."

Mr. Oatmeal, given name Harold, stands and shakes my hand. He sports the look most men have when they first meet me "in real life." Slightly stunned. I'm so used to my face, to this body, that I almost forget the effect they have on people. Also, the fashion world is an alternate dimension, populated by a species of gorgeous, lissome perfectly maintained superwomen where I am the norm. I rather enjoy not being the most striking person in the room from time to time.

"And this is his business partner, Trevor Bishop."

Walsh steps back, and I have my first close-up of the fish I'm here to catch. Only I'm the one hooked, immediately. I'm careful not to show it, but that stunned look I'm used to seeing on other people's faces? All over my inside face.

This force of flesh and bone and muscle wrapped in heat *looms* over me. Trevor Bishop's presence burns holes in my composure. I could tell from across the room that he was attractive and built like a mountain lion, lean and strong and broad. But it's only now, with proximity, that his absolute confidence meets mine head-on. He tilts his head to the left, his chocolate-colored eyes steadily considering me, and I swear he knows. Even though I'm sure my face doesn't give it away, I swear he knows that as I stand in front of him, inhaling his clean scent and waiting for his first smile, windmills turn in my belly.

"A pleasure to meet you, Miss Baston." His lips, wide and full, give me a smile punctuated by dimples. And he has a Southern drawl.

Fuck me now.

That's not a figure of speech. I quite literally want him to toss me over that hulking shoulder, find a dark corner somewhere, and screw me so deeply into a wall we leave a dent. Or in a bathroom stall. Hell, he could drag me over to the elaborate buffet table and take me from behind right there by the ice sculpture.

One brow, a few shades darker than his hair, rises. Holy crap, I haven't responded yet.

"Um, nice to meet you, too, Mr. Bishop." I take my time so my tongue doesn't betray the muddled mess of haywire hormones I am right now.

His eyes drift over my shoulder, forcing my mind and manners back to Rip.

"Oh, yes. I'm sorry. How rude." I turn to Rip, who immediately claims my elbow and draws me into his side. All of a sudden he's territorial. I can't blame him. If my girlfriend was within five feet of this man, I'd handcuff her to me for the night. "This is Michael Ripley."

"Great game Sunday." Trevor shakes the hand Rip isn't manacling me with. "I'm a Falcons fan myself, but I can appreciate a good toss no matter the team. That's some arm you got there."

Rip's hold on me relaxes a bit. Clever Trevor, disarming him that way. Well played. Will I be able to strip this fish of his defenses as easily?

Once seated, Rip, Trevor, Harold, and Walsh fall into a discussion about football I don't even try to follow. Apparently neither does Kerris. She's texting someone with a small frown on her face, and mumbles something to Walsh about a sitter. I settle into my seat beside Trevor, taking a few moments to compose myself and strategize how I can get that hook in his mouth.

"So you were in Dubai?"

The question startles me a little, I was so lost in my musings. I turn slightly in Trevor's direction, creasing my lips politely.

"For a shoot, yes." I toy with the clamp on my clutch, which rests on the table. "And my friend Ardis married a prince over there. I like to visit her every once in a while."

"A real live prince, huh?" He teases me with a quirk of those full lips.

"Don't be too impressed." I lean a few inches closer to him and lower my voice. "He's a prince in name only."

"If he's a prince in name only, what does that make him in deed?"

I can't hold on to the humor when I recall the bruises shackling Ardis's throat and wrists, or the black-and-blue mark on her cheek like a brand. I refocus my eyes and sober my mouth.

"A frog."

"I thought you ladies kissed all the frogs to find the prince."

"It happens that way in fairy tales, not in Manhattan." I sip my champagne. "Or in Dubai, apparently."

"So that accounts for your tan." His dark eyes make a slow, thorough inspection of my features.

"Hmm. What accounts for yours?" I toss a skein of silvery-blond hair back so he gets an eyeful of the bare line of my neck and shoulder. His eyes move down my neck, warming the skin like a touch, before he looks back into my eyes.

"Haiti." He laughs a little, lounges back in his chair, and links long fingers across a flat stomach I imagine is corded with muscle. "Well, and my father is Lumbee, so some of my tan's natural."

"Lum what?"

He laughs again, his teeth white against his skin. I really like that it's because of something I said.

"Lumbee Indian, a tribe found mostly in Lumberton, North Carolina."

"So your mother's responsible for the red hair?"

"She is." He brushes a hand over his neat hair, disrupting it into a coppery spill on his forehead. "I was spared the freckles, though."

"I'm sure there's one or two."

His eyes are suddenly hot chocolate, heating up a little as they hold mine.

"You're welcome to try to find them."

I'm supposed to be flirting with *him*, baiting *him*, but he's casting the line. I don't like it. I need the pole in my hand. I break that steamy contact, lowering my eyes to the cocktail ring I'm twisting around my finger.

"What took you to Haiti?" I ask. "It's miserably hot this time of year."

He pauses a moment before answering, the press of his lips against a smile acknowledging my conversational feint.

"You've been?"

"Sofie's been to our orphanage in Haiti several times for the foundation," Walsh interjects from Trevor's other side.

I wonder how in on this little plan of Daddy's Walsh actually is. He is a great guy, but when it comes down to it, he's as much Martin Bennett's son as I am Ernest Baston's daughter. Both of us descend from ruthless corporate raiders.

"She's our celebrity ambassador," Walsh continues.

"Really?" A new light enters Trevor's dark eyes. It could be respect. I'm not sure.

"Kristeene, Walsh's mother, recruited me years ago to do it, and they haven't gotten rid of me yet."

Though there were a few times I wondered if the Walsh Foundation board of directors might have ousted me had I not been Baby Girl Baston. And right on cue, Daddy takes a seat beside Harold. Maybe Oatmeal is his assignment.

"Sorry, I was detained making plans for a surprise guest." He takes a sip of the white wine at his elbow. "Now, Harold and Trevor, you're both Princeton men, right?"

"In a manner of speaking." Trevor offers a self-deprecating laugh, sharing a grin across the table with Harold. "We dropped out our junior year to start Deutimus Corp."

"It all worked out, though." Harold pushes the glasses back up his nose with an index finger. "They conferred an honorary degree on us last year."

"Well, that was nice." Daddy points a fork in my direction. "You wouldn't know it, but Sofie here was accepted to Princeton."

My lips purse against the groan that wants out so badly. Not this again.

"And Sarah Lawrence," Daddy continues. "And UCLA."

"Yes, but somewhere along the way I got confused and thought it was my life." I dash saccharine on the smile I offer my father. "And that I could do what I wanted with it."

"You mean running all over the world having your picture taken?" Daddy lowers his fork to his plate and his eyebrows into the frown I'm used to seeing when we discuss my misspent youth.

"It's actually worked out quite well for me, Daddy."

I'm one of the highest-paid, most sought-after models in the world. That means something to me, if not to him. I won't let him piss on it.

"We saw your billboard today." Harold passes the words and a kind smile to me across the table.

"I hope it was the one where she's wearing clothes." Daddy slices into his tender steak and any pride I might feel for my accomplishments, as they were.

An awkward silence pools around his words. I feel Trevor's eyes on me, assessing if Daddy's words have found their mark. Good luck cracking this safe, Bishop. I offer a laugh that tinkles like a champagne toast.

"Daddy, that's the BARE campaign." I'm sure he's not bringing up the *Playboy* spread I recently did for my birthday. Not in front of his fish. "It's very tastefully shot."

Harold forks an asparagus spear. "Was that the one we saw, Trev?"

"Not sure." Trevor moves his broad shoulders in a careless shrug.

"If it was Times Square, it's BARE, a skin-care product I endorse." I push a chunk of hair behind one ear. "In the other one I'm actually wearing clothes."

"Where's the other billboard?" Trevor raises his glass of water to his lips while he waits for my answer.

"In the Meatpacking District." I'm taking the pole back and baiting the hook. "But you don't have to try to find it. You have the real thing right here."

He doesn't bite, but smiles and gives me one last look before turning to answer a question Walsh just posed.

"Where's your mom?" Rip asks from his seat beside me.

"Probably scolding a server." I pierce a scallop and pop it into my mouth. "After years of practice, she's very good at that."

"Your mother is actually making some seating chart adjustments so our special guest can sit here with us," Daddy says.

That special guest again. As long as it's not another sheikh. The last time I entertained one of Daddy's sheikhs, he followed me to the bathroom and got handsy. He didn't speak a word of English, but I translated knee to groin perfectly.

"Here they come now." Daddy wears a pleased expression on his usually hard-to-satisfy face.

I see my mother first, and I can only hope, with all my creams, exfoliations, and serums, to look as beautiful as Willimena Baston—Billi to her friends—does in twenty years. Like my father and me, she's blond. Where my hair is naturally almost Nordic bright, hers is a buttery gold. Her hair color and nature are much softer than mine and Daddy's. And where our eyes are emerald green, with not a speck of hazel, hers are pewter gray.

By all rights, living with my father—his callousness, infidelity, and neglect—should have lined Mother's face with pain, but her skin radiates age-defying youth. By necessity, I have toughened my heart's tender places, but I've always wanted to be like her in some ways. Always wanted us to be closer. Maybe I remind her too much of my father for her to really love me. I glance at Daddy, who barely registers her approach because he's fixated on the "special guest" accompanying her.

I shift my attention to the special guest.

Everything in me goes still. My fingers freeze around my fork like rigor mortis has set in. My breath stalls in my throat. My heart refuses to beat for a matter of seconds, depriving me of blood to the brain. That must be why I'm light-headed. Why my hands go cold and my feet go numb. It is circulatory, not long-buried fear. Not never-forgotten disgust. Not deeply embedded shame.

I want to believe the man at my mother's side is not who I think he is. Is not who my body thinks he is, but he goes still, too, and makes me certain. He stops walking toward us, his steps faltering for a heartbeat and his eyes widening when they tangle with mine. We share memories, memories that tortured my dreams into nightmares. Memories that, even now, as he regains his composure and continues his steady pace toward my table behind my mother, twist his lips into a smile.

CHAPTER TWO

Trevor

W ho is this girl?

Obviously, I know who she literally is, but what stirs beneath that polished, placid surface? When Harold told me Sofie Baston would be here tonight, I expected to be impressed with her physical beauty, but I didn't expect to be…intrigued.

Even though I saw her on a billboard earlier, that colossal image a hundred feet in the air is somehow dwarfed by this woman in the soft, silky flesh. My preconceived notions of her have been broadened and lengthened by what appears to be a quick wit and sharp intelligence.

I've been fighting myself not to just stare at her ever since she and that punk-ass quarterback walked in. I mean, yeah, Rip's got a great arm, but he hasn't *fully* lived up to the promise he showed in college when he won the Heisman. Okay. He *was* MVP last year. I gotta give him that. Let's face it. I'm just sour because he's with her. I've never been one to go after another guy's girl, and I won't start with this one. But I'd trade places with him, even if just for a night.

In the high-risk ventures that have made Harold and me richer than we ever imagined when we walked away from our Princeton scholarships, I sink or swim on my instincts, on my gut-level assessment. Based on what I see, Rip bores her. He has no idea how to handle a woman like Sofie. That silver-blond hair, those bottle-green eyes, that pale gold skin—all make you think she's an icy goddess, but even our brief exchange showed me the truth. There's fire beneath that perfectly cool façade. She isn't feisty or sassy. Those words are too girlish somehow for what I sense in her. She is...bold. And I've decided that I like her.

I've been rationing glances, allowing myself to look over at her only every so often. I don't want her to think I'm one of those idiots who run behind her with their noses wide open. I'm not that guy. Harold and I have been so focused on building Deutimus over the last decade that there's barely been time for dating, relationships, or any life really outside of creating these entrepreneurial incubators all over the world. But even I haven't been so far under a rock I don't know a gorgeous woman when I see her.

Okay. I've waited long enough. I've earned another look.

I turn in her direction, ready for more flirting and to tease out that fire I sense hiding, but everything about her is now frozen. Her smile has hardened into an icy curve on her face, and I watch it splinter into a thousand icicles that leave her lips a straight, dead line. Her hand is a cold claw on the table in front of her. And her eyes, frozen over like a winter pond, fix on the man approaching with her mother.

Walsh leans across me, touching Sofie's hand and tugging until she shifts her glance to him.

"I had no idea, Sof." His eyes and whisper are urgent. "I didn't know he would be here. I don't know why he is, but I'll find out. I'll handle this. I promise. Are you okay?"

This is the softest I've seen her so far. Not in a magazine, not on that billboard, not tonight has she been less than certain. Less than the runway moniker I've heard they call her—the Goddess. But for a second, in a flash, she looks completely, humanly lost. Those icy eyes melt when they meet Walsh's, and she bites her lip hard enough that when she releases it, blood rushes to the surface, color flooding the lips that had gone white around the red lipstick.

"I'm fine, Walsh." Piece by piece, she reassembles herself, layering confidence and dispassion around her like veils. "I promise I'm fine."

She slides her eyes to me like she's just remembered that I'm there, between them. I was never supposed to see that weak, lost moment. She is naked on the Times Square billboard, but I just saw her completely exposed, and she doesn't like it. She pulls her brows into a V, her soft lips tightening.

"I'm fine." This time she aims the words and the hardening-by-the-second eyes at me.

"Walsh and Sofie, here's the surprise guest I mentioned," Ernest Baston rises from the table to give a quick kiss to the gorgeous woman I know is Sofie's mother. He slaps the surprise guest on the back. "You both remember Kyle Manchester, right? I believe you were at Hanover together, right?"

Harold and I met Manchester last week. I wasn't impressed then and remain unimpressed now. He's an opportunistic cretin who pretends to care about the issues of the moment that carry weight on a ballot. He's social tofu, absorbing the flavor of any cause that will gain traction with voters. If he has any personal integrity, I didn't detect it. Somehow he has convinced the American public he's the best thing since sliced bread, and he is so incredibly popular, he'll probably be New York's next senator. Coming from a powerful, wealthy family probably doesn't hurt.

Kyle splits a cautious glance between Walsh and Sofie, seeming to gauge their reception of him. Walsh's jaw is locked tight and hard as diamonds. He glares at Kyle and looks at Sofie, concern softening his expression.

What the hell is going on here? And am I the only one feeling this tension?

"Yes, Daddy." Sofie passes one hand over the silvery fall of hair caressing her shoulder. "Don't you remember Kyle took me to the prom?"

"That's right." Ernest Baston narrows his eyes at Kyle like he's seeing him for the first time. "How could I have forgotten that? Well, he's come a long way since high school, huh?"

"Haven't we all." Sofie's eyes linger over Ernest's hand on Kyle's shoulder before dropping to the table. She reaches for her glass of champagne, only to find it empty. Without missing a beat, she grabs mine.

"Oh, that's my—"

She holds my eyes with hers, gulping back the bubbly, intoxicating liquid like it's water before slamming the delicate flute so hard I'm surprised it doesn't shatter.

Screw it. She obviously needs it more than I do.

"You're looking at the great state of New York's next senator." Ernest motions Kyle to the empty seat made available at the last minute for him.

"Let's not get ahead of ourselves." Kyle settles into the seat, snaps open his linen napkin, and lets it float over his knees under the table. "There's an election to get through."

"Oh, that's a formality, my boy." Ernest gestures that everyone should resume eating.

"Your support means a lot." Kyle glances at Sofie again, who doesn't look up from the fingers tangled in her lap. "It's a long road ahead. I just hope I can hang in there."

"You will, son." Ernest studies his daughter, with that same look on his face as when he talked about the schools Sofie didn't attend. "We respect quitters about as much as those who never even try."

Sofie's shoulders stiffen and she raises her eyes to meet her father's. She reaches for my glass again, but it's empty now, too. Her eyes scan the room, almost like she is looking to escape. Her fingers open and close around her small purse, a compulsion of which she seems unaware. Her eyes collide with Kyle's across the table, exchanging some message I wish I could decode, but it's garbled and embedded in whatever secret they harbor between them.

"I hope our future senator can count on all of your votes." Ernest smiles around the sip he is taking and looks around the table.

An awkward silence falls over the group. I glance at Sofie, who rolls her eyes and sits back in her seat, folding her arms under her breasts.

"Kerris, the women's vote will be crucial." Ernest softens his shark grin for Walsh Bennett's petite wife, who has seemed distracted much of the night.

Walsh frowns, shooting a protective glance his wife's way.

"Oh, well." Kerris lays her phone in her lap, but looks down once more at the screen and nods before speaking. "I...I'm not really very political."

"Understandable." Manchester's smile condescends.

"But I do wonder where you stand on equal pay for women."

I hide my grin behind a napkin, wiping away something imaginary. This should be interesting.

"Ah, well…I didn't think you worked, Mrs. Bennett." Manchester's smile slips a little.

"I've been in the work force since I was fourteen years old."

"Yes, but you no longer work, correct? Maybe we should talk about my stance on charter schools or—"

"I *do* work." Kerris raises both brows and rests her elbows on the table. "I'm a business owner, and I would never pay a woman less than a man or a man less than a woman doing the same job."

Never able to resist a scrimmage, I add my two cents.

"It's a great question, Manchester. I'm interested to hear your answer."

The look he aims at me is loaded with quickly veiled malevolence. We only met recently, but it didn't take long for us to dislike each other.

"What are you, Bishop?" he asks. "A feminist?"

"Aren't you?"

"Excuse me?" Manchester's brows elevate.

"By definition, a feminist is someone who believes in social, political, and economic equality between the sexes." I pause, giving him the condescending grin he gave Kerris a few moments ago. "Surely any reasonable person in this millennia, in this hemisphere, certainly at this table, would be a feminist."

Harold clears his throat, the "shut your damn mouth" signal we've worked out between us. He thinks Manchester could be an ally. I don't believe in keeping my enemies that close.

Sofie stands up without another word, drawing questioning eyes from everyone at the table.

"Powder room." Her voice comes out strong, but I'm close enough to see the mad pulse thumping at her throat. "I'll be…I'll be back."

When Harold and I were last in Kenya, we went on safari and saw a ravenous lion pursuing an antelope. There had been no hope of safety for the beast. The kill, inevitable and savage. The lion, a beautiful predator, greedily devoured the prey before our eyes, not even acknowledging his rapt voyeurs. As I watch the slim, vibrant line of Sofie's body fleeing the room, I have no idea why, but I feel that same guilt. Like I'd stood by and watched something awful without raising my hand or voice to help.

CHAPTER THREE

Sofie

I study my reflection in the bathroom mirror, but I don't see a polished, poised woman with sleek hair, a pop of matte red lipstick, and lash extensions. Instead another girl, younger, with smudged lips, hair spilled around her shoulders, and angry, red welts at her wrists stares back at me. I hear her jagged inhalations, the way her breaths drag over her quivering lips. The stench of her fear churns the dinner in my stomach, and nausea floods my mouth. I swore I'd exiled her for good. She was handled. She was dealt with, but now she's back.

Weak bitch.

I thought I had gotten rid of her once and for all, but it only took him slithering back into my life to open the door for that weakling child to come out whimpering. I grit my teeth and close my eyes. When I open them, I am determined she will be gone.

I open my eyes and jump a little when I find Kerris's amber-flecked gaze reflecting back to me in the mirror over my shoulder. The last time we were in a bathroom together, we weren't exactly sharing lipstick and tampons. She'd told me that Walsh was hers and she had no plans of letting him go—ever. I hated her that night, but maybe I also respected her a little for the first time.

"We have to stop meeting this way, Kerris." I tug at the plunging neckline of my dress. "Walsh sent you?"

Kerris leans against the wall by the door and bites her bottom lip before speaking.

"He was worried about you." She clears her throat and a path for the next words. "He's outside in the hall."

I check my hair one last time.

"He has nothing to worry about."

"You seemed…I don't know, disturbed. Was it that Kyle guy?"

"Kyle Manchester does not disturb me." I turn to face her, propping my backside against the marble counter. "Why would he? You can let Walsh know I'm fine."

"Or you could come out and tell him yourself." Kerris doesn't look away from my steady, blank stare.

I'm just now realizing that what I took for timidity in Walsh's little wife might be quiet strength. Our lives couldn't have been more different. She spent her early years in foster homes, bounced around and abused. I was cultivated like a pearl, protected from harm and born to rule. She doesn't know we may have more in common than she would assume. More in common than I want to share.

In the six years since I first met Kerris, a lot has changed for us both. I had so much to prove to the world, to myself, to my parents, most of the time I didn't care who I trampled to prove it. With Kerris, looks like I tried, but didn't trample her. There's a confidence in her now that has little to do with the money that comes with Walsh, and a lot more to do with the way he loves her.

"Tell Walsh I'll be out in a minute," I say.

With a quick nod she turns to go, but I surprise myself by stopping her with, of all things, a compliment.

"That's a fabulous necklace, by the way."

With her hand on the door handle, Kerris goes stiff and looks at me over her shoulder like the Wicked Witch of the West just gave her a Christmas present. She must think my compliment might explode at her feet.

What made me stop her? Maybe it's a diversion, a distraction from what's out there. Or maybe I just love fabulous jewelry. It could really be a little bit of both.

"Um, you mean this necklace?" She runs her fingers over the rounded stones strung together like pearls around her neck, but colored a distressed teal.

"Yes, it's unique. Where'd you get it?"

"It's one of mine actually." A small smile tugs at Kerris's lips.

"Obviously it's one of yours, but where'd you *buy* it?"

Maybe she *is* slow.

"No, I mean it's from my Riverstone Collection. I make the jewelry myself."

Oh, so *I'm* slow. I forgot about her jewelry line. I wasn't in the city when it launched, but I'm sure I wasn't invited. We don't exactly socialize outside of Bennett functions.

"Nice." I wave my hand like a scepter toward the door. "You can go now and tell Walsh there's no need to wait. I'm fine."

I should have let her go when I had the chance; now she's lingering. Hesitating. Grappling with her misplaced compassion.

"That's the closest to a moment as we're likely to have, Kerris." I plasticize a smile. "You should probably go before the full moon comes and I turn bitch again."

She must believe me because she leaves without so much as a chuckle. I need the quiet, the space she left behind, to pull what remains of my shit together. Mentally, I reach for the affirmations my therapist taught me all those years ago. Those words that empowered me to, day by day, reconstruct myself, but I'm empty-handed. It's been so long since I needed them. Now that I do, they elude me.

"You haven't needed them." I turn back to the mirror to tell my reflection. "And you don't now. They're just words. I don't care who's out there."

Who's in the mirror? The leather-tough, butter-smooth woman I've spent the last fifteen years creating? Or that sniveling girl who used to wake up screaming and shivering and sweating because of *him*?

It's me. The version of myself that did whatever it took to survive. I marshal all my forces and step into the hall. Walsh straightens from the wall and approaches me, concern all over his face. How did he end up such a good guy? With Martin Bennett as a father? I really want to know, because I haven't figured out how to escape my DNA. It must have been Walsh's mother who tempered that ruthlessness that lives in Martin. And in my father. And in me.

"I had no idea Kyle would be here." Walsh shoves his hands in his pockets. "I haven't seen him since high school. I didn't know we had any business with him."

"Daddy's buying himself a senator." I lean against the wall Walsh just abandoned, flexing my toes in the beautiful shoes that are starting to hurt. "Think of all the legislation we can corrupt with a senator in our pocket."

Walsh huffs a heavy breath and runs one hand through his dark hair. He knows I'm right.

"We should have handled this years ago, Sof, when you told me what happened."

I focus on the span of floor between our feet. I can't look at Walsh right now without seeing that girl, without feeling her shame and despair. And with that monster only a dining room away, I cannot afford those emotions. They'll cost me, and I need every advantage at my disposal.

"We did handle it, Walsh."

He tips my chin up with a gentle finger, his green eyes dark and tortured.

"I've never forgiven myself for not turning him in."

"By the time you found out, it was too late. It was my choice, not yours, and it was the right choice for me."

"But he never *paid*. He never *answered* for what he did to you. He—"

"Don't you dare say it." My voice is an outraged hiss in the confines of the hall. "Don't you ever give him that much power over me again, Walsh."

"But, Sof, he's about to become a damn senator. We could still tell the truth about what happened and—"

"I didn't want to fifteen years ago, and I certainly don't want to now. If it hadn't been for a drunken night in Paris, you wouldn't even know." I rest my fists on my hips. "It happened to me, so it's still up to me, right?"

"It's not right to—"

"You don't get to determine what's wrong or right *for me*." Anger and frustration, maybe fear, sharpen my tongue and dull my discretion. "You have your perfect life. Bennett Enterprises will be yours soon. You have your perfect wife. Your perfect kids with another perfect child on the way. Why do you give a damn what I do or don't do?"

Walsh's eyes narrow and his jaw hardens the way I know means he's about to sort my shit out, but a small motion behind us grabs our attention. Kerris stands there, eyes wide, gripping her phone.

"Speaking of your perfect wife," I snap, rolling my eyes. "Here she is now."

Kerris doesn't know what to make of me. A few minutes ago I was complimenting her taste in jewelry and acting the closest I've ever come to being nice to her. Now the bitch is back. My head is spinning, too, honey.

"Um, the sitter just called." Kerris trains her eyes on Walsh, ignoring me. "The girls have a fever."

Walsh squeezes the bridge of his nose, something I've seen Uncle Martin do a thousand times. He palms his neck, head bent toward the floor, and looks up at me.

"I have to go." He lays a gentle hand on my shoulder, a gesture I don't deserve after the vitriol I just spewed at him. "We still need to talk about this. If your father knew—"

"Don't bother." I jerk back from his hand and press my shoulders into the wall. "I'm not changing my mind."

Kerris hovers just down the hall, wearing the anxiety for her little girls between her eyebrows and around her tightened lips.

"Go to your family, Walsh. I'll be fine."

He hesitates, but after a few seconds moves down the hall and grabs Kerris's hand. He kisses her fingers, wrapped around his, like he can't help it. Like when he's that close to her, he can't resist expressing how much he loves her. It is salt in a wound that shouldn't still hurt. I don't love Walsh anymore, if I ever really did. It's so hard to sort out the imaginations of our youth from what's real. When we're young, we feel things so deeply, how could it not be real? How could it not be right? But as I look at them, hands twined, walking so close even light doesn't intrude, I know what right looks like.

"Hey, Walsh," I call out against my better judgment.

He stops and looks back at me. So does she.

"I'm…I'm sorry."

Walsh grins, that rakish slash across his handsome face that has grabbed more than one heart. That once held mine.

"You know I know that." He keeps walking, but waves over his head at me. "You want me to make your excuses so you don't have to go back?"

"Yeah, send Rip here and we'll leave through the back."

I don't have the energy to wriggle on a hook for that prize-size fish Trevor Bishop. He's the kind of man who requires all your wits, and mine are scattered all around me. As handsome as he is, as intrigued as I am—I can't tonight. Daddy can catch his own damn fish.

CHAPTER FOUR

Trevor

Harold and I have endured ceremonies in developing nations, on other continents, that lasted days. Interminable rites of passage. Festivals we thought would never end, but none as intolerable as my time at this table with Ernest Baston and Kyle Manchester. Maybe I'm hasty in saying this, but I don't think so. They *might* quite possibly be two of the biggest assholes I've ever encountered, and considering the corrupt leaders in the nations where we do business, that's saying something.

I stopped following Kyle's diatribe on redistricting about ten minutes ago. I'm considering fake choking, thinking the Heimlich maneuver would break this shit up nicely, when Walsh and Kerris return to the table. No Sofie in sight. I look over Walsh's shoulder to make sure. A woman who stands nearly six feet tall barefoot would be hard to overlook, especially one who looks like Sofie, but I check anyway.

"We need to go. The girls have a fever." Walsh frowns while Kerris grabs her bag from the table. "Where's Rip?"

"He saw an old college teammate," I answer, grateful my vocal cords didn't atrophy during Kyle's filibuster. "Said he'd be back in a few. Everything okay?"

Walsh's frown deepens, his eyes narrowing when they connect with Kyle Manchester's. Gotta give it to him, Kyle gives him glare for glare. What's up with these two? Seems to be more than the typical alpha male, my-dick-is-bigger vibe, but I can't figure out what.

"When he gets back, tell him Sofie's ready to go." He directs the response to Sofie's mother. "She's not feeling well, Aunt Billi. Rip can find her outside the restrooms."

"She's not coming back?" Billi Baston crinkles her blond brows. "I'll go check on her."

"I don't think there's any need for that." Kerris offers a kind smile. "Seems she just needed some air and time to recover, and is really tired. Maybe just send Rip back and it should be fine."

Something's not right. The unease on Walsh Bennett's face is about more than just his twin girls' fevers.

"I'll see you two tomorrow, right?" Walsh splits a look between Harold and me. "Bright and early at Bennett?"

"Yes." Harold's smile is a little too eager for my liking. "Nine o'clock. We're looking forward to it."

Harold's ready to move on. Do something different. Something that doesn't keep him in developing countries half the year, with limited access to ESPN. We've made a helluva lot of money since we left Princeton, and he's ready to enjoy it. I get that, but we didn't start Deutimus primarily to make money, and that won't be the deciding factor in why or to whom we'll sell it. So Bennett Enterprises and any other takers can flash vulgar amounts of cash in our faces, should they choose. I'm not moved by it.

"Did I miss the memo about the meeting, Walsh?" Ernest scowls.

"Our assistants spoke, I believe. Celeste should have it on your calendar." Walsh takes Kerris's elbow. "Karma confirmed with her. We need to get home. Good night."

Ernest's frown only deepens as he watches Walsh and Kerris walk away. It can't be easy for him to see Walsh, a man half his age, taking over the company he built right alongside Walsh's father. While I feel for the older man, I don't much like him, and probably wouldn't consider Bennett Enterprises at all if Walsh wasn't at the table. For one thing, the way the man treats his daughter rubs me the wrong way.

Speaking of…

"I'll be right back." I scoot away from the table and stand.

"Where are you going?" Harold looks at me over his spectacles like a librarian.

"I know we've been friends a long time, Smith," I say with a grin. "But I'm still not ready to go to the bathroom in pairs like girls."

Harold's face reddens and he rolls his eyes.

"I'll be ready to leave when you get back, I think." He spoons up some of his crème brûlée. "Henri wants to meet at seven tomorrow morning."

Henrietta runs a tight ship. Even now she's back at my sister's place in Brooklyn, prepping for tomorrow's meetings and our trip to Cambodia. I've been looking forward to getting off this continent, but meeting Sofie tonight makes me wish we didn't have this three-week interruption in our New York trip.

"I'll be right back."

Why am I seeking out Sofie? What is this about? So she's the most gorgeous woman I've ever seen in real life. Looks count for something with me like most men, but not for everything, and from what I've heard, she probably doesn't have much else to offer. But there's this gulf between what I've heard and the woman I met tonight. Maybe the gulf is filled with my preconceived notions.

I see her slumped against the wall as soon as I round the corner, shoes kicked off and wiggling her bare toes. Even witnessing her posture less than perfectly straight, perfectly erect feels like a violation of her privacy. She looks up, squinting into the semi-dark passageway. I can see her much better than she can see me.

"Rip?" She straightens from the wall, her expression becoming annoyed when she realizes it's not the quarterback. "You've got to be kidding me. How many more people have to come through here? What is this? A parade?"

"Oh, I'm sorry for stumbling into your private boudoir." I lean one shoulder against the wall beside her, stepping close enough to smell the fresh scent she's been tantalizing me with all night. "I thought these were public bathrooms."

She holds my gaze in the dim light for a few seconds, not even blinking. Then her lips twitch and spread over the smile people pay to see. From a billboard, that smile hits you like a gut punch. This close, the impact is practically atomic.

"Boudoir?" A husky chuckle suffuses the space separating us. "Did you seriously just break out 'boudoir'?"

She props her butt against the wall and bends at the waist, slipping on one shoe and then the other. Even the high arch of this woman's foot is sexy. Every detail I uncover makes me want to go deeper until I've discovered them all.

"I like a woman who can laugh at herself."

My eyes follow the impossibly long line of her legs over the subtle curve of her hips and the surprising lushness of her breasts until I finally reach her waiting gaze, which asks if I've looked my fill.

"I wasn't laughing at myself." She grins again and inclines her head toward me. "I was laughing at you."

"I'll settle for that. Long as you're laughing."

She's not anymore, the humor falling away as quickly as it came. She looks back down the passageway, sleek brows knitting together.

"Did Walsh tell Rip to come?"

"Rip saw a college buddy and stepped away. I'm sure he'll be down as soon as he gets back to the table and they tell him you're ready to leave."

She moves over to a padded leather bench against the opposite wall, seating herself and crossing one leg over the other. She shifts her eyes from me to the men's room and back again.

"I thought you needed that public restroom." She gives a regal nod of her head toward the bathroom. "It's right there."

"I don't actually have to use the bathroom."

I leave it there, waiting for her to ask the obvious question, but I get the feeling Sofie Baston never does the obvious. She leans her back into the wall and narrows her eyes, waiting for me to go on.

"I came to find you."

She tilts her head and raises both brows, conducting a wordless conversation using only her patrician features.

"Can I ask you a question?" I continue.

She nods, confirming that I still haven't earned words yet.

"Why are you with Rip?"

She sinks deeper into the wall, sliding a few inches down and stretching her legs in front of her to cross them at the ankles

"Why wouldn't I be?" she finally asks. "Haven't you read the papers? We're the perfect couple."

"He bores you out of your mind."

"No, he fucks me out of my mind."

If she was going for shock value, that did it. Only our eyes lock and I realize she's not trying to shock me. She's just telling the truth. Her gaze is frank and honest.

"That's all you want in a relationship?" I hazard a step closer before dropping to the other end of her bench and leaning my back against her wall.

That husky laugh permeates the air in the passageway again.

"Look, Dr. Phil, I'm not one of those sweet girls looking for some man to sweep me off my feet and put a ring on it." She crosses both arms over her flat stomach, a cynical twist corrupting the beautiful curve of her mouth. "At least not anymore."

"Kissed too many frogs?"

"Make no mistake about it. Those frogs and I did more than kiss." Her smile exudes a sexual confidence I'm unused to from the women in my circles, but that I find by the second I more than like. "It's not so much that I can't find my prince, as that I'm no princess."

I take in the symmetry of her face, the elegant arch of her brows, the vibrant green eyes, the high slant of her cheekbones, and that lush curve of lips like a splash of passion on an otherwise pristine plane. The graceful bearing, even relaxed against the wall, commands attention and respect. She looks like nothing if not a young queen.

I'm just about to tell her so when approaching footsteps cut our conversation short. I turn, disappointed to see Rip striding quickly up the hall. Sofie stands immediately, grabbing her clutch from the bench and looking down at me. Our eyes connect, and I wonder if she wishes we had a few more minutes alone. Probably not, but there's something hiding behind those eyes, green as leaves. Curiosity? Interest? Whatever it is, it would take longer than two minutes for her to trust me with it.

"Sorry, baby." Rip's huge quarterback hands almost meet around Sofie's slim waist when he pulls her close. "I saw Don Siemer from college. Can you believe that? Small world, right?"

She smiles and gives a quick nod.

"Can we just go?" She gives a practiced pout of that lush mouth. "I'm exhausted and have to be up really early."

"Of course," Rip says. "The car's waiting. We can stay at your place."

Rip looks at me down on the bench. That last comment was for my benefit. He's marking his territory. I should tell him Sofie was much less subtle about his virility, but I don't bother. There isn't much more to Rip than what you see. All-American good looks. Athletic and not too bright. But Sofie? She reminds me of one of the African mines we've visited, diamonds so deeply embedded in the earth children risk life and limb to retrieve them. That's Sofie. Somehow even after just tonight, I know her diamonds are buried deep, and retrieving them would prove dangerous and rewarding.

You don't meet someone like Sofie Baston every day, and I wonder if this will be the only time we encounter each other. If it will be a story I tell my grandchildren. I met that famous model once. She wasn't a bitch at all. She was beautiful and funny and honest, and I wanted to punch her boyfriend in the face every time he touched her. I just met her the one time, but I'll never forget.

Rip guides Sofie down the hall toward a rear exit, and she looks back over her shoulder, our eyes connecting for an extra few seconds before she looks straight ahead and is swallowed up by the dark. I could be wrong, but I think she would have liked five more minutes with me. As eager as she was to leave, I might intrigue her as much as she increasingly intrigues me, and like I do with everything else in my life that counts, I make up my mind quickly, decisively.

No, that won't be the story I tell my grandchildren.

CHAPTER FIVE

Sofie

*D*amn, *Sof. For someone so skinny, you've got great tits."*

He paws my breasts and pinches my nipples so hard it feels like needles piercing the flesh, sharp and painful. He shackles my wrist, but I jerk against his strength. My heart slams into my breastbone. I'm a live wire soaked in water. I'm—

"Sof, wake up!"

The voice, insistent at my ear, jerks me out of the nightmare I was buried alive in. My eyes snap open, immediately colliding with Rip's blue gaze above me, his toned bare chest hovering over me, his arms caging me on either side. My nightgown is pulled back to bare my breast.

"I'm sorry." Rip frowns, easing away and off me a little at a time. "I know you like to fuck first thing in the morning and I was just—"

I shove him harder than I meant to in my haste to get out of the bed. I flip back the quilted comforter and scramble across my bedroom and into the light-filled bathroom. Nausea churns everything left in my stomach from last night before propelling all four courses into the toilet. I curl my legs beneath me on the cold tiles of the bathroom floor, resting my temple against the porcelain seat.

Rip didn't mean to. He's right. I do like sex in the morning, first thing. I like to wake up in the middle of an orgasm, if I can. Rip was just doing what he always does, not realizing he played into the nightmare I haven't had in years. I can't even remember the last time that demon visited my bed, but seeing Kyle last night stirred it all up again. Brought all the things I thought dead and dormant back to horrible life.

"You okay, Sof?" Rip asks from the bathroom door, his voice uncertain.

We aren't that couple who discusses real shit. We don't share real things. We're that couple who smile for cameras and pose together and screw each other's brains out, but don't know each other's birthdays or middle names. And I like it that way. Correction, I *liked* it that way. After seeing Kyle last night, I wasn't in the frame of mind to deal with breaking things off with Rip. Frankly, I'm still not, but it's coming soon.

"I'm fine, Rip." My eyes drift over his well-conditioned body in just briefs. Maybe I'm not all right if that package doesn't even stir me. "Sorry about that. I guess I was having a bad dream or something."

He saunters over, stopping beside me, dick right at my mouth. His morning wood doesn't care that I had a bad dream. He's ready for a good blow. Typically, I'd accommodate. I give good head. I'm sure all my former lovers would write glowing letters of recommendation for me based on that skill alone, but I'm not in the mood this morning.

I don't even acknowledge his erection, but stand up and cross over to my closet with its shelves of shoes, rows and rows of dresses and jeans, drawers and bins of accessories. I toss my nightgown into the hamper and start the shower, Rip's eyes on my naked body doing nothing to change my mind. I'm soaping up when I feel him hard at my back, not just his muscles, but his dick.

"Sof, we could do it real quick." His husky voice almost gets lost in the shower spray and steam. He nudges between my butt cheeks. "Come on, baby."

I can't. I still feel that dream like hot breath on my neck. My nipples still ache from the phantom pain. And though it's empty, my belly twists with nausea again at the thought of anyone inside me.

"I'm late, Rip." I turn toward him, careful to insert space between our bodies. "Maybe later."

I start shampooing my hair without waiting for his response.

"Something wrong, Sof?" A frustrated breath huffs across his lips. "You didn't want to last night either."

Now he's getting on my nerves. No one is entitled to my body. I choose who I share it with, on my terms. We just had sex yesterday morning. He can't go twenty-four hours without making himself and his dick a nuisance?

"I said I'm running late, Rip." Still lathering my hair, I face the shower wall and sprinkle steel shavings into my voice, warning him in the subtlest way I can to back off. "Now are you planning to shower, or are you just in here taking up my steam?"

"Sorry, Sof, I—"

"Could you close the door behind you?" I give him a semi-sweet smile over one bare, soapy shoulder, ignoring his eyes roving my naked back and over my ass. "Thanks."

I have to end this. Anytime you're kicking out a man who looks and fucks like Rip, it has gone too far or you have gone insane. And I know I'm not crazy.

Once I'm dressed in slim black pants, stiletto ankle boots, and a silky mist-colored camisole under my black lambskin blazer, I feel a little more like myself. Clothes always add an expensive, protective layer to cover up whatever I need the world to overlook.

Rip's stayed over enough that he has a few things here now, so he's at the kitchen bar dressed in jeans and a Jets T-shirt, eating a slice of cantaloupe. I pack my iPad and essentials for today's meetings, mentally running the schedule as much to clear my head as to make sure I don't forget anything.

"So should I pick you up tonight?" Rip asks between juicy bites.

"Sorry." I tuck a few stray hairs into my high-swept ponytail. "What?"

"The rooftop party Bennett's throwing." Rip looks like he will whine if I say I've changed my mind about attending. "We are still going, right?"

"Of course." I pick up my bag and check my phone. "Baker's downstairs waiting."

"Should I pick you up here tonight?" Rip frowns, maybe starting to sense me pulling away. About damn time. I've been about as subtle as a hooker in heels.

"No, I'm not sure how my day's going. I'll probably dress at the office." I curve my lips just so. "Let's meet at the party."

I'm out the door and at the elevator before he can protest anymore. The black Infiniti QX80 idles in front of my apartment building, Baker, my father's driver, waiting to open the back door for me. I peck his cheek just to see his face redden and his stern mouth yield a tiny smile.

Baker's been driving my father all over this city for twenty years. If Walsh were ever unable to run Bennett, Baker probably knows just as much as my father and could step in without a hitch. He's overheard and forgotten more about Bennett Enterprises than most of its executives will ever know.

"Thanks for the ride, Baker." I meet his eyes in the rearview mirror. "I suppose Daddy's been at the office for hours already."

"He went in rather late this morning, Miss B. Not until eight."

Over the years, Martin Bennett and my father set a high bar for everyone else, always at their desks and decimating other companies by six most mornings, seven on slack days. I know for a fact Walsh arrives even earlier than that many mornings.

We fall into a comfortable silence, and I look over my notes for the meeting ahead. Soon we're in front of the Bennett building, and Baker is opening the back door for me to exit.

"Will you need a ride to the party tonight?" Baker takes my hand to help me down to the sidewalk. "Or will Mr. Ripley be taking you?"

"Neither, actually. I'll make my own way."

"You often do, Miss B." His face and tone relax. "May I ask if you and Mr. Ripley are still…together?"

He's earned these personal questions. When I was growing up, my father had time only for Bennett Enterprises, and my mother thrived at the epicenter of New York City's social scene. Sometimes Baker ended up being the closest thing to an actual parent I had, answering awkward adolescent questions and making sure I made it home from rowing practice each afternoon.

"We're still together for now." I glance up the bustling block before looking back to Baker's deliberately stoic features. "You don't like him very much, do you? Rip, I mean."

"He's not for me to like or not like, Miss B." He crinkles only the corners of his eyes. "He does have a great arm."

I tease him with a wicked smile.

"It's not exactly his arm I'm interested in, Baker."

Nothing like seeing a grown man blush, and Baker makes it fun to be outrageous.

"Why, I think you're blushing, Baker."

"One day I'll figure out how to make *you* blush again, Miss B."

"Me blushing would be my face's idea of sarcasm." I straighten my blazer and glance at my watch. "I need to get on in. Thanks again for the ride."

The elevators at this time of morning take forever, so when I see a set of doors open, I rush across the lobby, stilettos and all, my runway experience coming in handy.

"Hold the elevator!" I call out with little hope that someone actually will.

A hand presses the door back, and I slip in, grateful words already spilling out of my mouth.

"Thank you so m—"

A set of dark chocolate eyes smile at me from under a spill of ginger-colored hair.

"You were saying?" Trevor Bishop stands there, smelling delicious and looking mouth-watering in a gray three-piece suit. I love men in pink, and his choice of a pink silk shirt beneath his vest, no tie, exposing the tanned strength of his neck gets my vote.

"Thank you," I finish, noticing for the first time that the elevator is crowded with other people, including Harold Smith and Karma Sutton, Walsh's assistant. "Good morning, Mr. Smith, Karma."

"Good morning, Miss Baston," Karma says, British accent crisp.

"I meant to tell you I saw you walk Chanel in London. You were flawless."

At her words, I sense interest pique around me as people realize it's not their imagination, but they do actually know me from a billboard or grocery store magazine. I'll be glad when the elevator car empties. I'm going to the top, so it should soon.

"Thanks, Karma." I fix my eyes on the climbing numbers illuminated above our heads.

"When is your next show?"

"Um, I don't have a show booked." I give her a smile, starting to care less if anyone else is listening. "I've been walking runways since I was eighteen years old. I think I'll leave it to the youngsters from now on. Maybe it's time to retire."

"But you're the Goddess." Karma sounds so dismayed I have to laugh a little.

"Fifteen years is a long time." I study my boots, determined not to look at Trevor Bishop, even though I feel those dark eyes pressing on me. "I'm ready for something else."

As much as I've enjoyed my run modeling, it's not a game you stay on top of indefinitely. A wrinkle here. Fine lines there. The bar is perfection, and no one can clear it forever. I want to exit gracefully and on my terms, not be chased out by some idiots who only want to photograph nineteen-year-olds.

We've stopped several times, emptying along the way until it's just the four of us now, headed toward the thirty-fifth floor, which houses Bennett's most senior level executives. And me for now.

"Is the office to your liking?" Karma asks.

"Yes." I give her a warm smile. "I appreciate your help. It's lovely, and exactly what my team needs."

"You have an office here?" Trevor asks, forcing me to at least give him a glance. Still mouth-watering, towering over us all, the breadth of his shoulders swelling in the perfectly tailored jacket. And what does he do to get those muscles in his thighs? No businessman should have all that body. His suit is like a silk cage barely containing a lion.

"Yes." No more. No less.

"I didn't think models needed offices," Trevor says.

"You pay him to think?" I direct the question to his partner, Harold, who swallows a laugh, his eyes twinkling back at me from behind his glasses.

"He doesn't pay me at all." Trevor's wide smile sketches dimples in the lean cheeks covered with a thin layer of cinnamon stubble.

Death by dimples. Just drive a stake through my vagina. It would be a quicker, less painful way to go.

"So what's your office for?" Trevor is persistent. I'll give him that.

"It's a temporary office while my permanent spot is being renovated." I wonder if he'll notice that I didn't actually answer his question.

"And what business do you conduct in this temporary office?"

I turn my head, giving him the full benefit of the face he's been staring at in profile ever since I boarded this elevator.

"It's a business I like to call mind your own business." My voice is saccharine, artificially sweet and might over time kill you.

Trevor's chocolate brown eyes narrow on me, but his smile remains even when Harold and Karma snicker. I know because my heart keeps tripping over itself every time he flashes those damn dimples at me.

Before he can poke his nose any further into my business, the elevator dings for the top floor. I divide a smile equally between the three of them, maybe giving Trevor a slightly smaller portion than Harold and Karma.

"Enjoy your day, gentlemen." I step off the elevator and turn right, knowing they're probably headed left toward Daddy's or Walsh's suite of offices. "Thanks again, Karma, for your help."

Every confident, long-legged step puts much-needed distance between Trevor Bishop and me. For some reason, I glance back over my shoulder. I'm startled to find him standing at the other end of the hall, hands shoved into his pockets, jacket pushed back to show that taut waist widening up to the long, broad torso. He's watching me walk away while Harold and Karma continue in the other direction. I don't stop, but aim a discouraging frown at him, hoping he gets the message to leave me alone. Maybe he misreads the message, because he merely grins and salutes me before he turns to follow his partner and Walsh's assistant.

He has a bad case of social blindness. I can't get much ruder without jeopardizing his business with Bennett. What does he want? Why is he acting this way? He was one of Daddy's fish. I was bait. I was just supposed to draw him out, convince him that Bennett was the best option. Let my breasts do the talking, except something went terribly wrong, and now I think I might like him.

I didn't expect to see him again. I didn't expect him to disturb me the way he does; to disrupt my equilibrium. And between the business venture I'm getting off the ground, a monster named Manchester reentering my life, and a past-due quarterback in my bed, my equilibrium has enough to manage without a lumberjack in a three-piece suit making my heart skip beats every time he's within dry-humping distance.

I shove those weak-minded thoughts aside when I enter my tiny, luxurious space at Bennett Enterprises. It's only mine for the next two weeks, but it's chic and gorgeous, decorated in icy blues and misty grays, glass desktops and delicate furniture populating the two rooms I've been temporarily assigned. As soon as I cross the threshold, a slim hand with rings on every finger except the thumb proffers a cup of steaming coffee.

"Ah, Stil, you're worth your weight in chocolate." I grab the coffee and slurp greedily. "I thought I was going to have to set up a caffeine IV. Thank you."

My assistant, formerly my makeup artist, is also formerly Stella Miller. Early on she was obsessed with all things Stila. All of us models teased her about buying Stila eyeliner when she didn't even have money for food. So over time, Stella became Stila, and Stila became Stil, and Stil has become one of my few true friends. In this transition from model to mogul, she's my right hand. She's helping me keep life on kilter.

She always had the most organized station at the shows, all her pots and potions and liners and lipsticks almost OCD level neat. She brings that same obsessive attention to detail to my life. Thank God someone can.

"The rest land in half." Stil follows me into the larger office, where we've placed my desk.

We have our own verbal shorthand, Stil and I. We can conduct entire conversations in a roomful of people and no one be the wiser of what we are actually saying.

"Oh, good." I settle behind my desk and into the lumbar-loving leather seat molding the line of my body. "Thirty minutes to do a few things. I'm ready when they get here."

"How was last night?" Stil leans her too-slim petite frame against the doorjamb. Pink strikes like lightning through her onyx hair, short and pixied. She's not too slim because she doesn't eat. The girl has a "man meets food" appetite. She just also happens to have the metabolism of a hamster on Ritalin.

"It was okay." I keep my face neutral. I really don't feel like rehashing being at the table with Walsh and Kerris, or seeing Kyle Manchester again, or why that's a bad thing. And I certainly don't want to talk about Trevor Bishop.

"Did you do it?"

"Do what?" I raise cautious eyes to Stil. We've been through some wild times together. There's no telling what she thought I was going to do last night.

"Break it off with Rip." Stil rests her fist on one bony hip. "Or was it an 'o' for the road?"

"Neither. I didn't break it off, and no orgasm as a parting gift. So the night was truly a bust."

"Tonight then?"

"Maybe after the party." I grimace, taking a sip of my caffeinated lifeblood. "The break, I mean. I think I'm done with the sex. It has to be soon. If he used his tongue only to service me, we could probably stretch this out, but he keeps—"

"Talking?"

"Yes!" I slap my forehead. "He keeps *talking*, and it's driving me batty."

"He could use that tongue for so much good." Stil shakes her head and sighs. "I'm sorry he doesn't know when to shut up."

"*C'est la vie*, yeah?"

"Yep. Just be gentle. He seems kind of fragile to me."

"Fragile?" I scoff. "Rip's tough as nails. We both knew this was no grand love affair. Just fuck and fun."

"Okay, well, you know what you're doing. I'm gonna get ready for the meeting."

"Me, too."

I take out my iPad, and instead of pulling up the figures for my meeting, seemingly without my permission, my fingers type "Trevor Bishop" in the search bar. He has a TED talk? Who has TED talks? The word "incite" snares my attention, and I click on the video link. He's addressing a group of college students at a university, dressed more casually than I've seen him so far. He wears a Kelly green T-shirt and dark wash jeans, his ruggedness more pronounced in the less formal clothing. He turns to a whiteboard to write, and my jaw almost hits the desk.

That ass. Tight and round and muscular, I want to take a bite. To pluck it like I'm testing ripe fruit. I sink my teeth into my bottom lip, imagining what he must look like without the wrapping. I need to know how a Princeton dropout turned businessman gets this body. I'm so caught up in how good he looks, I almost miss what he's saying, but the urgency of his tone arrests my attention.

"It was my junior year at Princeton." He faces the lecture hall packed with students. "As part of a course study on international business, my then-roommate Harold Smith and I spent the summer visiting Southeast Asian and African countries. I was struck by how lands so rich in natural resources had such poverty. We were just a few days away from returning to the States when I experienced an inciting incident that would change the course of my life."

He props himself on the desk, connecting his dark eyes with as many of the students as he can from his spot at the front of the room. He folds his arms, biceps straining in the short sleeves, across his chest before continuing.

"We were in Indonesia. I'd never seen such hunger and poverty, unlike what we call poverty here." Trevor's whole expression hardens, so far from the teasing lighthearted man I've seen over the last two days, I barely recognize him. "Our global economic system had failed the people there so badly. I'm not one who believes we can take responsibility for everything that goes on everywhere in the world, but dropping food in a place like this was like spitting on a forest fire."

Trevor pauses, swallows, stands, and shoves his hands in his pockets.

"A little boy died right in my arms that day. Just breathing one minute and not breathing the next because of hunger. Because of malnutrition. Harold and I just...well, we just cried that night."

A bomb could go off downstairs and I probably wouldn't move. I'm as silent as the students listening whenever this was recorded, with bated breath waiting for his next words. I'm rapt, and it has nothing to do with how good he looks, or his tight ass, or those broad shoulders. His words are like a fist reaching into my chest and squeezing my heart, massaging the muscle until it beats, maybe for the first time in years.

"And that's when we started envisioning Deutimus Corp," Trevor says on the video. "We derived it from the Greek word *dunamis*, which means an act of power. Natural power and capability. We didn't just want to drop aid or food or resources onto people in developing nations, but we wanted to *restore* power to them, to economically and intellectually empower them so they could generate their own resources. Indigenous people generating indigenous solutions. We used our business understanding to establish these profit-bearing ventures in developing nations all over the world, run and managed by the people in those contexts."

"Everyone's here," Stil says from the door.

I fumble to stop the video, but Trevor's deep voice continues for a few seconds, electrifying the air around us.

"Who's that?" Stil steps deeper into the office, leaning over my desk to see Trevor on my iPad screen. "Shit, I'd climb that mountain."

I take the screen dark, irrationally irritated by her comment. I needed a bib for my drool at the dinner table last night when I saw Trevor for the first time, but hearing him discussed that way after what I just heard feels wrong.

"You said they're here?" I put on my business face. "Bring them in. We've got a lot of ground to cover."

I grab the iPad, stand, and cross over to the glass-and-steel conference room table on the other side of the room, surrounded by chairs just as delicate and tensile as the one at my desk. Soon every seat is filled with the people I've handpicked to help me with what Stil and I call my passion venture. It's hard to think of something that's this much fun as business.

"So Haven, as you all know," I say, leaning back and crossing my legs at the head of the table, "is a lifestyle website along the lines of Goop or Preserve, but with an edgier, more fashion-insider angle. Me, of course, being the fashion insider."

Everyone at the table grins or chuckles. Some of them are interns or come-uppers I plucked from fashion houses, but most of them are what I like to call texperts—the technical experts who will be the engine behind the glamour. One of them, Marlee, interned with the

Walsh Foundation last summer. A Columbia graduate, she'll help build the charitable arm of the website.

"We have all of our artisan partnerships nailed down." Stil levels a hesitant glance across the table at me. "All except one."

"Which one?" I tip my coffee cup all the way back, begging gravity to release one more drop, but nada. "Who haven't we secured?"

"Well, we all love this one jewelry line," Sera, a girl I snatched from Calvin Klein, says. "So unique."

"Show me." I stretch my hand out for the iPad Sera slides across the conference table. I swipe through the pictures, loving each one more than the last. The use of crude stones in classic settings is especially clever. And oddly familiar.

"I've seen these." I squish my brows together. "Where have I seen these?"

"It's the Riverstone Collection." Stil clears her throat and brushes nonexistent stray hairs back. "By Kerris Bennett."

Dammit.

Everyone at this table, everyone in this building, everyone in New York, hell, everybody who is anybody, knows my history with Walsh Bennett. To think I want to work with his wife; the woman who essentially usurped the place I always thought would be mine…

I glance at the iPad again and remember the piece Kerris was wearing last night at the charity dinner. Remember, too, her concern in the bathroom. Whatever I felt for Walsh wasn't much more than an heirloom my parents passed down to me. The sex was great, but I saw them together last night. What Walsh and I had is on a different planet from his connection, his commitment, to Kerris. They have a family, and I've moved on. I have…well, I don't actually have very much besides my work with the Walsh Foundation and this site I'm starting.

"Put that on my list." I don't look up from the iPad. "I'll talk to Kerris myself about partnering with us. Anything else we need to discuss?"

"I'm in communication with Jo Walsh Mitchell about the partnership with the Walsh Foundation," Marlee says. "We're discussing co-promotion opportunities, brand placement, and other ways we can link the two entities."

"Sounds great." I scribble my name in one of the Moleskine journals I keep handy all the time lately.

"And that illustrator you were interested in using for the site will be at the party tonight." Stil takes a sip of her chai tea latte. "Maybe try to cozy up to her at some point."

"Oh!" I look up from my scribblings, a smile taking over. "She does those Megan Hess kind of drawings, right? Yeah. I'll meet her tonight."

I stand, signaling the team that our meeting is over.

"Let me know if you need anything from me. Good meeting, guys. You're doing an amazing job."

I take the seat behind my desk, not looking up from the profit projection spreadsheet we distributed during the meeting as they all drift out of the office. Stil pauses at the door, resting her shoulder there.

"François Gerrard sent over some things for you to consider wearing to the party tonight," she says.

"Oh?" I slide my spreadsheets to the side. "Lemme see."

Stil steps back into the lobby and rolls a garment rack back in. I count six options. Two immediately stand out—a black strapless jumpsuit with dipping cleavage and narrow legs, and a caramel-hued long-sleeve minidress that would probably mold every curve I've got.

"I'll probably get ready here, so his timing couldn't be better." I run my hands over my sleek ponytail. "What do you think for my hair and makeup?"

Stil tilts her head, squeezing one eye closed. She'll always be a makeup artist at heart, and I trust her opinion completely.

"You're doing it yourself?"

I nod. After fifteen years in the hands of the world's greatest makeup artists and stylists, I know all their tricks and can achieve the same effects when I have to. We talk through a few options until a clear vision for the night emerges.

"I guess François wants you in his stuff as much as possible now that the Goddess deal has been inked." Stil grins, the stud in her left nostril glinting. "Can you believe you're gonna have your own perfume, Sof?"

I hold my chin in the palm of my hand and tap my fingers against my face. François was one of the first designers to give me a chance when I was eighteen and had never even walked a runway.

"Well, it's *his* perfume. He's just using my face to sell it." I circle my index finger around the lip of my empty coffee cup, setting aside my cynicism long enough to smile about something I never would have seen coming. "It is pretty cool, though. We should see if he's willing to sell it on Haven."

"Oh, connect the dots." Stil turns toward the outer office. "I'll call his people and set up a convo. Want a salad from the bistro downstairs?"

"Yes, please." I pick up my iPad to review the items we discussed at the meeting. "I'm starving already."

Stil's Loubs echo across the floor as she leaves the suite. Down the passageway, I hear the elevator ding for the doors to open. As soon as I know she's safely descending toward the bistro, I flip back to my Google search of Trevor Bishop. I watch three more videos, all of them captivating. It isn't the hint of stubble coating his square chin, or the dimples hole-punching his lean cheeks. Nor is it the intimidating breadth of his shoulders. It's not even that ass that has me watching video after video, reading post after post, article after article about him.

Trevor Bishop tempts me, intrigues me, even inspires me. Few men have managed to do that all at once. He's a species I've rarely encountered in my years of hurried hookups, illicit affairs, and dead-end flirtations.

He's a good man. I have no use for good men, and despite what they may think when they look at me, they have no use for me. A good man should have a good girl.

And that I've never been.

CHAPTER SIX

Trevor

I'm not sure this will work.

Walsh Bennett is sharp, brilliant, resourceful, and, from what I can tell, a man of integrity. He lives up to and even exceeds his reputation. Unfortunately, so does Ernest Baston. I'm not sure I can do business with that man. He's ruthless, heartless, and I'm pretty sure underwent a conscience lobotomy decades ago. After spending the morning meeting with him, I could use a full-body soak in hand sanitizer.

"So what'd you think?" Harold asks as we wait for the elevator.

I know Harold wants this deal to happen, but we've worked too hard to get Deutimus where it is, achieving what it's doing for the people it's helping, to take the first offer that comes our way. We're not desperate. We're in pole position. We've made the smart moves to put us there, and Ernest Baston won't fool me into thinking differently.

"I didn't like Baston's body language when I mentioned keeping indigenous workers," I say. "Even when it might be more cost effective to use workers from other nations like India or China."

"He didn't *say* it would be a problem, Bishop." Harold gives me that long-suffering look he reserves for my "gut" reactions.

"You know as well as I do that most of communication is nonverbal." I lean against the elevator wall while we wait for the elevator car to come. "He isn't saying what he's thinking because he knows we'll walk away."

He knows *I* will walk away. There is already a conflict brewing between the inner warriors tucked neatly away behind our suits. Baston doesn't like me, and I don't like him, and we both know it. But we'll just keep grinning until we can put the pretenses aside and bare our teeth at each other.

My guess, based on Baston's pattern, is that he's digging around for something he can hold over us to force us into his way of thinking before he shows his hand. I don't operate that way, and I'd rather get out before he starts tampering with the people and things that mean something to me. That wouldn't end well.

For him.

The elevator dings, the doors open, and Harold steps in. It takes him a second to realize that I'm still out.

"What are you—" Understanding dawns on his face. "Aw damn, Bishop. Leave that woman alone. She's not your type."

"I'll catch an Uber home." I grin at him and turn to the right, the direction I saw Sofie go this morning. "You take the car."

"You'll take an Uber all the way to Brooklyn?" Harold asks as the doors are closing. "That'll cost a fortune."

"Didn't you hear?" I say over my shoulder. "We're rich now."

I can only hope there aren't many options down this hall. I could end up looking ridiculous poking my head in every door until I find Sofie. It's a cause I'm willing to look the fool for, though. Even though Harold's right. She's not my type. The last woman I dated...hell, I almost married, graduated from Oxford and leads a global clean water campaign. Half Kenyan, half British, she speaks four languages and will probably be an ambassador before she's forty.

And the whole time we dated, the whole time we were engaged, never did I feel what I felt in the sliver of time I've spent with Sofie. Like she's an impossible table puzzle with a million pieces I could spend all afternoon assembling, and never get quite right. Like I'd get to the end, and still have these tiny empty spaces where pieces hiding under the couch or lost in the attic should be.

I know people instinctively. Call it a curse or a gift, but I see things they try to hide from me. My dad is just in touch enough with his Native American forefathers to believe the Great Spirit guides us in these things. I have no explanation for how or why I can cut through what people present to who they really are, but I always can. I never fall for bullshit.

And though Harold's right about Sofie not fitting the usual profile of women I'd be interested in, my feet still follow the path I saw her take. That path ends at an open space with a glass reception desk of sorts. No one is seated there, but a clear carry-out container rests on the large, wide marble lip above the desk. It's a grilled chicken salad, and on the container there's a note.

"Sorry, Sofie," I read aloud. "No artichoke hearts today."

I look around the small, neat lobby. I'm in the right place.

"Stil, food!" a disembodied voice booms from the adjacent room. The door is slightly ajar, and through the crack, I see Sofie's gilded head bent over a stack of papers on her desk. Without a second thought, I grab the container and walk into the office.

"It's about damn time." Sofie doesn't lift her head, but jots down a note in a Moleskine notebook. "Now I'm hangry."

"Well, they're out of artichoke hearts." I set the container on the desk in front of her. "Hope that doesn't make it worse."

Her eyes fly up from her work, meeting mine and widening.

When they say this woman is beautiful, they're not telling the half of it. Or maybe they just leave out the most important part. It's not the perfection of her features that captivates me. It's all the things hidden behind those green eyes. Like water so vibrant and clear you can see all the way down to the ocean floor, but somehow as you dive deeper, there's all this life teeming beneath the surface that managed to remain undetected until it brushes up against you.

That brief surprised widening of her eyes is the only moment she yields to me, my last advantage. She recovers quickly, leaning back in her seat and crossing one long leg over the other, clearly a move that usually distracts horny men long enough for her to manipulate them. If she were wearing a skirt, I might have even fallen for it.

"Are you lost?" She raises one dark blond brow.

"No more than everyone else." I settle one butt cheek on the edge of her desk, mostly for show because I'm afraid my full weight would topple the little glass table.

"Oh, is this a philosophical discussion then?" Her full lips bend almost undetectably.

"If you'd like, I'm down for that."

"Men don't usually want to have philosophical discussions with me."

"I bet they're missing out."

"No, they're not." She uncrosses one leg, scoots them both under the desk, and rests her chin on folded hands. "What can I do for you, Mr. Bishop?"

"First, you can call me Trevor, or just Bishop." I give her a grin. "All my friends do."

She doesn't bounce a grin back to me.

"How nice for your friends. And you're here because?"

"I was wondering if you're coming to the rooftop party tonight."

She tilts her head, giving me an unblinking stare.

"And that matters to you why?"

"I'm leaving for Cambodia tomorrow, and I wanted to see you again."

A small frown knits her eyebrows together, and her lashes drop to hide her eyes.

"I thought you and Harold were staying in New York for a while."

"We are when we come back, but have some business there first." I reach out to lift her chin, forcing her to look at me again. "So will you be there tonight?"

She turns her head, subtly freeing herself from my grasp.

"You know I'm dating Rip." She lifts her lashes, giving me the full impact of those green eyes. "Are you in the habit of pursuing another man's girl?"

"No, I have a definite rule about that. I never go after another guy's girl." I shake my head. "This isn't pursuit. This is early level mild interest."

"*This* is early level mild interest?" She leans forward a little, extending her neck for the question. "Following me to the bathroom? Staring at me rudely in elevators? Asking probing questions in front of strangers? Tracking down my office and arriving unannounced? I'd hate to see pursuit."

"I actually think you'd like to see pursuit, but we won't know until you kick the quarterback. When's that happening, by the way?"

"I told you he's still fucking me out of my mind. Why stop now?"

She watches my face closely for the response she wanted from her words. Little does she know it's not my face that's responding. Every time she says the word "fuck" my dick goes hard as granite, even though she's talking about it with someone else.

"I think the only way a guy like Rip can hold on to a woman like you is to keep her fucked out of her mind, so that's probably his best strategy. If you stop fucking him long enough to come to your senses, I'd like to take you to dinner."

"Dinner?" Her laugh is like cream, rich and decadent. "Why don't you say what you really want?"

"I just did. I always do."

"Well, it's a moot point since I'm with Rip and you're off to Cambodia and I doubt we'll cross paths again."

"You didn't answer my question. Will you be at the rooftop party tonight or not?"

Her smile fades to nothing and she blinks several times.

"I'll be there with my boyfriend."

"I'll respect that, of course." I straighten from the little glass structure I almost crushed. "But once he's out of the picture, which we both know he will be soon, all bets are off, and I'm formally warning you that we go from early level mild interest to full-on pursuit."

"You can pursue all you want, but that doesn't mean you'll succeed."

"That's like pouring gasoline on a kitchen fire with somebody like me. My high school guidance counselor told me that about going to Princeton, but I got in on a football scholarship. My own parents warned me about leaving college to start Deutimus, and it's turned out pretty well for me."

"Is that what I am to you, then?" She looks at me unsmilingly. "A challenge? Something to be achieved?"

"I think you're a woman who hasn't even begun to show the world who she is." I consider her for an extra second. "I think in some ways that's something you're still trying to figure out yourself, and people engaged in that process fascinate me."

"*I* think the world and I both already know who I am." The look she gives me is supposed to be a dismissal, but I'm too much of a stubborn goat to read it as one. "Now if you'll excuse me, I have work to do."

So I'll see her once more before we fly out tomorrow. Another chance to chip away at that sparkling armor. I walk back toward the door, pausing by the garment rack. My imagination puts her in the dark brown minidress, and I practically drool.

"I like the brown dress, by the way."

I shouldn't have said it. She'll wear something else just to spite me. That's okay, though. With this woman, even spite is an aphrodisiac.

CHAPTER SEVEN

Sofie

It's not quite five o'clock when I make my way toward my father's office, hoping I can speak to him before he leaves, if he's leaving. He usually has clothes here so he doesn't have to go to the house. Over the years, he and my mother have devised all manner of ways to avoid being at home at the same time.

Celeste, Daddy's assistant, and probable longtime mistress, is packing up when I approach my father's suite.

"Ms. Baston, good evening." Celeste adjusts the strap of her bag on her shoulder. "Your father's wrapping up a call."

"Thanks, Celeste. Will you be at the party tonight?"

"Wouldn't miss it." Celeste offers a parting smile before walking out. "See you this evening."

When I was a little girl, this office seemed so massive. I felt like Alice in Wonderland, with everything oversize and fantastical. Now when I walk in, knowing the kinds of deals Daddy does behind these doors, it just feels like the black hole Alice tumbled through.

"Keep me posted." Daddy speaks into the handset, glancing up at me as I cross the threshold. "Yes. Just let Celeste know."

I sit down in the chair across from Daddy's desk. Anxiety swells inside my throat, not unlike the day I sat in this very office and told him I wouldn't be going to Princeton, but was heading to Paris for my first runway show. That bastard Kyle Manchester was a dark undertow in that pivotal conversation, just like he is in this one. Only Daddy didn't know it then.

The secret I've been carrying around for fifteen years hovers on the tip of my tongue, lured out of darkness by necessity. I had put this behind me. After two years of therapy and more than a dozen years living strong and making my own choices, I put it behind me. But now it's rearing its ugly head again, and though I won't expose it to the world, I have to tell Daddy. If he knew what Kyle Manchester did all those years ago, I have to believe he wouldn't do business with him.

"Sofie, this is a surprise." Daddy shifts his attention to a stack of papers on his desk, giving me a cursory look. "Shouldn't you be on your way home to get ready for tonight's party?"

"I'm dressing here at the office." I fold my hands in my lap. "Leaving from here."

"So did you need something?"

Right to the point. No affection or concern. My father doesn't deal in either of those, and I should be used to it by now, but somehow I never am. I should lower my expectations of him, as he has done of me.

"Could I ask you...well, how deep are you in with Kyle Manchester?"

I've spent my whole life studying this man, trying to figure out how I can best please him. I can never seem to get that quite right, but trying has taught me a lot about him. And I recognize, even though his face remains completely relaxed, a certain alertness enter his eyes.

"Why do you ask?" Daddy flips open a file, running his eyes over it, but not really seeing it. Not fooling me. I have his full attention.

"He's not a good man, Daddy."

His eyes flip up to mine, narrowed on my face.

"Neither am I, Sofie." A band of steel runs through his soft words. "Neither are half the men we do business with. Neither is Walsh Bennett, if it comes down to it."

"You're wrong about Walsh." I tug the corner of my mouth between my teeth. "But Kyle…"

I inch forward until I'm literally on the edge of my seat.

"Daddy, what if I told you that Kyle hurt me?"

A frown pinches his brows together.

"Hurt you how? When?"

"On prom night, he—"

"High school, Sofie?" His sharp laugh dices my confidence. "Next year this man will be one of the most powerful politicians in the country, and you're talking to me about prom night? Really, Sofie. I expect better of you."

"No, Daddy, listen." I lick dry lips. "On prom night he hurt me. He forced me. He ra—"

"Stop." Daddy slams his hand on the desk, rattling a bin of paper clips, rattling my nerves. "Don't say it, Sofie. Not to me and not to anyone else. Have you repeated this nonsense to anyone else?"

"It's not nonsense, Daddy. If you'd just listen to what happened—"

"And you're just now telling me something like this fifteen years later?" He stands, walking back and forth and rubbing his chin between his fingers. "No, I think that time and memory twist reality. It's understandable. You probably expected more from your…encounter with Kyle, and maybe you were upset when he moved on."

"That isn't what happened at all." I borrow some of his steel, weaving it into my words. "I know exactly what happened that night."

"I can't let you endanger a man's career because of something you *think* happened more than a decade ago."

"Daddy, please listen to me." His dismissal whittles my voice, my heart, down to a nub.

"No, you listen to me, young lady." No one seeing this man's face, hearing his voice, would think I'm his daughter. There is nothing soft or protective in how he looks at me, in how he speaks. "I am on the cusp of the most important deal of my life, and Kyle Manchester is the linchpin. No one, not even you, will ruin that for me."

"I don't want to ruin anything, I just…I just thought you should know that—"

"That he's not a good man. I heard you." His face softens, but it's a calculated yielding. A deliberate act to put me at foolish ease. "Sofie, let sleeping dogs lie, and don't repeat this nonsense to anyone else."

"Will he be there tonight?"

"No, he's on vacation with his wife and children." His mouth pulls back to show his teeth. "He's a dedicated family man like me."

"You do your deal, Daddy. I won't get in the way since it's obviously more important to you than I am." I stand, shoving down the hurt long enough to make my face a rigid reflection of his. "But I will not be in the same room with that man again. Ask me to, and I'll become difficult."

Daddy crosses around the desk and intrudes into my space so quickly, I'm forced to recoil.

"Difficult?" He snaps, disdain distorting the distinguished face and filling the green eyes so like mine. "You haven't seen difficult, baby girl. I don't need you in the same room with him, especially now that I know the kinds of delusions you're concocting in that pretty little head of yours. Stay away from Kyle altogether, or you'll regret it."

"Wow." I walk to the door, turning to say the last words I plan to say to him for a long time. "I came here to tell you that vermin raped me, thinking it would make a difference, and *you* protect *him*."

His face tightens at the word "rape." A word I've so rarely even said aloud. And never to anyone, but my therapist, applied to me.

"Sofie, you have to understand. This deal—"

"Stop." I lift my hand, blocking his excuses, which cannot possibly be good enough. "Just stop, Daddy. I'll stay out of your way and you keep Kyle out of mine. It's worked all these years. Why stop now."

CHAPTER EIGHT

Trevor

She didn't wear the dress I liked. That's okay, because what Sofie decided to wear has me, and, I suspect, every man in her immediate radius, adjusting myself discreetly in my pants. It's some one-piece pantsuit thing with no straps that fits her body like she was sewn into it, plunging into a V that displays the tops of her high, firm breasts and leaves her shoulders bare. A mass of onyx and pearls hangs around her slim throat. Her hair, fair as white gold in places, is piled high in messy splendor, a few tendrils caressing her neck. In her heels, she probably stands only a few inches shorter than my six five.

"You're catching flies, Bishop." Harold stands with his back to the bar, elbows up on the surface. "Mouth hanging open over that woman again."

"Fuck you, Smith." I knock back the last of my scotch. "Shouldn't you be back at the manor convincing Henri to finally give you a shot?"

Harold has a massive crush on our assistant, Henrietta. For a long time, it seemed destined to be forever unrequited, but lately she's shown signs that maybe she's feeling him, too.

"Shows how much you know." Harold grins, making his face even more boyish than usual. "I'm taking her to dinner as soon as we get back from Cambodia."

After two years watching him pine over her, I can't even bring myself to teasingly deflate him. I extend my fist for a pound.

"Good work, Smith. So, where you taking her?"

Harold's eyes go wide with panic, and all his color washes away.

"Hey, you've got time." I pat him on the back. "We'll figure it out. Don't break out your inhaler."

He nods, as if reassuring himself, the color slowly returning to his blanched face. He *really* likes Henri. Just as I'm about to ride him about it at least a little, I see a guy near Sophie who looks like he's screwing up the courage to speak to her. Get in line. Actually, there isn't a line. Only me. She just doesn't know it yet.

"You okay there, buddy?" Harold nods to the end of the bar, where Sofie waits for her drink. "Need my inhaler?"

I nail him with a deadly look and then make my way down to her end of the bar before the guy can make his move. She glances up, doing a double take when she realizes that I'm so close.

"You again." She cuts her eyes up at me. "Shocking."

If I wasn't so sure this woman likes me, I'd put on a Kevlar vest before every conversation.

"So what're you drinking?" I ask.

She grins, taking a sip from her martini glass.

"Perfect Ten."

"Why am I not surprised?" I signal the bartender. "Scotch, please. So where's your quarterback?"

"On his way." She peers over the rim of her glass as she sips. "Don't worry. You won't have to keep me company for long."

"Oh, I don't mind." I step close enough for her scent to wrap around me. "But then you know that, don't you?"

Our glances tangle for a few seconds before she lowers her lashes.

"I know what?" she asks.

"That I like you."

"Why?"

"Why what?"

"Why do you like me?"

I laugh a little, enjoying this perplexing woman more than I have anything in a long time.

"I don't know yet, to be honest."

There's no time to name the emotion that flits across her face because she hides it so quickly.

Before I can make any more progress with Sofie, a large hand falls on my shoulder. I'm almost shocked to see Martin Bennett standing there, since he's been so scarce during our negotiations. I know he suffered a heart attack a while back and has been less involved in the company, but he hasn't been in any of our meetings since we arrived in New York.

"Bishop, good to see you." He drops a quick kiss on Sofie's hair. "I didn't know you'd be here, Sof. Haven't seen you in so long."

"Too long, Uncle Martin." Sofie leans into Martin's shoulder for a second before glancing at me and pulling back.

"How have negotiations been going?" Martin asks me, looking so much like Walsh I have to remind myself I haven't sat across the negotiation table from this man.

"They're going." I keep my reservations out of my voice. "We've got a ways to go and lots of options to explore."

"You're in good hands with Walsh." He flicks a quick glance Sofie's way. "And Ernest, too, of course."

"Where's Walsh tonight?" Sofie asks.

"The girls are sick, and he wanted to relieve Kerris." Martin offers a rueful smile. "Wish I'd done more of that when I was his age. Too busy building empires."

My father spent a lot of time with me growing up. I'm as close to him as I am to my mother. He didn't have an empire to pass along to me like Martin has for Walsh, but I wouldn't have achieved anything I have had my father not invested as much in me as he did. He never missed a game. Made sure I was prepared for every test. Stayed close, but gave me space when I entered my rebellious stage as a teenager. I know Walsh and Martin never had that, and right now Martin looks like he'd trade all he's amassed to have what I shared with my pop.

"Walsh seems to have turned out all right in the end," I tell Martin.

Martin gives me a long, considering look before nodding and giving another rueful smile.

"You know, you remind me a lot of Walsh." Martin takes the club soda Sofie secured for him at some point. "Thank you, Sofie."

"I remind you of Walsh?" I lean against the bar. "How so?"

"He's always looking for ways to mesh business and philanthropy. Got that from my wife." Martin's face pinches for a moment. "From his mother, that is, Kristeene."

I've heard Martin took Kristeene Bennett's death hard, even

though they had been divorced for years. His face betrays all the things he's been publicly reticent about: that he loved his ex-wife very much. That he still misses her. That he probably always will.

"I'm hearing great things about Bennett Charities," I say into the heavy silence that follows his comment.

My words seem to flip a switch inside the older man, his face becoming animated as he talks about the work he's overseeing with the relatively new charitable arm of the company he founded.

"I'm enjoying it a helluva lot more than I thought I would." Martin grins at Sofie and me. "They can barely get me in the office for anything else lately."

He says it jokingly, but if I had to call it, I'd say this legend in the corporate raiders hall of fame just isn't as interested in it anymore. I'm not foolish enough to think, when he has to be, that he's any less ruthless than when he founded Bennett Enterprises, though. Sofie grew up with men like Martin and her father in this cutthroat world of high stakes and few qualms. So different from the way I was raised. My father, a postal worker, and my mother, an elementary school teacher, instilled in all seven of us kids things like integrity, compassion, and humility. I'm almost afraid to find out what Ernest and Billi Baston instilled in Sofie, in case it all took.

"I better get going." Martin squeezes Sofie's hand. "Keep up the good work with the Walsh Foundation, too, Sofie. They're lucky to have you."

"Thank you, Uncle Martin." Sofie's face is softer than I've ever seen it. "I'm lucky they haven't kicked me out yet."

Martin chastises her with a look.

"Well, that *Playboy* stunt came close." He chuckles when Sofie at least looks abashed. "Walsh went to bat for you on that score."

"He's done that more than once." Sofie takes another sip of her drink, flipping her chin toward the bartender to signal for another. "Your son has a hero complex, I think."

"Yeah, well, he didn't get that from me." Martin waves to someone a few feet away, motioning for him to come over. "I better go. Glad you're here, Bishop. Enjoy New York."

"So *Playboy*, huh?" I ask as soon as we're alone again.

Sofie meets my eyes as bold as a summer sunrise, shrugging her bare shoulders.

"It was tastefully done. My body, my business."

Before I can dig into that anymore, a young girl approaches us. Maybe mid-twenties. How am I ever supposed to make any headway with Sofie before the quarterback shows up with so many interruptions? She probably wants to know where Sofie got her shoes.

"Mr. Bishop, hi." The dark-haired girl wears a shy smile, flicking a nervous glance at Sofie. "Ms. Baston, sorry to interrupt, but I wanted to come thank Mr. Bishop."

"Thank *me*?" I eye her more closely. "Have we met?"

"Not exactly. I'm Marlee Simmons," she says. "I heard you lecture at Columbia a few years ago."

"Oh, yes." I return her smile. "I remember that talk."

"You spoke about inciting incidents in our life and global good and world citizenship." Marlee's smile grows wider. "It changed my life. I was a senior about to graduate with a degree in business, but I knew there was something missing. I'd never experienced much to make me passionate about anything, but you said if nothing has incited you, seek it. Position yourself to be impassioned. After your lecture, I graduated and did two years in the Peace Corps."

"That's amazing." I shake my head, still astounded and humbled when people tell me stories like this. "Good for you."

"I want to spend my life finding ways to leverage my business training for the greater good." She smiles at Sofie. "I interned with the Walsh Foundation last summer, and I'm helping Ms. Baston with charitable ventures for Haven."

Sofie deliberately looks away from me to the other partygoers. What's Haven? How is it connected to charity? What's Sofie up to?

"Again, sorry to interrupt." Marlee nods her head toward a table at the rooftop entrance. "I better get back over there, but just wanted to say thank you. You look lovely tonight, Ms. Baston."

"Thanks, Marlee," Sofie says with a small smile. "See you tomorrow."

Marlee leaves behind a silence packed with questions and impressions I need to sort through, but I don't have enough time. I'm about to ask Sofie about Haven when she surprises me with a question of her own.

"What's that like?" Her voice is low and clear, free of sarcasm and the snark she usually dishes out. I hear only genuine curiosity.

"What's what like?" I ask.

"To have people see you that way." A laugh at her own expense slips past Sofie's lips. "Uncle Martin compared you to Walsh, which for him is the highest compliment he could pay a man, and he talked to me about my *Playboy* spread. And Marlee, whom I've worked with for weeks, gushed that you literally changed the course of her life with one lecture."

Her unblinking stare rests on my face.

"I'm just wondering how it feels to affect people that way."

I could spout some self-deprecating drivel, some false modesty, or pull out some trite phrase that would make me seem like it's old hat to me now, but I don't. If I want to see what's going on beneath Sofie's surface, I have to show her what goes on beneath mine.

"I'll never get used to it." I shake my head, sliding my hands into my pockets. "And I always want to check for a hidden camera because I assume Harold's punking me."

Sofie smiles, relaxing against the bar. I lean back beside her, waiting for her to say the next thing. To make the next move. I can tell she likes to take the lead, and I guess I can let her take it until she shows me she doesn't know what to do with it.

"I heard that lecture, you know," she says so softly I almost miss it in the party conversation going on around us. "The inciting incident, I mean."

"You heard that?"

I've addressed Congress, done TED talks, and spoken before dignitaries and kings from all over the world, but at her words, I'm replaying that lecture in my head, wondering if she thought it was any good.

"I listened to it today." She looks into her drink instead of at me. "Four of them actually."

Did she say four? Today? And then it clicks for me—the thing I sensed teeming beneath the surface, the thing she's hiding from the world. Maybe even from herself.

It's hunger; a voracious appetite for more in a woman who has everything and who, I suspect, is starting to realize it will never be enough. Don't underestimate the power of dissatisfaction. When someone like Sofie, who's had everything culture tells us should make us happy—money, fame, prestige—realizes it doesn't, one of two things happens. She dives deeper into cynicism, gives up on meaningful pursuit, and continues down that path. Or she starts poking around inside herself and at the world around her to see if there is more to this life than the things we acquire, the things we achieve. I believe, even though she may not even realize it herself, Sofie has chosen the latter. She's searching for significance. That's what draws me to her, because I recognize that. I *remember* that.

"Sofie, did you see the way Martin Bennett's face lit up when he talked about Bennett Charities?" I wait for her nod. "And Marlee, the way she came alive talking about the Peace Corps? They're doing what I call following the fire."

"And what is that, exactly?"

"It's figuring out what burns inside of you, and then letting it guide you." My eyes probe her face. "What guides you, Sofie? What's your fire?"

A tiny frown puckers her expression as the question challenges her.

"I'm not sure how to answer that."

"Maybe not yet, but you will."

She holds my glance for a few seconds before looking at the floor.

"So you think Uncle Martin has found his fire, huh?"

Does she think I don't realize she deftly redirected the conversation away from her? Just this once, I'll let her get away with it.

"Honestly, from what I observed tonight and have seen over the last few weeks," I say, "I think not only has he found his fire, but that it's going to guide him right into retirement even earlier than everyone thinks."

Her eyes snap to my face, and maybe she knows what I'm about to say, but I'll say it anyway.

"And that will bring this power struggle between Walsh and your father to a head sooner than later."

"There's no struggle." Sofie licks her full lips, a quick swipe to make way for the lie she's telling herself, but that doesn't fool me. "Daddy knows Bennett Enterprises passes to Walsh."

"You don't believe that any more than I do." I hesitate before giving a mental "screw it" and going all the way. "And Deutimus won't be trapped in the crosshairs of that. It's not just jobs at stake. Wrapped up in our company, there are lives, there are families. They're people I made a commitment to, and I have no intention of letting them down."

Sofie and I stare at each other in the dimming light of the rooftop lanterns, in the waning light of the moon.

"Bishop, you have the kind of mind, the kind of heart, that changes people's lives when they meet you, and I'm just a model. I smile and look pretty." Sofie's gaze wanders over the partygoers around us before returning to me. "But can *I* give *you* a piece of advice?"

I nod, eyes fixed on the resigned expression she wears.

"If you care about those families, about those people who depend on you, whatever you do," she says, eyes as sharp and bright as the rare diamonds in our African mines, "don't trust my father."

"What do you mean?" She has my full attention, because when it comes to the people who rely on me for their livelihoods, I can't be too careful.

"He uses the things and people you care about against you to get what he wants." Sofie's mouth cracks into a hard smile. "Since he cares about no one but himself, not even his own daughter, he doesn't have those pesky liabilities."

"Did he hurt you?" The desire to squeeze the breath out of Ernest Baston's body takes over for a few seconds, surprising me with its intensity.

She looks from my scowling face to the hand clenched around my glass.

"Not in any way you would imagine, no."

"Why are you telling me this? Warning me about your father?" Even though I had ascertained this information for myself already, it means something to me that she's sharing it.

"Because you're a good man." She crooks that wide, beautiful mouth a little. "And there aren't enough of those out there. Mostly frogs, from my experience."

"If I'm such a good man," I say, going in for the kill, "once you've dumped the quarterback, and we both know you will, have dinner with me."

Sofie's laughter strikes a discordant note in the cooling night air.

"You just don't give up, do you?" She lowers her lashes and shakes her head. "A good man should have a good girl. I'm not a good girl, Bishop. Take out someone like Marlee. You two can talk about the Peace Corps and the world's starving children."

"Don't do that."

"Don't do what exactly?"

"Put up that guard and pretend to disparage something you want because you're not sure how to get it."

Her face tells me she's shocked by how much I see. So much so that she has to pretend I'm wrong.

"You don't know me and you have no idea what you're talking about."

Sofie pushes away from the bar, sets her glass down, and turns to walk away. I grab her elbow, gently and firmly. She tilts her head back, connecting our eyes.

"I see you, Sofie." I dip my head the few inches to bring our eyes level so she can read me as easily as I read her. "You're not just a pretty face and a tastefully done *Playboy* spread. There's a lot more to you than that."

"Sofie!" a voice calls over a few heads.

We both follow the direction of that voice.

Aw, hell.

I grit my teeth when I see Rip heading our way. Sofie pulls away, but not before Rip's eyes draw a line between me and his girlfriend, a frown settling on his commercial-ready face. This guy has no idea who Sofie is. I doubt he cares if she hungers for significance. That she wants to be more than just a walking, talking beauty brand. I can see how he and everyone else would assume that's all there is to her because she hasn't shown them anything else. I see her with unexpected clarity, though, like a gem under a loupe lens. Guys like Rip will never challenge her to be any more than the girl on his arm and in his bed. She's more than that. She's worth more than that, and I want her to know it.

Dumb move on my part, but I follow her, and when she's only a few steps away from Rip, I grab her gently by both elbows, pulling her into me until her back is flush to my chest. I lean down so that my words will reach only her ears.

"Sof, I'm leaving for Cambodia tomorrow."

Her long, slim body stiffens against me, but she doesn't glance up or back to look me in my eyes.

"If you haven't gotten rid of him by the time I get back, you know that rule I have about not going after other guys' girls?"

She does look up at me then, eyes guarded and uncertain, yet somehow knowing.

"I'm breaking it."

CHAPTER NINE

Trevor

I miss the ocean.

My arms feel like overboiled noodles barely dragging me through the electric blue, chlorinated water in the Brooklyn athletic club up the street from my sister's house. I long for the tumult, the capriciousness, the wild beauty of water deeper and wider than this tame rectangle marked in feet and inches. I want fathoms so deep I'm not sure when I'll reach the bottom, or if I ever can.

I've lost count of how many laps this makes. When I was a kid, I had so much pent-up energy, I couldn't focus and ended up in fights. Just as doctors started recommending medication, my father got me into football. And basketball. And swimming. Physical activity has been my drug of choice ever since. It focuses me, centers me, in a way nothing else ever does.

I haul myself onto the edge of the pool, chest heaving and arms trembling. I can tell I haven't been training. I stopped counting laps, but I know I can usually do more than I did this morning. Out of habit, I run my hands up my face to push back my hair, but there isn't much hair to push away. I buzzed it down when we were in Cambodia. Harold and I just got back two days ago, but I'm already pining for the open waters of the Atlantic down at Tybee Island, where I have a beachside property I don't get to use nearly enough.

The pool door opens, and Harold strides over to me, dressed in gym shorts and a T-shirt. He sits down beside me, taking off his running shoes and socks, dangling his legs in the pool.

"I figured I better come make sure you hadn't drowned." He hooks a towel around the back of his neck. "Man, you've been in there forever."

"Have I?" I snatch a towel from a nearby stack, wiping water away from my eyes and face.

"I knew you'd need to burn off some steam after that meeting with Ernest Baston." Hesitation settles on Harold's face. "Are we pulling out of negotiations?"

I consider my partner and best friend, holding my words for a few more moments. This was never meant to be permanent. We were twenty-one years old when we started the Deutimus journey. We said we'd give it five years to see if it succeeded, and it's surpassed all our expectations. Helped more people and made more money than either of us ever anticipated. But it was never supposed to be forever. We're both eager to find a partnering business that shares our values and can take Deutimus to the next level, but we can't compromise on commitments we made to the people all over the world who bought into this vision. Who have, in many ways, staked their futures on it.

"I'm kind of relieved Ernest showed his hand yesterday," I say.

"Well, he didn't as much show it as couldn't hide it when you started probing."

I pressed Ernest on keeping indigenous workers, on making sure that Bennett wouldn't use employees from other countries to cut costs since restoring economic power to the people in developing nations was the whole point. Not just amassing more economic power for ourselves. Ernest's polite mask fell away, and the ruthless businessman showed the ugly mercenary truth. I know it's about the bottom line for them, but that just means they may not be the right company to partner with.

"So are we done with Bennett?" Harold tries to hide the disappointment in his voice, but I hear it.

"I'm done with Ernest Baston," I correct. "I still think Bennett Enterprises *could* be the right partner."

"But Ernest—"

"Ernest's last name is Baston, not Bennett." I stand and dry off. "Walsh is the future of Bennett Enterprises. Him, I'll stay at the table with."

"If he'd been there yesterday like originally planned," Harold says, "things would have gone differently."

"Yeah, I think Ernest thought so, too. That's why he pushed to still meet even though Walsh got held up in Hong Kong."

"So what do we do, Bishop? We have other offers."

"I'm not ready to abandon Bennett yet. I think we wait. We made our position perfectly clear. Let's see what their next move will be."

"Sounds good." Harold stands. "I'm gonna shower. You coming?"

"In a little bit. I want to get some steam first."

Stripped down to just a towel, I lean back against the wall in the steam room. I draw a deep eucalyptus-infused breath, letting the steam soothe the muscles I stretched to the limit. The door opens, and I close my eyes. I'm not in the mood for some near-naked guy who enjoys a good, steamy chat. I hear him settle on the other end of the bench, but just slump my shoulders against the wall, hoping he takes the hint.

"Funny meeting you here."

My eyes snap open when I recognize that voice. Not much surprises me anymore, so I'm not sure why Walsh Bennett in my steam room should.

"Bennett, you're quite resourceful, aren't you?" I lean my head back against the wall, but remain alert. "I know you aren't a member here, so to what do I owe this dubious honor?"

He grins at me through the scented steam.

"I heard things didn't go well yesterday with Ernest," Walsh cuts right through the steam and the small talk.

"If you would say Hiroshima 'didn't go well'—I cross my arms over my chest—"then, yes, that's how I would characterize yesterday's meeting with Baston."

"Look, I know he can be a bit of an asshole."

I open one eye, cock one brow.

"Okay." Walsh chuckles, settling back against the wall. "He's a total dick, but what if I can guarantee you deal only with me?"

I lean forward, elbows to my knees, and give him my most candid look.

"Only you can't make many guarantees right now, can you? Not with things about to become so unstable at Bennett."

Speculation narrows Walsh's eyes.

"What have you heard?"

"It's not what I've heard. It's what's obvious to anyone paying attention." I pour a portion of eucalyptus into a small pot against the wall, intensifying the scent. "Your father is at the end of the road, and when he retires, the transition of power won't go as smoothly as he had hoped. Am I right?"

A muscle ticks in Walsh's jaw, but his face gives me no other indication that I'm even close.

"I propose that we take a back channel approach," Walsh finally says.

So he's going to ignore what I said, only confirming that I'm right.

"Back channel?" I lean into the sweating wall. "What are you thinking?"

"I need it to look like you're walking away from this deal." Walsh lifts one brow and one corner of his mouth. "But don't. Don't talk to anyone else. Wait for me to get things settled at Bennett, and then once I'm in charge, we resume talks."

"Where do you expect opposition to come from at Bennett?"

"Everywhere." Walsh scoots forward, until he's barely on the bench. "But don't worry. I'm ready for whatever Ernest and anyone else throws at me."

"You sure about that?"

"Always." Walsh leans back, stretching his long legs out in front of him and linking his hands behind his head, his casual posture not fooling me. "So what'll it take for you to agree to this? We can't put any of this in writing. It has to stay off the books, but I trust you."

"Why do you trust me?" He *can* trust me, but I'm interested to know how he figured that out so quickly.

"Let's just say I never go into a deal without knowing who I'm dealing with."

I've heard that anyone working with Walsh should expect to have their past and present excavated because he digs so deeply.

"So what'll it take?" he presses.

I love it when opportunities fall into my lap like apples. Harold and I had already decided we would wait for their next move, that we'd stick with Bennett for now. I'm getting something I want in exchange for something I was already prepared to give Walsh. It's great being me. I also love that as prepared as Walsh likes to think he is, and as much as he likes to think he has dug up on me, I'm about to take him completely by surprise.

"We'll stay in play if you give me Sofie Baston's number."

Walsh just blinks at me for a few seconds, until the request registers. A frown settles between his eyebrows. His mouth tightens.

"I don't think that—"

"That's it. Not much to ask."

"Sofie?" Walsh's frown goes deeper if possible. "Sofie Baston?"

"About this tall." I bring my hand up as high as my nose. "Legs that go on forever. I think you know her."

"Look, Bishop, I get it." Walsh grins at me. "Sofie's beautiful, obviously. And lots of guys—"

"I don't care about lots of guys." My voice comes out harder than I expected. Obviously harder than Walsh did, too, judging by the sharp look he levels at me. "You give me that number, or today we start calling all the other companies prepared to meet our terms."

"That doesn't make any conventional business sense."

"Says the man ambushing me in a steam room to do business wearing nothing but a towel. Neither of us got where we are being conventional. We both know what we want, and go after it."

"And you want Sofie?"

"Obviously." I don't sprinkle sugar on it. I don't explain it to him because it's none of his damn business what I want with Sofie.

"I wouldn't have pegged you for—"

"Trying to peg me would be a mistake, Bennett. Waste of your time and insulting to me."

Walsh stands up, gripping the ends of his towel together at one hip.

"I'll get you the number, but let me warn you." He turns at the door. "I know Sofie seems tough, but she's been through a lot. Guys have hurt her in the past."

"Like you did?" The question is a dart I aim through the scented air.

Walsh might punch me if he could. Only the business we still have pending, the twenty pounds and couple of inches I have on him, probably stop him.

"Yeah, like I did," he finally responds. "Sofie and I grew up together, and dating her was a mistake, but we're still friends. She's not an easy woman to know."

I hope the smile I give Walsh doesn't come off as cocky, because right now I'm feeling pretty satisfied with myself.

"Which is why I need your help."

"One more thing, Bishop." Walsh angles his head down, looking at me from beneath a slash of dark brows. "Because of my, shall we say research, I think I know what you want to do next."

"Next?" I focus on keeping the line of my shoulders even and relaxed. "Not sure what you mean."

"One of the things I admire *most* about you is that you, like me, actually want to change the world, and are foolish enough to think you can do it. You understand that even as much good as Deutimus is doing, it's sometimes like blowing on a wildfire."

He presses his back to the door, pushing it ajar and releasing some of the steamy air trapped in the room.

"You need to work from inside, to be in a position to influence those corrupt bastards leading these countries and making it hard for their own people to thrive."

"Let's say you're right," I offer. "What does any of that have to do with me and Sofie?"

"I know what you want next, and you can't have scandal if you're going to get it. Sofie draws scandal like bees to honey. I'm just saying you may not be able to have both."

"Walsh, your father recently told me that I remind him of you. I'd like to test that theory. How do you respond when someone says you can't have something you want badly?"

A lopsided grin skews Walsh's lips. He turns to leave, tossing his last words over his shoulder.

"I'll get you that number."

CHAPTER TEN

Sofie

Not him again.

I've been ignoring my cell all morning, but if I see Rip's name flash on the screen one more time, I may hurl the phone through my office window. And it's a new phone. A new window, for that matter.

"Rip, hey." I lean back in the office chair I managed to smuggle from Bennett Enterprises in last week's move.

"Sofie, I've been calling you all day," Rip says, voice petulant.

"Have you? Sorry, I've been slammed here at the office."

"Did you see what the *Post* wrote about us? They're reporting that we're done."

"Is that what they said?" I massage one temple. In just the week since our split, I'd almost forgotten what a recalcitrant child Rip can be.

"How'd it get out so fast? I haven't told anyone because I've been hoping you'll rethink the breakup."

"What can I say? We live in a bubble. Hard for people like us to keep secrets." I check a chip in my manicure. "And I have thought this through, Rip. I told you that last week when we ended things."

"But I thought maybe we could just take some time apart and figure things out."

"I just think we've come to the end of our road." I draw a deep breath, making a conscious effort to gentle my voice. "We can still be friends, but that's all I want."

"Is there someone else?"

Trevor Bishop's face, the square jaw and lean cinnamon-scruffed cheeks dented with those damn dimples, splatters itself all over my mental canvas. Not a day has gone by since that man traipsed off to Cambodia that I haven't thought about him. It's really irritating.

"There's no one else, Rip. Just me. It just needs to be me for a while." I let that sink in before checking to make sure he understands. "Okay, Rip? Friends?"

"Friends for now, Sofie," Rip says. "But you know how hot it was between us. I'll try not to rub it in when you come knocking wanting more."

Don't flatter yourself. Don't hold your breath or your dick.

"M'kay. Take care, Rip."

Why did I answer? His call has thrown my schedule off, and I need to get across town to meet with François's team about the unveiling of the Goddess scent. I'm gathering a few things to work on in the car while I ride when my cell rings again. I don't recognize the number, but I called a few artisans for Haven. It could be one of them returning my call.

"Hello?" I don't give more information than that in case it's a wrong number.

"Sofie, hi."

That voice pours over me like a vat of honey, and just those two words run down my body, leaving a trail of goose bumps in their sweet, sticky wake. I'd know that voice anywhere.

"Who is this?"

Trevor's deep chuckle rumbles from the other end.

"You don't recognize my voice, Sofie? I'm hurt. Truly."

"How'd you get my private number?"

"I'm a well-connected man."

"Are you back in New York?" Even though I have no intention of seeing him, I'm curious if it's even a possibility.

"Got back yesterday. Sorry it took me so long to call." A small pause hangs between us. "I read that you dumped the quarterback."

"Did you now?"

"Which brings me to the reason for my call."

"Which is?" I brace myself to refuse anything this man asks of me.

"Have dinner with me tonight."

"I'm busy tonight."

"Tomorrow?"

"No."

"Uh…the next night?"

"Sorry, no." I heave a sigh. "We talked about this. Go find yourself a Marlee."

"But I want myself a Sofie." I hear the grin in his voice and want to slap myself across the mouth for grinning back.

"We all want things we can't have."

"That's not my mantra."

"You have a mantra? How very pretentious of you."

The low-timbered laugh from the other end tightens my nipples in the silk cups of my bra.

"I can't remember ever being called pretentious before."

"Oh, then I'm your first. I promise to be gentle with you."

"No." His voice dips and goes a shade darker. "Don't be."

Damn, it's hot in here. I fan myself with the report Marlee sent over this morning.

"I have to go, Bishop. I'm already late for a meeting."

I hang up before anything else on my body goes wet or tight. Just two minutes of that Southern drawl has me making battery-operated plans for tonight.

"Was that Rip again?" Stil places a mint green and white shopping bag on the corner of my desk. "Here's a few pieces from Kerris Bennett's Riverstone Collection, like you asked for."

"Oh, thanks. Yeah, she and I are supposed to meet soon. Can you confirm?" I peer into the bag at the three boxes stacked neatly. "And, no, that wasn't Rip. Well it was, and then it wasn't. Two calls."

"Rip's still not getting the message?" Stil drops into the seat facing my desk. "Even after we went to the trouble of leaking the story to the *Post*?"

"Yeah, even still. I'm done being subtle and sweet." I grab my floppy leather clutch and my iPad, standing. "Remind me again why I'm not at least experimenting? Men aren't worth the trouble."

"I'm sure I can find you some girl-on-girl."

"No, thanks." I pair a wicked smile with a wicked wink. "I like riding stick too much."

"Ain't that the truth." Stil giggles. "You said it was and then it wasn't Rip. Who was the other call?"

"Oh, the *other* call." I lower my head and bend over, focusing on slipping my heels back on. "That was Trevor Bishop."

"Ooooh." Stil rubs her hands together vigorously enough to make fire. "We like him."

I make my face stern.

"No, we don't."

"Yes, we do." Stil's face softens. "I can tell you do, Sofie. You should give him a chance. I would."

I stand up straight and give her my "you better not ever" eyes.

"You won't."

"Oh, is my girl jealous?"

"Never." I grab my wrap for the October breeze that snuck into the city over the last few days. "You know I don't do good guys."

"You forget I've seen that good guy, and I bet he could do you good."

You're telling me…

"Well, he won't get the chance, will he?"

Stil has this way of just staring at me when she knows there's more, waiting for me to give it to her.

"Stil, everyone would ask what he saw in me. What he's doing with me." I grab the bottled water from my desk. "I've never been that girl, and I'm sure as hell not starting now. We don't fit. We make no sense."

"You never know."

I smile at her over my shoulder on the way out.

"And I never will."

CHAPTER ELEVEN

Trevor

*H*aven.

The scripted writing on the office doorplate makes me smile. I never did find out what Sofie was up to. Guess I will today. A mahogany reception desk takes up a good portion of the cool-toned lobby. A man, slim, brown-haired, early twenties, is on the phone. He holds up an index finger, silently indicating that he'll be right with me, and then waves me toward a set of sleek leather chairs. What's with all the skeletal furniture? A guy as big as I am needs something wooden and sturdy. I'm afraid I'll squash Sofie's little leather sofa.

"How can I help you?" The receptionist runs his eyes up my legs and over my chest before finally reaching my face. "I'd *love* to help you."

Well, this is awkward already.

"Um, hi." I stand and approach the guy at the desk. "I'm here to see Sofie Baston."

He glances from an iPad on his desk back up to my face.

"I don't see an appointment."

"Yeah, she must have forgotten to put it down." I hope the smile I'm giving him is actually persuasive.

"Yeah, sure. That must be why she left for the day." He rolls his eyes, but still looks interested. "You could leave a card with me."

I don't want to leave a card. I want...after three weeks, I'd just like to see Sofie. In a short time, I've grown to enjoy the way she layers sarcasm and testiness to hide what she's really feeling. She may as well be using cellophane, that's how apparent it is to me that she wants to explore what this could be between us.

"No card, but thanks."

I'm headed toward the exit when a petite woman with dark, pink-streaked hair enters the lobby from the hall presumably leading to the offices.

"Gil, were those illustrations delivered?" A frown puckers her eyebrows together. "Sofie needs those for her meeting tomorrow."

I hover near the door in case she drops information I may be able to use. She flicks a glance at me, looking away and then back again, eyes focusing on me.

"Have you been helped?" she asks.

"He was looking for Sofie." Gil does air quotes, skepticism lining his otherwise unlined face. "An appointment that she must have forgotten."

"I keep Sofie's schedule," the little lady says. "She didn't have an appointment this afternoon."

"Miscommunication, obviously." I head for the elevators.

"Trevor?"

My name called stops me in my tracks. I turn to find the lady smiling now.

"Trevor Bishop, right? I thought that was you." She grins, gesturing for me to follow her down the hall. "Come on back."

What happened? Am I missing something? Only one way to find out. Little lady leads me back down the hall into a spacious office decorated in shades of gray and green. She indicates another tiny chair that looks like it probably can't hold me.

"So I finally get to meet you," she says.

I freeze, halfway down to the narrow seat.

"Finally? You obviously know my name." My brows go up as I sit down. "And you are?"

"Call me Stil." She sits on the edge of her desk, her sharp eyes taking in my shoes, gray slacks, and dark sweater. "You're even better in person."

"Excuse me?" I manage a quick, self-conscious laugh. She doesn't hide the admiration in her eyes, but I don't get an interested vibe from her at all. "How do you know me?"

"Sofie watched some of your talks." Stil rolls her eyes and grins. "Actually a lot of them."

I run my palms over my knees, keeping my face neutral so she won't know how much that information pleases me.

"She did mention that." I look at her like I fully expect her to answer my next question. "Where is she?"

Stil gives a husky laugh and wags a finger at me.

"Oh, no, buddy. I'm not that easy." Her face drops any sign of amusement. "What are your intentions toward Sofie?"

"My *intentions*?" I run a hand over my closely cropped hair. "Does she have a dowry I should know about? Are we be betrothed now? What do you mean my intentions? I want to get to know her."

"A lot of guys want to 'get to know' Sofie, but I was hoping you were different." She stands, her mouth a straight line, and raises blue, disappointed eyes to me. "I'll show you out."

"I like her."

The words spill out before I have time to think better of it. I don't even know this little sprite of a woman, but it's apparent to me that she cares about Sofie, that she knows her. And the fact that she knows more about Sofie than I do means I should take her question seriously.

Stil slowly settles back onto the edge of the desk, a small smile playing around her lips.

"What do you like about her exactly?"

I wasn't prepared for a Sofie pop quiz.

"I like that she is absurdly honest," I say. "Like rudely so."

"You *like* that?"

"I hate bullshit. I hate having to figure out what people really mean behind what they say, and she's not like that." I shake my head and give a quick laugh. "Except for the fact that she pretends not to like me."

Stil lifts one pierced brow.

"Confident, aren't we?"

"Would she want a man who wasn't?" I return her grin before continuing. "So will you help me? Tell me where she is?"

"No, I'm sorry I can't tell you where she is."

I stand up, ready to head out. As much as I want to find Sofie today, Henri will be calling soon reminding me about the meetings that take up the rest of my afternoon. The reason I'm actually in New York.

"Well, it was nice meeting you, Stil." I start toward the door.

"Wait."

I look back to find Stil walking toward me, eyes fixed on her phone.

"I can't tell you where she is now." She glances up from her phone to offer a conspiratorial grin. "But I can tell you where she'll be tomorrow."

CHAPTER TWELVE

Sofie

No pain. No gain.

Really, I put myself through this pain so I *don't* gain. Even though I'm retiring from runway, I'll have opportunities for years to come, if I play my cards right. If I expect to still fit the sample sizes my favorite designers send over, I'll keep pressing through the pain of these crack-of-dawn workouts.

These are the things I recite to myself as I walk to Bodee Barre Studio a few blocks from my apartment building. I, along with just five other women, take private barre classes from Jalene, a former ballerina and the tyrant we voluntarily submit to at least four times each week. I hang my coat up in the small coatroom at the back of Jalene's studio, tugging off my UGGs and pulling my gripping socks out of the bag. My black capri leggings and hot pink halter top are both from a line I'm test running for Haven. It seems like everything I eat, do, or wear lately connects to Haven. I'm not complaining. With all the crap going wrong in my life right now, Haven feels like the only thing going according to plan.

"Morning, Sofie." Anna, one of the girls in the class, walks in and starts the same ritual I just completed, hanging up her coat and slipping on her barre socks. "How are things going?"

"Great." I pull my hair into a high ponytail and manage to grin at her despite the early hour and lack of caffeine. "How'd the audition go?"

Anna spends the next few minutes telling me about her upcoming Broadway show while we walk back out into the studio. The other three girls have already assumed their places at the barre.

"Morning, ladies." Jalene's bright eyes and smile defy the early morning hour. "Hope you're ready to work hard. We're supposed to have a guest, but I don't see—"

The door behind me opens, ushering in some of the brisk October morning air.

"Ah, here he is now." Jalene's aging-but-still-lovely face breaks into a girlish grin.

I glance back to see the guest who elicits such an uncharacteristic response from the termagant ballerina.

Unbelievable.

Trevor Bishop's eyes locked with mine are like hot chocolate on this cool autumn morning, steaming up the room around me. I'm trying hard not to eat this man up with my eyes, but after three weeks, the way he fills out the sweatpants dripping from his hips and the Princeton sweatshirt pressing against those massive shoulders, has me greedily taking in every detail. I still feel his eyes on me when I make myself turn away.

I miss whatever Jalene says about him joining us today. It doesn't matter. Whatever flimsy excuse he offered to get into my class doesn't interest me. We both know why he's here. I search for anger, frustration, irritation—something more appropriate than the tiny shoot of pleasure springing from some secret part of me that has hoarded images of him for the last few weeks. That part that should know better than to think things could work between a woman like me and a man like Trevor.

I face the barre, adjusting my socks, tugging on my leggings, tightening my ponytail—anything to occupy myself while he walks past me and into the coatroom without a word to stow his things.

"Glad I showed up for class today." Anna glances over her shoulder at Trevor, her eyes running up then down his body as he walks back to the coatroom. "They don't make 'em like that anymore. Not sure I'll be able to focus on any positions this morning but the ones I'd like to have him in."

I swallow a cutting reply. I have no right to be peeved over Anna's appreciation for Trevor's body. Wasn't I just doing the same thing? And yet I want to strangle her with my towel even after she turns away to chat with someone else, the thespian hussy.

Something wide and hard and warm at my back makes me go completely still.

"Mornin', Sof." Trevor's breath in my ear sprouts goose bumps all over my arms that have nothing to do with the slight chill Jalene maintains in her studio.

I turn to face him, ready to snap and hiss for this unconscionable invasion of my privacy, but every word dries up in my mouth at the sight of him. So this is what he's been barely hiding under those perfectly tailored suits. The heavy slope of his shoulders strains the thin white T-shirt clinging to rungs of muscle in his abs. Arms and legs thick and cut up with muscle stretch from his sleeves and shorts. And if his big body wasn't enough assault on my senses, his scent—something clean and unabashedly masculine—makes me wetter and weaker by the second.

"Cat got your tongue, Sof?"

Trevor's words don't even snap me out of my lusty inspection. Forget the cat. Trevor can have my tongue anywhere he wants it. Every reason I shouldn't give this man a chance burns away under the heat of those dark, laughing eyes.

He's too good for me, but I'm going to have him. At least once, and maybe only for a night, but I will have this big, beautiful creature.

And then I'll walk away like I've always done before.

That certainty settles inside me. It slows the mad race of my heartbeat. It eases the ache at the apex of my thighs. It emboldens me.

"Bishop, so good of you to join us." I step closer, becoming the aggressor, reaching up to run my fingers over the reddish brown pelt of his hair, lightly scraping my nails over his scalp. "You cut your hair. I like it."

He draws a deep breath that brushes his wide chest against mine. My nipples predictably spring erect, tightening under the fitted halter top. His eyes drop to my breasts, slide over my hips, and caress the length of my legs before meeting my waiting gaze.

"Cat got *your* tongue, Bishop?" I ask, my voice husky.

He narrows his eyes at me and catches my hand, still touching the silkiness of his hair. He senses the shift in our dynamic but is trying to figure it out. Trying to figure me out.

Don't worry, Mr. Bishop. I'll clear it up for you soon enough.

"You're not angry that I showed up in your class?" He releases my arm, and it drops to my side, a small frown furrowing those thick brows.

"Angry?" I feign surprise, touching the exposed skin of my chest where the halter dips, drawing his eyes back to my breasts. "Why would I be angry? I'll warn you, though, Jalene's tough. This class is not for the faint of heart."

"Somehow I think I'll be fine in your little ballet class."

The road to humility is paved with cocky grins like the one he gives me as he looks from the slim barre at the mirror to the slim woman assuming her place to lead our class. A body like his doesn't just happen, so I know he works hard at keeping fit. But barre requires something different; it will test muscles he probably doesn't usually use in ways he's never used them.

This should be fun.

I turn around. Between Jalene's kick-ass barre routine and my ass in his face for the duration of the class, he's in for an hour of torture.

"Good luck, Bishop." I bend over to touch my toes, giving him an unobstructed rear view that has inspired poetry and prose from more than one melodramatic suitor over the years.

Did he just groan behind me? Already, and I'm just getting started.

And that's not his last groan. Over the next hour, from the first position, through each grand plié, to the grand relevés responsible for all the killer calves in Jalene's class, Trevor groans and grunts through a routine that, even after a year, still leaves me aching and sore. Jalene has no mercy on him, ruthlessly correcting his posture, adjusting his positions, and demanding his attention, all while I do my best to distract him with every stretch and lean of my body. Poor man must be exhausted, physically and mentally, but he brought this on himself.

And boy is he gonna get it.

"Excellent class, ladies." Jalene concedes an appreciative grin for Trevor. "And gentleman. I'm impressed, Mr. Bishop. Beginners don't usually fare as well in my classes."

"If that was faring well," Trevor drawls with a chagrined smile, "I'd hate to see crashing and burning."

All the ladies laugh at his remark, and Anna is practically coquettish. She walks over to Trevor as everyone disperses.

"I'm Anna, by the way." She appears so small and delicate beside him. I can't stand petite women like her who look like they need saving all the time. Anna bats her lashes, lays a hand on Trevor's arm, and even giggles. I'm so glad I haven't had breakfast yet.

Have you no self-respect, woman?

And besides, I have plans of my own for Trevor Bishop.

I'm just about to break up that little tête-à-tête when Jalene stops me.

"Sofie, I'm sorry I didn't call you back yet." Jalene blocks my path to Trevor and Anna.

"Call?" I lean subtly to the left, just in time to see Anna following Trevor into the coatroom.

The hell.

"Yes." Jalene raises her penciled brows expectantly. "You asked me about a series of instructional barre videos for your new lifestyle website, remember?"

"Oh, yes." I try to focus on the conversation, but can't help wondering what's going on in that coatroom. "Of course."

"I was afraid I wouldn't have time, but I can do it."

"That's awesome, Jalene." I give a quick smile. "My assistant Stil will contact you to set up details."

"Great job in class today, Sofie."

"Thanks." Having Trevor behind me added a little something to my usual enthusiasm. "I need to grab my coat. Thanks again, Jalene."

I speed walk to the coatroom, jerking the door open like I might catch Trevor and Anna in the middle of a compromising position. They are both fully dressed, though. Both layered up for the cool morning and laughing over something I'm sure I wouldn't find funny.

"Sofie, hey." Anna leans into Trevor, her head well below his shoulder. "I was just inviting Trevor to opening night for my new show."

"Really?" I lean against the wall by the door. "And what did Trevor say?"

"I hadn't gotten around to saying anything yet." Trevor walks over to stand in front of me, taking my hand. "Maybe we could go together."

Just past his shoulder, the dismay on Anna's face is almost humorous. I'm sure when she invited Trevor, she wasn't thinking he'd bring me along. And he won't be.

"See you Thursday, Anna." I address her, but my eyes cling to Trevor's. Will I have to climb the man for her to take the hint?

"But, Trevor and I—"

"Thursday, Anna." My eyes and words cut into her sentence like a razor blade. "Good-bye, Anna."

She's out the door without further protest.

Trevor rests one arm against the wall by my head, his scent and the warmth of his body sheltering and stimulating me, making me feel safe and completely vulnerable at the same time. He stares down at me, waiting for my move. I've never taken a step in his direction, and the fact that I sought him out obviously pleases him, but he knows me at least well enough to guess there must be a reason.

I reach behind me to lock the door. Trevor's eyebrows lift, but he otherwise remains still. I reach up to rest an arm on his shoulder, sliding my fingers into the short, soft hair close to his scalp.

"Let's get straight to the point and not play games, Bishop."

His hand, wrapping around my waist, cupping the curve of my back, lays warm and heavy through the thin fabric of my workout clothes.

"I don't play games, Sof." Trevor leans down to whisper in my ear. "I'm a man who goes after what he wants and usually gets it."

He pulls back, dark eyes not laughing, close to sober.

"Am I getting what I want?" He drops his other arm from the wall, bringing that hand to my side, and pulls me close enough to feel his hard body through the sweatpants and hoodie he's put on. "Say yes."

I'll do better than saying yes. I'll show him.

I tug his head toward me until our mouths touch. Those full lips are softer than I imagined. He opens me up with his tongue, delving into my mouth slowly, like he's savoring the first taste of me as much as I'm savoring my first taste of him. He groans into our kiss.

"God, Sofie. I knew you'd taste like this."

His words drop off and he pulls my bottom lip between his, every suck and pull a direct hit between my legs. My wandering hands explore the strong neck, the broad shoulders, the bulge of his arms, the tight waist. Even though he can never truly be mine, I'm claiming him for these moments at least. I open my mouth wider, stretching for him, pulling his tongue deeper into my mouth.

A warning flutters across my heart. This isn't what I planned. This hot, sweet communion of a kiss. Part pure, part drug. You don't model as long as I have without seeing drugs, maybe even sampling, and that's what this kiss is. Like that first hit of cocaine, heady and entering your bloodstream with claws that sink in and steal all control before you know you're addicted. This first kiss is that addictive. It's not the hardness pressed to my stomach. It's not the way my nipples pebble against his chest. Those things feel so damn good, but that's not what I could become addicted to. It's the feeling of rightness that could grab hold of me and never let go.

He skids his palms down my sides and over my hips to cup and squeeze my butt.

"When can I pick you up?" His question is a heavy pant against my lips.

"Now." I curl one leg around him, waiting for him to hoist me up against the wall. "Pick me up now. We've got a little time. The door's locked."

I miss his breath on my lips as soon as he pulls back and peers down at my face. I don't even try to hide the absolute need that must be burning from my eyes and smeared all over my face. Every part of me burns for him, wants him urgently, but only like this.

He cups my neck with one hand, his fingers slipping up to caress the skin there while his thumb plays over my lips. A smile softens his mouth and his eyes.

"No, Sof, I mean for our date. What time should I pick you up?"

I haven't been as clear as I thought. I slip shaking fingers into the waistband of his sweatpants and wrap my hand around his thick cock. Lord above, he's big. My mouth waters at the thought of him holding my head still while he's pushing down my throat. I squeeze the impressive length that might daunt a lesser woman, but not me. I slide my hand up and down until he squeezes his eyes shut, his mouth falling open as he leans into me and rests his forehead against the wall beside mine.

"Fuck me, Bishop."

He goes still against me before pulling back, eyes narrowed on my face. I lift my lashes, giving him a glimpse of how uninhibited I'll be once he has me under him.

"No date. Let's just fuck."

He smiles only a little, running his tongue across those full, sculpted lips.

"Um…as flattering as that offer is," he says, carefully extracting my hand from his pants, "I had a little more in mind."

"Are you saying you don't want to?"

"I'm saying I'd like to get to know you a little first."

"First? So you *do* want to?" I just need to know it will happen, because I've never wanted anyone this badly.

"Is there any doubt?" He shakes his head, his smile deepening until the dimples pop in his cheeks.

"Haven't you ever heard of a one night stand?"

"Yeah, I have." He nods, dark eyes wicked and teasing. "Even had a few."

"And?"

"And I've had enough to know they don't interest me at this stage in my life." He leans an inch closer, his minty breath misting my lips. "Besides, I think you'll want me more than once."

The look he pours over my body, the promise behind his words, penetrate me as surely as if at any moment I'll feel him move inside.

I've never felt this before. He doesn't want one night stands at this stage in his life? Well, I don't want complications.

"I don't know what you want from me."

"Yes, you do. It's just that no one's ever asked you for it before." His lips straighten and his jaw clenches as his eyes skim my face. "You want a quick fuck, but I want more."

More. Dammit. He's making me do this.

"Look, I'll sleep with you, but anything more is getting too personal."

His lashes fall to cover his eyes, but not before I read disappointment there.

"Then this is as far as we go." He steps back, inserting a chill between us. His pupils are dilated and a swallow works the muscles of his throat, but those are the only clues his body offers that I may be affecting him as much as he's affecting me.

"You're saying you don't want me?"

He grabs my hand, his thumb caressing my fingers. He squats until our eyes are level, and I don't know what he's looking for, but I drop my eyes before he can find it.

"I'm saying I want more, Sofie."

I reach between us and wrap my fingers back around the lengthened stiffness hiding in his sweatpants.

"This tells me you'll settle for what *I* want, Bishop."

He blinks once, but his face remains otherwise unchanged.

"My dick doesn't rule me, Sofie, and neither will you. I have two heads, and that's not the one in charge."

I tighten my fingers around what is, even by my standards, an impressive stretch of inches.

"You sure about that?"

"I do Ironman triathlons."

"And I enjoy long walks on the beach. Are we just sharing random facts about each other now while I hold your dick, or did you have a point?"

"Not random. I *do* have a point." He pushes my hand away from his pants. "Do you have any idea how much discipline it takes to do an Ironman triathlon?"

"I can only imagine a great deal, but I fail to see how that relates to us screwing this out of our systems."

"A great deal of discipline, yes," he says, barreling past my words. "And I take it to another level."

"Why am I not surprised?"

"When I'm training, I abstain."

"Abstain?" I frown so deeply I'm sure I almost unibrow. "From what?"

"Sex."

"Well, that's just uncalled for. All that build up can't be healthy."

He laughs and shakes his head, his hand finding the sensitive skin of my nape.

"Fighters do it all the time."

"For outrageous amounts of money, yes." My voice thins to a breathy whisper as his fingers trace the downy hairs on the back of my neck. "Who voluntarily does that?"

"Lots of people do." He drops his hand back to his side, depriving me of his touch. "My point is that I'm used to going without. I *can* go without."

"But you've never had this. Never had to go without this."

I'm done playing games. I grab his hand and slip it into the band of my workout pants, positioning his huge hand to cup the bare mound between my legs, willing him to penetrate me with at least one of those thick fingers. He doesn't. A heavy arc of lashes falls to conceal his eyes. I don't want him hiding from me. I want to see the lust overpower his resolve. I want to see want knock down those walls, but he doesn't give me that. He takes his hand back and steps out of my reach until I'm left empty-handed. He puts a few feet between us before looking back at me, the same determination in those dark eyes and in the locked jaw.

"Dinner. Let me know when you're ready, Sof."

"Oh, I'm ready now. If you had put those fingers to good use and explored the landscape down there, you'd know just how ready I am."

"I think the problem is you've been sleeping with boys who settle for just what's down there."

"Settle?" I give a short laugh so harsh it's like a tiny razor in my throat. "Oh, I'm sure they don't see it as settling. They'd tell you it's the grand prize."

"That's the other problem. I think you actually believe that. Who convinced you the best thing you have to offer is in those expensive panties of yours?"

"How dare you?" I snap, eyes wide, brows jerked together.

"How dare *you* assume I'm anything like anyone you've ever had?" Irritation heats up his dark eyes. "Judging me by the assholes you've been with before."

"They may be assholes, but they'll have something you never will, apparently."

"Well, that's fine, because I want something *they* never had."

"And what's that?"

"Have dinner with me and I'll show you."

"These are the terms." I set one hand on my hip. "We fuck or we don't, but there's nothing else on the table. Are we clear?"

"No, we're not clear. I told you I want to get to know you, and that's what I meant."

"Let's just skip the part where you pretend to find me fascinating and get right to the part where we fuck, you get to say you had Sofie Baston, and we go our separate ways. Isn't that the endgame?"

His brows settle into a frown low over his eyes.

"This isn't a game, Sof. I want—"

"No, you don't," I cut in, words like a blunt instrument. "You think you want. It's not happening."

"So you'd date that quarterback, but you won't even have dinner with me?"

"That about sums it up." I sigh and roll my eyes. "Look, I'll admit I've felt this itch ever since we met, and we can scratch it, but that's all. No dates. No promises. No relationship. This is every man's dream."

"Don't presume to know what I dream about, Sofie." He steps close again, his body caging me against the wall, his breath on my lips. "Dinner or nothing."

I'm through with this shit. He may be one of the most beautiful men I've ever seen, and his dick would probably thrust me into another stratosphere, but I've heard the lectures. I've heard him talk about following the fire and being incited to do something you're passionate about. Beyond the bedroom, this man is more than I can handle. I'll admit that only to myself. He's good and brilliant and sees way too much. I truly think he does find me fascinating, wondering what's beneath my guard, but when the layers finally fall away, in the end he'd wonder what he was even looking for.

"Then it's nothing," I say.

I fumble with the lock behind my back until it turns. I grab my coat and bag, slip on my UGGs, and leave without giving him a chance to protest anymore. We're done. I wish he'd just go back where he came from so I can forget about even the possibility of him.

The studio is deserted. Jalene is probably in her office. I'm through the door and on the street, walking back toward my Fifth Avenue penthouse that sits atop the world, a symbol of all I've accomplished. Without my parents. Without a man. Without anyone but myself. I've learned that I'm the only person I can depend on. A man like Trevor Bishop could make a woman forget that, and it's the only thing that has kept me moving forward, one foot in front of the other, all these years.

And that's what I'm doing now. Pressing through the early morning crowd, now out and on their way to offices and jobs, avoiding touching whenever possible. Maintaining the force field around themselves you need to survive in a city that could swallow you whole like you never existed without anyone knowing you were ever there. One step at a time puts as much distance between Trevor and me as possible when a hand breaks the rules, grabbing my elbow. Trevor pulls me around to face him, as wide and strong as a wall with the crowd rushing around him like water.

"Dinner, Sofie."

The intensity of his eyes on my face. The gentle way he holds me, like he'll let me go if I want, but he hopes I won't pull away. The determined set of his jaw, like he's fully prepared to fight for this. Only I know once he has what he thinks he wants, he'll be disappointed.

"I said no." I make my voice as hard as it's ever been, and it's been hard before. "Maybe this kind of thing works on the country bumpkins you usually take on sweet dates, but not on me. Back off. Is this the same man who spouts all those lofty principles?"

"Sofie, stop." His eyes, soft and hot on my face, cool and harden. "I know what you're trying to do, and—"

"You don't know what I'm doing. You don't know anything about me, and if you have any of the self-respect I *thought* that guy from the videos had, you'll stop. You're just making a fool of yourself now, and it's beneath you."

I gesture to the people milling around us, several slowing their steps to study me closely.

"Everyone walking past us right now knows exactly who I am. I don't need a scene in the middle of the street with some do-gooder who wants to take me to dinner before he gets his rocks off. Now do I need to get a restraining order? 'Cause I will."

I hate how hard his face has grown. Whatever he thought he wanted from me, I'm sure I've convinced him now it doesn't exist. That I don't exist outside of billboards and *Playboy* spreads and runways. That what you see is all you get. That what you see is all there is. I think he believes that now because with one last livid look, with a press of his lips so tight the dimples pop in his cheeks, he turns on his heel and walks away.

And I should feel good. Watching the broad back and shoulders headed in the opposite direction, hunched into the Princeton hoodie against the morning chill, I should feel good. This is what I wanted; the only way. I should feel satisfaction that he finally got it through his thick skull.

Then why do I feel like a petty bitch who just tossed something precious away like trash? Tossed out the possibility that what he thinks he sees in me, might actually be there.

I see you, Sofie.

He said it to me on the rooftop, and those words tugged something in me up and forward in a way no one's words ever have. What exactly does he think he sees? Whatever it is, he may be the only one who's ever seen it, and I just shoved him so hard I don't have to worry about him ever looking back.

Panic grips me by the throat, strangling anything I would say to stop him. I can barely see him now, a distant shock of cinnamon bobbing over the people around him. He'll be gone soon, and the look on his face when I landed my last verbal blow tells me he's not coming back.

I don't know if it's a decision I make, or if that part of me that's keeping secrets about how I feel about this man from the wiser, saner parts of me takes over, but across the dense, bustling crowd, a stone's throw from Fifth Avenue, I call his name loud enough for anyone to hear—doing exactly what I accused him of doing. Making a fool of myself.

"Trevor!"

It feels like everyone on this street looks at me except him. He keeps moving forward, every step taking him farther away. I'm gripped by a sick urgency that I'm letting something special die before it draws its first breath. If that kiss in the studio was the first time I moved in his direction, then this is the second. I'm rushing after him now. Plowing through shoulders, bumping against briefcases without so much as a pardon me.

"Trevor, wait!"

He still doesn't stop. Maybe his resolve shifted that fast from having to have me to being determined to never see me again. I don't know, but I have to find out. I stop in the street, lean over, and press my hands to my knees to work up a scream that he can choose to ignore but will have no choice but to hear.

"Bishop!"

I bellow it. Even over the horns blaring and the collective hum of the early morning commute, he hears it. I know he does because he turns around, not even a block away, and stares back at me. He makes no move to meet me halfway. He won't. The angry set of his mouth, the stiffness of his posture, the fists balled into the front pocket of his hoodie—all signals that if anyone's taking steps this time, it will have to be me. I ignore the stares of everyone around us on the sidewalk and eat up the block in rushed steps until I'm right in front of him. I'm so close I feel his displeasure like a heat wave in the cool morning air.

"Bishop, I'm sorry."

Every time he's looked at me, I felt like he was searching for something. Probing, plumbing, diving deep with every glance. Not now. His eyes are flat, guarded, not letting me in and not asking anything of me. Maybe waiting to be done with me.

"I…what I said back there about…" I can't finish.

"You mean about my having no self-respect?"

Even though his words are so deep and low no one else could hear, I feel exposed and want him to stop immediately.

"What I meant—"

"Or maybe the part about my making a fool of myself?" He tilts his head, lifts both brows over dark, flinty eyes. "No? Oh, you must mean when you threatened to take out a fucking restraining order. Is that what you're sorry for, Sofie?"

"Bishop, I—"

"I kept telling myself there had to be more to you than what everyone said, but maybe that was my imagination. Maybe you are just a pretty face and a great set of tits. I'm so sorry I was making things complicated for you by thinking there was more. By wanting more than just a quick fuck, which is obviously what you're used to. I just thought I saw…forget it."

He turns around and starts to walk away again.

"What did you see?"

I don't even care anymore that people still mill around us, that they know who I am. I have to know what he saw to make him chase me all over this city when even I know I'm probably not worth his time. He stops walking, standing still facing away from me for a few moments. I wait, wondering if he'll just keep walking, but finally he turns back around and stalks toward me until he's standing close enough for me to see the anger has drained away, but I can't tell what's left.

"Hunger." His eyes never leave my face, like he's searching for glimpses of it again. "An appetite for significance. To feel like you're contributing something, adding something. I thought I recognized it in you because I remember it in myself. Remember wondering where I fit in all the needs around me."

I'm not sure how to respond. He's articulated something that's been skulking about inside me for months, maybe longer. I'd never put a word to it. Never really given it much thought, but as I look back at the things that mean something to me—the Walsh Foundation, Haven's charitable partnerships—maybe he's right, but I'm still not sure. Not of me. Not of him.

I drop my eyes to study the cracks in the sidewalk instead of looking at him, wondering how to crack the wall he's raised against me.

I ask, "But you were wrong?"

He's so quiet the moments stretch out and open, gaping enough for the sounds of the city to intrude. Everything around me is frenetic, but I'm still while I wait for him to let me know if he was wrong about me. He reaches out to cup my face, lifting my chin, his thumb tracing my cheekbone, his eyes searching mine.

"Was I, Sof?" He steps closer until the width, the height, the breadth of him, blocks out the scene around us. And it's just us. "Was I wrong?"

I'm not sure how to respond without risking more of myself than I can afford to lose.

"One dinner." I hold his eyes with mine as long as I can, dropping them before his eyes show triumph or satisfaction.

"When?" His question doesn't break stride, as if he hasn't gone through a gamut of emotions to end up right back at the request that started it all.

"Um...I don't know." I shrug, catching the eye of a woman staring at me. I smile politely like I don't realize she recognizes me. "When do you want?"

"How about tonight?" His eyes are still serious, the smile I've gotten used to still nowhere in sight. I didn't realize how much I'd grown to like that smile until it's nowhere to be found. I want it back, so I say the thing I hope will restore it.

"Sure. Tonight works."

He doesn't smile, but leans in and down to kiss my forehead and then to lightly brush his lips over mine. The heat that's been set to simmer between us flares up in me again, responding to his faintest touch like a nerve sliced open. I've had sex in public bathrooms and once, in Milan, almost fell from a balcony screwing, but I've rarely felt this exposed. Like I'm standing naked on Fifth Avenue, giving everyone a show. Or worse, showing him more than he should see.

"Seven o'clock then." He turns around and walks away.

There was no smile. No dimples, no laughter, but I could have sworn in those dark eyes, there was pleasure. It's a little scary how much pleasing him, knowing he's not angry with me anymore, pleases me.

CHAPTER THIRTEEN

Trevor

I spent my morning at the UN negotiating diamond mine rights with leaders from the Democratic Republic of Congo, and tonight I'm trying my damnedest to dechoke artichoke hearts. Give me the UN any day. I'm good at that. This? This tiny paring knife and my big ol' fingers? Give me delicate negotiations over delicate fruit any day.

Are artichokes fruits or vegetables?

I'm still pondering this and life's other mysteries when Harold and Henri come down the staircase, both dressed for their first date. Henri's wearing her contacts. Harold's ditched his glasses, too, but he's squinting and bumping into the couch. And he's wearing aftershave. Nerd mating rituals.

"You ready?" Harold squints in Henri's general direction but is actually talking to a large plant in my sister's foyer.

He looks calm to the naked eye, but I've known him for almost fifteen years. I know a river's probably running under his armpits. Hope he wore a T-shirt.

"Sure." Henri frowns. "Actually, let me go grab a wrap."

She turns and dashes back up the stairs. When Harold comes into the kitchen and nearly breaks his neck stumbling over the trash can, I have to intervene.

"Smith, where are your glasses? You know you can't see three seconds ahead of you without them."

"I just thought I'd—"

"Go get them." I set the artichokes aside, afraid I'll pare my index finger if I have to focus on the food and Harold at the same time. "Henri's seen your glasses before, and she still said yes."

"But I think that—"

"Do you want to face Zimbabwe's minister of finance with a sprained ankle or worse tomorrow?"

"Of course not. My vision—"

"Is nonexistent. Get your glasses, man."

Harold squints at me for a few more seconds before slumping his shoulders and turning back to march up the staircase.

"Tell Henri I'll be right back."

I've never seen Harold this way over anything. Not even his spreadsheets and algorithms. I'm trying again with the artichokes when Henri comes back down, peering through the living room and into the kitchen, brows knit again.

"Where'd Harold go?"

"He forgot his glasses."

"You convinced him to wear them, huh?" She grins and props a hip against the counter. "Thanks. We probably would have ended up in the ER if he tried to leave this house without those glasses."

"You just better hope he doesn't put on more aftershave while he's up there."

"You're evil." Henri tosses a blueberry from the bowl on the counter at me. I block it so it plops uselessly to the floor.

You could easily be fooled into thinking Henri unremarkable. Button nose, sprinkled with freckles. Narrow chin widening into a heart-shaped face. Shoulder-length hair, not quite dark enough to be brunette, but nowhere near blond. That's Henri in repose. Henri on a mission, solving a problem, figuring out how to get fresh water into a droughty region or food to a starving village—that's Henri on fire. The challenge and reward illuminate her face. She all but glows, and that's what Harold fell hard for.

I have five sisters, so it's not like I need another one, but Henri feels like number six. She studies me performing open-heart surgery on the artichoke hearts with my tiny knife.

"Gimme that." She takes the knife and deftly peels away the delicate leaves, tossing them into the bowl of olive oil. "You roasting these?"

"Yeah." I grind salt and pepper into the mixture. "Oven's already preheated."

Henri finishes the task, mixing it all together and tossing it onto the pan. I place the pan in the oven, turning to find Henri studying me a little too closely.

"Special occasion?" Henri grabs another blueberry and pops it into her mouth. "You haven't cooked once since we've been in New York."

"My mother started a catering business when she retired." I shrug, hoping she'll drop it.

"What's that got to do with the price of tea in China, Bishop?" Henri hops onto one of the leather bar stools at the counter, sharp eyes darting from my dark green shawl collar sweater to the black pants and boots I just shined. "Is someone coming over? Do you have a date?"

I knew I should have ordered in. That wouldn't have raised Henri's antennae. She's a mini pit bull.

"A friend's coming over for dinner." I season the steaks I bought from the butcher up the street, not looking up under Henri's scrutiny.

"This friend wouldn't happen to be Sofie Baston, would it?"

My hand stops mid-shake, poised over the raw meat, and I finally look back at Henri.

"What makes you think that?"

"Well, Harold said—"

"We should really get going, Henri, don't you think?" Harold cuts in from the kitchen archway.

"Oh, no. Don't rush off." I fold my arms over my chest and cock my head, enjoying Harold's discomfort. "Hen was just telling me that you said, what exactly, Henrietta?"

Henri's wide eyes flick between her two bosses.

"Well, just that…" Henri bites her bottom lip. "Just that you…"

"That I…" I raise my eyebrows, waiting for her to finish the sentence. "What?"

"That you kind of have a thing for Sofie Baston," Henrietta says defiantly. "That you like her."

"Is that a fact, Harold?" I glance at my friend, enjoying seeing him squirm even as I'm irritated by his flapping gums.

"I just said that you, well, that I had never seen you like this about a girl before."

"This?" I ask. "Like what?"

"Chasing her all over the city and—"

"I did not chase."

Harold tilts his head, giving me a knowing look.

"Okay, maybe there was a little chasing." I chuckle just as much at myself as at the face Harold makes.

"I just never thought of you as one of those guys, Trevor." Henri presses her lips together, something dangerously close to disapproval on her face. "I mean, a supermodel?"

It raises my defenses immediately, as much on my behalf as on Sofie's.

"You don't even know her, Hen."

"Neither do you, Trevor," Henrietta shoots back.

"You're right." I turn to open the oven, checking the artichoke hearts. "Thus dinner."

"I guess she does have a certain appeal." Henri looks like she can't for the life of her understand what it might be.

Harold and I exchange a quick look. A "certain appeal" doesn't begin to describe what Sofie has, and a red-blooded male in a coma would recognize it. Harold wisely just clears his throat and places a hand at Henrietta's back.

"Ready?" he asks. "Our reservation is for seven thirty, and I think I heard the car outside."

"We're not grabbing an Uber?" She smiles sweetly.

"No, I ordered a car for us."

They grin at each other for a few seconds before heading toward the door.

"Don't wait up," Harold yells back to me from the stoop of my sister's brownstone.

"Hadn't planned on it."

I can't help but smile while I continue the preparations once they're gone. I know it's only their first date, but I hope it will turn into more. First, things could get really awkward with Henri being our assistant if things don't go well. Second, Harold deserves some happiness. He's sacrificed a lot over the years. We both have, and I'd love to see him enjoy himself a little.

Hell, I'm ready to enjoy myself, too.

I pull a basket of blackberries from the fridge, only to realize I'm missing something very important. I retrieve my cell phone from my pocket, pressing the number I was supposed to call two days ago. I brace for an earful.

"Trevor!" my mother says from the other end. "I'm so glad you called. I've been worried."

"I know. Sorry. Things have been hectic here in New York."

"So you *are* back?" Her tone chides a little. "I thought you'd call when you got back from Cambodia."

"Mama, don't start." I press the phone between my shoulder and my ear, walking the steaks out to the grill on the patio.

"How are things going with Bennett? You think they're the right fit?"

Mama's not who you would expect to be on top of foreign policy and business, but she could probably hold her own in half of my meetings. She's the main reason I'm *in* those meetings at all. She has been tracking with every step Harold and I have taken with this Deutimus transition.

"Walsh Bennett's all right." I place the steaks over the flaming grill. "We're not ready to make a decision either way."

"What about the indigenous workers clause? Are they fine with that? You can't compromise on that, son."

"Mama, I know." I chuckle, heading back inside to the kitchen.

"We won't. Look, I didn't call to talk about Deutimus. I need a recipe."

A brief silence follows my statement.

"A recipe?" A smile creeps into my mother's voice. "Well, well, well. So you're finally putting some of my training to good use. I've been worried about you and Harold eating out so much with no woman to take care of you."

"Henri's here with us, Mama, but she doesn't cook much either."

"Girls these days." She sighs. "So what recipe can I help you with and why?"

I pause in front of the oven, the last part of her question making me cautious. Using the oven mitt, I pull the artichoke hearts out.

"Remember that black and blue cobbler you make sometimes? You made it last Fourth of July down at the beach house?"

"Oh, yes. That's a hit. Easy, too. Why do you need it?"

"I wanted to bake it, Mama, of course."

"Don't 'of course' me, Trevor." She laughs heartily on the other end. "You haven't cooked anything in ages, and you call me out of the blue asking about cobbler? On a Wednesday night? Fess up. You're cooking for someone."

"Is that a crime?" I grin and toss the artichoke hearts with capers, yellow peppers, red onion, and parsley. "I thought you'd be happy about me making a home-cooked meal."

"But the question is *why*, son?" Curiosity soaks right through the short silence on the other end of the line. "Is it a girl?"

A girl? Sofie? I'm sure she was a girl once, but it's hard to think of her in those terms.

"Yeah, it's a girl, Mama, but don't make it a big deal, okay?"

"Wait till I tell your sisters."

So much for it not being a big deal. I'll have a six-way FaceTime with them all before the week is over to discuss this.

"Could you just not?" I check the refrigerator for the vinaigrette I picked up this afternoon.

"Trevor, you haven't really dated anyone since Fleur, so I—"

"We're not dating, Mama. It's dinner. Our first, by the way."

"But you like her."

The statement stops me in my tracks. I've been in constant motion since I argued with Sofie this morning in the middle of a busy city block. Meetings all day, and then zipping into nearby shops to get things for tonight's dinner. I haven't stopped, but that question from my mother stops me. She really wants to know, and I've never been less than honest with her.

"Yes, ma'am, I like her a lot."

Maybe my response is too quiet. Too serious. Something steals Mama's words for a few seconds at least.

"Well, tell me about her, Trev."

I get going again, heading out to the patio to check the steaks.

"Nothing to tell, Mama."

"Is she pretty?"

God, is she.

"Yeah, she's attractive."

Understatement.

"And what else? I know you want more than a pretty face, Trevor."

"She's smart." I pull the steaks off, plating them and heading back inside. "She was accepted to Princeton, Sarah Lawrence, *and* UCLA."

Mama's all about education. Broke her heart when I dropped out of Princeton.

"Impressive. Pretty and smart. Those are a dime a dozen, though.

There must be something that sets her apart considering you haven't shown much interest in anyone since Fleur."

Mama loved Fleur, and I broke her heart *again* when I called off our engagement last year.

"She's…I don't know. Confident. Honest. Ambitious. Funny."

Rude. Sarcastic. Vain.

"She sounds sweet."

I don't correct my mother, but I'm not sure "sweet" is accurate.

"What's her name?"

I don't know what my mother's heard about Sofie Baston, the supermodel, and I don't want it to taint what she still has to learn about Sofie, the woman I'm still getting to know myself.

"Uh…Sofie." I heft generous portions of the grilled artichoke salad onto the plates beside the steaks.

"Sofie. That's lovely. Maybe you could bring her to Thanksgiving at the beach this year."

Oh, that'll happen. Sofie down on Tybee Island with all my sisters, not sure if they should waterboard her or ask for fashion tips. My brother begging her to sign his copy of *Playboy*. Mama asking where she stands on global warming, or some shit. And my father? If he isn't making sure we remember the actual meaning of the holiday instead of the commemoration of a Pilgrim fantasy, he'd probably be the only normal one of the bunch.

"We'll see." I set the plates on the dining room table. "It's our first date."

It feels odd to say I'm having a date with Sofie after fighting so hard to make it happen.

"What's her last name?" Mama is just getting started. "What does she do for a living? I want to know all about her, Trev."

The doorbell ringing comes just in time.

"She's here, Mama." I give the table one quick glance. I'll light the candles later. "I gotta go."

"I'll email the recipe. Check your phone in a li'l bit and call me tomorrow."

"Busy tomorrow. Call in a few days. Tell Pop I said hi. Gotta go. Love you."

I disconnect before she finds another way to hold me longer. I open the door to find Sofie on the stoop, looking up at the house number, a small frown etched between her dark blond brows. She looks back to me, confusion evident on her face.

"This is Brooklyn."

"You know, I'm from out of town," I say, allowing myself a grin, "but I believe you're right."

She holds my stare, making no move to come inside. It gives me a chance to study her right back. She's scooped her hair into an artfully messy knot behind one ear. Her face is lightly made up, not too heavy, which I like. The flawless texture of her skin isn't suffocated by a bunch of stuff. The purity of her features is truly remarkable, but I know Henri is wrong to think I'm one of those guys who's most interested in Sofie's beautiful casing. This outward shrouding, as beautiful as it is, is easy for her to share. She shares it for a living. It's all the stuff she wants to hide, wants to keep to herself, that intrigues me.

"I thought you said we were going out." She steps into the house, walking past me to inspect the foyer and large front room.

I step onto the stoop and wave the car on. I'll call him back later for the ride home.

"I didn't say we were going out." I close the door and lean against it. "I said we'd have dinner. See the difference?"

"I do now." Sofie glances around the Brooklyn Heights brownstone foyer, looking beyond it to the warm comfort of the living room with its dark leather tones and Persian rugs. "Nice place you got here."

"My sister's actually. She and her husband and the kids are in Berlin for his job." I shrug. "Worked out perfectly. He's there for two years, and I stay here when I'm in New York."

"This big place all to yourself?"

"Actually, Harold and Henri, our assistant, stay here, too. We work out of my brother-in-law's office."

"Cozy." She gives the room another glance before looking back to me, waiting for my next move.

"Well, come in."

She walks ahead of me, smelling incredible and looking even better. A dress, the color of chocolate mousse, hugs the dips and curves of her long body. It's short, mid-thigh, leaving the length of her legs bare. It plunges so low in the back that she's naked from her shoulders to the curve of her waist, an expanse of creamy skin begging to be touched. It's a dress made of silk and drama and sex, woven together to draw and hold a man's attention.

I'm only a man.

And this particular dress…I remember it from her office the night of Bennett's rooftop party.

"So I dressed up for nothing?" She glances at me over her shoulder.

I take her wrist, pulling her around to face me again. Our eyes catch and hold, and I realize the molecular structure of our relationship has changed after our argument this morning. The air still sizzles between us, but there is something softer, more vulnerable, uncertain, behind Sofie's eyes. And she can't hide it from me anymore. I'd like to think she doesn't want to, but I know better.

"Not for nothing. You dressed up for me." My eyes glide down nearly six feet of perfection and back up to meet her eyes. "Isn't this the dress I liked?"

She drops her lashes, pressing her lips together against a smile.

"It was already at the office, so…"

"Hmmmm. Convenience. I get it." I gently pull her by the wrist toward the dining room. "Well, you look beautiful."

"Thank you." She stops when she sees the table, set with our dinner, fresh flowers, and candles. "This is…wow."

Her eyes climb the few inches separating us before looking back to the table. Walking farther into the dining room, I pull her seat out and then take the one across from her.

"I would have come to get you, but the day got away from me and I needed to cook dinner, so I sent a car."

"No problem. My day was chaos, too."

"Your timing was perfect." I gesture for her to eat. "The steaks are fresh off the grill."

She's just staring at the food, and something occurs to me. Dammit, Sofie's a model. She may not even eat meat. She may barely eat anything to stay in that kind of shape, as far as I know.

"Do you not eat meat?" I'm halfway out of my seat. "I bet there's something in the freezer I could—"

"I eat meat." She picks up her fork and knife, slicing into the tender steak with relish. "I eat it all, and I'm starving. I was just surprised. You made this?"

I inch back into my seat with a grin, digging into my own food.

"It was nothing. Just steak and a salad."

Her moan of pleasure sends my blood pressure through the roof and has me wondering if she'll moan for me like that when the time comes.

"Artichokes." She closes her eyes, relishing the forkful of her salad. "My favorite."

She's not the only one who remembers details. Point one for Bishop.

"What made you decide to cook dinner for me at home for our first…date?"

I wanted you all to myself.

"I thought we gave New York enough of a show this morning."

I expected her to grin, to laugh about it, but she puts her fork down, wipes her mouth at the corners, and looks at me directly.

"I want to apologize again for the things I said." She studies her hands in her lap. "I just…I'm not the kind of woman you'd usually date, and I'm not sure what you want from me. Guess I overreacted."

"How would you know what kind of woman I usually date?" I set my own knife and fork down.

"Maybe I don't." A small smile teases her full lips. "I just assumed."

"Well, tonight is about us getting to know each other so we don't have to assume anymore." I give her a straight look, no smile, but not hard. "You won't ever have to wonder what I want, Sofie. I don't play games. I told you I want to get to know you, and that's what it is."

Her eyes probe mine for a few more seconds, trying to discern the validity of my statement. She finally picks up her fork and resumes eating, gobbling up the artichoke salad without another word.

"I'm sorry." She laughs, covering her mouth with one hand. "I'm so greedy, but I skipped lunch today by mistake, and I love artichokes."

She narrows her eyes.

"But you know that, don't you?"

I grin, going at my steak without acknowledging her comment.

"You know a lot of things," Sofie continues, taking a sip of the red I pulled from my sister's cellar. "How'd you get my private number, for instance?"

"Oh, that." I lean back, sipping my wine. "I can be very resourceful."

"Now that I don't doubt."

Her husky laugh does things to me. Caresses my ears. Drifts up her throat and over my skin like the pads of her fingers might—lightly. Most of all it just makes me want to laugh, too.

"And my barre class?" She frowns even while a smile plays around her mouth. "How are you feeling, by the way? Jalene's class is no joke."

"I'm sore in some unusual places," I admit, capturing her eyes over the rim of her wineglass. "But it was worth it."

She blinks a few times before setting her wineglass down.

"We'll see if you still think that by the end of the evening." She leans forward, propping her elbows on the table and resting her chin on folded hands. "Now that you have me, what exactly do you want to know?"

I'm like a kid in a candy store, not sure where to start, so I figure I'll start at the beginning. Or close to it.

"What did you want to be when you grew up?"

I find that this question sometimes tells me a lot. Not what people say, but how far from it they landed in adulthood. It helps me get to their dreams and the things that drive them.

"You want the honest answer?" Her brows are all the way up, eyes serious.

"I want nothing but honest answers."

"When I grew up I wanted to be Walsh Bennett's wife." Her lips lift at one corner, bitter on one side, sweet on the other. "That's what I thought I was supposed to be almost from the beginning."

"I knew you two dated briefly," I say with a frown, "but I didn't know it was that serious."

And I don't like it. It's unreasonable how much I resent that she had deep feelings for Walsh. She told me to my face she was fucking Rip, and it didn't feel like this. Maybe because I know Walsh could handle her, and Rip never could.

"My mother raised me to believe that Walsh would be king and I would be his queen, and we would rule Bennett Enterprises and as much of the world as we could acquire." Sofie shakes her head. "I accepted that as my path, and decided I would love Walsh till the day I died."

Her bitter laugh disrupts the quiet of the house.

"Except he fell in love with someone else." Sofie shrugs her slim shoulders. "But even before Kerris, it wasn't me. Not really. He'd always been in other relationships, and so had I. I thought we'd sow our wild oats and then settle down together. Only he's settled down, and I'm still sowing."

"Should I worry that you're still in love with a married man?"

Sofie's eyes widen and snap to mine.

"A married man? What? Who said…what?"

"Walsh, Sofie." Who did she think I meant? "Do you still have feelings for Walsh?"

"Oh! No, of course not." What looks like relief settles over her face. "I mean, for a long time I resented Kerris because I thought she took something that should have been mine, but I realize it never was. It took me a while, but I got over it."

"But you and Walsh did date for a while, right?"

"Briefly, but it was right after Kerris married Cam, Walsh's best friend. I sensed Walsh had feelings for her and swooped in. Kind of a rebound thing. It didn't last. Between Walsh and me, nor between Kerris and Cam. He's married to Walsh's cousin Jo now."

"Wait. Kerris used to be married to Walsh's best friend? And Cam…what?"

What kind of twisted mess have I stepped into?

"It's complicated." Sofie laughs and shakes her head. "I guess everyone ended up where they were supposed to be in the end. The four of them paired off, and me…"

She pulls her bottom lip between her teeth.

"Well, me right back where I was before." She raises guarded eyes. "Me, playing the field. On the loose. Emphasis on *loose*. Isn't that what they say about me?"

"Why would I listen to secondhand information when I have you here and can get it from the horse's mouth?"

"Oh, I'm a horse now, am I?"

We share a smile, both returning to our plates and our own thoughts for a few minutes.

"What about your parents?" I venture after a few more bites. "Were you close growing up?"

"Not really." Sofie drags her fork through the remains of her salad. "You've met them. We weren't exactly the model family. My father...well, let's just say the only deal he needed me to close, I never could, and that was Walsh."

She shrugs, glancing around the room before returning her eyes to me.

"I didn't help matters by deciding not to go to college, modeling, living the way I have." Sofie's lashes drop, casting shadows on her cheeks in the candlelight. "I'm over disappointing him."

No she's not. It's obvious that she's a daddy's girl to a daddy who doesn't care enough. If I didn't have reason to dislike Ernest Baston before, I have it now.

"You're so successful, Sof." I reach across and hold her hand. "He should be proud."

"Well, he's not." A fake laugh slips between her lips. "Not sure my mother is either, frankly. I think she was more disappointed about Walsh than my father and I were."

"You two weren't ever close either?"

"I always thought I was too much like my father for my mother to like me." Sofie gestures to her face and hair. "Physically, yes, but maybe deep down, I'm just like him, and she sees it. And being as close to him as she is, knowing him the way she does and how he's hurt her, I can't imagine she'd want to risk it with someone so like him. At least that's why I assumed we were never close."

"You're not like him." I squeeze her slim fingers. "I don't believe we're held captive to our parentage. We make choices about who we want to be. Everything isn't in our control, but the most important things are. Kindness, compassion, character. If I thought you were anything like your father, you wouldn't be sitting here now, no matter how gorgeous you are."

Sofie looks at me, humor alive in her vibrant green eyes.

"Good to know you're not *completely* immune to my looks."

My eyes travel over the flawless face, the silvery hair, the fine bones in her shoulders, the high, full breasts. I'm not immune. Matter of fact, if there's a vaccine for the way I feel when I look at Sofie, I don't want it.

"I wouldn't say immune, no."

She drops her lashes and dips her head, freeing her eyes from the connection burning the air between us across the candlelit table.

"So enough about me," she says. "Let's talk about you."

I set my elbows on the table, holding my chin in one hand.

"I'm an open book. What do you want to know?"

"Family?" She widens her eyes and smiles. "Please tell me yours is better than mine."

I feel my face relax and an almost involuntary smile take over.

"My family is amazing."

"Figures."

We laugh together for a moment before I continue.

"There's seven of us kids."

"Seven?" Sofie doesn't try to hide her astonishment. "That's like a litter."

I can't help but laugh.

"Mama didn't have us all at once like puppies, Sofie. My mother's Irish Catholic. There were gonna be lots of kids." I shake my head at how different our upbringings were. "There's five girls and my brother and me."

"I always wanted a brother or a sister. A big family sounds kind of great."

"It had its moments." Memories of our fights and squabbles and good times as kids make me smile. "We didn't have much. Mama was a teacher, and my pops was a postman, so with seven kids, every dollar was stretched pretty thin. Lots of hand-me-downs."

I grin to make sure she knows it wasn't so bad.

"You should have seen me in my sister's dresses."

Our laughs wrap around each other across the table, blending in a way I like the sound of. Making me consider how it'll feel to wrap my arms around her again. That kiss in the coat room haunted me all day. She's haunted me all day. Hell, who am I kidding? Sofie's haunted me since the moment I saw her on that billboard in Times Square.

"Are they like you? Successful globetrotters?" she teases.

"Ha! Yeah, right." I shake my head. "Three of the girls are stay-at-home moms. They wouldn't have it any other way, and love it. One sister is a junior at Duke, studying math. She wants to teach. The other sister is a senior, about to graduate from Michigan State. She's pre-med. Knowing Darcy, she'll end up doing Doctors Without Borders or something. And my brother, that idiot, is a sports agent."

I pull out my phone because I'm that guy who has pictures of his family everywhere all the time.

"Wanna see my nieces and nephews?"

She nods, smiling at me. I cross over to take the chair beside her, flipping through pictures of us at Christmas, at my beach house on family vacations, at dance recitals for my nieces, and at little league baseball and pee wee football for my nephews.

"They're all beautiful." Sofie swipes back to a picture of my parents, studying them before looking back to me with a soft smile. "You're the only ginger in the whole litter."

I grin, brushing a hand over my tightly cropped hair.

"Yep, me and Mama are the only redheads. Everyone else took strongly after my father."

"You did, too." She reaches over to run a finger across my cheekbone and then my chin. "Your strong bone structure and height are from your father."

She traces my bottom lip with her thumb.

"Those dimples are all your mother, though."

Am I supposed to ignore the fire in her touch? Every smile, every look, blows on the embers from this morning. I want to take this slow, to get to know her, to want her for the right reasons, but I'm not neutered.

I capture her hand, bringing her soft palm to my mouth, running my tongue across her lifeline, sliding my lips down to her wrist, suckling the pulse pounding through the scented skin there. She watches me possessing those extremities with my lips and tongue, her eyes going dark and hot with the same feeling I've been fighting since she stepped through that door looking like dessert.

I lean forward until there's nothing but a breath between us. Our eyes are still connected, open. With my eyes on hers, I close the gap, tugging the fullness of her bottom lip between mine, nibbling at the softness until she opens for me with a whimper. My hands cup her face, holding her perfectly still so I can taste the sweetness that's left me hungry all day. I lick into her mouth, running my tongue over the roof, teasing her into kissing me back. Her tongue brushing up against mine, seeking mine behind my lips, wanting mine, is driving me past restraint. I pull her deeper into me, groaning when her breasts press against my chest. Her lashes drop, breaking the contact between our eyes, but deepening the heat between our mouths, leaning into me harder and sweeter.

Hunger drives my hand down over her shoulder and across the naked, silky expanse of her back. Her skin is like silk and velvet, softer and smoother than anything I've touched before. She slides her fingers into my hair, caresses my neck, grips my biceps, all the while sucking my tongue down the tightness of her throat, imitating something my dick is throbbing for, but I can't even let myself consider if I'm going to make it through this night without screwing Sofie on my sister's dining room table.

I pull back, but she recaptures my mouth, the sweet suction stronger, her hands gripping tighter. I pull back again. If I don't, this is over and we'll be upstairs in my bed before dessert.

"Sof," I whisper against her lips. "Wait."

She drops her head until her forehead rests against mine, her breaths as heavy as mine. She lowers her long lashes, shadowing the delicate skin beneath her eyes.

"You must think I—"

"Want me?" I laugh against her lips, converting it into a kiss. Forcing myself to pull back. "I like how much you want me, but it's not nearly as much as I want you."

"I don't know about that. I bet I could give you a run for your money." She smiles, leaning forward to kiss the dimple in my cheek. "Was that dessert?"

It helps to think about something other than how hard I am in my pants.

"Um, dessert." I sit back, clearing my throat, running a quick hand over my hair, gathering my thoughts. "Yeah, like I said. The day got away from me, so I didn't get to make it, but I thought we could bake it together."

"Me?" Sofie raises her brows, a smile stretching between her cheeks. "You want *me* to cook?"

"I have the recipe."

"Oh, well then we're home free." She adds a laugh to her sarcasm, shaking her head. "I'm not much of a cook, Bishop."

She gestures at the dress I'll be dreaming about stripping off her tonight when I'm in my cold bed alone.

"And not really dressed to cook."

"You can throw on something of mine." I grin, pulling her to her feet. "It'll be fun."

"I think we have different definitions of fun."

I risk pulling her close, setting my hands at her slim hips, breathing in her clean scent.

"I think we can meet somewhere in the middle."

She rests her elbows against my chest, leaning into me, green eyes open and teasing.

"I really like meeting in the middle," she says, her tone light but her voice husky.

"So do I, Sof." I drop a quick kiss on her soft lips. "But first, dessert."

CHAPTER FOURTEEN

Sofie

I held Trevor's dick in my hands twice today before the sun was up, but baking a cobbler with him makes me nervous?

One of his T-shirts hangs almost to my knees, and my brown dress is laid out on his king-size bed. I glance around the room, taking in the shades of ebony and cream, punctuated with splashes of raspberry. I know it's a guest room, surely decorated by his sister or some designer; I know that this isn't his home, but I still find myself searching for clues to the man who, as open and genuine as he is, remains a mystery.

A desk takes up one corner of the room, its surface neat but peppered with stacks of papers and files. Pictures of his family are everywhere—on the desk, on the nightstand and shelves. It's sweet how much they mean to him. I've never had that connection with my parents, and seeing how he loves his family only strengthens his appeal.

One picture in particular catches my attention. Trevor is hugging his mother from behind. They're both looking into the camera laughing, the ocean behind them no more vivid than their smiles and ginger-colored hair.

"That was taken at my beach house on Tybee Island," Trevor says from the doorway, startling me.

"Sorry." I step away from the desk. "I wasn't snooping. Just curious."

He walks fully into the room, taking in the oversize Princeton T-shirt and my bare legs peeking out from beneath the hem.

"I guess that's a little big, huh?" He pushes back the hair that has escaped from the knot I haphazardly pinned behind my ear.

"Just a little." I tug at the shirt, conscious that though everything is covered, I'm wearing only underwear underneath. I've posed nude for *Playboy*, but one man catching a peek at my business makes me self-conscious?

"Are you nervous?" He ducks his head, capturing my eyes and smiling.

"A little." A breathy laugh slips past my lips. "Is that so hard to believe?"

"Not really." He glances between me and the large bed, his smile widening. "This is a dangerous place to be if I want to stick to my guns."

"Now who's nervous?" I tease, a smile I can't stop on my face.

"Don't mistake caution for nerves." He leans down to leave a kiss I want to deepen on my lips. He pulls away, a knowing smile on his face. He knows damn well how wound up he has me, that if he wanted to have me on that bed right now, he could. This taking it slow thing is new to me, especially when I want someone as badly as I do Trevor.

Only I can't remember wanting anyone like this. It's not even that package of his, though I haven't been able to stop thinking about him thick and hard in my hands. There's more. Maybe the more he wants from me is the same more I want from him. It feels foreign, knowing that even if we had sex right now, it wouldn't be enough. What I want from him goes deeper than that. I want to know why he's so passionate about developing nations. He told me not to assume I know what he dreams about. What *does* he dream about? If he believes in following the fire, what burns so bright that his whole life shines, inspiring other people to find their own fire?

And could he inspire me?

It scares the living shit out of me.

"I've got the recipe." He shows me his phone, an email containing the recipe for dessert.

"Black and blue cobbler?" I lick my lips. "That sounds very Southern. Very fattening. And very delicious."

"Are you sure you're a model?" He presses a warm hand to my back, ushering me out of his bedroom and into the hall. "'Cause you kinda eat like a horse."

"That's the second time you've called me a horse tonight, Bishop." I laugh as we take the stairs back down. "My fragile self-esteem can't handle it."

"Fragile?" He snorts, turning on the light to illuminate a gorgeous kitchen decorated with cherry cabinets and shades of lemon and cranberry. It shouldn't work, but somehow it does. The granite counters are clean, save a few cutting boards evidencing Trevor's meal preparations. No man has ever cooked for me. It makes me feel special.

He makes me feel special.

"So we're taking a shortcut," he says.

Trevor assembles the ingredients—sugar, flour, butter, vanilla extract, a cup of blackberries and a cup of blueberries, eggs, and packaged pie crust.

"That's for the topping. My mama would skin me for not making it, but we're pressed for time and this is what my sister had."

"You usually make the crust? Like make it, make it?"

He grins, opening the crust and sliding it toward me.

"Yep, but since it's your first time, I'll be gentle with you."

I grin, recognizing my words to him from yesterday.

"Touché." I point to the pie crust. "What am I supposed to do here?"

"You'll cut that into strips for the cobbler, while I mix all this together." He walks over to the oven, turning a knob. "That's preheating."

He glances up at me, his dark eyes dancing with mine across the counter.

"You ready?"

"Um, no, but when have I ever waited to be ready to do something?"

He surprises me, leaning over the counter to drop a quick, sweet kiss on my mouth.

"This time, with me, you'll wait until we're ready, right?"

One minute we're talking about cobbler, and the next we're talking about his timeline for sex. I think?

"How will you know we're ready, Bishop?" I hold his eyes with mine, refusing to release him until he answers.

"We'll both know, Sof." He turns his attention back to the ingredients. "You, pie crust. Me, mixing."

For the next few minutes, we work and talk. It feels so natural, the way we talk about our day, laughing at things that aren't even really that funny except because the other said it. I'm doing something I've never done before. Making cobbler, yes, but I'm sharing myself with him in a way that feels as intimate as anything I've ever done, but new and fresh. Like a gulp of ocean air, revitalizing me. Clearing my head.

"Okay, that goes in for forty-five minutes. We got a while before it's done." Trevor turns from the stove, leaning against the counter and looking devastating.

He took off the hunter green sweater he was wearing earlier, and is wearing a plain white T-shirt, which contrasts with the naturally tanned skin he inherited from his father. His face is a riveting geometry of sharp angles and straight lines, softened by the dimples that appear every time he smiles.

"So tell me about Haven." He settles onto a stool of mahogany and dark brown leather. "What's that all about?"

I take the stool beside him, crossing my ankles and resting my feet on the lower stool rung. The T-shirt rides up to about mid-thigh, and his eyes run over the length of my legs. I don't pull it down. I love seeing him want me, even if he won't do much about it yet.

"Ever heard of Goop?" I ask.

"Gwyneth Paltrow?" Trevor scrunches up his face in thought. "Her website thing?"

"Yes, her website thing."

I tug at the pins digging into my scalp, securing my hair in the knot behind my ear, until my hair falls past my shoulders. Again, I enjoy his eyes on me, taking in the silky fall of hair to the middle of my back. I look up to find him studying me, his eyes dark and warm and admiring.

"Haven is my Goop." I offer a small smile. "It's a lifestyle website, but mine has a heavy fashion emphasis."

I gather some stray flour between my fingers, sifting it and rubbing the velvety texture.

"We partner with artisans and designers who create products specifically for our site. Part of the appeal from their perspective is that half of the profits go to charitable partners."

He stares at me like I've grown horns before opening his mouth and then closing it again.

"Charitable partners?" he asks. "Which ones?"

"The Walsh Foundation, obviously." I pull a clump of hair across my mouth, a girlish habit I never kicked. "I've been their celebrity ambassador for years, but I want to work with other organizations, too. I'm being really careful about which ones, though."

I look up at him through my lashes, feeling more exposed to him than when I brashly shoved his hand into my panties this morning.

"Maybe you could help me? I mean, to find the right charitable partners."

"Of course." He reaches over, toying with the ends of the hair hanging just above my breast. "I'd love to."

"Really?" A wide smile takes over my face. "Marlee's heading up the charitable effort, and the rest of the team handles everything else. You wanna see what we have so far?"

"Sure." His eyes flick from my eyes to my mouth and back again. "Show me."

I find myself hunched over his laptop in the office, pulling up the site my team has been working on.

"I love it, Sof." He navigates across the various tabs. Some empty, some already filled with content.

"I'm taking a very hand-drawn approach to the aesthetic." I point to the sketches for the various aspects of the site. "Along the lines of Megan Hess. In keeping with fashion sketches and design."

I perch on the desk, pulling one leg up and resting my bare foot on the edge.

"And after this initial stage, I want to expand Haven into my own clothing line, home goods, furniture. The works."

"Sofie, that's brilliant." He runs a finger over my hand, resting on the desk for support, the simple contact lighting fire to the goose bumps his touch arouses. "You're brilliant."

"We've all got our things." I shrug, of all things embarrassed, and look for something to draw his focus away from me. A glass jar filled with tiny kernels on a shelf behind his desk provides the perfect distraction.

"What's that?" I point to the glass jar.

Trevor reaches for it, stretching across me to grasp it, bringing us closer. He smiles at me, acknowledging the magnetic tug between us.

"This is my seed jar." He points out the script writing etched across the front, handing it to me. "That's a Ugandan proverb."

"Sow seeds in your garden; wait and see what comes with the rain," I read, tracing the faint letters with my nail. "What are these seeds from?"

"Everything we do isn't diamond mining or some grand venture." He pulls a seed from the top of the pile, holding it in his palm. "A lot of the places we visit are still primarily agrarian, and the best thing we can do is introduce the farmers to modernized agricultural techniques, show them how to more effectively grow their crops, and, subsequently, provide a better livelihood. Knowledge is the greatest charity because it continues giving."

"Who said that?" I ask, trying to place it.

"I just did." He grins and plops the seed back into the jar. "So every time we work with a new village, a new farmer, I keep one of the seeds we plant. I guess it's a collection of sorts. Even though they all blend together, and I couldn't tell you which one belongs to which village now, every one is special to me."

"That's really cool." My response sounds lame compared to his impassioned eloquence, and I drop my head, chewing on my bottom lip, feeling like the vapid girl people assume I am.

He tips my chin up, smiling at me until I smile back.

"You're right. It is pretty cool."

His eyes fall to my lips, darkening to that delicious shade of chocolate I'm coming to crave. Just as I'm sure he'll kiss me again, and wanting it so badly, the oven timer goes off, signaling the cobbler is ready. Desire tugs taut between us like hot wire. I've never let it simmer this way. I've always just given in to it, but there's something about this slow build, this spark that grows hotter and brighter every time we look but don't touch. Every time we smile but don't kiss.

It makes me want him more.

"I may be biased," I say around a mouthful of warm black and blue goodness, tempered by cold ice cream, "but I think this is the best cobbler I've ever had."

"Have you had much cobbler, Ms. Yankee Supermodel?"

"No, can't say I have." I laugh, turning the spoon to cup my tongue. "But I bet it's some of the best ever. We did good."

"Things taste better when you make them yourself." He scrapes his almost-empty bowl. "Just like things feel better when you build them yourself. I guess. I've never had anything handed to me; I've always built everything from scratch, so I don't have much to compare it to."

"Well, you're right." I slide my bowl over to him, still half full since he keeps eyeing what I can't finish. "I've never felt as good as I do at the end of my workday now. Knowing I'm doing it all myself."

He digs into my cobbler, nodding his agreement.

"I have to work out extra hard tomorrow after all this," he says.

"Oh, will we see you in barre class again?" I grin, my chin resting on the heel of my hand.

"No, back to my Ironman regimen tomorrow." He stands and steps close until his sweet, berry-scented breath brushes my lips. "Besides, I got what I wanted from the class."

"What was that?" I lean forward another centimeter, tempting him to come the rest of the way. "A date with Anna?"

He looks confused for a moment, and then he understands.

"Oh, sorry. I forgot her name. Sweet girl, but no." He inches in, his lips touching mine with his next words. "Was there ever any doubt why I was there? Who I wanted?"

He closes the tiny gap separating our lips, the berries barely disguising the deliciousness just beneath that is all him. His tongue, his lips, his mouth. So sweet. So addictive. I want much more. I'm throbbing between my legs for him. I'm soaking through my panties for him. I'm falling apart inside for him, and it's the merest brush of our lips. The softest tangle of our tongues. Imagine how wonderfully devastated I'll be when he fully unleashes himself on me.

Voices in the foyer burst our bubble, the one our kisses fashioned around us.

"Damn," Trevor mutters against my lips. "Harold and Henri are home."

I smile, easing forward again to nip his bottom lip. His groan vibrates against my mouth.

"And if they hadn't come home"—I pull back, lifting one challenging brow—"what would you have done, Bishop?"

"You mean what will I do, don't you?" He cups my head, threading his fingers into the long tresses falling around my neck. "There's still the ride home."

These panties are done. I hate that I'm seeing Harold again and meeting Trevor's assistant for the first time in sopping wet panties and a giant college T-shirt, but I've made worse first impressions.

Henri's a neat little thing, and by the way her eyes go all judgmental when they meet mine, she's not a fan. She and I would be at opposite ends of the pole, for sure, but the easy and obvious affection between her and Trevor softens my attitude. She's probably just protective of him. I like him too much to hold that against her.

"Nice to meet you, Ms. Baston." She peruses my long, bare legs. I refuse to explain or feel at a disadvantage.

"Likewise, Henri." I shake her hand like I'm dressed to walk the runway. "I hear you hold things together around here."

Her face softens only a little. She's not one to be flattered out of her preconceived notions. I'll have to prove her wrong. I usually can't be bothered convincing people I'm anything other than what they expect, but for her, for Trevor really, I might make an exception.

After we've said our good nights to Harold and Henri, and I'm back in my dress and we're in the backseat of the car, heading to my apartment, my stomach twists and turns, flips and flops, like this is the end of my first date. Like I'm not sure I'll be ready for my first kiss.

"Thank you for riding back with me," I venture into the quiet of the car as we speed through the night, the East River glimmering through the window.

"You knew I would." He slides across the seat until our bodies are flush. "How else could I collect my good night kiss?"

"Oh, you want a kiss?" I smile, my lips tingling with anticipation, full and throbbing and waiting for him.

"I want a lot more than a kiss, Sofie," he breathes over my lips. "But we'll stay there for now."

I glance at the privacy window, closed and sealing the driver out.

"This legendary self-control of yours." I shake my head, locking our eyes together. "I'm not sure I like it."

"Believe me, you're testing it."

He slips one hand up into my hair, drawing me toward him until our lips touch, burning up all control. Restraint falls away, unshackling the desire we've held at bay all night. His tongue is so deep I can barely breathe, and I love it. The impossible choice of breathing or having more of him. I pull air through my nose, determined I won't give up even for a second the sweet, hot melding of our mouths.

He caresses my thigh, pushing up my dress and cupping my ass. My answering touch, over the strong pecs and the tight muscles of his stomach and then the broad back, elicits a groan.

"Touch me, Sof."

Don't have to ask me twice.

My hands relish the brawny beauty of his body. The wide shoulders and thickly corded arms beneath his sweater. I slide my palms over the warm, smooth skin of his back, raking it lightly with my nails. He tugs at the neckline of my dress until it falls away, baring one nipple. He just looks at me in the dim light of the car, barely illuminated by the city lights rushing past.

"My imagination did you no justice." He runs one thumb over my nipple. It goes painfully tight and I press my eyes closed. I can't take it. If he doesn't take me in his mouth, I'll die.

But then he does.

He licks the pink-ringed areola, sampling me before his mouth consumes the whole, waiting bud. I thought I'd die if he didn't taste me, and I'm sure I'll die now that he has. The pleasure washes over me like a flood, covering me from head to toe. Soaking me. Drowning me. Just as I'm sure I'll go under, the car comes to a halt in front of my building.

We can't stop. There's no way we can stop. There aren't enough cold showers to cool me down. To ease this burn.

"Come up." I whisper the words into his mouth, sharing a breath with him. Diving back into the warm, dark depths of him for another kiss. Another stroke of his tongue that licks fire down my throat. His mouth is urgent on mine, and I'm sure he'll give us both what we want, but he slows the kiss, little by little, until it is mere brushes of our lips against each other.

"I'll walk you up, of course, but then I should go."

The Southern gentleman.

Disappointment congeals in my stomach. All the way up in the elevator, I say nothing. My throat burns with rejection. I study the swirl pattern of the marble floor, so glad when the doors whisk open to the penthouse level.

"This is me." I step off the elevator, not even sure he'll follow, but he does.

At the entrance to my apartment, I turn to face him, my back pressed to the door.

"Thank you for a lovely evening."

"Aren't you polite?" Trevor dips his head, trailing kisses down my neck and over my collarbones until his lips are at my ear. "Do you think I don't want to, Sofie?"

I shake my head, pushing my lips into a self-deprecating smile.

"I guess you don't want to as much as I do."

This man continues to surprise me. He takes my hand and slides it down to the bulge in his pants. My breath catches at how thick and hard he is under my fingers. I squeeze to assure my libido it's all him. It's all real, and soon it'll be all mine.

"All the time, Sof." He leaves kisses along the underside of my jaw and whispers them across my lips. "That's how I feel all the time around you."

"Then why—"

"More." He pulls back and peers into my eyes, still searching for something I don't even know that I can give him. "I want more from you than you've ever given anyone else."

"What if I can't give it?"

He smiles, tracing a finger over my brows and down my chin, finally touching my lips.

"Have dinner with me again tomorrow night."

That look is back, the one that pokes at my surface and tugs at my stitching, loosening me, freeing me a little more every time. Of all the pleasures I imagine with him, it's this look I'm finding hardest to resist.

"Okay. Tomorrow then."

CHAPTER FIFTEEN

Sofie

I've gone all out.

Last night at Trevor's place was incredible. It was intimate and warm and private. Tonight is our first time...out, unless you count our argument on Fifth Avenue. I don't go much of anywhere without being recognized. Even before I modeled, Walsh and I were in the public eye by virtue of who our fathers were. Everyone, especially me, assumed we would end up together, and the media started tracking us early on. Even my debutante pictures appeared in *W* magazine. I don't even think about it anymore really. But tonight, they'll know I'm with Trevor, and I want him to be...I don't know, proud. I'm used to walking into a room and knowing every man wants me. I want everyone to know that *I* want Trevor. That I'm dressed for him. That at least for tonight, I'm his.

One last glance in the mirror confirms that I've done Stil proud. She was more anxious about tonight than I was. She cleared my schedule for a wash and trim, facial, and all-over body wax. I didn't have the heart to tell her the Brazilian would probably be wasted tonight.

My hair falls past my shoulders, silver and gold. I went dramatic with my makeup, eyes fully smoked out. My lips are pale petal pink, almost nude. My leather skirt grips my body from waist to knee, then flares to a peplum hem. The blush-colored silk blouse sheaths my arms tightly and plunges just below the curve of my breasts, offering flashes of skin but no nipple. I don't think Trevor would like that. I've finished the look with classic black Louboutins and a simple clutch. At the last minute I slip the pink diamonds Daddy gave me for my sixteenth birthday into my ears.

Just as I'm giving myself the final *final* perusal, the wall intercom buzzes. I press the button to answer.

"Ms. Baston," Clive from the front desk says. "You have a visitor. He's not on your list, so I wanted to check before I sent him up, of course. A Mr. Bishop."

"Yes, send him up, Clive. Thanks."

I take a steadying breath and shake out my hands. I used to feel this way before rowing competitions. Excited. Nervous. Eager. I was a teenager then. Over the years, I've shooed away all the butterflies, but they're back tonight, fluttering in my belly with acrobatic turns. When I open the door for Trevor, they flap their wings triple time.

"Hi." His smile is my favorite thing about this day so far.

His flawlessly tailored suit is black and again Tom Ford. It's another three-piece, this time with a silvery blue shirt and a complementing tie. François would eat this man alive. Most of the male models I know are slim or "gym" muscled. François would love the challenge of dressing this man with his big, tight body. I love the challenge of him for a completely different reason.

He leans down to kiss my lips lightly. I enjoy the brief contact, but don't press for more. I've decided I'm just going to let this happen. Let him set the pace. He knows I'm ready when he is.

"You look…" He trails off, tilting his head to one side like he's considering. "You'll do, I guess."

I chuckle, pleased by the way his eyes belie his words. He hasn't looked anywhere but at me since I opened the door. It feels good. I've lived with this shell so long, I take it for granted except as a means to my ends, but tonight he makes me happy that I look the way I do. Happy that my appearance pleases him.

"So where to tonight?" I ask from the backseat of the car as we pull off.

"There's this new seafood place called Minnow. Have you heard of it?"

"Yeah." I whistle. "Tough to get a last-minute reservation. It's on everyone's list right now."

"Yeah, tough unless you're a sheikh." Trevor takes my hand, rubbing his thumb over my knuckles. "One of Walsh's friends got me a reservation on short notice."

"Sheikh Kassim?"

He nods. "Yeah, he loves Walsh."

"Are you okay with such a popular place?" He bends his brows into a frown. "We could go somewhere less public, if you prefer."

"It's fine." I twist my fingers so it's my turn to rub his knuckles. "I'm excited about tonight. I haven't been out in a few weeks."

"Since the quarterback?" His voice remains neutral, but his eyes tell me he doesn't like the thought of me with Rip. I can't undo my relationship with Rip, or with any of the men I've known over the years.

"Yeah. Not since Rip."

"How did he take the breakup?"

"He's still taking it." I laugh, but there isn't much humor because I actually feel bad about how things with Rip ended. Not bad that I called it off, but that it ever started in the first place.

"Is he giving you problems?" Trevor's frown grows heavier and darker.

"And if he *was* giving me problems?"

"I'd solve them."

He doesn't grin or follow up with some phrase to lighten the moment. He leaves it heavy with his honesty. He means it. I haven't had anyone interested in solving my problems for me in a long time. On the one hand, it has taught me independence. On the other, it's left me in many ways alone.

"We're here." He steps out, reaching a hand back to help me from the car. This place opened only a few weeks ago and became an instant hot spot. It's crawling with celebrities, so I'm hoping I'll go unnoticed. New York isn't LA. The paparazzi aren't assaulting you as soon as you step into the street. They're more subtle, but no less thorough. I'm sure there's some camera discreetly aimed my way right now. I hope this outfit looks good on Page Six.

A long line stretches from the maître d's podium to the door. I see a few flashes and recoil inside. I don't want everyone speculating about what Trevor and I are to each other. They probably don't know too much about him, so they'll dig, and I already know what they'll find. A brilliant philanthropist and businessman with a conscience. A good man. If I'm honest, I really don't want them speculating on what he sees in me. Probably because I'm not sure myself.

"Let me check on the reservation." He grabs my hand and starts forward.

"Can I wait here?" I ask. "It's a bit of a crowd up there, and I just saw a few people I don't want to run into."

He searches my face, looking for the solid truth behind my flimsy excuse.

"Okay." He leans down to kiss my temple. "I'll be right back."

"I'll be right here." I reach up to run an affectionate hand over the short ginger hair.

With a quick grin, he sets off, broad shoulders pressed forward, and people stepping aside because he walks like they should move when he's coming through.

Someone touches my hair. Random touches in public make me nervous. I've had stalkers before. I didn't mean it when I threatened Trevor with a restraining order, of course, but I've had to do it before. More than once, and someone touching my hair reminds me just how vulnerable I am in situations like this. I jerk my head away from the touch, looking around to see who dared.

"Sofie?" A dark-haired man about my height, maybe a little shorter when I'm wearing my Louboutins, stands behind me. "I thought that was you."

"Esteban?" My heart drops like mercury in a thermometer, plummeting from tropical to subzero.

"I can't believe it's you." He pulls me close, an arm around my waist before I can stop him. "It's been years."

He dips his head to smell my hair, a long inhale like he's absorbing me through his senses. I'm still frozen. Every fiber of my being screams at me to pull away, but my body can't move, can't catch up to the alarms going off in my head.

"I *hoped* I would see you." His accented voice is husky in my ear. "But after all this time, I didn't think I actually would."

He pulls back, just enough to study my face, but keeps our bodies interlocked. His dark eyes probe mine, searching for trace elements of what we had in Milan years ago.

He won't find them.

"Let me go, Es." My body finally wakes up enough to struggle against his tight hold.

"Sofie, we should talk." His eyes become earnest, a familiar desperation I used to think was all about me, but isn't. Everything with Esteban is about Esteban. "I've missed you. All these years, I've missed you."

"I asked you to let me go, Es." I harden my voice so he'll know I mean it. "I don't want a scene tonight."

"A scene? No, of course not." His hold relaxes, but he doesn't relinquish me. "Are you alone, *querido*?"

"No, she's not," Trevor's deep-voiced reply comes from behind us. He stretches his hand to me, eyes sliding between Esteban and me. For a second, Esteban's hold tightens, like he won't let go, but after a few moments of Trevor's hard eyes drilling into him, I'm free. I step away, taking Trevor's hand gratefully and putting much-needed space between my former lover and me.

"You okay, darlin'?" Trevor's eyes soften on me.

"I'm fine," I whisper up to him, a small smile crooking my mouth. His returning smile lasts only a second before he goes back to studying the silent man watching us.

Esteban's eyes drop to my hand linked with Trevor's, a humorless smile curving his sensual mouth. How I used to love that mouth and the wicked things he used it for on me. I loved his swarthy skin, his dark eyes. Now I can't look at him without feeling sick to my stomach. We had some good times, but the bad cast a wide, dark shadow over anything good we ever shared. It was all lies. *He* is all lies.

"Sofie, aren't you going to introduce us?" Esteban's eyes rake my body with familiarity before drifting to Trevor. He isn't subtle, and I feel Trevor tense at my side.

I clear my throat, wanting to get this over with so we can just go to our table and try to salvage an evening that started with such promise, but has soured and curdled like milk gone bad before the expiration date.

"Of course." With my free hand I gesture toward Esteban. "Trevor, this is Esteban Ruiz, a photographer I worked with a lot when I first started out. Esteban, this is Trevor Bishop. My date."

I say the last two words deliberately, being as clear as I can that I want nothing to do with him anymore. It hasn't worked in the past. He is part of the reason I'm so protective of my cell number. He always manages to find it. Always manages to find me. After all these years, I'd hoped he'd stopped looking, stopped trying. Has he been following me?

Esteban extends a tanned, slim hand to Trevor, a smug smile on his handsome face.

"Nice to meet you, Mr. Bishop."

Trevor ignores the hand politely extended, turning his attention back to me.

"Sofie, our table is ready."

The obvious snub has no effect on Esteban except to make him smile wider as his hand drops to his side.

"I'm ready."

I look up at Trevor, searching for the easy warmth we shared before this skeleton from my past slithered out of the closet. His eyes, though, are cold and stony on Esteban. What does he sense in him? Trevor sees more than most men. He's more discerning than most men I've met. I know from very personal experience that Esteban is not a good man. From the way Trevor looks at him like he's a rodent at the dinner table, I think he sees past the handsome façade to the rotten core.

We're turning to leave when another voice from the past cracks into the tight silence the three of us occupy.

"Sofie Baston?" A petite, dark-haired woman demands from Esteban's side. She might be coming from the ladies' room or from the street. It really doesn't matter. All that matters is that Seville Ruiz is here now, her eyes as alive with hatred for me as they were the last time we saw each other.

"Esteban, *bastido*," she hisses, her voice heavily accented, hurt and anger clouding her dark eyes. "Our first night in New York, a city with millions of people, and you manage to find *her*. Did you know she would be here?"

"No, Seville." Esteban remains calm in the face of his wife's impassioned rebuke. "I had no idea. Purely coincidence."

"I don't believe in coincidence." Seville turns those turbulent eyes on me. "Stay away from my husband, *puta*."

Trevor swears under his breath before taking an ominous step toward the couple.

"Listen here, lady," he says, his Southern accent thickening with the anger practically vibrating off him. "Sofie's with me. I brought her here, and she didn't even know where we were eating. So she didn't arrange to meet your husband. I don't hit girls, but if you insult her again, I'll take it out on your little man here."

He raises both brows, looking between the husband and wife.

"We clear?"

They both just stare at him before nodding.

Trevor invades Esteban's space in a few steps.

"And if I catch your hands on her again, you won't be taking anyone's pictures for a long time. Got it?"

Esteban stares back at Trevor, not agreeing or disagreeing, just smiling like he knows something Trevor doesn't. And it's true. He knows things I don't want Trevor to know, but will probably have to tell him after this. But not here. No one's really paying attention. This near-disastrous tableau played out with little to no drama. With the dinner crowd none the wiser, but I can't stay. Without another word, Seville and Esteban walk off, presumably to their table. I turn to Trevor, swallowing the dregs of my anxiety. The more room between Esteban and me, the better I feel, but I still can't answer Trevor's questions in this room full of people. And it's obvious from the firm, straight line of his mouth and the hard eyes that he wants his questions answered.

"Could we go?" I ask, hoping he won't question me about that, too.

"Sure." Trevor's eyes follow the path Esteban and Seville took into the dining room. "Can't say I want to be the same room as those two. I can call the car service, and a car will be here in a few."

That encounter shoved me back into a stuffy, dank room I haven't been inside for years. I could use the air.

"Or we could walk." I squeeze his hand, offering him a hopeful smile. "My place is just a few blocks away."

"And we'll eat what?" Finally a teasing smile appears on his face.

"Don't expect me to cook." I try a laugh that sounds close to normal. "But I have a variety of delivery menus for us to choose from."

"So I dressed up for nothing?" He tosses my words from last night at me, and I volley right back.

"No, you dressed up for me."

"Yes, I did." He bends until his forehead rests against mine, laying his hand in the same spot at my back Esteban touched moments ago. The heavy weight of his hand is so different from Esteban's, whose hands on me made my stomach heave.

We start the short walk, and I thank God I broke these Louboutins in a few months ago, or this would have been a really bad idea. Trevor swings our hands between us, the gesture somehow innocent. Pure. So different from the story I have to tell him before the night is over. Practically before it's even begun.

"Who was that man to you, Sof?" Trevor drops the quiet question between our swinging hands.

"Can we just walk?" I watch our linked fingers. Mine almost lost in his grip. "We'll talk at my place. Is that okay?"

Trevor nods and drops my hand, pulling me closer, sliding his arm around my waist, tucking me under his shoulder. I burrow into the scent and strength of him. I wish I could hide from my past here in the shadow of this mountain of a man, but I can't. First Kyle Manchester and now Esteban. Karma's a bitch hot on my heels, gaining ground. Outpacing me.

Dread pricks the lining of my stomach. My past with Esteban isn't pretty. I can't tell Trevor all of it, the things no one knows, but even the part I will share might make him want me less. Because I know Trevor doesn't want me for my face or my body or the blond hair that always fascinated Esteban. It's the promise, the possibility, that there is something behind the Goddess persona worth touching, worth having in his life. I'm afraid my story will convince him otherwise.

I'm afraid he'll walk away.

All these weeks I thought I wanted that. I pushed him to leave me alone. Now the thought of him giving up on me scares me, disappoints me more than I want to admit.

When we're young, we live for the good times, setting moments on fire, laughing and dancing in the flames. We're invincible. No one tells you the memories may haunt you like ghosts, knocking around when the house is quiet and you're alone with your regret. No one tells you about the rubble of your destruction. No one tells you that you'll get burned, and those fiery moments become your mistakes. At least no one told me. I wish they had. With this good man at my side who deserves more than the ashes of my transgressions, I wish more than anything someone had told me.

CHAPTER SIXTEEN

Trevor

I'm not a huge fan of Indian food, but Sofie's eyes lit up over that menu, so that's the one I chose. I'm just hanging up with the place around the corner when she comes back into the living room, dressed down. As good as she looked dressed to kill, I think I prefer the yoga pants and off-the-shoulder sweatshirt she wears now.

"Sorry I don't have anything that would fit you." She laughs up at me, shorter without her high heels. "Glad you made yourself at least more comfortable."

My suit jacket, vest, and tie are draped over the couch. I've rolled my sleeves up to my elbows and even poured myself a scotch. I'm the picture of relaxed male, but inside I'm still seething over what happened at the restaurant. That weasel touching Sofie. That woman calling her a slut. I've been keeping a rein on my temper, but it's fraying. Every time I think about the way Esteban Ruiz looked at Sofie, about his proprietary touch, I want to smash something. Preferably something shaped like his head.

"I ordered the food." We sit down on the couch beside each other. "Are you sure the rice and vegetables will be enough? Where's my horse tonight?"

"Oh, it'll do." Sofie pulls her long hair up and off her neck before letting it fall around her shoulders again. "The horse has a shoot in a few days, and it takes more than barre classes to look good naked."

Her eyes fly up to meet mine.

"Not actually naked. I'll be wearing panties."

Okay.

"And, well, that's it. Just the panties." She scrunches up her face. "Sorry. It's my job."

"I get it."

I don't like it, but I get it.

She's nervous. I could make small talk until our food arrives, but I'm not good at that. I want to know who Esteban is…was…to her. If they weren't lovers, I'll eat my shoe. I know Sofie's not some shrinking virgin. She's confident and unashamed of her sexuality. I like that about her actually, but there was more to Esteban. It seems that I'm always looking for more when it comes to Sofie, but this time I'm not sure I'll like what I find.

"You're dying to ask me about Esteban, right?" Sofie teases me, but her eyes can't quite catch up to her tone.

"Yeah, li'l bit."

I scoot close enough to pull her head down to my lap so I have an aerial view of her face. She relaxes some, flipping her legs up and letting her feet dangle over the arm of the couch at the other end. She closes her eyes and sighs before looking up at me.

"I left home right after high school." She pulls a chunk of her hair across her mouth before speaking again. "I needed to get away from here, from this city, from this life. To do something nobody saw coming, not even me."

"Is that why you turned down all the college offers?" I stroke the hair back from her face, tracing her silky eyebrows with my thumb. "Just needed a different direction?"

"Well, and remember I thought I was biding my time until Walsh popped the question." Sofie rolls her eyes. "I could have worked at the 7-Eleven for all I cared. It was just temporary. Something fun to do until Walsh came to his senses."

She gives a quick shake of her head.

"Such a fool." She shrugs. "Anyway, I left New York altogether and lived in Milan for a year or so. I didn't know it would become all that it did. A career that lasted this long."

"At eighteen?" I shouldn't be so astounded. By twenty-one, Harold and I had started Deutimus, but fresh out of high school living on her own in Italy? "Your parents let you do that?"

She blinks up at me, a frown crinkling her smooth skin.

"How could they have stopped me? I was making so much money modeling, and honestly, they just didn't care."

My mother sent me care packages every month my freshman year. I can't imagine my parents being that detached.

"In hindsight, I wish they *had* found a way to stop me." I barely hear Sofie's addendum it's so quiet. "They left me to my own devices, and I got in a lot of trouble."

"With Ruiz?" I go still while I wait for her answer. Even though I suspect they were lovers, I hope she'll say no.

"Yes, with him."

I hope I hide my disappointment, but maybe I don't because she sits up abruptly, pulling away from me and leaning her elbows on her knees, avoiding my eyes.

"We met at a shoot on the Riviera when I was barely twenty," she continues, eyes on the carpet, on her bare feet, on everything but me. "It was our first time working together, but after that, he would suggest me, request me, recommend designers use me. People started calling me his muse."

Sofie stands up, shoving her fingers through her hair, linking them on her head and blowing out a breath.

"I was so stupid, naïve. Flattered." Her bitter laugh breaks the silence. "He wanted me and I wanted him. It was that simple, but I had no idea how complex things would become."

"What happened?"

"We had an affair." She drops her arms to her side, looking at me unblinkingly, her eyes not hiding a thing. "I knew he lived in Barcelona, but he was with me so much in Milan, I didn't ask questions. At least not the right questions."

"He was already married."

It's a statement, not a question, because I can see how a man would betray his vows for a woman like Sofie. I would never do it—could never do it—but a man like Ruiz seizes every opportunity, even the ones that don't belong to him. And it's only now I understand that Sofie responded so strongly last night when I asked if she still had feelings for a married man because she wasn't thinking about Walsh. She was thinking about Ruiz.

"I didn't know." Sofie drops her head back, fixing her eyes on the modern light fixtures overhead. "And no one thought to tell me. We weren't even discreet because I didn't think we had anything to hide. It's only now, looking back, that I realize how clever he was. Living freely in another country, but managing to keep our relationship relatively quiet in another. I wasn't nearly as recognizable then as I am now, but still…"

"But things blew up eventually?"

"Boy, did they. We were at Fashion Week in Paris, and I assumed we'd go to dinner after my show, but Seville had decided to surprise him." Sofie licks her lips. "There was a horrible scene. Everyone heard her calling me…well, what she called me tonight. She's high strung and, from what I can tell, emotionally unstable. I wanted to break things off with Es, but he told me their marriage had been over for a long time."

"So you continued the affair after you found out about his wife?" I want her to say no.

"Yeah, I did." She looks at me and then away, swallowing before continuing. "It was…complicated. When I finally did come to my senses, he still wouldn't leave me alone for a long time."

She sighs, dropping her eyes to the floor and chewing one corner of her mouth.

"Right before I broke things off for good, Es and I had lunch in Paris, and pictures were taken. Pictures got out." Sofie runs her palms over her thighs in the yoga pants. "Seville saw the pictures and apparently tried to kill herself. Came pretty close. She took some pills. It was everywhere. All over the papers. I was barely twenty years old and I was already labeled a home wrecker. I eventually put it behind me. Moved on to someone else. Hell, I even had my shot with Walsh, but this thing with Esteban will always follow me. "

She hazards a glance up at me, eyes braced for judgment.

"Say something." An ugly twist of her lips interrupts the flawless face. "Tell me how wrong I was. That I should be ashamed of myself."

She shakes her head, aggravating the corner of her mouth with her teeth.

"Won't be anything I haven't heard before from everyone else." She sighs. "From myself."

I once got the chance to view a king's private collection of artifacts. Everything was ancient, fragile. Some of the items looked as sturdy as the day they'd been created, but that wasn't true. If I'd handled them too roughly, without care, they could literally have shattered in my hands. That's how this feels. Some of Sofie's hurts she's been carrying around since she was still a girl, and she may appear tough, but I sense that how I handle this moment sets the tone for how we go forward. Despite what she just told me, I *want* to go forward. The last thing I want is for Sofie to shatter in my hands.

I stand up to take her hands between mine. She doesn't look up from our fingers joined together. I take her chin between my fingers gently, tipping up until she has to look into my eyes.

"We all make mistakes, Sof," I say softly. "I hope people won't judge me forever for the stupid stuff I did when I was twenty years old."

"Yeah, by twenty-one you and Harold had already started Deutimus." She shakes her head, dropping her eyes again. "You don't have to make up stuff to make me feel better. Like I said, you're a good guy, and I'm—"

"I am a good guy," I cut in before she can bring up the old argument again. "But I'm not perfect. Just like you made mistakes, but aren't a bad person. We learn from our mistakes so we don't make them again. It sounds like you learned from yours."

She nods, but doesn't elaborate. I have many more questions, but they are put on hold when the intercom buzzes for our food coming up. We don't talk about Ruiz while Sofie eats her vegetables and rice, or while I devour my curry chicken. I think it's deliberate, and that Sofie redirects our discussion on purpose.

"So I told you about Haven." She takes a long draw from her bottled water. "Tell me what's next for you."

I set aside the other questions I have about Milan and Ruiz and his bitch wife because I'm still learning Sofie, but I think she's reached her limit for tonight. All my life I've pushed until I get what I want, but with Sofie, it's clear to me if I push too much, she'll just walk away.

"Next? What do you mean?"

"After Deutimus." She sinks into the deep cushions of the cream-colored couch, pulling up one knee to wrap her arm around it. "I know you're not just riding off into the sunset, so what's your next step?"

I hesitate because my next steps are…still forming, and the wrong person knowing or saying anything or mishandling the information could ruin everything. I study Sofie for an extra minute, and I might be crazy, but there's nothing in me that sees her as the wrong person.

"It's confidential."

She nods, shifting both feet to the floor.

"I understand if you—"

"So I need you to keep this to yourself."

A small smile settles around her lips, and she nods again, looking at me while she waits.

"All right. I can do that."

"There's an organization called the Collective." I slide closer, taking her hand and linking our fingers. "It's an international organization that aligns leaders from the spheres of business, philanthropy, and politics to financially empower people in developing nations."

"Wow." Sofie's eyes widen. "That sounds exactly like what you wanted to do through Deutimus, right?"

"Yes, it is." I nod, twisting my mouth. "And even though we've seen the financial success, our efforts are sorely hampered by corrupt, selfish, short-sighted governments more concerned about a privileged few than about the whole."

"I remember Walsh running up against that in Haiti with our orphanage there."

I smile at her use of "our." She really does care about the Walsh Foundation.

"Haiti and just about every other country we're trying to help," I say. "Politicians with integrity and their country's best interest at heart are the missing link. There are some, though, and the Collective identifies and works with them to achieve our goals."

"Our? You're part of the Collective?"

"Yeah." I lean forward, resting my elbows on my knees before looking at her. "Once Deutimus is sold, they want me to consider leading it."

A wide smile illuminates Sofie's face, and with so little makeup, her hair falling around her shoulders, and the casual clothing, I imagine she doesn't look much different than she did when Ruiz first met her. First lied to her. I know she wants to talk about something else, but it's all I can think about.

"Bishop, that's incredible." She squeezes my hand, dipping her head to study me more closely. "Right?"

"Right. It's not a done deal, but right."

"What's left to do?" A small frown touches her face.

"I'm not their only candidate." I shrug and turn down the corners of my mouth. "There are a few other people they're considering. I'm sure my age is a concern."

"Because you're so old?" She grins and wrinkles her nose.

"Excuse me? I'm thirty-five. In their world, I'm a puppy."

"Thirty-five?" She stretches her eyes wide. "That old? I'm surprised you could keep up in Jalene's barre class."

"Is that so?"

I inch toward her, flattening her back into the cushions until my chest presses her back completely. She's so tall it's easy to forget how slim she is. She feels fragile under me, like I could break her, and I pull back just a little. She reaches up to run a hand over my head, digging her fingers deliciously into my scalp. Damn, that feels good.

"So that's what you want to do next?" she asks.

"It's what I hope to do next, but there's a vote." My hands find the silky, warm skin of her back beneath the sweatshirt. "I really don't want to talk about the Collective right now, Sof."

She relaxes into my hold, relinquishing herself to me, if only in this small way.

"What do you want to talk about?" Her voice drops, husky with quick-building heat.

"I don't want to talk at all."

"That so?" She leans up, taking my bottom lip between hers, eyes wide open and fixed on me. "What do you want to do then?"

I answer with my mouth, with my hands, with a kiss. Her fingers skim my neck, my shoulders, until she's cupping my face and kissing me slowly, each stroke into my mouth deep and deliberate. My hips push into her, into her soft heat, and she pushes back. We moan into each other, my hand cupping her head, holding her still so I can penetrate the hot, wet heat of her mouth over and over, deeper every time. Her fingers work at my shirt buttons until her hands brush across my chest, making my nipples tight and hard. I feather kisses across her shoulder where the sweatshirt falls away, pulling the soft skin into my mouth. I push at the material with my chin until my mouth reaches her breast, the nipple already tight and plump before I even start sucking.

I don't know what to do with this. I've never wanted a woman with this intensity. It's more than the softness of her breasts pressed into me. More than the long slim legs that bracket my hips as I stretch her back on the couch. More than the heat of our bodies seeking each other. This feels so good, and there's only one thing I want more than to be inside her body right now: to know what's in her heart, what's in her head. But I can't stop. For the first time in my life, I literally don't think I can stop. Me, the master of control, is spiraling into this heat so deeply I can't remember why I should stop.

I *won't* stop, and she won't stop me.

But my phone stops us. Harold's damn ring tone sings from my pocket.

"Dammit," I mutter against her lips. "It's Harold."

"Don't answer." She reaches down, gripping my dick. "Stay with me, Bishop."

I will. I dip my head to take her mouth again while her hand pulls on me through my pants. Just when I'm sure I'll explode in her hands, the strident ring tone shatters the passion, no matter how much we try to ignore it. Sofie breathes heavily and pulls back.

"I think I remember him disturbing us last night riiiiiiight around this time." She gives me a quick peck, pulling the sweatshirt up to cover her breasts. "You better get it. And tell Harold he's a cock blocker."

We both laugh, and I reluctantly pull away from her warm body, sitting up and pulling my phone from my pocket.

"The world better be on fire, Smith."

"Were you busy?" Harold asks.

"Uh, I'm on a date, remember?"

"Oh." A pause while he remembers Sofie. "Ohhhhhh. Sorry, man, but I thought you'd want to see this story on CNN. Are you near a TV?"

"Yeah." I look at Sofie. "Remote?"

She opens a drawer in the ottoman in front of the couch and pulls out the remote, offering it to me.

On-screen I recognize Marcus Clarke, a South African business-man and current leader of the Collective, right away. He's being led away in handcuffs, and the headline mentions financial misappro-priations and sexual misconduct.

"Dammit, they found out," I say to Harold.

"Yeah, so much for people thinking Clarke was just seeking other opportunities. I know you were hoping the truth wouldn't come out, but looks like it has."

"Thanks. Guess I'll be dealing with this all day tomorrow." I blow out a frustrated breath, flopping back into the cushions and watch-ing the footage. "See you when I get home."

"Yeah, we can compare dates." His voice turns eager. "Henri and I had dinner again."

"That's a great idea, Smith. And maybe then we can give each other manicures and braid our hair." I can't help but laugh at him, but he can take it. We've been giving each other a hard time for nearly fifteen years. "What the fuck?"

"Okay, you're right." He laughs at himself and probably at me. "Night."

"Yeah." I hang up and study the shit storm playing out on Sofie's flat screen.

"This is bad, right?" Sofie scoots close, leaning her head on my shoulder.

"Yeah." I settle back, wrapping my arm around her. "We knew about all the things he'd done. We're actually forcing him to resign, but we didn't want to expose all of his misappropriations and other shit, not to protect him, but to protect the integrity of the Collective. So much for that."

She tilts her head back, eyes concerned.

"What's this mean for you?"

"Nothing." I kiss the corner of her mouth before pulling back, studying the flawless bone structure and wide mouth that so obsessed Esteban Ruiz. "It just means the leader we choose will have to have a clean nose. Spotless, actually. Be above reproach in every way."

"Which you are, right?" She smiles, resting her head back on my shoulder.

"Far as I know." I brush my hand over the cool silk of her hair. "I—"

The next story catches my eye, and I stop to tune in.

"Wow, it's a night for scandal, apparently." I nod my head toward the screen. "I wonder how that prick Kyle Manchester will handle this. I knew I didn't like him for a reason."

Sofie stiffens beside me, pulling away completely and sitting up on the edge of her seat, eyes glued to the screen.

The headline proclaims that some intern is accusing Kyle Manchester of raping her years ago. Apparently the statute of limitations is up, but Shaunti Miller wanted to step forward and speak out before Manchester is elected senator next year.

"Brave girl." I rub Sofie's back, but it's not soft and yielding. The muscles are tight like marble under my hands. "Sof? You okay, darlin'?"

The endearment keeps slipping out. Chalk it up to my Southern roots. Or maybe the fact that my dad always called my mom that, and…shit. I need to slow down. My mom and dad? If Sofie even suspected that's where I went in my head, she'd probably change her phone number. But right now, that seems to be the least of her concerns. She's on her feet, walking in tiny circles like a wind-up toy. Pushing her hair back. Wrapping her arms around her body.

"Sofie, are you okay?" I stand and stop her pacing, holding her by the shoulders. "What's wrong?"

She lifts her eyes to me and lies. Just as sure as I know my own name, I know she's lying.

"Nothing." She creases her mouth into a smile as fake as the tofu in her takeout. "I'm fine. Just tired. Mind if we call it a night?"

I look back at the screen, seeing pictures of Manchester smiling that too-white politician smile and the young woman accusing him of rape. I was so distracted by the Collective drama, it's taking me time to assemble things in my mind, but now I remember Sofie's reaction to Manchester at the dinner the night we met. The silent messages they exchanged with each glance until she left the table like she was being chased.

Motherfucker.

"Did he hurt you?" It comes out harsher than I intended, the abrasion of my tone making her jump slightly. "Sorry. I didn't mean to…Sofie, did Kyle Manchester hurt you?"

She drops a curtain over her eyes, over her whole face, and lies to me again.

"No." She shakes her head adamantly. "No, of course not. I just…we went to high school together. He's one of my father's associates. So, I was, um, shocked, of course. That's all."

"Sofie, you know you can tell me if—"

"I have early meetings." She steps out of my hold, adjusting her sweatshirt until her shoulder is covered, gripping the fabric with white knuckles. "Can we talk tomorrow?"

This is another time when I want to push because if he did what I think he did, I'll crush Kyle Manchester. But Sofie looks more fragile than I've ever seen her. Strain paints a tight, white circle around her mouth. Her eyes are dark, the pupils stretched like she's in shock. And when I take her hands and raise them to my lips, they're cold. She is like ice, so frozen she could shatter with just the slightest pressure. So I don't press right now. I just drop a kiss on her hair and walk out the door.

CHAPTER SEVENTEEN

Sofie

I stare at the sketches splayed across my desk, but don't see them. I haven't really seen anything since that report last night on Kyle and the woman accusing him of raping her eight years ago. His face and hers burn my retina, leaving a phantom impression that eclipses everything else. His face—confident and smug. Hers—resolved, but frightened.

I give up. I'm useless today.

I push away from the desk, spinning my seat around to consider the busy street outside my window. I could have been uptown, in the heart of New York City's business world, but I chose Soho for my office. A little slower. A hub for artisans. Charming. It's a little more of a drive each day, but Baker doesn't mind having the extra minutes with me, I don't think.

"Sof," Stil says from my office door.

I drag my eyes away from the street below, forcing myself to meet my friend's stare.

"Yeah, Stil. What's up?"

"Walsh is on the line." She raises one brow and runs her tongue over her front teeth. "He says he's been calling your cell all morning."

"I've been busy." I shrug, glancing at the phone on the edge of my desk.

Stil walks into the office, running her fingers over the same three sketches on the desk's surface from an hour ago.

"Yes, I see you're making so much progress here."

I shake my head, collapsing into my seat again.

"Tell him I'm in a meeting and that I'll call him later."

"Before I deliver that message, he said to let you know if you brush him off, he's coming to Soho."

"Son of a…" I scoot forward and pick up the handset. "Line two?"

"Yep," Stil says, closing the office door behind her.

"Walsh, heard you needed me?"

"I needed you two hours ago." Irritation almost outweighs the concern in his voice. "But you've been ignoring my calls."

"Maybe I've been busy all morning."

"Sof, it's me." He lets out a frustrated breath. "You saw the news last night? About Kyle Manchester?"

"Yeah, I saw." I lean back, crossing one leg over the other and tapping my shoe against the desk. "We've talked about this, Walsh. If Shaunti Miller wants to tell her story, then—"

"She's not."

My foot stops tapping. I sit up, resting my forehead in one hand.

"But last night—"

"That was last night." Walsh's deep voice goes softer. "This morning, she withdrew her accusations."

"But why? What happened?"

"If I were to guess, Manchester's people found something to force her back in the closet."

A rock, hard and cold, sits in my chest where my heart should be. I can't let myself feel anything because if I feel anything, I'll feel *everything*. And it's too much. After all these years, it's too much.

"Walsh, what do you expect me to do?"

"What do you *want* to do, Sof?"

What I want to do is hard. It's dangerous. It thrusts me into the center of a horrific storm. What I want to do, I don't think I'm strong enough to try.

"I want to keep doing what I've been doing for the last fifteen years," I finally answer, keeping my voice steady. "Put this behind me. Keep moving forward."

"Sof, if someone as high profile as you are came forward, it might encourage Shaunti to tell her story in spite of what they have on her. Or there could be women we don't even know about who are afraid to tell their stories."

"I can't." Panic crawls up from a dark hole in my belly.

"At least tell your father. He's aggressively selling Manchester to the board as a sure thing."

How do you admit your own father doesn't care that you were raped? That he is actively pursuing business with the man who did you such harm?

"He knows, Walsh. I told him."

The silence on the other end puffs up with Walsh's outrage, his anger, his disappointment. All the things I felt at first, but have gotten used to.

"And he…" Walsh falters. "Ernest knows what happened and is still doing business with that bastard?"

"He thinks I'm remembering it differently than it probably happened. He—"

"Bullshit," Walsh snaps. "You may have been drunk when you finally told me about it, Sof, but you told me enough. The bruises, the—"

"Stop." I don't need him to detail any of it. I've spent all this time doing a great job of forgetting. "Just leave it alone, Walsh."

"I swore to you then I wouldn't expose this," Walsh says. "I won't expose your secret if you're not ready to, but I'll work around it."

"What does that mean?" I lean forward, barely sitting in my seat at his words.

"It means that Bennett's not doing business with a rapist." Walsh pauses before going on. "Sof, your father is setting himself against me at every turn, on every front. This could get ugly."

"Trevor seemed to think Uncle Martin's retiring soon, and that you and my father would end up battling for leadership of Bennett."

"Trevor?" Something lightens in Walsh's voice. "Trevor Bishop?"

Ugh. No. Me and my loose lips.

"You've been seeing Trevor Bishop?"

"Walsh, a date or two. Nothing serious."

"He's a good guy. Maybe you should pursue something serious with him. Better him than Rip."

I don't answer because I kind of want to keep whatever is happening between Trevor and me just between us for a while. Me, whose whole life has been lived in front of cameras, half the time half clothed, wants something that no one else sees.

"I think he really likes you, Sof."

"Well, he…" I know devious when I hear it. "Walsh, did you give him my phone number?"

His deep laugh on the other end is all the answer I need. Instead of being angry, a grin spreads over my face.

"You idiot. That man hasn't left me alone since he got back from Cambodia."

"And you like it."

I do like it…now, but I'm not telling Walsh that.

"Sofie, just because you and I weren't right for each other doesn't mean you aren't right for someone else. Someone who'll be good to you and call out the best in you. Bishop's good at that."

"What if there isn't a best, Walsh?" I swallow past the lump of uncertainty in my throat, forcing myself to ask the question that holds me back. "What if this is as good as it gets?"

"I think there's good in you, a strength in you that you haven't tapped into."

"You really believe that?"

"Why else would I still be your friend?"

"Well, no one really knows that."

We laugh for a moment together, and I think I can finally just be Walsh's friend without the shadow of my parents' misplaced hopes looming over us.

"Sof, please think about at least talking with Shaunti."

"I'll think about it," I agree, but I'm still not sure I can.

For another half hour after Walsh and I talk, I still can't focus. I'm just about to give up and go home for the day when Gil buzzes me from the reception area.

"Sofie, honey."

"Yeah, what's up, Gil?" I ask absently, packing up my laptop and iPad.

"Someone's here to see you." Gil's voice drops. "A very big and handsome someone."

"Did you drool on him, Gil?" I'm not sure if it's my crazy receptionist making me feel lighter, or the fact that Trevor's here to see
me. Doesn't matter. I haven't been able to feel better on my own all
morning.

"Maybe a little," Gil says with a grin I hear in his voice.

"Send him in." I smooth my hair back into the high ponytail and
check the wide-legged pants and fitted heather cashmere turtleneck
I put on this morning.

Trevor strides in, closing the door behind him and turning the
lock. He's on me in seconds, reversing our bodies so that he's
propped against the desk and I'm standing in the V of his powerful
legs. The palm of his hand rests under my chin as he commands my
mouth in a slow kiss that starts a fire in me I know won't be extin-
guished in the only way I'll find satisfying.

"Hey, you." He drops kisses over my chin and down my neck
until he reaches the edge of my sweater. A knowing grin creases his
mouth, and he tugs the turtleneck aside to inspect the mark he left
there last night.

"I like this," he says, eyes piercing mine.

"So do I, that's why I'm not sharing it." I lean a few inches in and
up until I can suck at the soft fullness of his bottom lip. "What are
you doing here? I thought it was going to be a hectic day with the
Collective."

His expression shifts from indulgent to irritated, and I'm glad it's
not me on the other end of that look.

"Idiots." He shakes his head and slides one hand down to the
small of my back. "I may have to go to South Africa."

My mouth slips into a pout. I don't want him to leave, but I just
nod.

"When?" I ask quietly, hoping I'm hiding my disappointment.

"We'll see." He shrugs, adding his other hand to my back and pulling me closer. "Come have lunch with me."

I glance at my iPad and purse, already packed and ready to go.

"Your timing is impeccable. I was just leaving."

"In the middle of the day?" He frowns and uses a finger to tilt my chin, searching my eyes. "Everything okay?"

I've never had much trouble lying to men before, but it's hard with Trevor. I look over his shoulder, avoiding his eyes while I answer.

"Everything's fine. Just trouble focusing."

When he doesn't answer, I flick my eyes up to find him studying me like I'm a problem it's taking him too long to solve.

"I think this luncheon is exactly what you need."

"Lunch*eon*?" I pull back, peering up at him. "I thought you said lunch. Is this a thing?"

"It's a thing you'll enjoy." He stands, letting me go, grabbing my clutch, and handing it to me. "But we'll be late if we don't get going."

I'm just about to dig a little more before fully committing when a loud banging interrupts us.

"Why is this door locked, Sof?" Stil demands from the other side. "Are you okay? Open it right now."

Trevor and I look at each other with wide eyes for half a second before busting out laughing. Stil is so dramatic.

Trevor walks over and opens the door, leaning one shoulder against the doorframe and blocking Stil's entrance. Her face is comical, transforming from concerned to dreamy-eyed in a millisecond.

"Trevor, hi." She practically blushes. "Sorry. I was worried about..."

She flicks a glance past his shoulder to find me leaning against the desk, grinning.

"That little minx there." She glares at me. "It's not like her to lock the door, and she's been off all morning, so I was worried."

My grin drops. I don't need her talking to Trevor about how off I've been this morning. He's too sharp, and he already suspects something happened with Kyle. I head toward the door, ready to get out of here.

"I'm fine, as you can see." I slip my arm through Trevor's. "And would you stop looking like that at my…"

Trevor's eyes drop to me, brows up, waiting for me to finish that sentence, which I can't do. I can't very well call him my boyfriend after two dates. I may *never* call him that.

"Just stop looking at him like that," I finish lamely.

"Screw you, Sof," Stil fires back. "I was just glad to see Trevor again and I—"

"Again?" I interrupt. "I didn't realize you two had actually met."

Now that I think of it, her greeting was awfully familiar for someone who's only seen pictures and videos. Stil starts stuttering, and I smell a rat with black and pink hair.

"Um, we…well, there was that time…we…" She looks at Trevor as if waiting for him to help, but he just grins, apparently enjoying my friend's discomfort as much as I am.

All my processes have been delayed today because of the craziness with Kyle, but I'm starting to catch up. Why didn't I realize this before? Only one other person knows my schedule, and she's standing right in front of me.

"It was you! You told him about my barre class." I put my hands on my hips, my clutch in one fist. "I should have known."

Stil looks like she's cooking up some lie, but she abandons that and just goes with the truth.

"Yeah, it was me." She slides a look up and down Trevor's suit-clad body. "You can thank me later."

"I warned you about those looks." I poke her shoulder and push her out of my way. "Back to work, peasant. We're going to lunch."

"Well, all right, your majesty." Stil follows us out past Gil and to the elevator. "And will you be back?"

"No, she won't." Trevor grins down at me, a hand at my back, ushering me into the elevator. "She's gone for the day."

He challenges me with a look, like maybe he's expecting me to protest, but I don't. I can't. I need to get out of here.

"You heard the man," I say to Stil as the doors close. "I'm gone for the day."

The luncheon is at Park Lane Hotel off Central Park. Traffic is insane, so we opt to walk the last few blocks. It's a brisk day, even though we're only mid-October. I should have grabbed at least a jacket, and a gust of wind makes me shiver. Trevor pulls me under his arm, shielding me from the wind.

"Cold?" He smiles at me, his warm dark eyes chasing away the shivers.

"Just a little chilly, I guess."

I love being this close to him, love his consideration even more than the warmth his body provides. We're almost at the door when someone calls my name.

"Sofie!"

I turn my head to see a man quickly approaching us. A boy, really. He's maybe only nineteen or so. The wind ruffles his brown hair, and his blue eyes are lit and eager and fixed on me. I'm not sure he even notices the mountain of muscle going stiffer and stiller and more alert the closer he gets to us.

"Hi, Sofie." His cheeks go pink, but he looks me straight in the eye. "I can't believe it's you."

"It's me." I smile, relaxing because I've done this about a million times since I started modeling. Since I was his age. "How are you?"

"I'm…I'm great!" he gushes. "I'm such a huge fan. I have all your *Sports Illustrated* bathing suit issues. And, of course, the *Playboy* spread."

His cheeks go even pinker when he mentions *Playboy*. He finally looks at Trevor, maybe realizing it's not the most appropriate time to mention seeing me nude.

"Um, yeah. Like I said, I'm a big fan." He glances between Trevor's unsmiling face and mine. "I don't want to bother you."

"But you already have," Trevor says, eyes flinty.

"Trevor, it's okay." I squeeze his hand. "What do you need…what was your name?"

"Barry." His grin is back, wider now. "The name's Barry. If you could just sign something for me."

I'm assuming he's not just carrying pictures of me around randomly, so I'm not sure what he wants me to sign. I hope it's not anything weird, or Trevor might snap him in the middle of the street.

From his backpack, Barry pulls out a pen and a subway map, offering them to me. I sketch a quick autograph and hand it back to him.

"Wait till I show the guys on the team." He carefully slips the subway map into his bag. "I just knew it had to be Photoshopped. Like I didn't think you could look like this in real life, but you do. You're the prettiest girl I've ever seen."

It's amazing how time changes your perspective. There was a time when those words would have meant the world to me, and now compliments about my looks are like single drops of rain in a deluge. They have no impact. Make no difference. Indistinct from all the other words people say.

"Thank you, Barry." I grab Trevor's hand. "We need to go. Nice meeting you."

Trevor doesn't wait for him to respond, but just starts walking toward the hotel.

"Does that happen a lot?" he asks, taking my hand in his.

We're holding hands. In public. Are we there yet? We've had only two dates, and they both ended up at home, but it feels like we've known each other for longer. For deeper. Maybe it feels like more already because Trevor set out to make it more. Whatever it is, my hand feels right in his.

"All the time." I can't help but laugh. "It used to give me a thrill. Now it's a little bit of a nuisance sometimes, but it usually doesn't take long to be nice. They build this image up in their heads about you. I at least try to be less of a bitch than usual."

He still isn't smiling, so I squeeze his hand and smile at him.

"It's not a big deal."

"It could be." Trevor frowns. "Some guy just like that could walk up with a knife or gun and hurt you before you have time to realize what's happening. Shouldn't you have security?"

"I do sometimes." I shrug. "Like for events and things when people know I'm scheduled to be there, but other than that, not much. This is New York. I've lived here my whole life. We New Yorkers can't be bothered."

Trevor gives me one more skeptical look before nodding and opening the hotel door for me.

"Now why are we here and what's for lunch?" I sit in the seat he pulls out for me at the table. "I'm starving."

"Ah, my horse is back." He pulls his chair closer to mine. Closer than the other chairs are to one another. "I have no idea what's on the menu. I only know I get to have lunch with you, and I love this speaker and this cause."

"There's a cause?"

His shoulder is within leaning distance, but I resist. I should be careful. I've just gotten out of a very public relationship with Rip. One the media is still speculating over. It will take only one picture of me cuddled up with Trevor for them to speculate that I was cheating on Rip. That I've moved on too fast. That I'm taking advantage of Trevor. Who knows what they'll say?

Well, I do because they've said it all before.

"Yeah, there's always a cause." He takes a sip of water and looks around the ballroom set in rounds of eight or so. The white tablecloths contrast with the bright floral centerpieces. The baskets of bread at the center of each table draw my eyes and my appetite.

"Bread," I growl. I reach for a roll, but drop my hand back to my side, thinking better of it.

"Thought you were starving." He reaches for a roll...and butters it, curse his head.

"I'll wait for protein." I sip my water, hoping it will douse the growl a little until the food arrives. "I have that shoot tomorrow."

"Oh, the naked one." His voice is neutral, but his lips go tight.

"Not naked." I lean into him for a second. "Remember the panties."

He relinquishes a small smile, but still doesn't look pleased.

"Does it bother you that I model in skimpy stuff, and sometimes..." I leave that sentence hanging, but he picks it up.

"And sometimes in nothing?" He sets his water down before looking at me. "I don't have any right to be bothered, do I?"

No, he doesn't, but it feels like he does. I don't know how he manages to make everything feel so intimate and new and familiar. Like an adventure I'm having for the first time with someone I've known forever, but just met.

"I just wondered...well, you seemed bothered when Barry mentioned *Playboy*."

"Why did you do it?" His voice and eyes hold no judgment. Just genuine curiosity.

"Really, I think I had something to prove." A low laugh slips out. "I think I wanted to prove that I still had...whatever I was supposed to be losing. I was in the best shape of my life in an industry that ruthlessly judges you by that shit."

Before he can reply, a few other people join us at our table. A couple of them do double takes when they realize who I am. I smile and shake their hands when Trevor introduces me. I'm too preoccupied with the salmon on the plate set in front of me to wonder what they're thinking about Trevor's bringing me.

"I'm so excited to finally meet Halima," the woman Trevor introduced as Isabelle says. "But you see her all the time, don't you, Trevor?"

"Some." Trevor chews the steak he opted for before speaking. "She lives in London now. I actually saw her more when she lived in Gambia."

"What a treat to have her here in the States," Isabelle's husband, Frank, says. "And while you're in New York."

"And is this your first Restore event, Ms. Baston?" Isabelle asks, her eyes toggling between Trevor and me.

"It is." I take a sip of my water, hoping I can disguise how ignorant I am about Restore and Halima, whoever she is, and Gambia in general. "I'm looking forward to it."

I frown at Trevor for throwing me in blind. He mouths "Sorry," but goes on eating. I'm finishing my fish when a young woman, dressed well but simply, takes the podium.

"Thank you all for attending our monthly Restore luncheon." She licks her lips, my only clue that the overflowing crowd might make her a bit nervous. "There are so many of you here today, and I think I know why."

She glances back at a woman seated behind her onstage. The woman has the most gorgeous skin I may have ever seen, the color of dark cocoa, not a blemish in sight. Her hair is cropped close, leaving her stark bone structure prominent. She is slim and dressed even more simply than the girl at the podium. The shift dress she wears is bright orange and contrasts beautifully with her dark skin. Her smile as she returns to the speaker makes her face glow.

"We are so pleased to have our guest with us today," the woman continues. "Her story, her courage, and her ongoing fight against FGM have inspired us all. She inspires thousands every year, and we are honored to hear her today. Please welcome to the stage Halima Mendy."

While I'm still using context clues to try to figure out what FGM is, everyone else applauds as Halima takes the stage. She receives a warm welcome and offers an even warmer smile.

"Greetings, all." Her soft voice, thickly accented, hushes the crowd. "I am honored to be here with you today. Thank you, Lisa, for that lovely introduction. Many of you have heard my story, but many have not, so I'll ask those who have to bear with me. Your story is your most powerful weapon. We must use our hurts to help, and so I tell my story every chance I get. Every time I do, I raise a fist against my oppressors."

I'm unprepared for her passion. She is soft-spoken, but her eyes gleam with the truth of her words. Even standing still, arms at her side, she has the look of a warrior.

"I was ten when they woke me before the sun was up," she continues, her eyes roving the crowd. "Me, my sisters, my cousins, girls from my village, all taken before daylight. One by one, we were held down, our legs spread, and we were cut. I have no words for the pain. I have never borne children, maybe I never will, but I am told this pain of female genital mutilation is greater than that. They cut away our pleasure and exchanged it for pain, for infection, for trouble that will follow many of us for the rest of our lives."

Her dark eyes scan the crowd. I don't know what she's searching for, but for some reason when she reaches me, it's like she finds it. Her eyes hold and lock with mine. And somehow I know it has nothing to do with the fact that she probably recognizes my face. It is that she recognizes *me*. Connects with something inside of me. I don't understand it, but I know it.

"I tell this story all over the world, but the one place I can never tell it is in my village in Gambia. My family has disowned me. If I ever go back, I will surely die for telling the truth about how our girls, not just in Gambia, but in Egypt, all over Africa, all over the world, are being abused, even right here in America."

Her mouth tightens as her fists ball at her sides.

"Yes, FMG is on the rise here in America. Vacation cutting is on the rise as those who have immigrated here send their young girls home to be cut, and they come back forever changed."

I'm stunned by the facts she shares over the next half hour. Shocked that I never knew this was happening. Mostly I am unsettled by her words.

Your story is your most powerful weapon. We must use our hurts to help.

I close my eyes against the images flooding my mind. Kyle's smug face, Shaunti Miller's frightened eyes. Memories from that night fifteen years ago that I have stuffed into a dark corner in the back of my mind, but Walsh's words from this morning and Halima's words now tug and pull at those memories until they are spread out before me, not dusty and wrinkled, but fresh and crisp like they happened only yesterday.

"Sofie." Trevor speaks into my ear as everyone else applauds the end of Halima's speech. "Are you okay, darlin'?"

I turn my eyes to him, meeting his concern finally with an honest answer.

"No." I shake my head and blink at the tears I've been keeping at bay since last night. "I'm not."

"Let's get out of here." He gathers my things and is pulling my chair away from the table when he's stopped by a hand on his sleeve.

"Trevor, you are going?" Halima asks, her smile warm and familiar. "I saw you about to leave and made my way over here quickly. It has been too long, my friend."

Trevor reaches down to hug her, his hands on her shoulders and a smile on his face.

"I was planning to call so we could see each other before you leave," he says.

"Where is Fleur? I've been meaning to call you both." Halima's eyes drift to me, standing close to Trevor. "Oh. I'm sorry. I…"

Who the hell is Fleur?

Confusion clouds her features for a moment, but she recovers, extending her hand to me.

"I'm sorry. How rude." She takes my hand, pressing it between hers. "I'm Halima."

"Hi, I'm—"

"Oh, Ms. Baston, I know who you are." Her smile somehow sets my rattled nerves a little more at ease. "One of the most beautiful women in the world. Even I know that."

"Thank you." I squeeze her hand back, looking directly into her dark, kind eyes. "What you said, your words, they…they moved me deeply."

"I could tell this." Halima's smile melts until her mouth is just a gentle curve. "When you speak as much as I do, you always know who's with you, and you, Ms. Baston, were with me."

I want to ask how she knew that. I want to ask her how she learned to fight. I want to ask her if telling her story, making it a weapon, is truly worth what it costs her, because I have a story I think I have to tell.

And it could cost me everything.

Before I can unload any of those questions on her, Lisa, the young woman who introduced Halima, appears.

"Halima, so sorry, but we need to go." She gives Trevor a smile. "Mr. Bishop, always good to see you. Thank you for your continued support."

"Of course. I wouldn't miss Halima for the world." He bends to kiss Halima's cheek. "But now we have to go, too."

"I leave for Los Angeles tomorrow," Halima says. "But I am back in New York in a few weeks before I return to London."

"Maybe breakfast?" Trevor hands me my things and rests his hand at my back, a reassuring pressure that draws Halima's eyes and smile.

"Yes, I can see we have much to catch up on. Much has changed since we last spoke."

Trevor grins, pulling me an inch closer.

"Yes, much has changed." He nods to Lisa, who is beginning to look impatient. "I think you have to go, and so do we. We'll talk when you're back in the city."

Trevor leads me out of the crowded ballroom and down the hall until we're in the corridor for the bathrooms. He sets me against the wall, facing me and clasping our hands together between us, taking my eyes hostage. I can't help but think back to the first night we met. He found me hiding from Kyle Manchester in a corridor similar to this one. I don't think I can hide anymore.

"Kyle Manchester raped me fifteen years ago." The words come out with no aplomb. No drama. I say them as matter-of-factly as if Kyle had stolen a parking space at the grocery store instead of what he actually took. My virginity. My dignity. My voice.

I don't know what I expected to find on Trevor's face—shock, anger, outrage. His face is stone—emotionless, prepared.

"I know." He cups my face with one large hand, his touch so tender I can't resist leaning into it. "Or at least I suspected."

I nod, not surprised that he's not surprised.

"Is that why you brought me here?" My bitter laugh joins us in the quiet corridor. "To convince me I should tell my story?"

"I brought you here so you would see that it's okay to tell your story. So you could see what it looks like to tell the truth when it's dangerous and hard."

"I don't want to do this." I shake my head, the air rushing up my chest in jagged puffs. "I'm stepping into the middle of a huge scandal. They'll eat me alive, Bishop. Who're they going to believe? The political favorite of the moment, with his sweet wife and two kids, or me? The woman who had an affair with a married man and posed for *Playboy*? And more. So much more."

I can't even meet his eyes when I think of all the things Kyle's camp will trot out about me. Not lies. The truth. The ugly truth of my reckless behavior and decisions over the years. Trevor tips my chin until I can't look anywhere but at him.

"I believe you. Shaunti Miller will believe you. People will listen. Halima said your story is a weapon, and you're going after Kyle Manchester with guns blazing."

He slips both arms around my waist, pulling me into him until my head rests on his shoulder.

"And I'll be right there with you."

Maybe that scares me the most. That when I fight Kyle Manchester, I won't be the only one with weapons. If my story is my weapon, my past is Kyle's ammunition. He won't hesitate to use it against me to save the life he's built and his promising future. And the thought that Trevor will be right there for all of it, witnessing the dirt and grime of my past, that thought scares me maybe most of all.

"Want to go back to your place?" he asks. "We could order something, or I could cook."

He pauses, and I can practically hear him choosing his next words carefully.

"Maybe you can tell me what happened." He pulls back to study my face. "And we can talk about what your next steps need to be."

"I want to talk to my mother before I go any further."

"And your father?" His voice softens. "I mean, I know he's not exactly father of the year, but if he knew that Kyle—"

"He already knows." I swallow the lump that's been growing in my throat since Halima took the stage.

"What the hell do you mean he knows?" Trevor grabs my shoulders, dipping his head until we're almost nose to nose. "He can't know, Sofie. He's still dealing with him. Still courting him for Bennett."

"Bishop, I told him." Shame and disappointment thicken the words in my mouth. "He…he doesn't believe me, or he tells himself that so he can stick to his plan."

"Unbelievable." Anger burns in his eyes. "What kind of man is he? To take that piece of shit's word over his own daughter's?"

"Don't." Tears burn my eyes and my throat swells with familiar hurt hearing him say aloud what I've wondered time and time again since I confronted my father about Kyle. "I'm used to it. It's just…him. Can we leave? Just go to my place?"

I muster a grin and tug on his lapel.

"And you can cook something good for me later."

He bends until he can whisper in my ear.

"I could get used to taking care of you."

I work against the smile that forces its way to my lips, but I can't resist it. I can't resist him. I'm not sure why I ever even tried. Who resists something this good?

"It's been a long time since anyone took care of me."

The smile I couldn't resist fades as the reality of my situation hits me. I'm not sure that once I expose Kyle Manchester for the douche bag rapist prick he is, anyone will be able to take care of me, to protect me. For the first time, I may not even be able to take care of myself.

CHAPTER EIGHTEEN

Sofie

I step off the elevator into the lobby of my apartment building the next morning like it's a normal day. Like I'm not setting into motion a series of events that could prove catastrophic for me. Like every other morning, Baker idles outside my building, waiting for me to start my commute to the office. Only this morning, I have a small detour.

"Baker, could we run by my parents' house first?" I set my slouchy leather purse and a bag of samples for Haven on the backseat beside me. "Do you know if my mother has plans this morning? Besides her usual, I mean."

Billi Baston is a woman of routine. Every morning she has her breakfast at nine o'clock sharp. Some variation of omelet, grapefruit, her Columbian coffee. Never in her robe or pajamas. Always dressed for the day, hair in place. God forbid our housekeeper, Millie, see her *dishabille*.

She and my father have a strange relationship. I don't see love between them, but something almost as strong binds them together.

I'm not sure what that is exactly, but it has kept her tethered to my father through infidelities, neglect, and downright indifference. My mother is a mystery wrapped up in another mystery. I've always wondered why she stays and why she turns a blind eye.

My phone buzzes from my bag, pulling me from the enigma that is my parents' marriage. In spite of the difficult conversation ahead, and the even more difficult days ahead once I go public with my story, I smile as soon as I see "Bishop" on my screen.

"Hey, you." I lean back in the heated seat, bracing myself for that warm Southern drawl.

"Hey yourself." I hear a smile in that deep-timbered voice. "On your way to the office?"

"Not quite yet." I pass a hand over my face, agitation returning full force. "I'm going to see my mother first."

"To tell her everything?"

I want to tell him no one ever gets *everything* with me, but I don't. It's easier to hide your secrets when people think you're baring them all. They don't dig as deeply or as hard. Some things will follow me to the grave, and with those secrets as my final bedfellows, I have no illusion that I'll rest in peace.

"Yes. I'll tell her what happened with Kyle, if my father hasn't already." I shrug even though he can't see me. "We aren't besties or anything, but she's still my mother. I want her to know her daughter was…"

I trail off, checking the rearview mirror to see if Baker is paying attention. Of course he is. That's what he does. Blends into the walls and furniture so you'll talk freely. He's a collector of secrets, even the ones he doesn't want.

"I just don't want her hearing anything on CNN she hasn't already heard from me," I conclude.

"Makes sense." Though only a few seconds, I hear his hesitation. "Look, about yesterday. I shouldn't have ambushed you with Halima and her story. This is a huge decision, and I never want you to think I'd manipulate you into anything."

"Trevor, I don't." I drop my voice to a whisper, an intimate breath between us across the airwaves. "I needed that. You have a way of inspiring me, and I like it. And thank you for last night, by the way."

"Oh, you mean cheap Chinese food and the documentary on the fight for women's rights in Kenya? The one you fell asleep watching?"

"I had a long day!"

"I fell asleep, too." His chuckle wraps around me, warming me more than the leather seat at my back. "It's okay."

"What I was actually thanking you for was not pressuring me to talk about...things last night."

I know that if I'm going public with this, I'll have to get used to resurrecting the details of that night, but I'm not ready to do that with Trevor. There is some small part of me that's afraid he ultimately won't believe me. My own father didn't. On some level, I don't expect more from my father. He's a ruthless, self-centered bastard. Always has been. Trevor has raised my expectations beyond what they've been with anyone else. The advantage of not expecting is never being disappointed. Over the last few weeks, Trevor has shown me what it feels like to expect.

"You'll talk to me about it when you're ready." Trevor's voice softens like there could be someone listening. "Can I see you tonight?"

"We've seen each other every night." A smile lifts the corners of my mouth and heart. "Aren't you tired of me yet?"

"No."

Just that. I'm not tired of him yet, either. As a matter of fact, I'm hungrier every day. Not just for him in my bed, but just… him. Being around him. Laughing with him. Learning things from him.

"I'd love to see you tonight, too, Bishop."

"You want to try going out again?"

"What if this is our third strike?"

"I'm not out, that's for sure, strikes or not." I can imagine the grin on his face that I hear in his voice, and it makes me grin in return.

"Maybe you should." My grin starts fading, and I wonder if he hears that in my voice, too. "Get out, I mean."

"What are you talking about, Sofie?"

I've weighted the conversation with my words, but it needs to be said. And as selfish as I am, as I have been, and as much as I want to keep doing what we're doing—do more—I have to say it.

"Things could get really ugly, Bishop. We could stop now before—"

"Is that who you think I am?" Irritation tightens his voice. "We haven't known each other long, Sof, but I thought you knew me better than that. I'm not abandoning you because things might get tough."

"And messy." I gulp back my fear. "There are things you don't know about me."

"And there are things that I do. I know you're brave, and despite your father's efforts, compassionate."

"That's not funny," I say, a giggle slipping from my lips.

"I know that you're beautiful." His voice dips, the sensual pull from the other line tugging on my senses, luring me into him even over the phone. "And that I can't be in the same room without touching you. I know I want to kiss you all the time and that I can't stop thinking about you."

What do I say to that? Do I confess that I feel the same? Only my thoughts go far past kissing. My thoughts go so far that I wake up sweating and twisting in the sheets for him, reaching for my vibrator, but I don't even try because I know it won't be thick enough, long enough. I know it won't go deep enough. I know it won't be him.

"Sofie?"

"I'm here." I clear my throat, sitting up straight and smiling at Baker, standing in the door to help me down. "I...um...I'm at my mom's."

"Okay." Humor and desire linger in his voice. "I vote that we stay in tonight so I can kiss you."

"Is that as far as we're gonna go?" I step out of the car, flashing Baker a quick smile as I walk into my parents' Park Avenue home. "Don't get my hopes up, Bishop."

My voice teases him, but he knows I'm serious. I'm ready when he is, and he knows it.

"Your hopes won't be the only thing 'up,' Sof, but tonight's not our night."

A chuckle percolates in my throat before spilling over, a rich sound only he could pull from me on the cusp of a conversation like the one I'm about to have with my mother.

"And you maintain that we'll both know when it's right?" I ring the bell even though I still have a key. My mother doesn't much like surprises, so I'll give her at least the warning of the bell.

"Yeah, I think we will." He pauses, his voice more serious with his next words. "And I think we're close."

He's saying two things, and I hear them both between the lines of what he's actually saying. Yes, we're closer than we've been to having sex. And halle-freaking-lujah for that. But he's also saying we're *close*. It's exactly the word I think of when I consider what we're doing, what we're becoming. We're becoming close. I'm letting him in, and I'm starting to understand that's what he wanted. He didn't want one intimacy without the other.

The door swings open, cutting off the things I want to say to deepen this feeling between us, even over the phone.

"I gotta go." I walk past our housekeeper, Millie, into the foyer with its black and white tiles.

"You'll call me when you're done?" Concern creeps into his voice. "As soon as you're done?"

"Bishop, I know how busy you are—"

"As soon as, Sof."

God, he makes me....

"Okay, as soon as."

"That's my girl."

He has no idea how good that sounds to me. What would it feel like to be *his girl*? To have all that care and sweetness and passion and fire aimed exclusively at me? I was the one resisting this, but now I want to lean into it so badly. This connection with Trevor is the silver lining in a very shitty cloud. I want to protect it from everyone who would question it, who would cheapen it, who would destroy it. The need to protect this connection rises so fiercely inside me that for a moment it steals my breath.

I walk deeper into the house and peer into the dining room, where my mother is already seated and eating her omelet. I drop my phone into my purse and walk in.

"Morning, Mother."

My mother looks up from her grapefruit, a frown worrying her brows.

"Sofie, did I forget we had an appointment?"

Not exactly how I wanted to start.

"It's good to see you, too." I sit down across from her at the dining room table that seats ten, but usually holds only one for breakfast. My mother prefers it that way, but she'll just have to put up with me for a little while today.

"Sofie, I'm not saying it isn't good to see you." That forced patience I've seen all my life enters her voice, settles on her face. "What can I do for you, sweetheart?"

We've never been close, and I regret that now more than I ever have. She was always beautiful and aloof, a maze of walls I could never figure out how to negotiate or scale to get on the other side. To get to her.

"Mom, I need to talk to you about some things that will be coming out soon." I shake my head when Millie gestures at the empty plate in front of me. "No, thank you, though, Millie."

I wait for Millie to leave the room before continuing.

"Things about...an incident from the past."

"Surely not Señor Ruiz again. I heard he's in New York." She rolls her eyes. "Sofie, please leave that woman's husband alone."

The serrated spoon she digs into the soft, pink flesh of her grapefruit may as well be plunging into my heart. That's how her comment feels. That's how it hurts. When that scandal broke I was barely twenty years old, and my mother had nothing but chiding for me. No guidance. No comfort. Only criticism and censure.

"I want nothing to do with Esteban Ruiz." My voice bounces off the walls of this cold room. "That's not what I'm talking about, though it will probably come back up."

"Sofie, dear, as much as I wish we had more of these little heart-to-hearts"—she glances at the diamond watch on her wrist—"I have a ten o'clock."

She's lying. Baker drives us all. He would have arranged a Bennett car for my commute if my mother had a ten o'clock appointment. He would have mentioned it. He would have known.

She wants to get rid of me. I wonder if my face disappoints her, the fact that I look like my father. If my actions, my life in most ways, have disappointed her. The chasm between us feels so deep and wide, I'm not sure my words will even reach her across it, but I have to try.

"Mom, fifteen years ago something happened that I never told you about, and it's going to come out."

My mother goes still, her pointy-tipped spoon hovering over her grapefruit. She places the spoon down, pushes her plate away, and sits back in her seat, eyes fixed on me.

"Go on."

I draw up enough breath to force the words out. Words I thought I would take with me to my grave.

"Kyle Manchester raped me."

I look up when there is not so much as a gasp. No sound, just those blue eyes looking back at me unblinkingly.

"Did you hear me, Mom? Kyle—"

"I'm sure you're mistaken, dear."

Shock and disbelief drag my jaw down and open.

"Mistaken?" Something I can't even call a laugh, it's so humorless, barges past my lips. "It's hard to be mistaken about a man forcing you to have sex, Mother."

"Sofie, I'm just saying that things get out of hand. People take things the wrong way."

"Exactly how was I supposed to take sexual assault?"

"This was fifteen years ago, so why are you just now coming forward? Why didn't you tell us then?"

I drag my mind back to that night. To Kyle dropping me off at the house like everything was normal. Like my wrists weren't ringed red from his belt wrapped around them. Like my breasts weren't on fire with marks from his teeth. Like I wasn't limping from the pain between my legs.

I'd felt filthy, and as soon as the door closed, I'd raced up the stairs to shower. I was a cliché, the victim huddled under a stinging spray of water that couldn't reach the parts that felt most unclean. I'd wept against the shower wall until my voice withered in my throat, and all I had left were whimpers and moans. I don't know how long I sat on my bed in my robe, catatonic, but eventually I knew I needed to tell my parents what had happened. I shuffled up the hall to their suite, but stopped at the door.

"You and Daddy were fighting."

"What?" My mother allows herself a small frown, not a deep one, because too much expression wrinkles skin.

"You and Daddy were arguing when I came home. I heard you, and I just didn't."

"So you didn't tell us you were raped because you heard us arguing?" Her face is skeptical, her voice condescending. "What were we arguing about? What was so important that you couldn't interrupt to tell us something like this?"

"I don't…I don't remember." My memory dredges up their raised voices; the anger and urgency of that argument, but no details. So many things about that night hide from me in the shadows of my subconscious.

"Now, Sofie, does that make sense to you?"

I can't explain to her that I always felt like an intrusion in their lives, like they weren't sure what to do with me now that they had me. Like they were just biding their time until I was gone. And that night, when I needed them more than anything, when I scrounged up the courage to go to them, I couldn't make myself intrude. Couldn't interrupt. Maybe I thought they wouldn't believe me. It was probably because I thought they wouldn't care.

As our eyes lock across the table, I realize for the first time that my mother is not an ally; I know that I was right on both counts. This isn't normal. A daughter tells her mother she was raped, and there should be tears. There should be hugs. There should at least be questions, but my mother acts like she already has all the answers.

"You knew."

Nothing on her face gives her away, but she blinks twice, a quick succession of reflexes. The only uncontrolled things about her.

"Sofie, listen to me."

"Daddy told you." Hurt climbs the walls of my belly, scaling my insides until it swells in my throat. "You've known for weeks and never even asked me about it."

"Your father did mention that you were confused about some events from the past with Kyle, yes."

"And you didn't even call me?" My voice rises, cracking the serenity my mother cultivates in this room for her morning meal. "You didn't even check to see if I'm okay? Or to hear my side of the story?"

"Sofie, things have been so hectic with the ballet and opera fund-raisers, and—"

"Just stop." I blink until the tears recede. "Don't pretend this is normal. That we're normal. We are not typical. This isn't right."

"Sofie, Kyle is a very powerful man, and you know he and your father have extremely important dealings right now."

"Kyle Manchester is a rapist, and I'm not the only woman he's done this to."

"But you're the only one who's talking about it, aren't you?" All civility drops away, and I realize my mother is angry with me.

"Be straight with me, Mother." I bounce her stony expression right back at her. "What's going on?"

"Whatever happened fifteen years ago is long over, Sofie, but what your father and Kyle are working on is right now. It may be the most important thing he's done. It's crucial to our future."

What the hell is going on? I prop my elbows on the table, dropping my forehead into my hands, trying to wrap my mind around this insanity.

"We can get you some help, a counselor, or—"

"I had help." I sit back in my seat and cross my legs. "I saw a therapist for two years after it happened."

"A therapist?" Her forehead pinches. "Who was this therapist? Where?"

"In Milan. I started seeing her while I was in Milan. She specialized in helping rape survivors."

"Sofie, you have to stop saying 'rape.' And you need to drop this. Boys lose their heads. Girls lead boys on. It's what happens in high school, but we can't afford to dredge up ancient history right now. I'm sure Kyle is sorry for what happened."

"Is that why he raped another woman? Because he was so sorry after the first time?" I lean forward, trapping my mother's eyes with my own, refusing to let her go. "He raped Shaunti Miller, too, Mother. And there's no telling who else."

"There's no telling because no one *is* telling, Sofie." My mother leans into our stare, her eyes hard and glinting like quartz. "And neither will you."

"You're crazy." I stand, bumping the back of my knees on the chair in my haste to get out of this house of horrors. I grab my bag and head toward the door.

"Sofie, this will be a circus, and you'll be the freak show." She picks up her serrated spoon and goes back to her grapefruit. "Not Kyle."

I'm almost at the door when I turn to look back at the woman I've longed to be close to all my life, but never found a way.

"I thought it was me." I shake my head, the breath bitter on my lips. "I thought I was broken, too much like Daddy for you to love me."

"Oh, God. Spare me the melodrama, Sofie." Mother sprinkles Stevia on her grapefruit.

"But it's you. You're the broken one." My lip quivers, but I get it under control. I won't give this woman any more weakness to use against me. "You're just like him."

"And so are you, little girl." Her eyes blaze in a face otherwise cold. "Don't get on a high horse now. Don't fool yourself that you're any different from us."

"Oh, I am different, Mother. I've learned that I have the capacity to actually care about other people, a secret I probably kept from myself to survive life with the two of you."

"You may have just started caring about people, Sofie, but no one cares about you. You're just a famous face and an overexposed body." She slices into her omelet, raising her fork to her mouth and her eyes to me.

"You've spent the last fifteen years being one thing. Don't expect people to all of a sudden think you're something else. Start telling this story about Kyle if you want. It'll be a bloodbath."

"Oh, I have no doubt there will be blood, Mother, but it won't be just mine. I'm going to bleed Kyle dry, and since you seem to be on his side, you might bleed, too."

I rush past Millie, hovering with her teapot, through the foyer with the sweeping staircase that leads to my childhood bedroom. I pull at the heavy door, letting in the light from outside. The fresh autumn air does nothing to clear my head, nothing to soothe my soul. I stumble into the backseat of the car waiting at the curb, tears stinging my eyes.

"Everything all right, Ms. B?" Baker asks from the front seat, his eyes seeking mine in the rearview mirror.

"Yes, I…" I don't know what lie I can come up with to cover this wound in my heart, bleeding out my illusions, an unstoppable flow, black with hurt and rejection.

My mother doesn't care that a man raped me. She offered no words of comfort. No horror that she never knew. I catch Baker's glance again in the rearview mirror, unsure what to say or how to explain that my mother doesn't love me, but his waiting eyes are soft with sympathy.

And I realize he knows. He's always known.

CHAPTER NINETEEN

Trevor

I've always enjoyed training alone. Things that make no sense in a room full of people, in a world filled with noise, crystallize in solitude. A way that seemed uncertain becomes straight as I'm pushing myself through water, meeting its resistance with my persistence, its force with my strength. On a morning like this with so many problems—the Collective scandal, the Deutimus sale, Sofie's revelation about that douche bag Kyle Manchester—it would be ideal to be alone. But as I touch the wall, coming out of the water to find Sofie already seated on its edge in her black bikini, her bright hair water-darkened, her lashes spiky, somehow I'm okay with not being by myself this morning.

"You cheated." I fold my arms on the side of the pool and match her grin. "There's no way you beat me."

"Why?" It's good to see those green eyes, so sober yesterday after her meeting with her mother, smiling back at me. "Because I'm a girl?"

"No, because while you're doing your squats and pliés or whatever the hell they are at the barre every morning, I'm here swimming. This is *my* thing."

"And since I beat you at *your* thing, you automatically conclude I must have cheated?" She leans back, arms straight and palms pressed to the concrete behind her. "That's some ego you've got there, Bishop. I beat you fair and square."

"How?" I'm too competitive not to frown. "I'm stronger."

"I'm faster." She sits forward to poke my shoulder. "And have less bulk."

"Bulk?" A laugh sputters on my lips. "Is that what I have?"

"Just saying maybe some of that muscle slowed you down in the water." She shrugs and points to herself. "Also, swimming scholarship."

"You were on the swim team?"

"And the rowing team. Two state championships." Her husky laugh bounces off the walls of the otherwise empty room. "The coach from UCLA? You should have seen his face when he realized he'd offered a scholarship to the daughter of Ernest Baston."

She kicks her feet in the water.

"I actually loved that he didn't realize who I was, and that I got that offer on the merits of what he'd seen me do."

I float into the canal between those long, slim legs, sliding my palms down her slippery calves.

"So you're saying you didn't cheat?"

Her lips, full and free of lipstick, tweak at the edges. She presses them against the laugher I see bubbling in her eyes. Finally, she flings her head back, howling with a laugh that comes from some part of herself she's quarantining from all the drama unfolding in her life.

"You little cheat!"

I drag her by her ankles until she's at the lip of the pool, then lean into her stomach, hauling her over my shoulder and wading back into the water.

"No! Bishop, no!" She beats my back with her fists, her laugh vibrating through my skin.

"You better hold your breath," I warn her.

"No, I…you…Bishop, don't you—"

I take us under, the water closing over our heads, sealing out the world above. I wish we had fins so we could stay under for hours, just us, breathing in the underwater utopia. Peaceful, as if a garish spotlight isn't about to turn on Sofie's every move. On her past. Our heads break the water's surface at the same time, both of us coming up gasping and laughing. Our eyes catch and hold until the air between us shifts, and even the cold water can't dampen the heat flaring between our eyes, between our bodies.

I find her in the water, sliding my hands over her hips to caress her thighs. A breath separates her lips as her hands climb my chest and slip into my hair. There's no one else here, but if there were, I'd have to say fuck it. This woman has had me tied in knots since she stared me down from a billboard, her face bare and her soul cloaked. And the more of herself she shows me, the more I want.

I plunge into her mouth, a treasure seeker. There's a moan, mine or hers, I can't tell, because I'm so busy making it happen again. Pressing into her, my hands lapping like water at her thighs, at her back, at her ass. She's so much of everything I want.

My hands slip under her bikini bra. I knead her breasts until her lashes drop, her head falls back, and nails dig into my scalp. She reaches around to unhook the bra so it falls away. I go down on my knees in the water, pressing my mouth to her breasts, nuzzling and suckling, pulling hard on her with my desperation to get as much as I can.

"Bishop, we should stop." Her words reach me on a ragged breath.

She's right. Anyone could come in, but my control is barreling downhill with no brakes. Hands gripping her butt, fingers sliding under the fabric of her suit until it's skin on skin. Tongue licking under the full curve of her breasts. Her skin, cool. My mouth, hot against her.

I don't want to stop, but I do when a noise catches my attention, the door opening. I'm instantly up and clutching her to my chest to cover her. I catch sight of her black bikini top floating just out of reach.

"Stay still, Sof. Don't move, darlin'." My voice is hoarse, and in my head I'm cursing myself for exposing her like this.

"Um, Bishop?" Harold asks from poolside. "You might wanna…"

"Got it," I snap, not bothering to look at him before he darts back out the way he came.

Her head drops to my chest, the deep breath she draws brushing her nipples against me.

That's not helping.

"That dude's such a cock blocker," she whispers.

We both laugh, loosening the passion that held us so tight moments before.

"I'm sorry." I pull back just enough to study her face. "I shouldn't have let it go that far in here."

She's not even blushing, the minx. She grins wide, pulling all the way back until she floats out of my arms. She faces me, topless for a moment, her nipples high and tight, before letting go of a lusty laugh, plunging underwater, and swimming over to retrieve her bikini top.

I run my hands over my hair and face, grappling for control and composure, when really I just want to take her under and make love to her on the pool floor. We might both drown, but what a way to go.

"For the record," she says, hauling herself to the lip of the pool, giving me a great view of the round, firm cheeks not completely covered by her bikini. "I did beat you fair and square."

She sits on the edge, long legs floating in the water. I swim over to stand in front of her, and we're back where we started, only my dick is a lot harder now.

"I'm not sure I can trust you," I say, cocking a brow.

Her smile fades until she's biting her bottom lip, lashes down to cover her eyes.

"You can."

I lean forward, lifting her chin with a finger until I have her eyes again.

"Goes both ways," I say. "You can trust me, too."

She still hasn't told me what happened with her mother, but I know it wasn't good. When she didn't call me, I called her. I could tell immediately that things had gone badly, but I didn't press. All through dinner at her apartment last night, I didn't press. And I won't. I have to believe she'll trust me. Is that what I'm actually waiting for? Looking for before we take this thing to the next level?

"I know I can trust you." She bends to trail her fingers through the water.

"I want to be there for you, Sofie." I catch her hand in the water and hold her eyes. "Let me."

"Okay." She nods, licking her bottom lip before looking at me squarely. "Will you come with me tomorrow to talk to Shaunti Miller's lawyer?"

"Yes." I'm flying to South Africa tomorrow, and I don't even know what time this meeting will happen. I'll rearrange the flight if I have to. "What time?"

"It's at ten o'clock tomorrow morning, but if you can't make it—"

"I can." I reach up to brush my thumb across her soft lips, brushing away any more protests. "I will."

She smiles, turning her head to kiss my palm.

"I do have a flight to catch." I drop our hands, clasped, to her knee. "But it's not until evening, I think."

She doesn't shutter her expression quickly enough to hide her disappointment.

"The Collective meeting in South Africa?"

"Yeah." I release a heavy breath. "Unfortunately."

"How long will you be gone?"

"We leave tomorrow, and come back sometime late next week."

She nods, eyes on the water.

"Hey." I tip up her chin until she can't look away. "I'll miss you while I'm gone."

Her smile is my reward, and despite the embers, still hot from our last kiss, I initiate another one. This one softer and slower, but still telling her that I can't wait much longer to have her. That I don't want to.

"Come out with me tonight," I whisper against her lips, still pressing soft kisses to her mouth.

"Are we really going to try that again?" She leans down, her fingers wandering to the back of my neck, pressing me in to deepen a kiss.

I pull back to answer her.

"Yeah. Come with me tonight."

She looks like she might turn me down, but I'm not having it.

"Say yes. It's important to me." I didn't want to play this card, but I will to get her to come. "I'm being honored, and I'd love for you to be with me."

"You're being honored?" Her eyes widen, a smile starting small and spreading over her mouth. "For what?"

"For my work with developing nations. Does it matter? I want you with me; now, are you coming or what?"

"Well I guess I am." Her smile melts, leaving concern behind. "And you're coming with me? Tomorrow, I mean?"

"I'm here for you, Sof. Nothing will shake me loose. Not lies or hearsay or scandal."

"What about the truth?" Her lips barely part to let the words out. "When it's not lies, but it's the nasty truth about something stupid I did a decade ago. Would that shake you loose? Because I wouldn't blame you. Wouldn't think any less of you if you want to get out of this now before it goes too far."

I pull her down from the lip of the pool, turning in the water and hooking her ankles behind me. I slip my hands under her butt to keep her floating with me, around me.

"This thing between us, Sofie." I dot kisses across her lips, under her chin, and over the long column of her neck. "Not only has it already gone too far…"

I pull back so she can see my eyes and know exactly what my next words mean to me.

"But I'm too far gone."

For a moment, I wonder if I've said too much, pushed too hard. But then she lifts those lashes, her green eyes soft and settled on mine. Her next words make me want her more, and make me so glad I waited to hear them.

"So am I, Bishop."

CHAPTER TWENTY

Sofie

I have no one to blame but myself for being in this position.

Technically, that's not true. As I step out of the car onto a freaking red carpet, to flashing bulbs and a receiving line of dignitaries, I realize I can also blame Trevor.

"You didn't tell me it would be quite so…" I pause long enough to smile for a photographer practically contorting to get the right shot. "Public. Such a big deal."

"Did I not?" Trevor squints one eye as if trying to remember. "I told you it was formal."

"Yes, but there's a red carpet and lots of media, and I think I just spotted a prime minister."

"Maybe one or two." He shrugs, broad shoulders straining against his well-cut tuxedo jacket. "Not a big deal."

I glance at him in a tuxedo. I must admit, we do make a striking couple. Him in his finery, and me in the midnight blue dress François sent from his evening-wear line. It reaches the floor and has deep cutouts under my arms, bares my entire back, and reveals the sides of my breasts. I study the other women here, and feel like I'm a little too much. They're all wearing evening gowns, but mine seems more glamorous, which isn't a surprise, but I don't want to stand out. I haven't blended in one day of my life, but tonight, I'd like to. It's Trevor's night, not mine. And the last thing I want is to become the center of—

"Sofie, who are you wearing?" a photographer yells from behind the rope.

It has begun…

"This dress was sent over by the fabulous François Gerrard."

Trevor and I take a few more steps before another reporter tosses out a question.

"Where's Rip tonight, Sofie?"

Trevor is standing close enough for me to feel him tense at my side.

"I have no idea." I offer a smile so plastic it should be recycled.

"So are the reports true that you and Rip are no longer together?"

"Michael and I remain very good friends, and I wish him well." Before they can fire another question, probably about Trevor, I continue. "Tonight is about my dear friend Mr. Bishop and this amazing event, and I want to keep it that way. Good night."

Another round of questions comes, but I dismiss them with a quick wave and another plastic smile.

Trevor wraps one hand around my elbow and lays the other at my back, directing me into the Savoy and toward the ballroom, where the dinner is being held. Before we reach the room, already packed and buzzing with people, I pull him into an empty hall to the side.

"Hey." I take both his hands, looking up to study the closed expression I've rarely seen on his face. "I'm sorry about that. It must've been awkward for you. They don't care about awkward."

"What was awkward," he says, reaching to brush the hair I left loose back over my shoulder, "was you calling me a dear friend."

I open my mouth and then close it, unsure how to respond.

"That's what has you bent out of shape?"

"I'm not bent out of shape."

I tilt my head, giving him a knowing look.

"Okay." His face relents a small grin. "I'm a little bent."

"You shouldn't be."

"Do you not want people to know we're together?"

"*You* shouldn't want people to know we're together, Trevor." I drop my eyes to the swirling pattern in the carpet. "Being with me…being seen with me…it draws the kind of attention I don't think you want."

"Sofie, I know what being with you means." He leaves a kiss behind my ear. "It means lots of takeout food."

He drops a kiss on my lips.

"Lots of cheating in the pool."

We laugh into the next kiss.

"And lots of blue balls."

I lean back so he can't kiss me.

"That, Mr. Bishop, is on you." I slide my hand under his tuxedo jacket until my hand cups his ass.

God, this ass.

"I don't believe in blue balls." My eyes match the sultry heat of his. "Matter of fact, I am fundamentally opposed to them in a relationship."

"Oh, so we're in a relationship now?" He teases me with a grin, even though my heart flutters at his words. My breath catching at what I just said. At what he just asked me.

"If that's the case, maybe I'm against blue balls, too." His fingers splay across the curve between my butt and my thigh. "Fundamentally."

I don't breathe. My heart thumps heavily in my chest. Is he saying…are we going to…is he…

Before I can ask, Henrietta rushes around the corner, eyes slightly panicked behind her glasses.

"Trevor, here you are." Her eyes drift to me and then snap back to her boss. "Oh, Sofie. I didn't realize you were coming tonight."

She doesn't sound too pleased about it. What's with her? Is it just my reputation? I gave her the benefit of the doubt the last time she was rude to me. Once more, and she'll find that when they call me a bitch, it's justified.

Trevor's hand moves slowly up to my back and a frown settles on his face.

"What's up, Hen?"

"Um…I don't think…" Her eyes shift to me again, hesitation on her face and in her voice.

"What's wrong?" Trevor's frown deepens. "Just spit it out."

"Okay." She gives him a look that says you asked for it. "Fleur's here."

"And that's a problem?" he asks.

"She's at our table." Henri's poor eyebrows look like they might fight their way through her hairline if they go any higher. "Like, now, at our table."

"It's fine, Henri." He flicks his chin back toward the ballroom. "Go on back in. We're right behind you. Just give us a second."

As soon as Henri turns to leave, I ask the question that got lost in everything that's happened since the Restore luncheon we attended two days ago.

"Who's Fleur?" I caress the lapels of his tuxedo, eyes fixed on his bow tie. "Halima mentioned her the other day, too."

He glides his hands over my arms and down to rest on my hips before answering.

"We were engaged."

My hands still over the lapels, and I lift my eyes to his. He searches my face, the dark eyes gauging my reaction to the words that just sucker-punched me in the gut. He was engaged to someone? There was a woman he wanted to *marry*? And she's here tonight? At our table?

"How long ago?" My hands fall from his jacket to hang at my sides.

"We were engaged for about six months, and I broke it off almost a year ago."

I look at him from under my lashes.

"*You* broke it off?" He nods. "Why?"

He glances back toward the ballroom, a small smile playing over his full lips, and shrugs.

"I guess we've got time for a little story."

He pushes his hands into his pockets, the jacket dragging back to display his broad chest and taut waist. I will not be distracted by how fuckable he looks, but with a little more time and a tad bit of privacy, I'd dry hump his leg.

"My mother moved to Lumberton, North Carolina, her freshman year in high school," he says. "Her father's job relocated them from Boston, and she was in my pop's homeroom class. She was outspoken, well read, sharp, and hilarious. He fell hard for her, and he never looked back."

Trevor's deep laugh and slow smile make my lips curve, too.

"Growing up, I saw my dad make a beeline for my mom every day after work." He shakes his head, grinning wider. "For a while, he drove a truck to make some extra money. He'd drive through the night to get home to her. We knew he loved us kids, but there was never any doubt that she was number one. He hated being away from her, and I don't think in forty years of marriage they've spent more than two nights apart."

"That's beautiful." I can't help but contrast that to my parents' separate vacations and the marriage that's felt empty as a tomb most of my life.

"I thought so." Trevor nods, his smile fading. "So last year Fleur had a special assignment in Ghana, and we didn't see each other for more than a month."

He drops his eyes to the carpet, twisting his lips and shaking his head.

"I was fine without her. I mean, I missed her, but I didn't have to fight myself from jumping on a plane to be with her every day."

"So there was no passion?" I ask, trying to understand exactly what he's saying.

"The sex was great." He meets my eyes unabashed, and I want to kick this girl Fleur in the stomach, or maybe lower, in her lady parts, for having Trevor when I haven't. "It's more than passion. More than great sex. It wasn't…urgent. I know what that kind of love looks like, and I realized we didn't have it. As much perfect sense as Fleur and I made on paper, we didn't have *that*, and I don't want to spend the rest of my life without it."

"So you broke it off?"

"I told her what I just told you—that though I cared about her, probably even felt some version of love, it wasn't what I needed to sustain a forever commitment. And that's what marriage is to me."

I hook my fingers around his wrists, even though his hands were still plunged into his pockets.

"I know that was hard for you."

"It was the hardest thing I've ever done." He sighs, hands abandoning his pockets to take hold of mine. "But it was the right thing to do. It's not just that I wanted that. She deserves someone who feels that way about her. She's a remarkable woman. This isn't the first time we've seen each other since we broke up. We move in the same circles. Her boss, David, is in the Collective, and is being honored tonight, too. I should have realized she'd be here."

He squats a little to drop a quick kiss on my lips.

"But I've been a little distracted."

I muster a smile, but I'm not looking forward to meeting the "remarkable" woman who's perfect for Trevor on paper and was *this* close to being his wife.

When we enter the ballroom and walk to our table, I hang behind just a little, wanting the advantage of even a few seconds to study Fleur before she gets to study me. I'm glad I do, because I see her eyes fixed on Trevor, unguarded at that first glance.

And I know she's still in love with him.

I can't even resent her, or be angry with her. My heart, that muscle that seems to have found new life since I met Trevor, actually aches a little for her. It would break any woman to lose a man like Trevor.

It might even break me.

She stands as soon as she sees him, and I revise my preconceived notions of what this "perfect for Trevor" woman would look like. I had envisioned a woman like Henri. Attractive in her own way. Bookish. Ordinary, with dashes of special here and there. This woman is no Henri. Beautiful women are as common as the cold in my industry, but Fleur is extraordinary even to my jaded eyes. Incredibly long, thick lashes fringe eyes the color of topaz. Her face, with high, molded cheekbones and flawless, latte-tinged skin, is arresting and framed by a cloud of dark, naturally curly hair. Her mouth, a tightly budded rose, opens up into a full-bloomed smile just for Trevor.

"I was wondering when you'd arrive." She grabs his hands, leaning up on her tiptoes to reach his cheek and leave a kiss there. "Congratulations. I'm so excited for you."

And she's British, her crisp accent softened by her sweet voice. More than anything I want to hate this woman, but I can't.

"Fleur, good to see you, too." Trevor pulls away from her hands and turns to me, his eyes checking my face, which I keep neutral.

She still doesn't realize we're together, hasn't even noticed me, and I'm a hard woman to overlook. She's so focused on him, it makes me sorry that I'm here and that in some ways, I'm about to shatter her world. I don't mean to. It won't be the first time I've stumbled into breaking another woman's heart.

"I'm here for a bit," she says. "Maybe we could grab a drink after this thing, or dinner before I fly back to London."

"I fly out to South Africa tomorrow," Trevor says. "And I probably won't be back until late next week."

Fleur's eyes go wide, a quick grin on her lips.

"That's right. The Collective is meeting this week. David's going, too, of course."

Trevor nods and steps back, reaching for my hand.

"Fleur, I'm being rude to my guest. I don't think you've met Sofie Baston, have you?" He gives a gentle tug to my hand, pulling me forward when I really just want to blend into the wall, maybe as a sconce or the wallpaper. "Sofie, Fleur Adeba."

As soon as our eyes meet, I know she knows. Trevor doesn't just pull me forward. He looks down at me, his eyes affectionate. His mouth widens into a smile as soon as our eyes connect. His hand goes to my back, gentle and possessive. I feel his absolute full attention turned to me, and I know she feels it, too. The natural smile withers on her face. She blinks several times, pressing her lips together against the emotion I hope isn't as obvious to everyone already seated at the table as it is to me.

"Hello, Miss Adeba." I extend my hand, a smile like wax on my lips. "So nice to meet you."

She looks at my hand for a moment before taking it, her fingers cold and stiff in mine.

"I didn't…" She licks her lips, bundling her hands at her waist. "That is to say, it's very nice to meet you, Miss Baston."

I'm not the kind of competition most women expect to run up against. Not me the actual woman, but the fantasy men build up in their heads about me. The illusion I've spent fifteen years constructing for the public. I want to confess to Fleur that no man has ever loved me the morning after. That it's all just bright wrapping paper, and once they tear it away, I'm that Christmas gift they forget why they even wanted so badly. I get cast aside and lost in the bright paper I came in. I want to tell her those things to make her feel better, but I know by the way Trevor looks at me that she wouldn't be convinced. Because when Trevor looks at me, it's not the brightly wrapped box he sees, but all the things I didn't even know I had inside. And if I can tell that, then surely this woman, with her sharp eyes and obvious keen intelligence, sees it, too.

I'm seated between Trevor and Henri. Fortunately, Fleur is across the table. Maybe it isn't fortunate, because she has an unobstructed view of us beside each other, and for the life of her, she can't seem to look away.

Conversation floats around me, giving me clues to this woman Trevor almost married. Apparently she works for an organization that supplies clean water to developing nations. Of course she does. I'm probably the only person at this table who's never dug a well. What am I doing here? I'm so out of my depth. Oh, I can follow the conversation about foreign policy, even though I don't contribute much. I'm not an imbecile. But everyone here has given their lives to service of some sort, and the only thing I've served in fifteen years, besides the Walsh Foundation, is myself. I feel Trevor's eyes on me, probing my reticence, but I only offer a smile over my wineglass. I'll just get through this and try not to draw attention to myself.

Trevor leans in to whisper in my ear, and I feel Fleur's eyes on us instantly.

"Are you okay?" His eyes run over my face, his concern an intimacy in itself.

"Of course, why wouldn't I be?" I take a sip of my white wine and give him a smile. It's phony, but maybe it will fool him and the others at the table.

It doesn't.

Throughout the five-course meal, I feel his eyes picking at the edges of the mask I drop over my face. The force of his stare pries at my façade until I'm not sure how much longer I can hold on to the image I'm so used to projecting, like a front on a theater stage. Painted beautifully, a backdrop for drama, but flat and propped up by spindly wood.

"Trevor," Henri says as the servers set dessert on the table. "They're signaling for the honorees."

Trevor takes one last sip of wine and tosses his napkin over his plate.

"Guess I better go." He dips his head to study my face, and I turn to look at him. "You'll be all right?"

I can't help it. He's found a way to, with just a look, tear down my defenses. I can feel my expression softening. Everything that's been pulled tight under Fleur's steady scrutiny all night loosens and gives when he looks at me.

"I'll be fine." I reach under the table to squeeze his hand. "Good luck."

He has that look he gets on his face just before he kisses me, and I will him not to. I will him to remember and to consider the heartbroken woman across the table. He narrows his eyes for a second, squeezes my hand back under the table, and walks off.

The table is silent for a few moments, and I realize that everyone understands the small drama playing out. These people knew Fleur and Trevor as a couple. This is their world, and I'm some exotic bird swooping in to light on the shoulder of one of their own.

"So Sofie, Ernest Baston is your father, right?" A gentleman with salt-and-pepper hair asks between bites of his cheesecake.

"Yes." I sketch a quick nod and smile, pushing away my dessert even though my panties-only photo shoot is behind me.

"He and Martin Bennett have done an astounding job with Bennett Enterprises." He gives a slow shake of his head, his mouth turned down in disapproval. "It's a shame that the young pup is going to take it after all your father has done."

Surprise makes me go still, hand poised over the cheesecake to at least bring the strawberry on top to my mouth.

"You mean Walsh?" I chuckle. "He's no pup. More like a Doberman. He and I grew up in Bennett Enterprises, and he's been working with his father since he was fourteen years old preparing for this transition. He's more than ready."

"But your father—"

"Has contributed greatly, and has always known Martin wanted his son to succeed him," I say firmly, steadying my eyes on the man questioning something he knows nothing about. "Walsh is a man of integrity, conviction, and unerring competence. I have all faith he's the kind of forward-thinking leader to take Bennett further than it's ever been."

End of story. My stare and tone tell him so, and he drops it, but I can't help but wonder how many others in the business community share those sentiments.

And if my father is the fire fueling them.

"I forgot you're the goodwill ambassador for the Walsh Foundation, right?" he asks.

"Yes, have been for many years. It's one of my favorite things I get to do."

"What does that entail exactly?" Fleur interjects, addressing me for the first time since our introduction. "Posing with some orphans and starving children, a few strategically placed flies buzzing around?"

I'm stunned. I literally gasp as her words dig into me like tiny talons. This woman, who almost married Trevor, who I'm sure does good all over the world, just hurled malice at my head like a snowball, hard and icy. I'm not the only one taken aback. Henri and Harold stare at Fleur, eyes wide, mouths slightly agape. Henri slides her eyes to me, and I see the closest thing to kindness she's ever shown me.

I get it. Trevor's a hard man to lose, but this little heifer has no idea who she's messing with. Just as I'm marshaling my forces, gathering fiery darts to return fire, she blinks several times, eyes bright with tears before she lowers her lashes, biting her lip.

I can't do it. This woman is devastated. She obviously thought there was still a chance with Trevor. It's not my fault. He'd decided that before he even met me, but I can't make her believe that. For once, mercy holds my tongue.

"Yeah, something like that."

She looks up at me, her eyes already sorry, but the speaker onstage takes our attention before she can follow through on the apology I see on her face. There's five people being honored, but I couldn't tell you what one of them looked like other than Trevor. I can't take my eyes off him. His hair is just growing back, but it's still a silky cap, molding his head like muted copper against his tanned skin. He's laughing at something the host says, his wide smile denting dimples in his cheeks.

I want him fiercely. Not the handsome face, or the tower of muscle and bone. I want his secrets. I want his dreams. I want his hopes. I want everything I've never cared about with anyone else.

I tear my eyes away from his face long enough to glance at Fleur, only to find her eyes fixed on him, too.

She wants him, too, and my heart contracts with something like sympathy for her. But she can't have him. I'm not that selfless.

Once the awards have been given and money has been raised for the various causes the night benefits, it's time to go, and I can't say I'm sorry to see this night end.

"You okay?" Trevor takes my hand as we wait outside for the car to pull around. "You've been subdued all night."

"I'm fine." I hope my smile reassures him, even though I'm still sorting through the things I learned tonight about Fleur, about him, about myself.

He takes an extra second to study me before looking down the long lines of cars queued up to collect the ambassadors, dignitaries, and leaders from tonight's gala.

"I think that's our car." He squints to see. "If so, we can walk down. I want to get you out of the cold. Wait here. I'll be right back."

He's only a few feet down the block when I feel a hand on my shoulder. I turn to find Fleur facing me. We stare at each other for a few moments before she finally speaks.

"I wanted to apologize for that comment I made." She looks at the sidewalk before looking back to me. "It was uncalled for."

"It's fine, Fleur. It was a difficult situation, and sometimes we say things we'd take back in times like that. Believe me, I've done it more than once."

"Thank you for understanding." She looks torn, but then seems to come to a decision. "He's a good man. One of the best I've ever known."

I don't reply, but just wait for her to say whatever else she still has to say to me because it's obvious she's not done.

"If you're just toying with him, then I think—"

"Stop right there." I run my tongue over my teeth before I

speak. "You don't know me, Fleur. You have no idea what's important to me or how I actually live my life. Only what you've read."

"Yes, but—"

"I repeat." I pause for effect, lifting my brows for emphasis. "You do not know me, and my relationship with Trevor is private."

"Relationship?" Dismay clouds her eyes. "Are you saying...are you saying it's serious between you two?"

Before I can answer, Trevor joins us, his smile stiffening when he sees Fleur beside me.

"That is our car, Sof." He links our fingers, but smiles at Fleur. "Good seeing you again, Fleur. I'm in London..."

He trails off, looking over Fleur's shoulder at Harold and Henri approaching.

"When are we in London, Henri?"

"Next month." Henri's eyes dart between Fleur and me like she's prepared to break up a fight if necessary. "At David's office."

"Next month at your office," Trevor finishes. "I'm sure we'll see each other then."

He bends to kiss her cheek, and like an involuntary response, her small hand reaches up to touch his hair. He pulls back immediately, wearing a rueful smile.

"I need to go, Fleur. See you soon." He steers us toward the car, tossing parting words at Harold and Henri. "See you two back at the house."

In the car, I have nothing to say. I can't shake my last glimpse of Fleur, her golden eyes, bright and devastated, glued to my hand holding Trevor's. I want him so badly, but he *should* be with someone like her. Everyone at that table tonight, everyone in that room probably, thought so. Wondered what a man like him was doing dallying with a woman like me.

"Sofie, talk to me." Trevor raises the privacy partition, leans forward to rest his elbows on his knees, eyes on my face. "Did someone say something to you? Was it Fleur?"

"No, I…" I look into his dark eyes, so confused by my feelings. Vacillating between what I know is probably best for him and what I selfishly want. "I was just thinking I'll be fine tomorrow on my own. For the meeting with Shaunti's rep, I mean."

He frowns heavily, his eyes searching my face.

"I'm going with you."

"No, you don't have to. I think I'll be fine." I look out the window, relieved to see we're in front of my building. "I can make my own way up. Have a great trip to South Africa. Be safe."

Before he can stop me, I jerk open the door and take long, swift strides into my lobby. I rush past Clive, giving him a nod, but not stopping.

"Sofie, wait," Trevor says from behind me.

I keep walking, even though it feels like I'm fleeing the thing I want more than everything else. His hand on my elbow pulls me up just short of the elevator door.

"I said wait." His voice is low and even, but emotion puckers below the surface.

We board the elevator together and I input the code for the penthouse level, neither of us speaking. He walks me to my door, and I turn to face him.

"Thanks for walking me up."

"I'm coming in." His tone warns me that I'm in for a fight if I refuse, so I open the door, walking in ahead of him.

"What's up, Bishop?" I school my features into an even mask, keeping some space between us because I lose my head every time he touches me.

"You tell me." He loosens his bow tie, allowing it to hang on either side of his neck. "I go up to accept the award, come back, and you're like a different person. What the hell, Sof?"

"I just…" I search my mind for an excuse that will get him out of here, but I have a hard time being anything but honest with him. "I just felt a little out of place tonight, I guess. Like I didn't belong."

"Didn't belong?" A laugh huffs over his lips. "How do you think I felt the first few times I was in the room with prime ministers and presidents? Me, the son of a postal worker and a school teacher? I'd think you'd be used to it by now, though."

"Yeah, not that kind of belong." I pull my hair over my shoulder, run my hands down my legs, shift my weight. "I meant like I didn't belong *with you.*"

"Not belong with me?" His expression goes stony. "Did Henri say something to you? Or Fleur?"

"It doesn't matter. I don't need them to tell me you can do better."

"I can do what?" He takes a step toward me, frowning when I take a step back. "What the hell do you mean I can do better? Than what?"

"Than me." I press my hand to my forehead, not because my head hurts, but because it's flooded with thoughts of how we could be together, of how he could be different from all the others, of how I could be different with him than I've ever been. And I'm not sure any of it's actually possible. And to know someone like him is out there and I might not be good enough, it makes me ache with unreasonable loss.

"Sofie, look at me." He pulls my hand away from my head, linking our fingers and resting our clasped hands against his chest. "It's not a matter of good *enough*. I'm good for you, and you're good for me. *That's* enough, and I really don't care what anyone else thinks or says about it."

He pulls me into him, resting his hands at my sides.

"And we're good together." He leans down to trail kisses over my jaw and down my neck, his cool breath somehow firing up my skin with his next words. "You believe that?"

"Yes." I can barely breathe with him this close. A pressure is building from the neediest part of me and spreading over every inch of my skin. It's a desperate desire I'm not sure how much longer I can suppress. "I...yeah...I, um, I do."

I don't even know what we're talking about anymore. When he shifts his hands so his thumbs rub over my nipples through the silk of my dress, thought is impossible. I'm a sea of sensation, and wave after wave of pleasure makes me wet. Makes me hot.

"Bishop." I lift my lashes, and his eyes are heavy-lidded and almost black, the pupils swallowing up everything. "I, um..."

"Can I stay?" he cuts in, dipping his head to lick into the shallow well at the base of my throat. "Let me stay."

I've wanted this for weeks; since I saw him that first night, and now that he's about to give me everything I wanted, I'm the one hesitating. I'm hesitating because it has to be right. My first experience with sex was brutal and against my will. It took a long time and a lot of therapy for me to try it again, and I discovered I love it. Love it so much I've been reckless with it in the past, but this means too much. *He* means too much for me to be reckless with an intimacy I know will mean more to me than anything ever has. I already feel closer to him than to any man before.

"Are you sure?"

He laughs against my neck, nudging the strap of my dress away from my shoulder with his chin and kissing the naked skin.

"Very." His hands come up to cup my face, and he parts my lips, dipping inside, possessing me sweetly, then harder and deeper with every brush of our tongues. I strain against him, moaning into his mouth, drawing his tongue in deeper.

"What's different?" I ask against his soft lips. "Why now?"

"Why are you hesitating?" His breath comes heavy as he pulls away the other strap of my dress until it gives way, falling to my waist, baring my breasts to him. His knuckles whisper over my nipples, and my knees almost buckle. I lean into him for support.

"Because…" I swallow, struggling to focus. "Because I want it to be right between us. It means too much not to be."

He leans down to whisper in my ear.

"That's why now."

CHAPTER TWENTY-ONE

Trevor

I didn't plan this. I didn't think it would be tonight, but now, hearing her wrestle with whether she's good enough for me, I know it should be. It has to be. Even though things were undeniably awkward with Fleur present, I loved having Sofie at my side tonight. Everything is richer and brighter with her. Awards and honors don't do much for me anymore. It's never been why I do the things I do, but my chest stuck out like a peacock's accepting that award tonight because *she* was there. Because *she* saw me receive it.

I loved seeing her in my world. It made me realize how much I want to keep here there, and even though her life is about to become a giant clusterfuck after this meeting about Manchester tomorrow, I want to be in it with her. No matter what. If I try to put this into words, I'll screw it up. I'll scare her away. I'll freak her the fuck out. But if I tell her with my body—with my hands, with my mouth, with any part of me that can reach any part of her—she'll know.

"Take me to your bedroom." I leave the breath-wrapped words, half plea, half command, in the fragile shell of her ear.

She looks up at me, and if it were anyone but Sofie, I'd swear her eyes are shy. The bodice of her dress hangs around her hips, and she crosses her arms over her breasts. Her eyes flit from me to the floor, then back up and around her apartment.

"You're sure?" She tucks the fullness of her bottom lip between her teeth.

I didn't think it would be like this. I'm not dumb or blind or stupid. I've known for weeks this is what she wants, and I can barely walk straight every time we're in a room together, so she must know how much I want it, too. I just wanted it to be the right time; when it would mean as much to her as it would to me.

And now it does.

I'm glad we waited and didn't just one-night-stand our way to something less than this will be. I turn her in the direction I know leads to her bedroom, pressing my chest to her naked back, crossing my arms across her waist and walking her down the hall. Her small steps forward are driving me crazy because I can't wait to unwrap this gift I've been saving. I content myself with nibbles at her neck and kisses across her shoulders until we enter her darkened bedroom.

She walks ahead of me, using one arm to turn on the lamp and one arm to cover her breasts. Is this the girl who posed for *Playboy*? The one who, without blinking, autographs the copies horny boys thrust in her face? If they could see her now. Actually, I'd want to gouge out the eyes of anyone who saw her now. Not just the half-naked perfection of her body, but the vulnerability of her eyes in these moments before I take her and she takes me. I want this just for me and just for her. These are the most intimate moments of my life and we still have our clothes on.

I walk deeper into the room and stop in front of her, pulling her arm away from her breasts. The cool air piques her nipples to tight, pink points. Or maybe it's my stare that does that, because I can't look at anything else for a few moments. My fingers find the zipper at the base of her spine, tugging until the dress falls to the floor.

I'm thirty-five years old. I've seen more naked bodies than I can remember, but everything, everyone else, is pale and distant next to this woman. The elegant slope of her shoulders, the full curve of her breasts with their pouty nipples. The dramatic cinch of her waist swelling into the curve of her hips. The long, toned stretch of those famous legs. I hate it when they call her the Goddess because she's flesh and blood and bone, and I want to know *her*, not just her body. But seeing her in this faint light, standing tall in nothing but a lacy black thong, I get it. I understand why they call her the Goddess.

I sink to my knees, looking up to find her eyes soft and hot on me. With our eyes still melded, I slide my tongue over the sleek muscles in her stomach. Her indrawn breath spurs me on to dip my head, with my teeth pulling the strips of lace at her hips aside and down. My fingers take over, pushing the panties over her thighs and knees until they land around her ankles, resting on her shiny shoes. She steps out of them, standing on one leg and kicking the other back to take off her shoes.

I give her a gentle push to the bed, prying her legs open and dusting kisses over the insides of her thighs, behind her knees, over the finely made ankles and the high arch of her foot. She's gasping, panting, whispering my name.

She tugs at my hair, pulling me up to her mouth and kissing me deep, her tongue pushing into my mouth and across my teeth. She's biting and sucking my lips. Her hands are frantic, pushing at my jacket, sliding it down my arms. She flicks the buttons of my shirt open. My breath stops in my throat when her nails scrape across my abs and then drift down to my zipper. She jerks it down, her eyes on me, all shyness absent. She pushes down my pants until they pool around my knees. Her eyes, hungry, hot, eager, touch on every part of me she has revealed.

"You are so beautiful, Bishop."

Her voice is soft, almost reverent. No one has ever looked at me like this, ever said my name quite that way. We've only touched, only kissed, and I'm already more satisfied than I've ever been with any woman before her, and yet still ravenous.

She stands, pulling me to my feet and then pushing me to sit on the bed. My pants and shoes come off, her hands caressing, her mouth worshipping the same way I worshipped her. When she reaches the band of my briefs, her fingers hover and a wicked smile takes over her sweet lips. She pulls them over my thighs, her eyes widening when she sees me for the first time.

"Oh me oh my." She sighs and wraps her hands around me, her grip sure and tight. "Tonight had its stresses."

What the hell is she talking about? I can't hold any sane thought with her hands stroking up and then down, up and then down. I grunt in response, my eyes tightly closed.

"It was so stressful," she continues, her breath hot on the most vulnerable part of me, "I skipped dessert."

Before I can tell her it may not be a good idea, that I might not last if she does this, she takes me in her mouth and down her throat.

"Fuck." Her mouth working at me, the pull and suck, wrench the imprecation from me. "Sofie...fuck."

"That's next"—she lets me go long enough to assure me—"I like my dessert first."

Just when I'm sure I'll erupt in her mouth, my fingers fisted in her hair, she releases me and stands to her feet, licking her shiny lips.

"You taste better than that cheesecake." A husky laugh passes her lips, and she runs the tips of her fingers over her breasts, down her stomach, and past her thighs. "Do you want to touch me, Bishop?"

I answer with my hands, running them over the muscles in her butt and thighs, sliding them over her breasts. I slip my hand into the tight cove between her legs, thrusting one finger into the slick heat.

Her head drops back, her hips flexing with the motion of my finger.

"Bishop, I'm ready. I'm so ready."

"Are you sure, Sof?" I ask hoarsely. "You seemed hesitant before."

She captures my eyes with hers, not blinking or letting them go as she settles her knees on either side of my legs. I can't believe this is finally going to happen.

"Dammit, Sof." I rest my forehead against her neck. "Protection."

A laugh drifts up from her throat.

"Are you going to think badly of me when I reach into my supply by the bed?"

I run my hand up her back, thrusting my fingers into her hair and holding her head still, holding her eyes with mine.

"Not as long as that's just *my* supply from now on."

Little pieces of her smile slowly fall away until her mouth is a sober line. She stretches to the bedside table, takes out and tears the foil packet, sliding the condom over me. Breath huffs past my lip at even that simple touch.

Eyes locked with mine, she slowly slides down over me, pressing her nose to mine.

"Only yours from now on, Bishop. I promise."

It's slow at first, a gentle rise and fall of her hips, but I'm pushing up deeper and harder with every motion. A small line sketches between her brows, and her top lip hides in the full curve of the bottom.

"Am I hurting you?" I ask.

"Good grief no," she gasps, tipping her head back until her hair brushes my thighs. "I'm just…fuck."

She rolls her hips into me, elbows hooked at my neck, breasts caressing my chest. Every thrust, every brush of our bodies, every slide in and out, stokes something between us. We become frantic, her cries, my pants, our breaths filling the room. I love how hard she rides me, how there are no inhibitions, only a complete immersion into this inferno of pleasure.

"Bishop, I…"She squeezes her eyes closed, her cheeks flushed pink, her lip between her teeth. "Ahhhh. Oh. Yes. Oh, yes."

And I'm right behind her, coming so hard my vision goes bright. I grip her hips, still pumping over me. My hands slide over her sweat-slick thighs, up to her back, pressing her as close to me as I can manage. I cross my arms at her back, melding our bodies until not even a breath separates us.

With my head buried in her silvery hair, and the soft kisses she leaves at my neck and over my shoulders as we come down, I know I want nothing to ever separate us again.

CHAPTER TWENTY-TWO

Sofie

That door looks so good right now. Sitting here waiting to meet Shaunti Miller, at the precipice of an irreversible decision that will throw my life into chaos, that door looks so good. Two things stop me from getting up and strutting out that door and all the way back to my apartment. One, Halima's words still have their hooks in my heart and echo in my head, provoking me to follow through on the conscience I've managed to ignore for most of my life. And, two, the man at my side, holding my hand and just being…there. Just being there for me, encouraging me to reach for that good Walsh assures me is in there somewhere.

If he says so.

Trevor's thumb stroking my hand distracts me for a few seconds. We've been touching each other all morning. Last night he kicked down some door, invading an inner sanctum no one's ever occupied. I can't evict him. I don't want to. Last night was…there aren't words. Only emotions. Only these *feelings* I've never had before. I think the hardest thing about this morning's meeting is the fear that it will get so bad once I go public with my story that I'll lose this thing with Bishop. And it's the sweetest, purest, most genuine thing I've ever had. Last night raised the stakes so high. Losing him now—I can't wrap my head around that.

And as much as I don't want to admit it to myself, it's not just my head. It's my heart, too. I can't wrap my heart around losing him.

"You okay?" Trevor leans forward to peer at me. "I know this is hard, Sof, but it's the right thing to do."

"I know." Nerves propel a laugh from me. "I'm not used to doing the right thing, so there's a little bit of a learning curve here."

Trevor brushes the hair back from my face, cupping my cheek and leaning forward to drop a soft kiss on my lips. I need more. I need something other than this sick panic gnawing through my insides, so I lean deeper into his kiss, hoping the hunger I always feel with him will distract me for just a little while. And it does, for a few seconds, as we nip and suck and lick into a kiss that both soothes and incites. He pulls away, laying his forehead against mine, his fingers brushing across my neck under my hair.

"Sofie Baston, you taste so sweet." His breath mists my lips. "I may just eat you alive."

"Yes, please." I lay one more kiss against his lips, holding on to this sensation for as long as I can.

When I pull back, we grin at each other for a moment. This is special. This is different from anything I've had, and I realize that what he wanted for us, it's happening. That we are learning each other, and loving what we learn, and wanting each other. We've become...I search for the word. For the way to describe how it feels to have my hand in his moments before I dive into a shit storm that could wreck everything I've worked for and everything I still want to have.

Close. There's that word again. We feel close. It didn't take long, and it's not fully formed, but I want to keep walking in his direction as much as he wants to keep walking in mine. And even though it's early, I know I want to be closer to him than I've been to the others.

The door opens. Not the one that offered me a way of escape, but the door that leads to chaos and mayhem and public humiliation. And maybe, finally, to some kind of justice.

"Sorry to keep you waiting, Ms. Baston." Karen Sims stands in her office door, motioning for me to come in. "I wanted to chat with Shaunti a little before you arrived."

I stand, surprised my wobbly legs support me. Trevor stands with me, his hand at my back. We start walking toward Karen Sims, Shaunti's lawyer.

"Just you, Ms. Baston." Karen firms her mouth into a straight line, her eyes flicking between Trevor and me. "Shaunti is prepared to speak only with you, not anyone else."

I'm about to yield, but the thought of going through this completely alone almost sends me through that other door. I need him with me.

"Ms. Sims, I really must insist that Mr. Bishop come in with me." I staunch the anxiety in my chest before it makes it to my face. "I came here without my lawyer, my publicist, my manager, without anyone from my team. I'm talking to you of my own free will, and I'm risking a lot. I'm risking things Shaunti isn't risking anymore, so again, I must insist."

For a moment Karen Sims looks like she'll rebuff me, but she must realize the line between my stony expression and the hand holding Trevor's is my line in the sand. My take it or leave it line. She doesn't look happy about it, but she nods and gestures for Trevor and me to precede her into the office.

Inside the office, Shaunti Miller sits in one of three seats across from Karen's desk. Trevor and I take the other two. I study her for a moment. A headband holds her dark brown hair away from her face. She wears a bit of pink lipstick and some mascara, but otherwise no makeup. She's paired a long-sleeved PTA T-shirt and a pair of jeans, faded in places. On her feet she wears pink-and-teal Asics.

She's staring at me, which I can't resent because I was doing the same. I offer a tentative smile, which she returns.

"Shaunti Miller," Karen says. "Meet Sofie Baston. Sofie's friend Mr. Bishop is sitting in, if that's okay."

Shaunti studies Trevor for a moment before nodding. She looks back to me, her eyes becoming more guarded.

"Sofie, you called to say you had information that we might find interesting given the claims Shaunti made last week." Karen sits behind her desk, leaning back to fold her arms across her chest. "What kind of information exactly?"

Trevor reaches for my hand, even though he continues to study Karen and Shaunti. For a moment I can't for the life of me remember why I would choose to do this—hurl my life into this typhoon. Then I think of Halima. They cut that woman's clitoris off. She'll live with the complications of that sloppy butchering for the rest of her life. She can't ever go home under threat of death, and yet she travels the world doing exactly what she challenged us to do that day. Using her hurt to help. Fifteen years ago I decided not to speak out against Kyle. There is at least one woman seated across from me who paid the price of my silence, and there are probably more.

"Kyle Manchester raped me when I was eighteen years old." I

press my lips together before continuing. "On prom night. Couldn't get more cliché, right?"

I just spat that out, but Karen and Shaunti both stare at me, eyes arrested and mouths slightly open.

"You're saying that…that Kyle raped you, too?" Shaunti asks.

"Yes. I never came forward. I never planned to." I cross my legs, tracing the stitching of my black skinny jeans. "But I'm prepared to speak out now."

Karen Sims leans forward.

"Sofie, we want to take that bastard down badly." She glances at Shaunti, tweaking one corner of her mouth before looking back to me. "We were pretty close, but his team dug up some things from Shaunti's past that she couldn't have come out."

"I have a husband and a six-year-old," Shaunti adds, her tone almost defensive. "One wild night in college and…"

She glances at Trevor, as if remembering that he's present.

"I just…those things couldn't come out. I had to pull back."

"We tell you this, Sofie, so that you understand Kyle's team will come after you with everything." Karen glances at Trevor, still holding my hand. "And to be frank, you have more than one wild night for them to dig up, most of them well-documented."

"Which should be an advantage in some ways," I say. "Everyone knows all my dirt. There's not much left to expose."

"The thing is, Sofie," Karen says, "The statute of limitations in your case, like in Shaunti's, has expired. This is purely a trial of public opinion. I'll be frank. As ridiculous as it sounds, being a woman who's posed for *Playboy* and been as open as you have about your affairs, your sexuality, doesn't make you a sympathetic figure in rape allegations."

Hearing it put that way, especially in front of Trevor, deflates me. You mean to tell me I worked myself up to speak out, to finally tell my story, only to be told my voice isn't good enough because I like sex? Because I'm not ashamed of my body? I'm about to speak up, when Trevor beats me to it.

"I'm glad you realize that sounds ridiculous, Ms. Sims," Trevor says. "I find it ridiculous that any reasonably intelligent person would be unable to differentiate between an adult woman having and enjoying consensual sex and an eighteen-year-old girl subjected to a violent crime."

"It's okay, Bishop." I squeeze his hand, wishing he weren't hearing this. It's embarrassing to be told everyone thinks you're too slutty to believe you ever turned down sex, even from a rapist.

"No, it's not." He looks at me, his eyes dark and flinty. "Sofie came here to see if she could assist with your efforts in exposing Kyle Manchester for the criminal scum that he is. If you don't want her involvement, I don't have to tell you her team is more than capable of handling this without you."

He leans back, resting one elbow on the seat's arm.

"But you'd regret that, wouldn't you, Ms. Sims?" A laugh laced with cynicism passes his lips. "The chance to attach yourself to such a high-profile figure in a case against a powerful man? A case that will garner national attention? You won't pass up that chance, will you?"

Karen Sims's cheeks go red. Her nostrils flare. Her mouth tightens.

"Now, you listen here, Mr. Bishop—"

"No, you listen here, Karen. May I call you Karen?" Trevor drops my hand and leans forward, resting a palm on the desk in front of us. "You've got about ten seconds to convince us that if Sofie comes forward she'll have your unequivocal support, and that you will speak with confidence on her behalf. If not, then I'll advise Sofie to walk right now. Because I can guarantee you there're a thousand others in New York just like you, but there's only one Sofie. One person with the kind of international instant recognition, with a profile higher than even Kyle's, who can actually fight him and win."

I'm blinking back tears. Why? Because he just stood up for me when no one usually does? Because there's no doubt he believes me, when my parents don't? When my parents won't stand up for me or with me? Because it's apparent he actually cares about me?

"I was merely advising Sofie that they'll come after her hard," Karen says. "And that there will be people who take his side. He's a very popular man right now. He's an Independent, but garners a lot of conservative support based on his fiscal positions. If he can rally conservative support against Sofie, it could get really ugly."

"I understand that," I say.

"I want to work with you, Sofie." Karen turns her words and eyes deliberately in Trevor's direction. "For the right reasons, but you need to know there's a lot to lose. Do your parents know about this? Your father has been very publicly aligned with Kyle Manchester lately."

"Yeah, they know." I lick my lips, hating that I have to say the next words, but it has to be said. "We can't count on them for support."

"Your parents don't believe you?" Surprise stretches Shaunti's eyes and lifts her brows.

"I think they believe me. They just don't care."

The silence that follows my statement is telling. I know what

Karen and Shaunti are thinking. If I can't count on my own parents to side with me against Kyle Manchester, how can I expect anyone else to?

"Okay, well then." Karen clears her throat. "I'm not asking this in a judgmental way, but just so that we can be prepared for anything."

"All right. Ask away."

"I did a little searching before you came." Karen steadies her eyes on my face. "Just some recon to prepare for your visit."

"I'm sure that was a fascinating Google search," I mutter.

"Besides the *Playboy* spread, a very public affair with a prominent married man." Karen clears her throat again, shooting a glance at Trevor that makes me scared to hear what dirt she's about to bring out from under the carpet. "A, ahem, threesome or two bragged about in the tabloids."

Trevor looks at me sharply, brows in the air, asking the silent question. I just shrug one shoulder.

"I was young and drunk."

"Which brings me to my next question, Sofie," Karen says. "Any drug use?"

"I'm a model, Karen," I reply. "If you're asking if someone somewhere may have a picture of me snorting a line of coke, that could happen. I'm not an addict, by any means. It would have been rare, but at a party or after a shoot, things happen. I'm not the one on trial here."

"And neither is Kyle, at least not criminally," Karen says. "We have to be clear about what a win is for us. Neither you nor Shaunti have a criminal case anymore, but with her allegations still in people's minds, and then someone as high profile as you adding yours, it will at least bring pressure for him to drop out of the Senate race.

And, hopefully, encourage some girl who *does* still have a criminal case against him to come forward."

"That's exactly what we've been thinking," I say.

"In the meantime, Sofie," Karen says, sympathy in her eyes and on her face. "They'll make life hell for you."

"It can't be worse than the night he raped me." My voice shakes only the tiniest bit, but from Trevor's eyes fixed on my face, I think he hears it. "For days afterward I had bruises and bite marks from his attack. I didn't take pictures, but I've never forgotten that."

"Did he bite your, um..." Shaunti glances self-consciously at Trevor. "Your breasts?"

"Yes." I look at my wrist, half surprised not to see red whelp marks ringing them. "And he belted my wrists."

"Mine, too," Shaunti whispers. "Did he ejaculate on your stomach at the end? I couldn't understand why he...he just...Did he do that to you, too?"

I can only offer a jerky nod, the memory of that humiliation sealing my lips together. Me tied to the hotel bed with his belt knotted around my wrists, his eyes locked on mine while he spent himself on my belly and rubbed it into my skin. Hours after I showered until my skin turned raw, I could still feel that wet stickiness violating me.

"If he did those things to both of us, maybe it's a pattern." Shaunti brushes a tear from her cheek. "And there's another girl who will hear your story and come forward, too."

"Would you be willing to share a detailed account, Sofie?" Karen asks.

"Yes, of course." I frown before going on. "The attack itself remained vivid in my mind for years, but the time afterward got hazy.

We tried to reconstruct those hours afterward in therapy, but bits and pieces of it just aren't clear."

"You saw a therapist?" Shaunti asks.

"Yes, in Milan." I rub the face of my watch, surprised at how much time has passed. I need to get Trevor out of here so he can prepare for his trip. "We don't have a lot of time left. We need to get going soon. Mr. Bishop has a flight."

"Of course." Karen jots down a few notes on a legal pad. "Start trying to reconstruct those hours following the attack, the ones you say remain hazy. People will ask why you're just now coming forward, and if there's anything in that time frame we need to speak about, we need you to remember it."

How different would things have been if I had come forward? Hadn't heard my parents arguing? Had knocked on their door with my bruises and bite marks, evidence of Kyle's brutality, instead of hiding it for days. Now it's just my word against his, but I'm determined he won't have the last word.

"We really do need to go." I stand and so does Trevor. "What's the next step?"

"You and I need to have a follow-up where you share a detailed account of the incident. I have Shaunti's account on file, and we need to have that for the record, but also for you to get used to recalling and articulating your story. You'll have to tell it soon."

"I'll coordinate with my assistant and get back to you with a time. She keeps my schedule."

"Fine, and give me a day or so. We'll craft a statement for release." Karen stands, too. "In the meantime, play this close to the chest. I know you want to apprise your team, but no one beyond that. We stand a better chance with Kyle's team having less notice."

"Well, my parents know I'm planning to do this." My lips take on a bitter twist. "They were very clear that they would not support me, and have probably already told Kyle about my allegations."

"In that case," Karen says, a frown puckering between her eyebrows, "Kyle's team is already digging."

"They can dig all they want. I've got nothing to hide."

A small voice I've managed to suppress until now reminds me there is one thing left to hide, left to find, but I dismiss that. *That* I did manage to bury. That won't come back to haunt me. I was too careful. Too discreet.

"Well, if there is, they'll find it. Secrets, especially for someone as high profile as you, are like bodies on the bayou. When the rain comes, the corpses rise above ground."

My belly clenches. That one secret is mine and mine alone. They can drag me through the mud, but that I'll carry to my grave.

"I recommend a small press conference with a live statement," Karen says. "That would have the most impact."

Shit just got real.

"I don't want a press conference." I level a look at Karen that tells her not to push me on this. "That statement you want to release is fine, but I need you to coordinate any written communication with my team. I have to bring them all up to speed. My lawyer will be in touch with you."

"And the press conference?" Karen persists. "You need to be ready to speak on this, Sofie, if you're serious about taking Kyle down."

"I am prepared, but maybe I could just record a statement from home or my office and release that. Then follow up later with an interview with someone I trust."

"Whatever we do, let's do it in the next day or so," Karen says. "Following Shaunti's allegations so closely with yours will raise a lot of questions, especially for those who know there must be some fire with this much smoke."

Shaunti stands, too, extending her hand to me. I take it, and she pulls me in for a hug. I freeze, unsure of how to respond.

"Thank you so much for doing this." She sniffs, squeezing me tighter before stepping back. "I wanted to take him down. If I hadn't—"

"Hey, don't judge yourself too harshly," I say. "I can't blame you. Your family comes first. If I had those ties, I'm sure I'd hesitate. Hell, I don't have those ties and it took me fifteen years."

We pass a smile, sympathy, back and forth to each other, uniquely connected by Kyle's cruelty, but mostly by our survival.

The elevator down is crowded, so Trevor and I don't talk about what just happened. In the press of bodies, he links our pinkie fingers, and it's enough. Even that tiny contact with him calms the roiling in my soul, but I break it as soon as we enter the lobby. I put a block of space between us while walking out to meet Baker on the sidewalk. Trevor reaches for my hand, but I step out of reach. He lays a hand at my back, but I walk ahead, outside and toward the car waiting for us. His hand shackling my wrist pulls me up just short of the idling vehicle and my faithful driver.

"You don't want me to touch you?" Trevor's voice is low and even, but his eyes reveal that it bothers him. "Did talking about that night do that?"

The people rushing past don't stop for us, but I still carefully extract my wrist from his hand.

"No, it's not that." I shake my head dismissively. "After fifteen years and lots of therapy, the night itself has very little power over me anymore. I'm more worried about the fallout from coming forward."

"Like losing endorsements?" He frowns. "That kind of fallout?"

"No, fallout for *you*, Trevor." I look away, not wanting to discuss this on the sidewalk. "You heard Karen. It's gonna get really ugly. I don't want that associated with you in any way."

He opens his mouth, and I can already hear his rebuttal even though he hasn't voiced it yet.

"Car's here." I walk toward Baker, who stands by the open back door. I give him my usual kiss on the cheek before gesturing toward Trevor. "Baker, meet Trevor Bishop."

The two men size each other up for a few seconds before Trevor extends his hand.

"Nice to meet you, Baker," he says. "How long have you been putting up with this li'l filly?"

The stiff lines of Baker's face relent, cracking with a small smile.

"Since she was a little girl, Mr. Bishop," Baker returns. "I've had that privilege for as long as she can probably remember."

"Lucky man." Trevor runs the backs of his fingers across my cheekbone.

An uncustomary heat spreads across my face at Trevor's gentle touch.

"Thought I'd never see the day again!" Baker full out chuckles. "Miss B, you're actually blushing."

I press my hands to my cheeks, frowning and stepping into the backseat.

"Am not. It's the cold. Your fault for keeping me waiting."

I can't help but grin as I settle into the back and wait for Trevor to climb in, since Baker's never had me waiting a day in all the years he's served my family.

As soon as Trevor's seated, he picks up right where we left off.

"I'm not pretending we aren't together because of your misguided sense of protectiveness." Trevor eliminates the space between us and drags me onto his lap.

"Bishop, stop." I struggle halfheartedly because pressed against this wall of reassuring muscle and bone and warmth and care is exactly where I need to be.

"I won't stop." He presses a kiss into my hair, his hands rubbing soothing circles on my back. "Not until you hear me. I told you I don't give a damn what people think or say, Sofie. You're doing a brave thing, and I'll be proud for people to know we're together. That I'm standing with you."

I lower my lashes to cover the sudden, foolish tears standing in my eyes. As much as it was his bulldozer obstinacy that got him that first date, it's his tenderness that draws and keeps me close. I can't help but wonder how different things could have been had I actually gone to Princeton, like originally planned. What if I had met Trevor there? Would he have helped me heal? Those first two years after Kyle, I was a wreck.

"You know, I didn't have sex for almost two years after that night with Kyle," I whisper into his neck, rubbing the lapel of his suit between my fingers. "I worked so hard to sort through my issues with sex after what he did. And I cried through the first few times I was with a man."

I laugh, my voice husky with the tears that better not fall.

"Those poor guys wondering what the hell was wrong with me." I shake my head. "I was posing in my underwear, selling fantasy, and flinched every time a man came near me in real life."

"Sofie, darlin', I'm so sorry." He strokes my hair back, concern darkening his eyes.

"No, it's okay. I just…it took so much for me to have a normal sex life. To even tolerate a man's touch, and now my learning to enjoy sex after Kyle ruined it for me is the very thing that will make it harder for me to put him away."

I look up, a sudden thought making me anxious.

"I'm not some nympho, Trevor. I'm a normal girl with a normal sex life. Mine is just splashed across every tabloid known to man."

"I know that, Sof. You don't have to…" He trails off, kissing my temple. "I know that."

"Thank you so much for going with me." I reach up to run my hand over his silky hair. "I couldn't have done that without you."

"I wanted to be there."

He drops a quick kiss on my lips. He moves to pull away, but that one touch is all it takes to light the match. His fingers slide into my hair, palming the back of my head, holding me still to control and deepen the kiss. I lean into his shoulder, returning every stroke of his tongue slowly, then more aggressively, until we are both panting into the space we give each other to catch our breath.

Trevor looks up, catching Baker's eyes in the mirror.

"We're giving Baker quite the show," he says quietly.

"Baker's used to me," I assure him, pulling him in for another kiss.

"Well, I'm not used to Baker." He raises the privacy partition, smiling at Baker in the mirror before the small window is all the way up. As soon as we're sealed in, Trevor's back, raining kisses down my neck, stroking me through my jeans. I push against his hand, hungry for the pressure. Desperate for relief.

"What do you have for the rest of the day?" He sucks my earlobe into his mouth, the sensual suction sending a quake to my core.

"Nothing I can't cancel to be with you."

"Good girl." He laughs against my neck. "You can come help me pack for South Africa."

"Is packing a euphemism for sex?"

"Yeah, pretty much."

"Well, let's go home and pack, because if how you packed last night—"

"And this morning," he whispers against my collarbone. "Don't forget this morning."

"God, yes, the way you packed this morning." The memory of seeing his head moving under the covers between my legs makes me shiver. "I could use a good pack before you leave me for the next week."

He pulls back abruptly, eyes fixed on me.

"To be clear, Sofie," he says, his voice losing some of the heat, "I'm the only man you're packing with. Got it?"

I lean in to kiss under his chin, pushing my fingers into his closely cropped hair.

"Are you saying we're exclusive, Mr. Bishop?" I tease.

His eyes are sober, going darker every second he stares at me.

"I'm saying you're mine."

Any trace of the smile I was teasing him with fades to nothing under the claim his eyes make on me. I've never abided possessiveness. I've been my own woman too long to be anyone else's, but the possessive heat of Trevor's eyes burns right through any protest because I want that, too. I want to be his. Any claim he lays to me is an absolute privilege.

"I'd like that" is what I say.

You're mine, too.

You'd think after what I just did in Karen's office, after what I've set in motion with Kyle Manchester, saying those three words aloud to a man who so obviously cares for me and wants to claim me, would be easy, but I can't seem to find the nerve.

CHAPTER TWENTY-THREE

Trevor

I've never considered myself a shallow man; I've never been impressed by a woman's superficial qualities. My mama taught me early on to look beyond the surface of a woman, and to search out her substance. I've taken that wisdom into every relationship I've ever had. Looks have never been that important.

But damn.

Watching Sofie sleeping in my bed, I can't help but thank every lucky star that my woman has substance *and* this body. The sheet has fallen away, baring her breasts and flat stomach. Her gilded hair spills over my pillow. We kissed away any trace of her lipstick before we even made it to Brooklyn, so her lips are bare and slightly swollen. Just thinking about what she was doing with that mouth an hour ago has me going hard again under the sheets. I won't even allow myself to wonder where she learned to give head like that. Thinking about the men in Sofie's past too long, too hard, will drive me out of mind. I'll just appreciate her particular talents and rest in the knowledge that I'm the only one benefiting from them now.

This is actually me. Back propped against my headboard, watching a woman sleep for half an hour because I can't seem to find anything I'd rather do. A knock at my door reminds me I have a shitload of stuff I *have* to do before we leave for South Africa.

I pad over to the door, naked as the day I was born, and crack it open just enough to see Henri in the hall, fully dressed.

"I'll be ready," I say, preempting her lecture on getting my ass in gear for our flight.

"You do that." She cranes her neck, trying to see into my bedroom. "Is someone in there? What's going on in there?"

"That information's above your pay grade, Hen." I laugh and close the door.

I turn around to find Sofie sitting up in bed, ivory sheets puddled around her waist, breasts playing peekaboo through the blond hair hanging over her shoulders, and eyeing me like the lunch we skipped.

"You, Mr. Bishop," she says, licking her lips and blazing her eyes over my naked body, "are a work of art."

I walk over to press one knee into the bed by her hip.

"So are you." I take one plump nipple into my mouth, tugging until it goes tight on my tongue. "Edible art."

"Do we have time?" She pulls my head up, kissing me deep and long before I have to pull away, shaking my head and breathing like I just finished one of my Ironman races.

"Sadly, no." I pull her to her feet, admiring my woman when she leaves the sheet behind, standing before me naked. Tempting me on purpose.

"Are you sure?" She lifts a little to kiss under my chin, her hand taking my dick in a tight grip and pulling. "I'm very persuasive when I set out to be. I can be quick."

"This I know." I have to step out of reach, or face a very irate Henri soon. "But I can't miss this flight."

"Oh, you're flying commercial." She shakes her head. "I don't know why people do that."

We both laugh at her ridiculous statement on the way to the shower. After I washed her and she washed me, Sofie had her way with me again against the shower wall. Or maybe I had her. Fuck it. We had each other, and if I could cancel this trip, I would. Not just for this, but to be with her over the next few difficult days. She's sitting on the counter naked, watching me shave, her breasts still flushed pink from the shower's steam.

"He bit your breasts?"

I know it's out of the blue to her, but the images of Kyle hurting Sofie have been torturing me since she shared them with Karen and Shaunti. It hurts to talk. Rage grates my voice up in my throat until it's barely a sound, but a syllabic growl.

The smile Sofie's been wearing almost constantly since we got here melts away. She just nods, reaching for a nearby towel and wrapping it around herself toga style. I wish I hadn't mentioned it. We've managed to enjoy these last few hours of being together without that meeting completely ruining it, but I can't *not* talk about it. The bastard tied her up and jerked off on her body. If he was that sick at eighteen years old, I can only imagine how more time, more power, more money have decayed him. The thought of him in the same room with Sofie sets off small explosives in my head.

I walk into my closet not only to sort clothes for my trip, but also to sort my thoughts and to regain my composure. I don't want to freak Sofie out, but all I can think about is her safety. What if that monster hurts her again when she exposes him? What if he finds a way to reach her, to retaliate?

"Do you have security, Sof?" I flick through a couple of suits, not even seeing what I'm selecting.

Sofie walks into the closet now wearing my Princeton hoodie, which falls about mid-thigh.

"Uh, yeah. Some. Like I told you before, usually just for events, but I'm sure we'll increase now." She scrunches her nose at the suits I pulled out. "Why are you taking those? Let me see what we've got here."

She steps in front of me, her damp hair just below my nose. My body wash smells so much better on her. My hands wander under the hoodie, over her waist to cup her breasts. She sinks back into me with a sigh, head resting against my shoulder.

"I thought you needed to get out of here." She looks up at me. "Keep that up and we'll be back in the shower, Mr. Bishop."

I nod and leave a kiss in her hair, moving down to grab some socks.

"Yes to this." She separates a dark suit from the others. "Is this Armani? Definitely yes to that. Where are your ties?"

She rummages through my closet, matching ties and shirts, lovingly caressing my shoes.

"You've got great taste, Bishop." She holds one of my dress shirts up to her chest.

"My sister does most of my shopping for me," I admit. "I just don't have the time. Nor do I much care."

"How can you not *care*?"

She drops her arms until the shirt hangs limply from her fingers.

I forgot who I was talking to. It's like I just told Gandhi he should eat a Quarter Pounder.

"I mean, well, of course I *care*..." I shake my head, unable to even fake it. "Yeah, no. I don't care."

"When you get back, we'll go shopping." Her green eyes sparkle like it's Christmas, so as much as that sounds like a root canal without Novocain, I kiss her head and nod.

"Sounds great."

"Besides, I'm not sure I like other women shopping for you." She frowns. "Even your sister."

"Are you possessive?" I button and belt my pants. "Because I'd love that."

"Not typically." She comes to stand in front of me, batting my hands away from my tie so she can do it herself. "But for you I could make an exception."

My hands can't help themselves. They're sliding up her thighs to cup her butt before I can stop them.

"I'm definitely making an exception for you." I pull back to consider her face. "And no more threesomes. I suck at sharing."

A laugh, dark and rich and rough like ground coffee, rumbles in her throat, and she looks up at me from under her lashes.

"Duly noted, and for the record, I don't even remember that threesome." She grins and shrugs. "After a bottle of tequila, that whole night is a black hole. I just took those guys' word for it when they told the tabloids."

"Guys?" I grab her shoulders. "It was two guys? Never mind. I don't want to know."

Sofie reaches up, hooking her elbows at the back of my neck and biting my earlobe.

"I thought a threesome was every guy's fantasy."

I settle my hands at her hips, slipping my thumbs under the lacy string of her thong.

"I've already got one thing most guys only dream about."

She leans up an inch more until our noses touch.

"Why are you so damn sweet?"

I lean my forehead against hers, not able or wanting to hide from her how much the last twenty-four hours have meant to me.

"Because I'm so damn happy to have you." I suck her bottom lip between mine. "Does that answer your question?"

She tilts her head, fitting our lips together, wrapping her arms around my waist. The kiss probably lasts only a few seconds, but I'm lost in it. Lost in her, until a knock on the door disrupts the kiss.

"Five minutes, Trevor," Henri says from the outer door. "Harold is already downstairs with his bags."

Well, good for Harold. He just wants to get in your pants.

"Okay, I'll be right out." I look back to Sofie, whose face looks about as deflated as I feel.

"Harold and Henri make the perfect couple." Sofie grins up at me, eyes mischievous. "The cock blockers."

"That's pretty good." I smile and shake her gently by her shoulders. "Ride with us to the airport. The driver can drop you off at your place after."

She nods, pulling away and going in search of her jeans.

"Can I keep this?" She lifts the neck of my hoodie, sniffing and smiling. "It still smells like you."

"It smells like me after a hard run." I shake my head and roll my eyes. "But you're welcome to it if you don't like, oh I don't know, deodorant."

She laughs and bends to slip on her jeans. I walk up and stop her.

"Fair's fair," I whisper across her lips. "What do I get to keep of yours?"

She holds my stare while she shimmies out of her panties and slips them into the inside pocket of my suit jacket.

"Don't say I never gave you anything." She pulls on her skinny jeans with a smile and walks out into the hall.

What am I going to do with that woman? I touch the silk stuffed into my coat pocket. Oh, any manner of things when I return from South Africa.

Once in the car, I wish Sofie and I had met Harold and Henri at the airport. I want to spend the last few minutes we have together with her much closer. I settle for holding her hand, and even that small gesture draws a disapproving look from Henri. What is her damn problem with Sofie?

"There's a picture of you on Page Six, Trevor." Henri lifts her eyes briefly from her phone, flicking a glance between Sofie and me. "And you, Sofie."

I've never been on Page Six in my life, and would have been fine going to the grave without that dubious honor.

"Let me see." Sofie holds out her hand for Henri's phone. Her smile disintegrates as soon as she reads the headline. "'The Sinner and the Saint'?"

"What?" I lean into her shoulder to see the screen, laughing as soon as I read the headline.

The Sinner and the Saint: Bad Girl Sofie Baston and International Philanthro-preneur Trevor Bishop Paint the Town for Good.

"Did they make up a word for me? That's kind of cool." I chuckle. "Which one am I supposed to be? Sinner or saint?"

"It's not funny, Bishop." Sofie hands the phone back to Henri, turning her face to the window, eyes straight ahead, mouth tight.

"Sofie, come on. Who cares what people think?"

"I guess I do." Sofie doesn't take her eyes off the water beneath the Brooklyn Bridge.

The rest of the ride is silent. Henri and Harold on their phones. Me debating how seriously I should take this. Sofie contemplating the city through the window.

"We're here," Henri slices into the silence. "Come on, guys."

"Right behind you," I say, not moving from my spot beside Sofie. "Just a minute."

Harold nods and gets out. Henri looks like she might crack the whip, but I give her a look to remind her who the boss actually is in this situation.

"Hey, you." I pull Sofie over my lap, bringing her knees on either side of my thighs so she's straddling me. "Don't let that stupid headline get to you."

"We just don't need this right now." She touches our noses together. "Not for the Collective or this case with Kyle. As good as this feels, as right as it feels, I keep wondering if it's the wrong time for us."

If I tell her what I'm feeling, I could scare her off. How do I tell her the feeling that was missing with Fleur, with every woman I've ever been with, that urgency my father told me about—I have it for her. I *feel* it for her. I have almost from the beginning. At first it was just a hunch that there was more to her than this body and this face. And then an urge to know for sure. It exploded into the possibility that I'll never feel this for anyone else. I can't say any of that. We haven't been together long enough. She'll assume it's the sex talking.

She'll assume that I see only what the other men in her life saw, what they thought they wanted from her. A good time until it was over. How do I tell her that there is no right time or wrong time, only *all* the time?

Because I don't see this ever ending.

I can't tell her that, so I just kiss her until we're both breathless. I press her into my body and trust that she'll hear my heart.

"Listen to me." I cup her face, holding her eyes even though it's obvious she wants to look away. "You're no sinner and I'm no saint. I don't care how other people label us or speculate about what we're doing. There's only one label you should worry about wearing."

"What's that?" she whispers, eyes softening the longer I hold her.

I lean into her ear and lace our fingers against my chest.

"Mine."

CHAPTER TWENTY-FOUR

Sofie

I miss Trevor already. It's impossible that after just a few days of having him in my bed I can't sleep without him, but last night I found myself wide awake, wondering how much longer before I would have him hard and warm at my back. I knew if he was with me, I'd have slept like a baby, feeling cared for and protected. Not to mention he'd probably have fucked me into exhausted oblivion. Man, was he worth the wait. He's insatiable and can't get enough of me. It's *so* mutual.

I have enough work to keep me busy, and a cold, lonely apartment awaits me at home, so I'll stay at the office as long as possible.

"I'm knocking off," Stil says from the door. "You coming?"

"Nah." I glance up from a prospectus one of our potential charitable partners sent Marlee. "I want to nail down at least our first four charitable partnerships before the site goes live. We've got the Walsh Foundation, of course. I want to talk to the team about Restore, one Trevor introduced me to last week. So that just leaves another two."

"You can do that tomorrow, Sof." Stil approaches the desk, purse already hanging from her shoulder. "Besides, I could use a ride home, and you got the wheels."

I roll my eyes but grin.

"Have Baker take you home. You're not far away. By the time he swings back through, I'll be ready."

"You sure?"

"Positive. Twenty minutes tops."

"Okay, better be." She heads back toward the door.

"Oh, Stil."

She turns, brows up, waiting for what's next.

"Um, could you pull the team together tomorrow?" I lick my lips and meet her questioning eyes. "Geena, Connor, Bill, you, and me."

Stil walks back to the desk slowly, a frown on her face.

"Why do we need your manager, publicist and the lawyer, Sof? What's going on?"

"We'll talk about it tomorrow, okay?" I try to reassure her with my smile, but it's so phony it probably does nothing to put her at ease.

"If there's something we need to handle, then—"

"Tomorrow, Stil." I drop the smile and put on my "I mean it" face. "It'll keep until tomorrow. Just see when they can swing by to chat and make it happen, 'kay?"

We've been together too long for my flimsy assurances to assuage her concerns, but I'm not prepared tonight to go into the scandal that is about to capsize my life. It'll be hard enough tomorrow, because what turns my life upside down ripples through all of theirs. The concern on Stil's face, in her eyes, only deepens, but she knows I'm done discussing it, so she goes.

Even so, when she leaves, the thickening silence in my office presses against my ears, squeezing away the peace of mind company manufactures. When Stil and my small staff buzz around the office, the laughter and conversation and energy cloak my fear and camouflage my uncertainty. With them gone, Trevor gone, just me here alone—the quiet exposes all, and I can't hide from my own unease.

I stand, walking around and doing what I've always done to settle my nerves. Shaking my hands like I'm about to dive into the water for a race or climb in the boat for a regatta. As an athlete, I had all these little rituals to prepare for competition: doing a hundred jumping jacks, eating one of Millie's Denver omelets, and, of all things, clipping my nails. But there's no ritual to prepare for the standoff that's coming with Kyle. I lean against my desk, rubbing the back of my neck where all my tension seems to gather.

I hear a sound in the outer office, and I lift my head.

"Stil, I told you I'm fine," I call out with a small smile. "Go on home."

Footsteps approach my office, confident and heavier than Stil's. For a moment, my heart lifts just the smallest little bit, irrationally hoping that by some miracle Trevor is here.

"Bishop?" The name slips past my lips before my brain reminds me that he is indeed in South Africa. He called me from there today.

"Is that who you're fucking now, Sofie? Trevor Bishop?"

What a betrayal of hope. Not Stil. Not Trevor. It's the man from my nightmares. The man whose handsome face and plastic smile disguise the lecherous violence Shaunti Miller experienced. That I experienced.

Kyle closes my office door behind him, and the sound of it clicking locked lands in my chest like a live grenade. The pin has been pulled, and it's only a matter of time before it blows. My composure disintegrates under his stare, which mesmerizes me like a snake poised to strike. The venom is in his eyes, and it paralyzes me, just as surely as if it's rushing through my bloodstream, attacking my central nervous system. My limbs lock, my breath seizing in my throat.

In the space of two blinks, he's across the room standing right in front of me, pushing the hair back from my face almost tenderly. His hands land on the desk before I can move, long arms bracketing my hips, trapping my body between his tall frame and the desk.

"Sofie Baston." His breath, cool and minty, settles over my lips. "It's good to see you again."

I cautiously straighten from the desk, but he doesn't move, so the motion presses our chests together. I can't struggle with this man, not with Jell-O in my knee caps and cotton in my mouth, so I settle back against the desk, creating a sliver of space between us.

"How did you get in here?" My voice comes out calm and low, no hint of the fear prickling my insides.

"Oh, I just took the elevator. My security detail is in your reception area, if you're concerned about that." His firm lips quirk. "We're safe in here."

Trapped in a room with a powerful man who raped me, who raped others, and the only security is here to protect *him*. I've never felt less safe. I stare back at him, making no sound or moves. I hate that fear paralyzes me, but I can't help it. The last time we were alone together, he tied my wrists, pried my legs apart, and ruptured me from the inside out. I thought those years of therapy cured me of this, but I fooled myself. I'm as frightened as I was on prom night. I'm just better at hiding it.

"What do you want, Kyle?"

"What a loaded question." A thin layer of lust films his eyes as they run up and then down my body. "So many possibilities with a woman like you."

"What do you want, Kyle?" It sounds no less confident when I repeat it, and it's no less a lie than the first time I said it.

One of the hands trapping me moves to my waist and slithers down to cup my ass. Everything in me rejects his touch. The hairs on my neck stand on end. My skin pebbles with goose bumps. My stomach heaves, but I'm afraid if I move, he'll hurt me, jerk me, and I can't invite his violence. My strength failed me against him before, and I'm afraid to test it again.

"Your father tells me there's some confusion about what happened between us that night all those years ago." He dips his head until his lips brush against my cheekbone. "We need to deal with that."

He's actually here to silence me. His balls are actually big enough that he came into my office to intimidate me, to charm me the way he does the public, to convince me that I'm confused. I crane my neck away from him, doing my best to escape his lips, his breath, his words.

"There's no confusion, Kyle." I force myself to meet the veiled malevolence of his stare. "How could there be when we both know you raped me?"

He inches forward, pressing his arms tighter against me, making sure I know he has me caged. Nausea roils in my stomach and floods my mouth with water as his erection presses between my legs. As much as I'm trying to disguise it, he senses my fear, and it's turning him on. He leans into my ear, his whisper burning my skin like acid.

"I didn't rape you, bitch. The way I remember it, you begged for it. I was your first, and there's a certain attachment to the man who pops your cherry." He laughs gruffly. "The way I remember it, when I told you I didn't want anything more than that one night, you threatened me with lies about rape. When you never followed through, I assumed you'd come to your senses. I was dismayed when your father warned me today that you haven't come to your senses at all."

His words sledgehammer me. My parents wanted to believe that lie so they can move forward with their agenda. In some corner of my heart, the last hope for support from my parents fades to dust.

"You really are something, though." He squeezes my ass, his breath releasing in a hiss. "I take a certain pride in knowing I had you first. I've never forgotten how tight your pussy was that night. How wet you were for me."

"I wasn't wet for you, motherfucker," I spit back. "I was so dry I bled when you rammed that tiny dick inside of me."

His eyes ignite with the violence he suppresses. His nostrils flare with it. The hand cupping my ass clenches into a fist, dragging me closer until his hardness digs into my thigh. If he could punch me in the face, he would. But he's smart enough not to leave any marks, smart enough not to say anything incriminating.

"I bet you wouldn't bleed now, would you, Sofie?" He pumps his hips slowly into me. I jerk back, pushing against his arms on either side of me, but they don't budge. "I may have been your first, but I certainly wasn't your last, was I? It must have been good because it really whet your appetite."

He licks behind my ear, laughing when I gag.

"Who's going to believe a whore like you was raped by a man like me?"

I can't stand like this with him another second. The last time we fought, he won. Everything in me resists the thought of another losing struggle, but I have to risk it. I shove at his chest, pushing him back just enough to lift my knee and ram it into the bulge in his pants. He doubles over, blue eyes watering with pain. I rush around behind my desk, rustling through the drawer until I find a letter opener. He stumbles toward me, face still red, lips yanked back with a growl.

"I wouldn't if I were you." I cock my arm back, letter opener gripped tightly in my fist. "This'll hurt a lot worse than my knee, and when I'm done you certainly won't be raping anyone else because that dick of yours will be tossed out my window into the street where it belongs."

"Bitch."

"You mentioned that." A calm, foreign but real, settles over me. Wraps around me until I actually manage to smile at my assailant.

"You can't stop me." I chuckle, leaning forward across my desk to taunt him with my eyes. With this irrational confidence. "You're the one with everything to lose, Kyle. Not me."

"We'll see about that." His lips peel back, showing his teeth like an alligator. "Seems to me you have *someone* to lose now."

My smile holds, but my heart stops. Trevor. I know that's who he means.

"We found all kinds of shit on you, of course," Kyle says, speaking easier now, his color returning to normal. "But him? Clean as a whistle. Not even a parking ticket."

I swallow, my smile melting away.

"I'll tell you right now, I got nothing on Bishop, but your shit will chase him away." He grins. "You had twenty years to close the deal with Walsh and you never could, and he can't hold a candle to this guy. This one? Oh, he's a saint compared to Walsh. You think he'll stay once the whole world sees what a slut you are? You think he wants that shit sticking to him?"

His grin drops, eyes almost earnest.

"It doesn't have to be this way, Sofie. Just tell me what you really want here, and it doesn't have to get so ugly. This can all go away. You can go on with your life. I'll be New York's next senator, and your father will be a very happy man. I'll make sure of that. Just don't come out with this ridiculous story."

I tell my story every chance I get. Every time I do, I raise a fist against my oppressors.

Halima's words, her battle cry, rises up to squash what's left of my fear and uncertainty.

"You raped me and you raped Shaunti Miller, and God knows who else," I say, not even a lump in my throat. "And you're going to pay for it. By the time I'm done, you won't even get elected PTA president."

His eyes narrow to reptilian slits, his lips falling back to bare his teeth at me. His face goes stony, hands clenching and unclenching at his sides.

"Why you little—"

"And I bet there's someone out there you've raped who still has a criminal case against you." I lean forward, fists resting on my desk, letter opener trapped in hand. "You asked me what I want. I want you to rot in prison, you miserable bastard."

His hand raises like he might strike me, but he catches himself and runs that hand over his perfectly coiffed hair.

"I'd take that hit, Kyle, to have proof of your brutality, so go ahead." I tilt my chin, offering my cheekbone to him. "Hit me like you did that night. You think I've forgotten the bruises I had the next day?"

"You're crazy if you think anyone will believe you over me." Disdain drips from his laugh. "Me, an upstanding citizen, a family man with a spotless record, or you, the slutty model who spreads her legs for *Playboy* and any man who'll crawl into her bed?"

"We'll just have to see, won't we? We'll have to see if your hollow marriage to your sweet wife is enough to get you out of rape allegations from one of the most famous women in the world."

He goes white beneath his fake tan.

"If you want to walk away from this unscathed," he says, "stop before you start."

A chuckle gurgles in my throat, spilling into the tension of the room.

"You may be the political darling in your little neck of the woods, Kyle, but I'm one of the most recognizable faces *in the world*. You can't just make me disappear."

"Everything you've worked for will be destroyed. You'll be a laughingstock."

"You first, Kyle."

"Bitch."

"Son of a bitch," I fire back. "You can't do anything to me that hasn't already been done. That's the advantage of living the way I have. Everyone knows everything. I'm not Shaunti, and you can't intimidate me."

I stride past him to the door, legs no longer trembling. I unlock and open the door, peering into the reception area, where two oversize men in dark suits sit flipping through magazines. I look back to Kyle, still standing by my desk, crimson crawling out of his collar and over his cheekbones.

"Get out of my damn office." I shift my weight from one stiletto to the other, grabbing my cell phone from my pocket when he makes no move to comply. "Get out now, or I'm calling the cops."

When I mention the cops, the two gorillas by Gil's desk stand and step forward. Kyle crosses the office with swift strides, but slows and stops in front of me.

"Your parents don't even believe you. What makes you think anyone else will?"

He doesn't give me the chance to respond, which is probably good because I have no comeback for that. My own mother is against me. My own father threatened me. With that thought hanging over my head, and Kyle and his gorillas gone, I look around the office and realize I'm still well and truly alone.

CHAPTER TWENTY-FIVE

Sofie

I'm in the privacy of my own home with Stil, my closest friend, nearby. My trusted team members—the lawyer, manager, and publicist who've been with me most of my career—sit just a few feet away. I should feel at ease. But how can I when one huge eye—the camera—opens up my home to millions of strangers, belying the illusion of privacy. Maybe my whole life has been an illusion of privacy, and this thing with Kyle will just expose the public as cruel voyeurs who watch and point and ridicule.

Or maybe they'll believe me. Maybe they'll sympathize. Maybe they'll be kinder than I expect them to be.

"You ready?" Karen Sims perches on the edge of my sofa.

"Is that a rhetorical, it's-too-late-to-turn-back-now kind of question?" I ask. "Or do you mean am-I-ready-right-now-to-do-this kind of question?"

"I think the latter." Karen laughs a little, something I haven't seen her do much in the last few days as we prepared for this. "It's not too late you know. This is a huge step, and it's a risk, Sofie. No one would think less of you for not doing it."

That's a lie. I would think less of myself. Meeting Shaunti made me wonder who else he's tied up and jacked off on and bitten. Who else has he humiliated and left broken? I got into counseling immediately and put myself back together. That night is a distant memory for me, but what if there's a woman out there for whom it's a fresh nightmare she keeps playing over and over in her head? What if she's afraid to come forward? What if, like Halima said, my hurt can help?

"And someone wants to speak to you." Karen proffers her phone, a small smile softening her thin lips.

I take the phone and say hello tentatively.

"Hi, Sofie," Shaunti says from the other end.

"Shaunti, hi." It's irrational, but tears spring to my eyes at the sound of her voice.

"I'm room mother today and my son has a game this afternoon. Too much to make it into the city and back in time," she says in a rush. "But I wanted you to know how much I appreciate this. I really wanted to do it, but when you love someone, sometimes you have to put them first. Above everything. And I just couldn't expose my husband and son to what Kyle's team had planned."

"Shaunti, you don't have to explain." I blink furiously, determined not to ruin Stil's perfect cat eye with tears. "I was just sitting here thinking that if I had spoken up fifteen years ago…"

My voice is so dampened by tears of regret and guilt, I can't get words out for a second. I clear my throat and try to finish.

"If I had spoken up fifteen years ago, maybe none of that would have happened to you."

"Don't take on guilt that is all Kyle's," Shaunti says, her voice tightening. "We're taking him down, Sofie, and you're the key. I have to go, but just wanted to wish you the best, and to say thank you."

"That actually means a whole lot to me, Shaunti. Thanks."

We hang up, and I just hold the phone for a few seconds like it's still emitting strength from miles away, and I can just absorb the conviction I heard in Shaunti's voice if I keep holding it.

"You ready?" Karen extends her hand for her phone.

"I'm ready." I fluff my hair around my shoulders, smoothing the simple green dress Stil and I agonized over. Green has become my signature color because it matches my eyes. It feels ludicrous debating my dress color considering the weight of this broadcast, but Stil and Geena insisted we go with green. Stil and Geena cared about it. I could be wearing plaid burlap for all I care right now.

Stil walks over to add a touch more lipstick, her hand trembling as she applies it. She blinks furiously, tears standing in her eyes.

"Hey." I grab her hand, pulling her to sit down beside me. "You okay?"

"Am *I* okay?" She strangles a laugh in her throat. "You walk around for fifteen years with this hanging over your head. You're about to take on this monster, and you're asking if I'm okay? Yeah, I'm fine, Sof. Just peachy. How 'bout you?"

"Look, I know you—"

"You could have told me," she cuts in, hurt and anger cocktailing in her eyes. "You *should* have told me. I'm your best friend. How could you not tell me?"

"I didn't tell anyone, Stil." I squeeze her hand. "I wanted to put it behind me. I fooled myself into thinking I could just walk away, but it doesn't work that way."

Stil nods, glancing around surreptitiously.

"Did you tell them that he came to the office?" Her quiet words rise only as far as my ears.

I glance at everyone in the room before returning my eyes to Stil.

"No, and I don't want to. It won't help. He was a jerk, but he didn't admit to anything. Didn't incriminate himself any further. And it is just more of what we already have. More of my word against his. I'm set on doing this. He didn't change that."

"But you'll tell Trevor, right?"

I pull my lips into my mouth, releasing a deep breath through my nose.

"I'm not sure. We'll see."

"You should tell him." Stil stiffens her lips in that stubborn way I hate. "Tell him or I will."

"You wouldn't." I aim a glare at her that seems to bounce right off. "This isn't the best time to discuss this, Stil. I'm about to tell the whole world Kyle Manchester raped me. Can we talk—"

"You're right." She pats my shoulder, her eyes softer. "You focus on this. Get through this, and we'll talk about it later."

I smile faintly when she stands. The last thing I want to do is tell Trevor. Clearly Kyle knows Trevor is my weakness and would love to see him involved in any way he can. He wants to drag him into this however he can. It'll be hard enough for me to see this through without worrying that Trevor will be hurt in the process.

My lawyer, Connor, walks over, squatting in front of me and taking my fingers in his bigger hand. He's not exactly been a father figure to me. He's only in his mid-forties, but definitely avuncular. He's as honest as Abe and a shark when he needs to be on my behalf, but never with me.

"Just stick to what's on the teleprompter," he says. "We've all agreed on that statement. It tells the truth, but doesn't give everything away yet. We need to roll this information out carefully."

"Teleprompter, got it." I glance at the large screen mounted above the camera with the words scrolling as Geena checks the statement one last time.

"Okay, let's do it then," Karen says.

At my very first photo shoot, I realized that I loved the camera. Everyone said it loved me back, and I'm counting on that today. The nausea churning my stomach, the sweat slicking my palms, the anxiety like a studded choker around my neck—all fall away as soon as soon as that camera goes live.

"Hello, I'm Sofie Baston." My hands lay relaxed in my lap. "Many of you know me from magazines, or the runway, or ads for your favorite perfume and clothes. I've been very fortunate to find success as a model over the last fifteen years. Modeling has made my life very public, but there is one thing I've never talked about publicly until now."

I draw a deep breath, knowing that once these words leave my mouth, I can't take them back. Once I level these accusations at one of the country's most powerful men, I can't rewind.

And he'll come after me.

When I think of how he hurt me that night—stole my virginity and stripped me of my dignity—and did the same thing to Shaunti and God knows who else, there is only one thought singing through my head.

Bring it.

"Fifteen years ago it was my high school prom night," I continue. "I was nervous and excited. There were pictures and dancing. All the things you hope your prom will be. I had no idea that it would be one of the worst nights of my life. That night, my date raped me."

I pause to swallow, the word "rape" curdling on my tongue.

"It was the most humiliating night of my life, and there are some things I've blocked, things I've tried to forget, but I remember who did it."

I tip my chin up an extra inch, eyes locked on the camera like it's a person right there I have to convince.

"It was Kyle Manchester, one of the leading candidates in next year's U.S. Senate race. I know many will wonder why now. Why, after fifteen years of silence, I've decided to come forward. I held back for the same reasons so many other women do. Fear. Shame. I was unsure that people would believe me. I was young and scared then, and trusted the wrong man. Last week someone else made this accusation, and seeing that person's courage spurred me to come forward, even after all this time."

The line on the teleprompter says that I should be saying thank you and wrapping it up, but I can't. Despite what Connor told me about sticking to the script, there is something I have to say that isn't written on that screen.

"And if there's anyone out there who might feel what I was feeling. Afraid. Ashamed. Unsure." I look down at my lap before returning my eyes to the camera. "Humiliated and dirty because this man did the same thing to you, I want you to know that if you come forward, I'll stand with you. When this happened, I felt for a while like everything that mattered about me was taken away, but I was wrong. I have my voice. I have truth, and no one can take that."

I narrow my eyes at the camera.

"Don't let him take that from you."

Now I'm not sure how to finish after my detour, so I go back to the line that is paused and flashing for me to read.

"That's all I have to say for now. Thank you for your time."

CHAPTER TWENTY-SIX

Sofie

I knew my announcement would make a splash, but I really had no idea it would be of "break the Internet" proportions. I find myself the center of a storm of my own making, but over which I have no control. Kyle's camp fired back literally within minutes of my video with denials and prepared statements. My parents have made no contact, other than a regretful message from Baker indicating that he has been told I'm no longer a part of his responsibility to the Baston family and will need to find other means of transportation. I guess that's my parents' way of disowning me.

Kyle's team has already resurrected the most scandalous of my exploits: the affair with a married man—*homewrecker*. The picture I knew could be out there somewhere, of me snorting a line of cocaine during Paris Fashion Week years ago—*druggie*. The two guys who claimed we had a threesome on that tequila-drenched night that I barely remember—*whore*. And, of course, my infamous *Playboy* spread—*exhibitionist*.

Mine.

Trevor said that was the only label I needed to worry about, but every day a new label is slapped on my back, each one weighing more than the last. I wish he were here, but I would never ask him to miss the Collective meetings so crucial to his future.

Every speck of dirt from my past Kyle's team could dredge up, they have. None of it's new, but one incident piled on another heaped on another has many people skeptical about the validity of my claims. It is definitely my word against his. Kyle's trotting out his devoted wife, their 2.5 kids and half a dog, along with all the work he's done "for the community" over the years, makes him look like a responsible, upstanding citizen and me look like a promiscuous, privileged wild child living a life so far beyond what the average woman could imagine, she just may find it hard to relate to me. Or worse, to believe me.

Well played, Kyle Manchester. Well played.

I'm sure it all hurts. My parents' condemning silence and all the accusations, the slurs virtually flung at me from Kyle's conservative supporters, the bloggers speculating. It probably all hurts when each blow lands on me, but one thing I've learned to do over the years like an evolutionary defense mechanism is to thicken my skin as needed. Only this time, the skin has grown so thick so fast, I can't feel anything. Even the support many rape advocates have expressed doesn't help much because I can't feel that either. I guess I'm numb. I'm really just afraid Kyle has a knife up his sleeve so sharp it will slice through those inches of protective layers, and I'll feel everything, and all at once, so deeply, I won't be able to stand.

"You ready for this?" Stil asks across from me in the backseat of the car we're sharing.

"Huh?" I look up from my phone to see Stil frowning.

"Stop reading those posts, Sofie. Kyle has those bloggers and re- porters in his pocket, so of course they'll take his side. There's a whole other group of folks already calling for him to withdraw from the race. Two women in two weeks accusing him of rape has hurt his image and his chances."

She grabs my purse and iPad from the floor, handing them to me.

"You're making headway, so keep your chin up, honey."

She flicks her head toward the quaint Tribeca brownstone where my next meeting takes place.

"You sure you'll be okay in there alone?"

"You mean without my guard dog?" I meet the driver's eyes in the rearview mirror. We've compromised a little on security, using one of the guys guarding me to double as a driver. I persuaded Stil I'd be okay inside this meeting without him, and that he can drive her on to the office.

"Miraculously, I don't think we've been followed," I reassure her. "And even if we have, I can manage the ten steps between the side- walk and the front door without being attacked."

"Get in there and close the deal with Kerris." Stil glances back to the brownstone where Walsh grew up and now lives with his family. "We all really love her stuff and want it on Haven's site."

"And you're afraid I'll what?" I've smiled so little the last few days, my lips barely remember how to do it, but they manage. "Claw her eyes out?"

"No, you two have some history, I know," Stil says. "But your head's in the game, and she's a sweetheart."

"Must be nice for people to think you're a sweetheart." I twist my lips and sigh. "Something I definitely won't be mistaken for anytime soon."

Stil sniffs the air.

"Is that self-pity I smell?" She wrinkles her nose. "I wouldn't think a woman with her own fragrance would abide a scent so foul."

"It's not my fragrance. It's François's, and it's not self-pity." I slump into the backseat. "I'm just feeling a little sorry for myself."

"Ahhhh." Stil nods her little black-and-pink head sagely. "I see the subtle difference between the two. Look, nobody said this would be easy, but do you think it will be worth it?"

"I know it will."

Her tough-love face softens.

"Then just endure." She reaches over to tuck a chunk of hair behind my ear. "And just think. Your new man will be back soon. Bet that'll make things better, right?"

Or worse. The only thing worse than all this public tarring and feathering from Kyle's supporters and his crafty team would be Trevor having a front-row seat for it. Or even worse than *that* worse, him being tainted by it.

"He'll be home in, like, four days."

An eternity.

"You guys talk every day?"

"For a little bit." I swipe through screens on my iPad looking for Kerris's designs. "There's a six-hour time difference, and his schedule there trying to sort out that Collective mess is even crazier."

"Well, once he's back in your bed, you'll feel better for sure." Stil sneaks a look at me under her falsies. "I mean, you guys have…you know. Sealed the deal. Dipped the stick, right?"

Now I do out-and-out grin.

"I'm not talking about this with you."

I've always been extremely forthcoming with Stil about my sex life. Once I even sketched a guy's junk for her when I realized he was uncircumcised. So, yeah. No holds have ever been barred until now. With Trevor...I just can't. It's so different with him. So intimate. So clean. So *right*. Talking about it like we're in a locker room would defile it somehow.

"You know I live vicariously through your vagina." Stil grimaces, and rightfully so. "That came out wrong, but you know what I mean. Just tell me if he's as hung as he seems to be. I mean, a guy that big has gotta be hanging pretty low, right?"

I gather my things, shaking my head the whole time. I reach for the door and step out onto the sidewalk, drawing my cashmere coat a little closer against the wind. I lean into the car for a parting shot.

"I'll only say that he delivers on the promise his body makes."

As I slam the door, I hear her screeching.

"I *knew* it!"

I'm still grinning when the door opens to Kerris standing there. There was a time when I pretended not to see what Walsh saw in this girl, but I do. She's petite and beautiful, with dark hair and a sweet nature. The opposite of me in every way, inside and out.

She's also very pregnant. That belly looks much too large for her small frame.

"Are you having twins again?" I blurt out, regretting it immediately. I can't believe I'm one of *those* people who says insensitive things to pregnant women. Next I'll be feeling up her belly in the grocery store.

She laughs good-naturedly, stepping back to allow me into their home.

"Um, no. Just one this time." She passes her hand over that mound of baby, a small smile on her mouth. "One little boy due any day now, but maybe he's just a big guy like his daddy."

She searches my eyes, looking contrite. At first I can't figure out why, but then I realize she must think this was my dream. To be home with two of Walsh's kids and another on the way in the brownstone where he grew up. No, this wasn't what I envisioned for Walsh and me. I certainly wouldn't have answered my own door. I'd have help for that. I wouldn't have dinner going, the house fragrant with my domesticity. I'd have some version of Millie for that. As for the kids…who knows how having children would have affected me?

"It's okay, Kerris." I walk deeper into the house, stopping by the bannister that leads upstairs. "I'm good and over Walsh. I realize now that if we had gotten married, we would have basically become our parents. He would have become his father, working around the clock and neglecting his family. I would have become my mother, glad to see the back of him and probably living a separate life."

I look back to Walsh's sweet little wife in her maternity skinny jeans and a simple tunic blouse. This place, with its shiny floors and little baby gate at the top of the stairs, the smell of something already cooking for dinner, shows me she is exactly what a man like Walsh needs. This house—*she*—must be a haven for Walsh after the cutthroat world he occupies all day. For a man who never wanted to grow up to be like his father, he married a woman who would make sure he never does.

"I practically grew up here, too, you know." I tap my shoe over a familiar nick in the floor. "Walsh and I used to slide down this banister like monkeys."

I open my mouth widely enough for her to closely examine my front tooth.

"I actually chipped my tooth here doing that." I laugh, tapping the tooth in question. "Mother was furious. We got it fixed the next day, of course, but Walsh teased me for the longest."

"I never realized that you and Walsh were…" She trails off, searching for the word.

"Friends?" I nod. "Yeah, even though my parents wanted us to be the cornerstone of the Bennett dynasty, and convinced me that I wanted that, too, we were friends first. Walsh has always been good to me."

"He's furious that your father isn't supporting you against Kyle Manchester." Kerris's face shows her sympathy, her concern. "I'm sorry, by the way. I knew there was a reason that man made my skin crawl."

She lifts her hands for the coat I'm sliding from my shoulders, hanging it on a vintage-looking coat tree tucked into a corner of the foyer. She walks back to me, hands slid into her back pockets and expression hesitant.

"I, um…well, I just wanted to say our situations are different, obviously," she says. "But I know what it feels like to be violated, Sofie. The man who hurt me had been dead for years by the time I spoke out. The man who hurt you is not only still alive, but powerful and prominent, with many people supporting him. I think what you're doing is incredibly brave."

I've never heard Kerris's full story, but I know she speaks from time to time for the Walsh Foundation about being molested as a child. She's sorry for me? I can't imagine the things she endured so young.

"I appreciate that, Kerris." Something lodges in my throat. Maybe it's the crow I need to eat. "Look, I know you and I have never been on friendly terms. I was a bit of a bitch to you. Old habits die hard."

We both laugh at my admission, and I wonder if one day we could be friends. I don't have many of those. Never have, but I sure could use some in this three-ring circus.

"But it's obvious that you make Walsh happy," I continue. "And believe it or not, ultimately, that makes me happy. This is probably as close to apologizing as I'll get, by the way."

Kerris meets my eyes, a fractional smile settling on her lips.

"Wow, Sofie." She toys with a slim necklace hanging at her throat. "I never thought I'd see the day when you almost apologized."

We laugh again, and I feel things loosen between us a little more.

"I gladly accept your almost apology." Still smiling, she gestures toward what used to be, and I assume still is, the kitchen. "Let me check on this stew I've got going, and then we can head downstairs to my studio. The girls' nap is over in about an hour, and nothing gets done once they're up. They're tyrants, both of them."

"It smells delicious."

I sniff the air appreciatively, sitting at the farmhouse table a stone's throw from the island and counters that make up Kerris's work space. I remember Kristeene Bennett's kitchen as warm and cozy, but dark. They've renovated, adding a skylight that ushers in natural light to brighten the space.

"I know I'm totally the housewife stereotype, Crock-Pot and all." She lifts the lid, stirring the savory-smelling stew. "But I'm a country girl. That's never going to change. Walsh had them install a small greenhouse on the roof, so I grow my own vegetables. All the veggies in here were grown right over our heads."

The distance between the wife I would have been to Walsh and the wife he needed continues to grow. Pictures of their girls, Brooklin and Harlim, decorate the refrigerator. Framed finger paintings hold a place of pride on one wall. A toy bin in the corner rests on a rug, and I can imagine the twins playing there while Kerris prepares dinner. It's a scene, a life of domesticity I'm not sure I could ever achieve.

Only…something feels good about it. Looks are deceiving because Kerris, in spite of her modesty, is anything but the typical housewife. She owns a thriving high-end thrift store back in North Carolina and has someone like me here courting her to design jewelry. It's apparent, though, that this is her first love. This life with Walsh and her children, it's her first priority. I never saw this, not in my home and not with my friends growing up. Walsh at least had Kristeene for a mother, and a greater woman you'd never find. She probably planted the seed for this vision in Walsh's head.

A peace deepens inside me as that dream my parents planted gasps its final breath, dying right here in the kitchen where Kristeene used to serve Walsh and me banana bread after school. There's no doubt in my mind I could never have satisfied Walsh. And honestly, he probably could never have satisfied me. He didn't want me enough, and I realize now, experiencing the way Trevor wants me, and for the reasons he does, how it feels to be wanted and prioritized that much, that way. I don't know that I can ever settle for less than that again.

"Come on down to the studio." Kerris washes her hands, drying them on a towel draped over the oven handle. "I'll show you the pieces I've been working on."

The jewelry is as delicate and unique as its creator. Several pieces lay on the windowsill, drying and in various stages of completion.

"I'd buy this right now." I touch a bangle studded with rough stones. "I love all of these, Kerris. You're really talented."

"Coming from you, that means a lot." A blush steals over Kerris's high cheekbones. "Thank you."

"I mean it. I'm pretty stingy with compliments." I grin to remove any possible sting from my comment. "So how would you like to be a Haven artisan?"

"Your assistant gave me a little of an overview." Kerris sits down on her workbench, gesturing for me to do the same. "But tell me more."

I unpack the Haven vision for Kerris the way I did for Trevor, including the charitable efforts and future plans to expand into clothing, household items, and furniture.

"That's amazing, Sofie." New respect creeps into Kerris's eyes. "I kind of always thought you were just a pretty face."

"Oh, I am a pretty face." I tap my finger to my temple. "I'm just also very smart. I keep that a secret because if girls knew I had that going for me, too, I'd have even fewer friends."

Kerris laughs, shaking her head.

"That's sadly true in a lot of ways," she says. "Okay, I'm in. What's the next step?"

"You're in?" I clap my hands, a wide grin taking over. "That's great. I'm thinking we call your line K. Bennett for Haven. Whaddaya think?"

"I love that." Excitement lights Kerris's face and eyes. "Let's do it."

We talk through a few details, both sketching ideas on a pad on her worktable. My phone dings with a text. I grimace when I read the message.

"Everything okay?" Kerris returns a few of the pieces back to the windowsill.

"My guard dog was just letting me know he's back." I slip the phone into my purse. "He dropped Stil off at the office and is outside when I'm ready. Apparently a few reporters somehow got wind of the fact that I'm here and are outside. Sorry about that."

"Don't even worry about it. Has it been awful?" Kerris asks. "I mean, I know some of his supporters have been especially…"

"Vicious?" I finish for her. "Yeah, they have, but no one has actually threatened me or walked up to me saying awful things. Mostly online. There's been a lot of support, too. The security is just a precaution."

"I heard you have one person's support you can absolutely count on." A teasing smile plays at the corners of Kerris's mouth. "Trevor Bishop."

"Does Walsh tell you *everything*?" I complain, mock exasperation in my voice.

"Pretty much." She laughs, walking toward the door, allowing me to leave ahead of her before turning off the light.

Something occurs to me. I've never thought there was much I could learn from a girl like Kerris. We're nothing alike. Our priorities live on different planets, but she makes it work with a man from a completely different background, who grew up driven by completely different things. They figured it out and have one of the happiest relationships I've seen.

"Let me ask you something," I say as we climb the stairs to the kitchen on the main level.

"Ask away." She straddles the bench at the farmhouse table, facing me. "And take a load off."

I sit, resting my elbows on the table before turning my head to look at her squarely.

"You mentioned Trevor Bishop." I pass my hand over my hair, feeling a little self-conscious. "We are…seeing each other, like you said, even though we're keeping it kind of quiet. We're just so different. The press is even calling us the Sinner and the Saint."

"Oh, gosh. Why can't people be as interested in their own lives as they are in everyone else's?"

"Well said and preaching to the choir." I laugh a little. "How do you and Walsh make it work? I mean being so different."

"I let our differences keep us apart for a long time, as I'm sure you remember."

She gives me a knowing look, probably because I exploited those differences to keep them apart in any small ways I could, too.

"I married Cam for all the wrong reasons," she continues. "We had such similar backgrounds, grew up with the same struggles, even survived similar traumas, but in the end, none of that kept us together."

"So what *does* make it work?"

"This will sound like an oversimplified answer." She leans forward, her eyes serious. "But it's love. I love Walsh more than I knew I could love anything, and I'm absolutely confident he feels the same way about me."

She laughs, dipping and shaking her head, dark hair caressing her shoulder.

"Me, the girl who comes from nothing and no one, who doesn't even know her parents, ended up with a guy who comes from everything and a family that everyone knows."

"It didn't make sense to me either," I tease.

"I still pinch myself sometimes, that this is my life." She waves her hand around the don't-be-fooled-by-the-quaint expensively outfitted kitchen. "Not all this. These are trappings. This isn't my life. My life is that man who works harder than anyone I've ever met, but tries to make it home in time to tuck in our girls. He doesn't always make it, but he wants to. He wants this life with me."

"But how does it *work*?"

"Because we want it to." She twists her wedding band and ring. "Because it *has* to. He's more important to me than I am to me, and I'm more important to him than he is to himself. We find ways to put each other first and to—even though we're so different—value the things that matter to the other. To make sure the other person is positioned to achieve what matters to them. Whether that's me creating a home for our family so Walsh can focus intensely on Bennett Enterprises, or him supporting my ventures and loving me unconditionally, making sure I'm fulfilled, too."

Her sweet mouth takes on a hard curve.

"I know what it's like being in a bad marriage with someone who makes perfect sense." She shakes her head. "Give me the challenges of making it work with someone who makes absolutely no sense, but I can't live without. It's that desperation that makes you fight for it because you realize you have no choice. The alternative is to be without Walsh, and I've done that. I found out that I can't do it. Or at least I never *want* to again. It's miserable, and you ache like half of you is missing. And it *is* missing because even though on the surface we're vastly different, he has my heart."

I'm not sure what to say. The concept of loving someone so much that I put them first is almost completely foreign to me. It's not the operating system I saw in my parents' marriage, or in any of the Upper East Side unions I saw growing up.

A plaintive cry comes across the monitor on the countertop. Kerris walks over and grabs it, turning the volume down.

"That's Brooklin," Kerris says. "And Harlim'll be next."

Sure enough another cry comes more faintly over the monitor she's holding.

"Productivity is about to go down considerably." Kerris smiles. "You're welcome to stay for a while, though."

"No, I'm sure you're busy." I stand and we head toward the foyer.

"Actually, it was nice talking to another adult." Kerris pulls my coat from the coat tree in the corner. "With Mama Jess and Meredith still in Rivermont, and the girls consuming so much of my time, it's been hard to connect here in the city."

Mama Jess is like the mother Kerris never had, and Meredith is her best friend and co-owner of Déjà Vu, Kerris's shop in North Carolina. I can imagine the transition into New York society without them has been challenging. I take my coat, meeting Kerris's cautious glance with caution of my own.

"Maybe we could…" Kerris looks to the floor, then back up at me as the two cries, nearly indistinguishable from each other, reach us from upstairs.

When I don't respond, but just stare at her blankly for a few seconds, she walks me to the door, a polite smile in place of the openness I've seen from her over the last hour. I would have bet my favorite pair of Loubs that we'd never be in this place, but I think we are. I think we're going to be friends one day. I turn from the open door to face Kerris briefly, giving her a small smile.

"Hey, Kerris?"

She looks at me with raised eyebrows, half of her attention already up the stairs and in the nursery.

"Maybe we could."

Our eyes hold for an extra second before she nods, smiles, and closes the door.

CHAPTER TWENTY-SEVEN

Trevor

Johannesburg is one of my favorite cites in the world. It's gorgeous and cosmopolitan and sophisticated, but those aren't the qualities that draw me to South Africa's crown jewel. The dark, ugly shadow of apartheid could have defined this country forever. By all rights, it should have, but the courage and endurance of one unifying figure made something that seemed impossible a reality in a nation divided by hate and violence and prejudice— *forgiveness*. Of course it wasn't just Nelson Mandela who abolished apartheid, but every revolution needs a hero, and he was theirs. He led this nation in a revolution of healing, showing the world that we don't have to be defined by our mistakes. We can be redeemed. We can do better.

As much as I love this city, I want to be done with our business so I can get back to New York. Back to Sofie. I can't help but think of the scandals of her past Kyle's team has resurrected. She may not be leading a revolution, but what she is doing takes tremendous courage. She's risking a lot; taking hard blows to see if her hurt has the possibility to help. Wondering if her past mistakes make her irredeemable. I know they don't, and I'm so damn proud of her.

I sip from the glass at my elbow, savoring the Vergelegen V, one of my favorite wines from the famous Cape Town vineyard. I raise the glass in a toast to Henri. She always makes sure I have it when we're here.

"Is it good?" She sips her merlot, eyeing me expectantly.

"Always." I flake off some of the blackened panga, a South African fish seasoned with turmeric, cumin, and nutmeg, before turning my attention to the man joining Henri, Harold, and me for dinner. "And your steak, Thurston? Good?"

"Very." He speaks between chews. "How'd you think the meetings went today?"

I take my time answering, savoring every spicy bite.

"Satisfactory." I set my fork on the plate, giving this exchange my full attention. "I'll be interested to see how some of the Collective members who have been around for a while respond to the transparency measures I outlined."

Thurston pauses, fork hovering between his plate and his mouth.

"Maybe you don't know, but I *am* one of the original members of the Collective, Trevor."

"I actually did know that, Thurston." I give him stare for stare until he finally grins, and I grin back.

"I see." Thurston resumes eating, eyes sharp and set on my face. "You're that rare man who doesn't deal in bullshit, Bishop."

"I'm not sure that I'm rare," I say. "But you're right that I don't have much tolerance for bullshit, so tell me how you think the transparency measures will fare when we vote tomorrow."

Harold and Henri exchange nervous glances, but my eyes never leave Thurston's face.

"Why do I get the feeling this isn't the casual dinner I thought it would be?" Thurston asks.

"No harm in making conversation over a delicious meal." I lean forward. "Thurston, you know as well as I do that the Collective can't afford another scandal if we're to maintain our corporate and philanthropic integrity. Members disclosing possible conflicts of interest and voluntarily submitting tax records, which are public anyway, are just a few ways we can protect the organization against corruption and self-interest, the very things we're fighting with most of these countries' leaders."

"And will you be disclosing information about your personal life, Trevor?" Thurston's tone is casual, but his eyes remain sharp. "Rumor has it that you've been making some very, shall we say, interesting personal alliances lately."

I push my plate away, and set my elbows on the table, linking my hands into a shelf I rest my chin on.

"To what are you referring exactly, Thurston?"

"Well, is it true you're seeing Sofie Baston?" Thurston drops his eyes to the meal in front of him, conveniently avoiding my direct stare.

"I'm the one who proposed the transparency measures, Thurston, and will be more than willing, of course, to fully cooperate within the confines of the requirements, which doesn't include who I'm seeing romantically."

"So you *are* romantic with Sofie Baston?" Thurston looks up, eyes gleaming for a moment with a light that is all male. "She sure is something. I can't blame you. Few men could turn that down."

I'd hate to bash Thurston over the head with the Michelangelo Hotel's fine china, but if he oversteps, I will.

"It's really no one's business who I'm seeing." I take another sip of my wine, using precious seconds to control my irritation with the direction this conversation has taken. "It has no bearing on my work with the Collective."

"Surely you're not that naïve, Bishop." Thurston's cynical laugher irritates me even more. "Just be careful. It can't leave this table, but you are definitely the leading candidate to assume leadership. Everyone loves your ideas. It's apparent you have integrity and vision. Your business and personal record are above reproach. You're young and vibrant, which is something we need. I'm in your corner. That's why I tell you to be careful. Ms. Baston has made a very powerful enemy. If you're involved with her, then so have you."

I'm just about to tell Thurston what he and the rest of his cronies can do with their sage advice and inappropriate concern, but Harold, who knows me too well, cuts in.

"I'm sure the transparency measures will pass tomorrow," Harold says. "It's good business practice and will go a long way toward restoring public faith that we remain committed to the best interests of the nations we've been tasked with serving."

Thurston and I lock eyes across our overpriced hotel food briefly before sharing a guarded smile. Henrietta further steers the conversation in a different direction with a few anecdotes from the last Collective gala, which eases more of the tension until we're all laughing, finishing our meal and considering dessert.

"None for me." Thurston stands, rebuttoning his suit coat. "I have to watch my youthful figure."

He shoots me a grin, patting his stomach where it pokes against his coat.

"We aren't all doing Ironmans in our spare time to keep fit."

I grin back and wish him a good night.

"Did he just stick us with his bill?" Harold looks from Thurston's scraped-clean plate to his departing back.

"Thurston's bill is the least of our worries." Henrietta sits straight as a line in her seat, folding her arms across her chest. "Did you hear what Thurston said, Trevor?"

"Which part?" I keep my tone casual in the hope that this isn't going where I suspect it will.

"Come on, Bishop." Henrietta's eyes narrow at the corners, her lips tightening. "We need to talk about this."

"No, Henri, we don't." I pick up the dessert menu, even though I'm sated and don't want another thing. I need something to look at besides Henri's disapproving face.

"Hen, leave it alone." Harold spears the last of his fish. He always was a slow eater.

"No, Harold, this needs to be said." Henrietta turns her resolved expression my way. "That woman is going to cost you everything, Bishop."

Oh, hell. I didn't want to do this here. Now. Ever, really. I lower the menu and meet her concerned eyes.

"Henri, I know what I'm doing."

"Do you?" It may be a question, but her expression already has the answer. "The man I've known for the last decade does not chase supermodels all over New York City."

"Hen," Harold half protests.

"He doesn't risk everything he's worked for, *we've* worked for," she continues, "because a beautiful woman gives him some attention."

"Henri, you have no idea what you're talking about." I keep my voice as even as I can with anger building in my chest like a brick wall. "Stick to the business at hand. The *real* business at hand, not my private life."

"And poor Fleur!" Henrietta's eyes go wide and outraged. "To be exposed to that woman at the event last week."

"*Exposed* to?" I snap. "Sofie's not a virus, Hen, and you'd best watch how you talk about her. And have you forgotten Fleur and I broke up a year ago? Am I supposed to mope about it forever?"

"You broke the engagement, and for no good reason, so why would you be the one moping?"

"My reasons are my own and none of your business." I crush the linen napkin in my fist, hoping it helps me control my temper. "Fleur knows why we aren't together, and my reasons existed before I met Sofie and still remain."

I lean forward, fixing my eyes on my friend of more than ten years.

"What exactly do you dislike about her so much?" I ask. "That she's beautiful? That she posed nude? That she's been in high-profile relationships? I know women can be petty and jealous about her, but—"

"Jealous!" Derision twists Henri's mouth. "That woman has nothing I want."

"Do you even know what she's in the middle of?" I demand. "The allegations she's leveling against Kyle Manchester, the 'powerful enemy' Thurston referred to?"

"I'm sorry if what she says happened to her happened, but—"

"It *did* happen to her, Henri." Tension knots the muscle in my jaw.

"How do you know?" She tilts her head, eyebrows up. "What if it's just a scheme to get more attention? Like posing for *Playboy*? And did you know she had an affair with a married man? Someone's *husband*, Trev."

"She didn't know he was married."

"Is that what she told you?" Henrietta rolls her eyes, disgust marring her face. "And of course you believe her."

"The woman was raped." The volume of my voice doesn't rise, but my displeasure is inescapable.

"If it's true, I sympathize with her."

"Aren't you a feminist? A defender of women's rights? Women who've been subjected to injustices like FMG? Why would you, of all people, vilify the victim?"

"It's hard for me to see Sofie as a victim, Trevor. You can't compare her to someone like Halima."

Yet Halima recognized the same strength in Sofie that I saw right away. I can't help but remember how she connected with Sofie at the event, and I know Henrietta is wrong about her.

"I know her, Hen."

"No, you're screwing her, Bishop," Henrietta says. "There's a difference."

"That's enough, Henrietta," Harold interjects harshly, eyes distressed behind his spectacles. "Drop it before you say something you'll regret."

"Oh, she already has." I lean forward, colliding my eyes with Henrietta's. "You've been a faithful employee and a great friend, Hen, but if you ever talk about Sofie that way again, things will have to change."

"You would choose that woman over your friends?" Hurt floods her eyes. "Over our friendship? You've known her what? All of two months? Been on a few dates?"

My phone vibrates in my pocket, and I slide it out to check the screen. I put an alert on Sofie's name to keep abreast of what's developing back in the States. These Collective meetings have consumed my attention and focus almost completely. The brief snatches of conversation with Sofie each day don't come anywhere close to reassuring me that she's okay. And I suspect she's not telling me all that Kyle's campaign is up to, how difficult they're making things for her.

"Trevor, are you hearing me?" Henrietta asks.

I hold up a finger, silently asking for a reprieve from our battle royal so I can peer at my screen. My teeth clench at what I see.

Model Behavior: Details from a wild past continue to cast doubt on Sofie Baston's allegations of misconduct by Kyle Manchester, front-runner in next year's U.S. Senate race.

The video that accompanies the article only affirms my suspicions. Sofie emerges from Jalene's barre studio to face a clump of reporters, throwing questions at her, snapping photos, pressing to get a better shot. The huge guy at Sofie's back can barely fend off the mass of people for the short distance from the studio to the black SUV waiting at the curb. Sofie's face remains composed even in the midst of the chaos. She slips the hood of the sweatshirt she's wearing with her leggings over her head, concealing her face. My Princeton sweatshirt.

These meetings and the delicate nature of the transition of power have required an inordinate amount of focus. I've always been that guy who doesn't have to be in charge, but usually finds myself in that position nonetheless. And this week has been no different. Someone had to step into the leadership void left by Clarke's arrest. One thing I've never been is hesitant.

Seeing the firestorm now surrounding Sofie in New York pushes me to the brink of that singular focus I've never had trouble maintaining. Frustration boils beneath the surface of the face I keep expressionless. I want to be there for her, with her. I want to hold her and reassure her that she's doing the right thing, to make sure she's not swayed by the dirt Kyle's hurling at her head. I want to be there.

And I will.

"I'm going back to New York." I flip my phone facedown on the table and prepare myself for all the objections Henri will make that won't change my mind.

"We all are in three days." Henrietta doesn't look up from the dessert menu, but I know I have her attention.

"I'm leaving tomorrow after our last meeting." I pour myself another glass of Vergelegen V. I need it.

Harold only nods, pushing away his plate and picking up the dessert menu. Henrietta drops her menu, eyes widen.

"You're leaving early? But why? We have more meetings over the next couple of days."

"All goodwill stuff. Checking on investments. Nothing new and nothing you two can't handle."

"You're seriously going back to New York?" She lets out a scoffing laugh. "Weren't you the one saying you couldn't wait to be done with that city? Oh, let me guess. Now it holds a certain appeal."

"Have I ever missed a meeting I needed to be in?" I run a steady hand over my face, exhaustion hitting me for the first time since we touched South African soil last week. "I'm tired, Hen. I've been going nonstop, and yes, I want to be there for Sofie. You may not believe she was raped—"

"I didn't say I don't believe her," Henrietta says, her voice softer than it's been. "Her past just makes things awkward."

"Is it awkward that Kyle Manchester raped her when she was eighteen years old and she's lived with that secret for fifteen years?" Just thinking of the story Sofie told Karen and Shaunti fans my anger, and I can't keep it out of my voice. "It took her years before she could even be touched by a man without…never mind. Sofie doesn't owe you an explanation, so I'm not making one for her."

I stand to leave, stopped by Henrietta's staying hand on my arm.

"It's not that I don't sympathize," she says. "I do. I just don't want this fling to jeopardize everything you've worked for."

"Who says it's a fling, Henri? What if it's more? What if she's the one?"

Henrietta closes her eyes and shakes her head.

"She's not, Trevor. Not for a man like you."

It sounds so much like the nonsense Sofie spouted before we left. I have to convince her that we are good together and that's all that counts, but I don't have to convince Henri.

"I think we all need some space." I gently shake her hand from my arm. "You guys take the house for a few days when you get back. I'm sure you could use some time together without me around all the time."

"Bishop, no." Harold shifts his eyes from me to the woman he's been in love with for years. "It's your sister's house. You and Hen just need—"

"Some space, like I said." I push my hands into the pockets of my pants. "It'll be business as usual in every other way."

"You don't have to do that, Trevor." Henrietta swallows and blinks back tears. "I'm only trying to help. You know I love you like a brother, and I only want the best for you. I always want the best for you."

I bend to kiss her head, squeezing her shoulder when she leans into me.

"I know, Hen." I straighten and look from her to Harold. "But you don't see what I see."

"And what's that?" Henrietta asks, voice still watery with her tears.

"Sofie *is* what's best for me."

Henrietta drops her forehead to her fist, eyes closed.

"I'll see you guys when you get back."

And with that, I leave the dining room, already feeling lighter because I know tomorrow I'll be exactly where I need to be.

CHAPTER TWENTY-EIGHT

Sofie

I thought work would offer an escape, and it does distract me from the pandemonium some, but I can lose myself for only so long before the situation with Kyle pokes a hole in the bubble, reminding me that every time I step outside, my picture is taken and splattered everywhere like mud dragged in from a storm. Every morning I wake up to new sordid details about my past, some true and some concocted. Every day another blogger posts about me, supporting or tearing down. It doesn't matter to me anymore really. I don't want my name on anyone's lips. The selective microscope I'm under magnifies every flaw, but somehow seems to overlook any good I've ever done.

I prop my elbows on my desk and cover my face with my hands. I knew it would be hard, but I didn't expect to feel so alone. Like I'm standing absolutely naked in the middle of an amphitheater, hungry lions licking their chops over me, their next kill, their next meal. Ironic, since exposing my body has never bothered me. But this exposure of the soul, it's gnashing at my peace of mind.

Three taps at my office door pull me back to the task at hand. Stil pokes her head in, a strangely eager light in her eyes.

"Hiya!" She walks into the office and places a salad in front of me. "How's the day going?"

I shrug one shoulder, pulling the salad toward me even though my appetite has been nearly nonexistent.

"It's fine." I pop open the clear plastic top, wrinkling my nose at the salad. "It has olives and feta."

"Yeah, that's how the Greeks do it, sweetie."

I roll my eyes, but can't resist a grin. My first of the day.

"Smart-ass."

"One of us has to be." Stil leans over the desk and snatches one the olives I have no intention of eating. "You used to love olives."

"That was in the early two thous. I haven't eaten olives in years. It's like you don't even *know* me."

"Bitch," Stil mutters, chewing her olive.

"Hussy," I mutter back, my smile growing even wider. I needed this. Something other than Kyle Manchester and the media breathing down my neck.

"François's office called." Stil crosses her legs and settles back into her seat. "He wants to meet tomorrow to finalize details for Friday's press conference to unveil Goddess."

"Is it still at the Gansevoort?"

"Yep, François wants a final fitting for your dress when we can squeeze it in."

"Can we do Wednesday instead? And see if he can pull a few things for me to consider from his evening collection for the Walsh Foundation's benefit next month."

My heart lightens at the thought of being involved in the foundation's work again, even in that small way.

"Sure thing, Sof."

My cell phone on the edge of the desk rings, and Stil reaches for it before I do. It's become a habit for her with so many people calling to ask me questions, express their support or skepticism. She's become the grand call screener. Thank God for her.

"Speak of the devil." Stil inspects the screen. "It's Jo Walsh."

"Perfect. I have some ideas I need to share for the benefit."

I reach for the phone, already smiling. After Martin and Kristeene Bennett divorced, Walsh spent his summers in Rivermont with his mother, her brother, and his cousin Jo Walsh. I, in turn, would spend half my summer there, too. I don't know that Jo and I were what you'd call close growing up, but we tolerated each other, which was more than we did for most girls. She was always too busy trailing after Walsh and his best friend, Cam, to show much interest in the things that fascinated me—namely makeup, clothes, and boys.

"Hey, Jo." I nod at Stil when she indicates that she's stepping out. "I was just thinking about you. Well, about the benefit."

"Really?" Jo doesn't sound like herself. I can only imagine that balancing her work with the foundation while being a new mom could be taking its toll.

"Yeah. How's Cam and the kids?"

"Amazing, really." Jo's voice noticeably softens when she talks about her husband and their children, a young girl they adopted from Haiti and the son Jo had a few months ago.

"Glad to hear it." I walk over to the wall comprised mostly of windows, affording me an unobstructed view of the narrow Soho street below my office. "Oh! I wanted to tell you about an idea I had for next month's benefit."

"Sofie, about that…"

"So there's this amazing floral designer who's working with my new lifestyle website, Haven."

"Sof."

"I was thinking we could get her to design these one-of-a-kind centerpieces for the tables. She's brilliant, I promise. And I could donate those. It would be great exposure for her, too, of course."

"That's…well, that's very generous, Sofie, but I really need to talk about something before we go any further."

"Sorry, Jo." With my finger, I absently sketch an invisible heart on the windowpane, writing Trevor's name in the center. "Shoot."

"First, I just want to say I'm so sorry for what happened to you all those years ago, for what Kyle Manchester did to you." Regret spills into the momentary silence Jo allows. "I wish you'd felt then like you could tell me or Aunt Kris. We would have helped you in any way we could. I hope you believe that."

"I know, Jo." My finger falls away from the window, and I turn to sit on the sill, back to the glass. "I just…I was all the way in New York. You were in North Carolina. We weren't talking a lot by then. I didn't tell anyone."

I didn't have anyone.

"I'm so, so sorry it happened," Jo says. "I left you a voice mail last week. Not sure if you got it."

"My voice mail is so full, I haven't checked it in days. Sorry, and thank you for reaching out."

"Of course. Cam and I are here for you however you need us. However you need *me*."

"Thanks, Jo." Gratitude swells my throat. "That means a lot."

"I wanted you to know how much I personally support you before I tell you what I need to tell you. I don't really know how to handle this except to just say it, Sofie. The board met today."

I clutch the phone a little tighter, draping my arm across my chest to grip my elbow with my free hand.

"I see," I say quietly, foreboding hushing my voice. "And?"

"It was an impromptu meeting, called at the last minute," Jo rushes on to say. "They voted to suspend your responsibilities as celebrity ambassador to the Walsh Foundation."

The words pound my heart like a hundred mallets beating away until it is bloody and tender in my chest.

"Daddy and I, of course, voted for you," Jo says. "And Walsh would have. I know they pushed the meeting because they knew it would be hard for Walsh to adjust his schedule at such short notice. By the time he called in, they had a quorum and the vote had passed."

"I see." I can't find other words.

"It's not that they don't believe you," Jo says, her voice tight and anxious. "They said that all the media attention and the coverage distracts from our mission, and that the benefit would become about all of that, and not our goals and objectives for the night."

"So they'd also prefer that I not attend next month?" It's not a physical blow, but I feel it like a kick in the stomach.

"Sofie, you can come, if you like, of course." Jo says. "But not in the official capacity of celebrity ambassador. None of the photo ops or interviews you'd usually do representing us."

I want to stomp my feet and throw myself flailing to the floor and scream that it's not fair. That I wanted to do something good, for once, by exposing Kyle, and all it's done is complicate and destroy things.

"I understand, Jo." I shove the hot lump of emotion back down my throat so I can get this out. "They're right, actually. I can't even work out at six in the morning without a press corps showing up. I believe in the foundation's mission too much to detract from it. I mean that, Jo."

This hurts like a motherfucker, but I mean it.

"Aunt Kris is probably turning over in her grave right now that we are making things harder for someone we should be protecting." Jo's voice goes watery. "I just...I'm so disappointed in them, Sofie. I'm so disappointed in myself for not finding a way to stop this."

"No, Jo, really." I straighten from the windowsill and walk over to my desk, collapsing into my chair. "I knew going into this it would be tough."

"Yes, but from Manchester, from the press, not from people who are supposed to care about you. Supposed to support you."

"Jo, let's be honest here, though." Cynicism bends my lips into a jaded curve. "Half that board has been wanting to get rid of me since the *Playboy* spread. You and Walsh barely held them off the last time. This was a final straw for many of them, and they took this opportunity to do something they've wanted to do in the past. Get rid of me."

Her silence on the other ends confirms that I'm right.

"Sofie, there's one more thing." Jo clears her throat. "There will be an official statement released tomorrow about it."

I close my eyes, one hand cupping the side of my face. It's standard procedure. I know that, but it feels like a public betrayal. First my parents don't support or believe me, and now the foundation

I've given years of service to publicly distances itself from me. Kyle's camp will have a field day with this. Everyone will interpret this as more doubt cast on my claims and character. Disappointment balloons in my chest until there's no room for breath.

"Hey, Jo. I'm gonna go."

"Sofie, please. I just want—"

"It's okay." I swipe furiously at the tears scalding my cheeks. "I, um, just have a meeting, and need to go. Do what you have to do. I understand."

"Sofie, I hope—"

"I still want to donate the centerpieces, okay? I'll have Stil contact your office. Give Cam and the kids my best."

"Sof, if you could just—"

I disconnect. Not just the call, but from Jo. From the world that keeps battering me. The skin that has been thickening hardens to a crust over my heart, protecting and insulating me from any more hurt. Arrows seem to be flying from every direction, even from people and places I didn't anticipate. It makes me feel like I can't trust anyone. Like I can't depend on anyone. I know it's not true. I have Stil. I have Karen and Shaunti. My team.

But I want Trevor. I've known everyone else longer than him, but he's the only one I want right now.

"Stil!" I yell, knowing my voice will carry to the outer office. "Sketches!"

Stil walks in holding a leather portfolio.

"How was Jo?" she asks. "Everything going smoothly for the benefit?"

"Um, yeah, about that." I take the sketches from her. "Nix the gown from François. I won't be needing it."

"Okay. You have another designer in mind? Or already have something to wear?"

"No, I won't, uh, I won't be attending." I glance up from the latest sketches for the website design. "But could we get Emily to design centerpieces for it? Connect her with Jo Walsh. I'll foot the bill."

"Back up." Stil leans her hip against my desk. "You're not going? I thought you were really looking forward to it."

I may as well just tell her. They're releasing the statement tomorrow, but it's still hard for me to coax the words from my mouth.

"I'm not working with the foundation anymore." I trail a finger over one sketch for Emily's section of the site. "She did a good job with these. Sign off on them for me."

Stil jerks the sketches off the desk, her eyes honed in on my face.

"Not working with the foundation?" she asks. "But you love it. Why...what?"

I run one hand over my face and tip my head back, a weary breath barely making it past my lips.

"Long story short, they don't want all the shit surrounding me right now to distract from the mission and the objectives, so they are suspending my responsibilities. They're releasing a statement tomorrow."

"Jo sanctioned this?" Anger shakes Stil's voice. "How could she do this?"

"It's not Jo's fault." I almost choke on a laugh. "She fought it as hard as she could, but she was outnumbered. Walsh wasn't there for the vote, but he barely won the last battle when I posed for *Playboy*."

"Can't a girl pose nude and still want to do good in the world?" Stil slams the sketches down on the desk. "What the hell is wrong with people? I mean, you come forward to say don't vote for this douche bag who rapes women, and everyone makes you out to be the bad guy?"

"Stil, I know, but it is what it is."

"No, it is not fucking what it is, Sof!" She starts pacing and shaking her head. Basically working herself up into a lather. "I'm so disappointed in people. So mad about how we vilify victims, especially women. How you're the one who was hurt, and yet find yourself on the defensive. I just want to punch the world right now for how you're being treated."

"Hey, slugger." I find a smile somewhere, as much for her as for me. "Stop pacing before you pull something. Sit."

I slide the salad toward her.

"Have an olive."

And just like that, we're giggling. It's not real, this temporary lightness I find with my best friend. It's a Band-Aid barely covering a bullet hole, blood gurgling over the sides, but I'll take it. It gets me through the rest of the afternoon of meetings, one fitting I squeeze in at my office, and a video call about, surprisingly, an upcoming photo shoot. For a model, I'm not modeling much lately.

"Go ahead and knock off, Sof." Stil glances at her watch. "Whistle's 'bout to blow."

I tap my phone to display the time. Only five thirty. All that's waiting for me at home is my cold, cavernous penthouse apartment and a stack of takeout menus. And my dusty vibrator, which is a sad substitute for the real thing and has been sorely neglected of late.

"I think I'll work a little longer." I wave my hand at the door. "You go on, though. We've been at it since eight."

"I'm not leaving unless you do." Stil sets her mouth at that mulish angle I know too well. "I've already called the car around."

There's nothing I'm doing here that I can't do from home, but I want to hole up and hide from the world a little bit. My hesitation costs me because Stil marches over and snatches the profit projection from my limp hands, tossing it into the trash.

"You threw it away!" I tip toward the trash can, dismayed to see vinaigrette dressing all over my document. "Stil!"

"Oh, keep your thong on. I printed the damn thing. You have a soft copy in your email, so don't go all nineteen seventy-two on me. Nothing's ever lost in the digital age."

"But, I don't want to go home." I bite down on my lip, feeling bruised by all the hard knocks of the last week.

"Yes, you do. I'd come with you, but I got a thing." A smile softens that obstinate mouth. "You can kick your shoes off and curl up by the fire with your profit projection."

I'd rather curl up by the fire with my...what do I call Trevor? I still haven't figured that out. Though he seems to know exactly what to call me.

Mine.

I miss the way his kisses persuade me to forget everything else. How his hands caress me until I'm burning for him, straining toward him. I miss the heat of his eyes on my body when he thinks I'm sleeping.

The light in my office goes off.

"Stil, come on. Turn the lights back on."

"Nope." She grabs my purse and props the door open with her back. "Get up. Get out."

She chatters all the way to her apartment, where we drop her off with waves and kisses and promises to see me in the morning. As soon as she's out, the temporary smile falls right off my face and lands in the quiet she leaves behind. There's nothing to sustain it. I raise the privacy partition between me and the driver/bodyguard person whose name I can't remember right now. I miss Baker. He was so much more than just my driver, and I feel the loss of him more than the loss of my parents, which says a lot.

I'm so grateful that we aren't ambushed by a group of reporters in my building's underground parking lot. That happened once, but we've tightened security considerably since then. What's his name takes the silent ride up the elevator with me, his eyes trained straight ahead with unswerving professionalism. I'm tempted to kiss him on the cheek to see if he would blush like Baker, but considering the slut factor Kyle's team has raised considerably, that could be misinterpreted.

"Good night." I unlock my door, turning to face him. "See you in the morning. I'll be fine."

"Are you sure, Ms. Baston?" He peers past me into the darkened apartment.

"Yeah, I only need security when I'm out." I step inside, hand already on the knob. "Have a good night."

As soon as I step into my apartment, I know something's off. The air feels charged somehow, not like the desolate box I left this morning that only I've been inside of for the last few days. And the smell permeating the apartment—heavenly. I would assume I'd left something in the oven, except I don't cook—ever. Should I call what's his name back?

Fool that I am, instead of fleeing the scene of a potential homicide—my own—I walk as quietly as I can down the hall toward the kitchen. It's bright in there for an ax murderer, and most psychopaths in my limited experience don't hum "Benny and the Jets" while sautéing dinner. As soon as I enter the kitchen, a well-muscled back and broad shoulders block whatever is cooking on the stovetop. Even though my potential perpetrator faces away from me, I'd know that burnished hair, the wide, hard slope of those shoulders, and *that ass* anywhere.

"Bishop?" I'm scared to say his name aloud in case he's some fevered hallucination the sound of my voice would dispel.

But he turns, a wide smile on those full lips, and opens his arms for me. That's the only invitation I need. I drop my purse and am across the kitchen practically before it hits the floor. His arms are the sanctuary I've needed. Standing here in this circle of comfort, completely enclosed by his scent and his warmth, I feel safe for the first time since he boarded that plane last week.

"You're here." I whisper into his neck. "I thought…you aren't due back for another few days."

"This is true." The deep timbre of his voice rolls through me like a tremor. He pulls back to cup my face in his hands and search my eyes. "I wrapped things up early."

Whatever. Couldn't care less. He could tell me South Africa floated into the wild blue yonder and he paddled all the way to New York on a piece of driftwood. I wouldn't ask any questions. All that matters is that he's here. My fingers wind into his hair, pulling him down and close enough to kiss. We skip slow, sweet kisses and cannon straight to desperate, our groans and panting the only sounds in the kitchen while we devour each other. I can't stretch my mouth wide enough. Can't touch enough of him at one time. I need more hands, more nerve endings, to absorb this thrill, these sensations.

Trevor hoists me up, and my legs wrap around his waist. He reaches behind him to turn off the food and walks down the hall and toward my bedroom. It's too far. I can't wait. I'm too empty. I need him to fill me right here, right now.

"Now, Bishop," I say against his lips. "Fuck me against the wall. I want…please. Right now."

Wordlessly, he turns me against the wall. I lock my legs around him tighter while he undoes his belt buckle. The sound of his zipper sliding open has me dripping, has my chest heaving with anticipation. He leans in, taking my mouth captive and then sliding his tongue down my neck.

"Your breasts," he mutters into the silk collar of my blouse. "I want to see them."

I brace one hand against his shoulder while the other scrambles to loosen the buttons on my blouse, baring the almost transparent bra. My nipples are so swollen from the thought of him, they press painfully against the sheer cups. I tug one satiny shell down to expose my breast. His eyes eat at my naked skin, and his hands slip beneath my arms, lifting me until my breasts are right at his mouth. His lips take my nipple, suckling me, the sound wet and erotic in the silent apartment. Every pull and tug churns the want in my belly, from my core through my heart until every part of me is electrified with need.

"Are you sure you're ready?" His words singe the delicate skin around my nipple.

I nod my head frantically, so hollow, so aching and empty waiting for him.

He pulls away to look at me, desire zip lining between our eyes.

"Check and make sure." He glances at the space where our bodies interlock, the juncture of my thighs, and then raises his stare back up to sear me.

My eyes never leaving his, I slide my hand beneath my skirt and into my panties, rubbing my fingers into the wet flesh there.

"Show me," he says, eyes almost black, his voice a husky rasp.

I pull my fingers out, glistening with my readiness. He takes my fingers into his mouth, dipping his tongue into the valley between my fingers, sucking me clean, groaning at the taste of me. He presses closer and reaches between us, shoving my panties aside and thrusting into me so deeply, so fiercely, my back pushes a few inches up the wall. He's so long and thick inside me, there's room for nothing else, not even thought, only this intense pleasure I had begun to think I dreamed.

"Ahhhhh, Bishop."

There has never been anything like this. The way he's in and out of me, the scrape of my blouse against the wall with every thrust, hot and fast like a piston. The erratic syncopation of our heartbeats. The intimate slip and slide of bare skin against bare skin.

"Fuck," he says, voice graveled with desire. "I'm not wearing anything. Are we okay?"

"I *promise, promise, promise* I'm tested. I'm in the clear." My breath chops up in my chest every time he pumps into me. "And I'm covered. Oh, God, please don't stop. It's so good, Bishop. So good. You can't stop."

He nods, eyes pressed tightly together, one forearm against the wall by my head while the other arm curves under my backside. His head drops beside mine against the wall, and he leaves dirty, sweet, desperate things in my ear, accompanying every word with a deeper, harder push into my body until I'm riding the shimmering line between pain and pleasure, an agony of passion that wrenches cries from my throat until it's raw. I can't get close enough, tangling my arms behind his neck, gripping his hips with my legs, eliminating any space separating us. Emotion and sensation quake from my core, fanning out and over every part of me.

My orgasm starts as a shiver and builds and rolls through me. Trevor pounds into me without restraint, without control, overtaken by the rhythm his body sets, rattling the frames flanking us on the wall. In the grip of this tumult of sensation, I can barely hold on. My body tenses, bracing for the pinnacle. My heart races ahead. The thick muscles of his shoulders and in his arms supporting me tighten as he joins me, all his hunger, all his passion, flooding and filling me.

Finally.

CHAPTER TWENTY-NINE

Trevor

I'm so far gone over this woman. Henri would roll her eyes, deeply exasperated with me, but I can't help it. And as good as Sofie looks in my shirt and nothing else, her shower-damp hair falling past her shoulders, it's not that. Even that face and those long legs crossed as she eats the fish I made for her wouldn't have me missing meetings. Her strength draws me. I love the unflinching way she looks, not just at the world, but at herself, the way she faces her mistakes and her flaws head on. She believes that even flawed, she can do good. Her willingness to change and evolve, but to never be less than who she authentically is. All of those things tighten the grip on my heart I don't think she even knows she has.

"This fish is delicious." She gestures to the panga I brought back just so I could prepare it for her. "Is this another of your mother's recipes?"

"No, I had it at the Michelangelo in Johannesburg, and requested the recipe." I rest an elbow on her dining room table, my chin on my fist. "Glad you like it."

"I love it." A smile takes its time spreading across her face. "Tell me how you came to break into my house two days earlier than I thought you would be back. We kind of skipped the conversation part of the reunion."

When she smiles at me like that, we could skip it again, if it were left up to me.

"I finished everything for the Collective, and felt confident Harold and Henri could handle the rest of our meetings."

"You skipped meetings?" She slows her chewing while she processes what that means. "To come back to New York?"

I get up from my seat and squat on my haunches in front of her, positioning myself between her bare legs, sliding my hands under the hem of my shirt to rest at her hips.

"I skipped meetings and came back, not to New York," I say, answering the questions in her eyes, "but to you."

Her smile fades, eyes dropping to her lap.

"Bishop." Her whisper dances across my skin. "I don't want to get in the way of what you need to do for the Collective. You deserve that position."

"There's something you should know about me." I take my hands from under the shirt, sliding them to her lap, capturing her slim fingers between mine. "When the people I care about need me, I'm there."

"I'm fine." She shakes her head, slipping her hand behind my head to caress my neck. "I don't want you putting all you've worked for at risk."

"It's not."

Maybe it is. I don't care what Thurston insinuated or what Hen said. I believe my record and my character will speak for themselves, and if they don't, fuck it. I don't want to lead an organization ruled by the same politics I have to work against to make a difference.

"I know you're okay, Sof." I push the hair over her shoulder, curving my hand around her jaw and forcing her to look at me when I bring up the bad news she told me earlier. "I also know it has to hurt that the Walsh board let you down. Has to hurt that your parents have turned their backs on you. It has to hurt that so many call your story into question because of things that have fuck all to do with what Kyle Manchester did to you."

She holds our stare for a few seconds before pulling away, turning back to her plate.

"And how'd you get into my place?" She looks at me, telling me with her eyes she's not ready to deal with all the hurts I enumerated. "No one can even get up here unless they're on my list, much less inside."

"A little birdie helped me with that."

"A little bitch birdie named Stil, I presume."

"That would be the one," I confirm with a grin.

"No wonder she was so eager for me to get out of the office."

"She texted me about twenty times." I grin when my phone lights up. "Actually, there she goes again."

"Tell her she's on my list."

My grin fades as I read Stil's latest text.

"What'd she say?" Sofie takes another bite of her panga. "This really is divine. Make it for me again soon."

"She says 'Welcome back. Did Sofie tell you about her visitor?'" I look up from the screen, a frown sketched between my brows. "What visitor?"

"Why that little…" Sofie pushes her plate away, reaching for her wine to take a sip.

"What visitor, Sofie?" My voice hardens. "And don't lie to me."

Sofie rolls her eyes, crossing her arms over her chest. She clears her throat, tongue swiping across her lips.

"It wasn't a big deal. I wish Stil hadn't—"

"What. Visitor."

"Kyle came to my office one night."

Rage blurs my vision and pounds the blood in my ears, drowning out everything else for a second.

"What the hell?" I demand, on my feet, fists clenched. "When?"

"The day…" She drops her words for a second, drawing and releasing a quick breath. "The day before I went public."

"But that was more than a week ago." I run agitated hands through my hair. "How many times have we spoken since then, Sof? And you never even mentioned it?"

"I wasn't going to…well, I didn't think you needed to know."

"Why the hell would you not tell me that?" I slam my fist into my palm, needing it to be Manchester's face.

"Because of that!" she points to my fist. "I knew you'd respond just like this, and it won't help a damn thing, Bishop."

"Won't help?" I lean forward until our noses almost touch and our breath mingles. "What did he say? What did he want?"

She doesn't back down, doesn't shy away, but meets my anger with her determination.

"He wanted to convince me that I had it all wrong. He wanted me to drop it all, and when I refused, he tried to intimidate me."

"Who was there with you?" My voice, gruff, growling.

"No one," she whispers. "It was just me. He came by after everyone had gone."

Fury, helpless fury, almost chokes me. This is exactly what I feared, that he'd find a way to get to her. That I wouldn't be around to protect her.

"You should have told me, Sofie."

"So what?" She gestures to the fist balled at my side. "So you could go beat him to a pulp?"

"Fuck yeah, and I still can."

"Good luck with that." Her laugh is brittle. "He had a security detail with him. If you can get through those thugs, then what? It won't change anything, Bishop."

She stands, her eyes wet with rare tears.

"You could beat him till the cows come home, but it wouldn't change anything. It wouldn't change the fact that he raped me. It wouldn't give anything back to me. It won't make this any easier."

And that's it. I want to make it all go away for her. It drives me insane that I can't fix this, that I can't protect her from, not a knife or a gun, but from words. From opinions. There is a part of me that wishes I'd never encouraged her to come forward, because it's killing me to see her suffer this way.

"Sofie, I have to do something. He should pay."

She reaches up, clasping my face between her hands, melding our eyes together with the heat of her conviction.

"He will pay. That's why we have to do this right. I don't need you to beat him up. I don't need you pissing circles around me, going caveman, comparing sizes." She laughs humorlessly. "Believe me. Yours is bigger."

I rest my forehead against her, managing only a breath before she goes on.

"You are my only vulnerability, Trevor," she says, her voice trembling over my lips. "You're the only spotless thing in my life, and if he can bring you down to his level, if he can ruin you, he knows it will throw me off. He knows I may give in."

"Sofie, I'm not spotless. I'm not perfect, darlin'. I'm not a saint."

"No, you're no saint." She closes her eyes, huddling against my bare chest, rubbing my back. "But in this fucked-up fairy tale, you're the only prince I've got."

"Baby—"

"I need you to hold me." A tear escapes from under her closed eyes, making its way down her cheek. "I need you to remind me that there's more to me than what they say, that there's good in me. I need you to take care of me in the ways that *count*. Can you do that?"

She lifts her head, rubbing my biceps with one hand, taking my hand with the other. I'm speechless. All I can do is grip her tighter to me. I sit down, pulling her across my lap, pushing the hair off her neck so I can leave kisses there. Shelving my anger, my vengeance, is one of the hardest things I've had to do, but I can do it for now. For her.

"Yeah. I can do that."

Sofie's phone vibrates on the table, Walsh Bennett's name flashing on the screen. Sofie rolls her eyes and shakes her head.

"I can't," she says. "I know why he's calling, and I just can't. He wants to apologize for what happened with the foundation. I have to put that behind me for now."

My phone vibrates on the table, too, but with a news alert. I pick it up to read the headline.

"That may not be the only thing he wants to talk about, Sof." I turn the phone to face her. "Martin Bennett just officially announced that he's retiring to focus on his company's philanthropic work."

Sofie tenses in my lap, eyes going wide.

"Oh, God, Daddy. He's going to challenge Walsh, isn't he?"

I nod my head slowly, placing the phone back on the table. Sofie reaches for her phone. When she listens to Walsh's voice mail, he apologizes for not being able to save her with the foundation and confirms that the Bennett board will vote soon on its new CEO because her father has challenged Martin's choice.

"Oh, God. Daddy's really doing it." Sofie stares unblinkingly at her phone. "He's challenging Walsh, and essentially Martin's wishes, to make a play for Bennett."

"Bennett Enterprises is not your responsibility. Walsh can take care of himself, and your father certainly can and always does." I press a kiss to the softest lips I've ever tasted. "You're going to take the next few days to take care of *yourself*. And I'll take care of you, too, in the ways that count."

She smiles against my mouth, angling her head to kiss me back. The touch and slide of our tongues raises goose bumps across my arms and incites my dick to readiness despite the heaviness of our discussion.

"I'm sorry." She squirms in my lap. "I can barely walk. You can't put that big thing inside me again so soon."

Our laughter shatters any passion the moment holds, and I can only shake my head.

"I'm serious, Sof. Let me take care of you for a few days. Take some time off."

She looks at me from under her lashes, capturing the corner of her lip between her teeth, considering my offer.

"I can't completely check out," she finally says. "I have a meeting with François Wednesday, and we have a press conference for Goddess Friday."

"I have a few things here and there, too, but they can be done from right here." I cup her face. "Let's be together for a few days. Say yes."

I slip my hand between the buttons of my shirt she's wearing, palming her breast, rolling her nipple between my fingers until it swells and pebbles. Her lashes drop immediately, eyes closed, head falling back against my shoulder. My other hand slides between her legs, finding the wet warmth I crave. My mouth waters at the thought of tasting her, eating the sweetness nestled between her thighs. As soon as I slip my middle finger inside, her legs fall open, her hips matching my rhythm.

"That's my girl," I whisper through her hair and into her ear.

"Are you controlling me with sex, Mr. Bishop?" Her breathy question is barely a sound.

"It's the only thing I've found that does the trick." I laugh against her neck. "Otherwise, I'd have no upper hand."

"Oh, I like where your upper hand is right now." A husky laugh slips past her pouty lips.

My hand goes still, the wet walls of her pussy still gripping my finger past the knuckle.

"So it's a deal? You'll give me the next few days? Forget the madness out there for a while?"

Her face clouds for a moment with something other than passion, and I realize until I mentioned it, she'd managed to almost forget the firestorm waiting for her outside these walls. I want that for her. Just for a little while. Just long enough to repair some of the damage this process has already done. I see it in her eyes, and the bruises don't show, but I know they're there.

"Sof, is it a deal?"

She lifts her lashes to look at me, a small smile budding on her face.

"It's a deal." She turns so that her long legs hang on either side of mine, straddling me in the chair. "And maybe I underestimated what I can handle. I'm ready if you are."

Oh, ever ready.

CHAPTER THIRTY

Sofie

How much bliss can one person take? It's rhetorical, a question I don't want to answer in case I've reached my limit. I'll just keep testing the boundaries of happiness with Trevor. I didn't know the world could be this bright, that sex could be this good, this meaningful. Every time we're together, he entrenches himself more deeply, seeping through my pores. He has worked himself into my crevices, woven himself into the pattern of my life so intricately, I'd have to pick him out slowly and painfully with something sharp to separate him from the fibers of my heart. I didn't know I had this in me, but Trevor has been digging around inside me, unearthing things I thought were for other women. Not for me.

"Well, that was fun," Trevor says, holding my hand in the backseat of the SUV as we leave François's atelier in the Meatpacking District.

"Yeah, that was supposed to be *my* fitting, but François spent more time oohing and aahing over those shoulders and that ass of yours." We share a grin, fingers locked and caressing. "I knew François would have a ball with a strapping fellow like you."

"I'm not sure I like the term 'strapping,'" he says. "Makes me feel like Paul Bunyan."

"That sounds about right." I laugh.

"You should see my father. He's taller than I am."

"Good grief. How tall?"

"Six seven." He shakes his head, a smile creasing his handsome face. "And my mom's a little bitty thing."

He hesitates, studying our hands before looking back up at me.

"I'd love for you to meet them."

Gulp. What? Walsh is the only man I've dated whose parents I met, and I "met" them at birth. They were my godparents. I don't *do* parents.

"Um…wow. I don't know. Maybe someday."

"What about Thanksgiving?" His eyes stay steady on my face, but I feel his fingers tighten around mine. "Based on where things stand with your parents, I wouldn't trust you with a carving knife around them. Doubt you'll be eating turkey at home."

"Yeah." I smile so stiffly it feels like a cramp across my lips. "Especially not after my mother's latest statement."

A reporter asked her about my involvement with Kyle Manchester fifteen years ago. Mother recalled me as "troubled" and emotionally unstable during that time. She said I acted erratically, abandoning my college plans and moving "on a whim" to Milan. She also added that I was under a psychiatrist's care around that time.

Yeah, after Kyle raped me I changed my mind about college and saw a therapist for two years trying to recover. My mother *would* distort and use that information against me.

"Sof?" Trevor brushes his thumb over my cheekbone, luring me away from my thoughts and back into the conversation.

"I'm sorry, what?"

"I said so why not spend Thanksgiving with my family?"

"That's in less than a month, Trevor." I pull my fingers away from his to toy with a zipper on my skirt. "We haven't been...well, we've only been..."

"Dating?" He leans forward, eyebrows lifted. "Is that the word you're searching for?"

"I guess that word will do." A nervous grin plays across my lips. "It's just...am I really the girl you want to bring home to mama right now? I'm freaking notorious, and I bet your mother teaches Sunday school."

"You called it." He chuckles, taking my fingers back. "Every Sunday for twenty-five years."

"You don't think she's read all the stuff Kyle's campaign has said about me?" I melt into the leather seat at my back, shame slinking through my belly at the thought of Trevor's churchgoing mother knowing all my exploits.

"I think she knows her son." He tips up my chin, plumbing my eyes. "She knows I'm not a fool, and that I'm an excellent judge of character."

"Maybe you're having a lapse of judgment." My harsh laugh cuts into the air between us. "I've been known to have that effect on men before."

"What have I told you about comparing me to them?" Irritation thins Trevor's full lips. "I don't care who you've been with before. You're with me now."

Every time I think I can get lost in this thing with Trevor, something reminds me that he deserves better. Avoiding blogs and working from home for a few days hasn't made my problems go away. And so far, no one else has stepped forward with allegations against Kyle. So it's just me, hanging out to dry, making a stand that might not even do any good. That might just leave my life in ruins, but not fix anything.

"I want you embedded in my life, Sofie." Trevor's fingers tangle in the hair at my neck, telegraphing tingles across my scalp. "And I promise you I'm going to be embedded in yours. Nothing will shake me loose."

He kisses me, sending his tongue diving deep, invading, marauding, taking his pleasure, all along the way giving me more than I think my body can withstand. This pleasure, this special brand of pleasure, is wrapped in tenderness, spiked with care, and lined with an emotion I'm afraid to name. Even when he moves to pull away, my lips cling to his. My hands hold his face so I can greedily take more, savoring him, savoring these moments because something this good can't last. Not for me.

"We're here, darlin'," he whispers against my lips. "I just need to grab a few things from my office, and then we can head back to your place."

I look at the Brooklyn brownstone I haven't been back to since he left for South Africa. I know Harold and Henri are back. I'm still smarting from the disapproval that bloggers, Kyle's supporters, and the media dish out virtually. I don't need an in-person dose from Trevor's assistant.

"I'll wait here." I reach down for my iPad, setting it on my lap.

"No, you won't." He pushes the iPad off to the side. "Come inside. Say hi to my friends."

"Trevor, they don't like me." I swallow the hurt swelling in my throat. "Henri doesn't like me, and I can't promise that my inner bitch won't show her ugly face if that woman pushes me too far."

"Does she have doubts?" Trevor leans his arms above his head against the car, looking back at me unwaveringly, honestly. "Yes."

I drop my eyes and reach for the iPad again.

He leans in and tosses the device to the floor mat, grabs my hand, and gently tugs until I'm standing sandwiched between his big body and the car.

"Do I give a damn?" He presses his forehead to mine, breath on my lips. "Nope."

"Bishop, I don't want to come between you and your friends."

"Then let's hope Hen doesn't make me choose." He clasps my waist, fingers splayed over my back. "Because she would get the very short end of that stick."

Even though I don't want to cause strife between Trevor and one of his closest friends, hearing that he would choose me is a feather floating in my chest. I'd choose him over so many things that have been important to me in the past. I can't help but remember Kerris's impassioned speech about putting the person you love before yourself because you know they're doing the same. I realize for the first time that I'd choose Trevor over *myself*, and that scares the living crap out of me. This is as close to selflessness as I've ever come, and there's only one thing I can blame it on.

I'm in fucking love with Trevor Bishop.

Only I would have this epiphany on a busy Brooklyn street.

"You okay?" Trevor studies me closely. "Let's get this over with so we can go back to your place."

"Um, yeah." I paint a fake smile on my face, feeling it dry and tighten at the edges. "Sure."

I follow Trevor upstairs to his bedroom, and can't help but remember the last time we were in this room. I lie down on his bed, the divan cool at my back, stretching my arms over my head. Oh, if this bed could talk it would moan. My eyes drift to where Trevor flicks through a stack of papers on the desk in the corner, his powerful shoulders hunched, concentration wrinkling his expression into a frown. Even his frowns turn me on. The man fucks like a matador. Or maybe he fucks like a bull, and I'm *his* matador, waving myself like a red flag every chance I get. Provoking him to lust and want and…

I can't fill in that blank. I had an epiphany on the street. Doesn't mean Trevor did. I know he cares about me. But *love*? That's huge. That's something I've never considered. I had the artificial version with Walsh, basically an overgrown puppy love I should have shaken when he didn't take me to the prom. But this? This is all grown up, all consuming, forget-what-you-thought-you-knew-about-love *love*.

It's a secret I want to lock in my heart under a trap door covered by a thick rug. If there's one thing Daddy taught me, it's that love is a luxury people like me can't afford. People with enemies. People with dark pasts. People with secrets. Love becomes a weapon, and I'm in the fight of my life right now. I won't have anyone using Trevor against me.

"Hey, I think what I need is downstairs in the office." Trevor makes his way over to the bed, running his eyes over my body, lingering on my legs where my skirt pulls up. He runs his finger from my knee up and over the sensitive skin inside my thigh. He dips until his lips hover over mine.

"You laid out on my bed like this," he says, eyes wicked. "Is that an invitation?"

I bend my knee so that his finger slides higher, closer to the heat centered between my legs.

"Do you accept?"

He chuckles and taps my nose.

"You will not distract me." He drops a quick kiss on my lips before straightening. "At least not here. Now when we get back to your place, you're all mine."

"Hmmmmm." I flick my eyes up to the ceiling and then back to his smiling face. "You keep saying that."

"I keep meaning it." He gives me a wink before leaving the room.

I relish the quiet that takes over the room, leaving space for me to hug my discovery close. I love Trevor Bishop. Who woulda thunk it?

Approaching footsteps bring a smile to my face. I bend my knee higher, sliding the other leg to the side so he'll see my pink silk panties as soon as he walks through that door.

"Changed your mind?" I lift up on my elbow, my sexy grin petrifying on my face when my eyes meet Henrietta's. I drop my knee hastily, sitting up and pulling down my skirt. "Oh, Henri. Sorry. I thought you were—"

"Yeah, that was obvious." She glances around the room. "I thought I heard Trevor in here."

"He went downstairs to look for something before we go."

"So he *is* staying with you?" Henri tsks, which I didn't think people could actually do, but she proves me wrong. "I hate that."

"You hate that he's staying with me?" My hackles rise little by little. "Why exactly?"

"I hate to argue with him." She gives me a long-suffering look over the round rims of her glasses. "In all our years of friendship, we've never disagreed like this. That's what I hate."

"What are you disagreeing about?" I scoot to the edge of the bed and smooth the skirt over my legs, the closest I can come to modesty.

"He didn't tell you?" Caution slows Henri's words and puckers her brows.

"Why don't you?" I have a sneaking suspicion this is about me.

"If you must know…"

"Well, now I must."

She licks her lips and straightens her glasses even though they sit perfectly centered on her straight little nose.

"In South Africa, concerns were raised." She clears her throat, looking at me directly. "About Trevor's relationship with you."

"With me?" I press my hands flat to my chest. "What kind of concerns? Who?"

"Several of the Collective members who want Trevor to be the next leader are concerned about the scandals he's adjacent to being involved with you."

"Adjacent?"

"It means—"

"I know what 'adjacent' means," I snap. "Are you saying that they would hold everything going on with me against Trevor? That it might affect whether or not he gets the position?"

Henrietta doesn't look away from the insistence of my words, my eyes.

"Yes, I'm saying as much. *Others* are saying as much, but he won't listen." Her eyes travel from my leather knee boots over my skirt and up my fitted sweater. "He won't see reason because all he can see is you."

"Trevor's a grown man." I narrow my eyes at her. "A smart man, not to be led around by the nose. Give him some credit."

"Oh, it's not Trevor I don't give credit." She tilts her head, a non-smile on her face. "He's worked too hard to see it all go down the drain because he's infatuated with some woman who can't keep her name out of the tabloids."

"Oh, you mean my salacious rape allegations?" Gloves off. Done with trying to gain this woman's sympathy. "How very naughty of me, going off and getting myself raped."

"It's not the rape, Sofie. I'm sorry that happened to you. It's all the things that keep coming out about you that have nothing to do with the rape charges."

"It's *all* about the rape charges, Henri. You know that."

"But it's your life. Your *choices*. Things you brought on yourself, and I don't want to see them brought on Trevor." She turns to walk out the door, but looks at me over her shoulder before she goes. "I think you actually do care about him. If you do, maybe think about how this will all affect his life when you're done with him."

Even minutes after she's gone, her slimy words stick to my skin. If I really love him, can I put his needs before mine, even when it might hurt us both? When he walks back into his bedroom, holding the file he went looking for, and his eyes find mine, tender with promises, I'm not sure I can.

CHAPTER THIRTY-ONE

Sofie

You're quiet." Trevor slides his thumb over my palm, concerned eyes on my face. "What's going on?"

"Nothing." I muster a fake smile. I hate being phony with him, but it's a hard habit to break. "Just thinking."

"About what?" He rubs my knee, pulls my head to his shoulder, and kisses my hair.

"About the Goddess press conference Friday." The lie comes easily to my lips, only affirming that I am too false for such an honest man.

"That dress François fitted you for today is gorgeous. You'll knock 'em dead."

"It is," I agree, the words barely registering. The only words I hear are the ones Henri dumped all over me at Trevor's house.

The privacy partition rolls down, surprising me. What's his name is so unobtrusive, I'm usually barely aware of his presence, but his eyes seek mine in the rearview mirror.

"Ms. Baston," he says. "Clive from your building just called.

There's some work going on in the underground lot. Will you be fine getting out at the curb, and maybe Mr. Bishop can walk you in while I park?"

"Of course, that's fine," Trevor answers before I can. He loves the fact that I have security, but feels like I need it only when he's not around. I think it offends his alpha sensibilities to think someone else is protecting me when he's here. His protectiveness has only intensified since he found out about Kyle's visit.

Trevor takes my hand, helping me step onto the SUV's running board. He keeps my hand as we walk toward my building. Before we can make it to the entrance, one reporter after another approaches, until we're surrounded by them, a shoal of piranhas circling us. All asking me the same question with one voice in a hundred different ways. I can't make anything out until my brain seizes on one word from the furor of their interrogation.

Baby.

I jerk my hand from Trevor's, turning wide eyes on him.

"You have to go. Bishop, right now, you have to go."

"What?" He sticks out an arm, fending off a reporter shoving a microphone in our faces. "What the hell are you talking about? I'm not leaving you. We're almost inside."

But not close enough. God, so close, but not close enough.

The last person I expect or want to see shoves her way through the crowd, eyes livid and mouth distorted into a scarlet slash across her face.

"Seville." I barely get the name out, the simple math of them asking me about a baby and Esteban's wife showing up here equaling disaster for me. And Trevor right here to witness it.

"You bitch!" Seville screeches, lunging for me, fingers extended like talons toward my face. Her nails rake over my cheek, leaving a trail of fire across my skin. Trevor grabs her around the waist, dragging her back. Panic tears at me, pulling at my seams, ripping any façade of calm away. Even as reporters block the door, hurl questions at me, I still try my best to calm her down.

"Seville, wait. I can explain, but not here. Come inside."

"Explain?" Her heavily accented English sags beneath outrage and pain. "*Si*, please explain to me that you had my husband's baby. That you killed my husband's baby! Explain that, *puta*!"

"Baby?" Trevor's eyes snap to my face. "Sofie, what's she talking about?"

"Sofie, can you address these new reports that you were pregnant with Esteban Ruiz's baby?" A reporter yells at me. "Is it true you had an abortion in Milan?"

I close my eyes and draw a shaky breath, hoping against hope that this is an old nightmare about long-buried secrets, and I'll wake up any minute. But when I open my eyes, it's still pandemonium, with reporters hurling questions and accusations at me. Seville is still straining against Trevor's strong arms, trying her best to maul me. Trevor's eyes still question me. I'm still a twig in a tornado, tossed madly to and fro.

"Do you know how long I have tried to give him a son?" Seville yells, tears streaming over her hollowed cheeks. "Fifteen years. Fifteen years I have tried, and you were with him what? *Months?* And you get my husband's child? You took that from me."

Her tortured cries grip and twist my heart. I had no idea.

"Seville, I'm so sorry, but I—"

"Now you have apologies?" Tears ravage her face, her hatred contracting and expanding with every labored breath. "You are poison in a man's blood. A man is never rid of you. You spit on everything that should have been mine. I spit on you, *puta*!"

She spits in my face, and cameras flash. I can't even flee the glare of what feels like a million lights. I'm stunned; a living, breathing affront trapped in this spectacle. I wipe her spit from my face, humiliation wrapping around my whole body, a vine winding from the ground and anchoring me to the spot.

"Sofie!" That voice penetrates the miasma of shame and horror enveloping me.

"Sofie," Stil says again, her eyes set on me, waiting for me to respond. "Let's get you inside, hon."

Details filter in like light through a dark cloud. Stil isn't alone. Geena, my publicist, and Karen are right behind her. All urging me toward my building. Stil grabs my arm and pushes through the wall of flesh and flashing bulbs. I look over my shoulder, seeking out Trevor. He stands in the middle of the mess I've made, Seville slumped against him, limp, weeping, distraught. I did that. I didn't mean to. I didn't know my photographer lover was her husband. I didn't know an ill-fated pregnancy would break her heart this way. I didn't know the man I love would end up holding the bag of my folly.

The man I love. Our eyes connect for what feels like the last time. I stop moving forward, turn back to him before I realize it.

"Sofie, go!" Trevor shouts, pulling one arm from Seville to wave me inside, ahead. "I'm right behind you. I'm coming. Just go."

"He's right," Geena says, speeding us toward the door of my lobby. "This is a disaster. Get inside."

I'm galvanized into action, rushing to the entrance, my team insulating me from the questions, surrounding me, protecting me.

Clive holds the door open for us, his eyes anxious.

"Ms. Baston, I'm sorry," he says. "If the underground parking lot had been done, none of this would have happened."

"It's not your fault, Clive," I manage to assure him.

"Let me know if there's anything I can do," he calls from behind us as they rush toward my private elevator.

I stop and turn, catching his eyes, resisting Stil tugging on my arm to pull me inside the elevator car.

"There is something you can do for me, Clive." The words queued up in my throat will hurt me like I'm cutting off my own arm, but they have to be said. If I love Trevor, they have to be said. "Take Mr. Bishop off my list, effective immediately. He's not to be let up."

I step into the elevator, a preternatural calm taking over my body, cell by cell. Now that Trevor is out of the picture, protected from the toxicity of my life, I can focus on taking that bastard Kyle Manchester down knowing that I'm the only one who will suffer the consequences. I swirl bitterness, rage, and indignation into a witch's brew I plan to force-feed Manchester personally.

I don't take my eyes off the numbers, lighting up one by one as I head toward my tower fit for a princess, even though I'm not one. Never have been. If anything, I'm the frog, and my prince is probably already trying to scale the wall I just erected, but he won't be able to. I've made sure of that.

"Sofie, what was that you said to Clive? Why would you do that?" Stil demands, her eyes like lasers on my profile as I study the ascending numbers headed toward my penthouse. "You're ruining everything."

"No, not everything." I harden my expression, freeing it from the pain soaking through my heart. "This time, I'm only ruining myself."

CHAPTER THIRTY-TWO

Sofie

I'm wearing green, my signature color. This is my signature hairstyle, the blond hair flowing past my shoulders, straight as a board to the middle of my back. Makeup—expert. Heels—high and outrageously expensive. The green dress François designed for me molds every curve like my body was a canvas he painted it onto. The skirt stops mid-calf, clinging from hem to throat. Even the sleeves fit my arms like skin. There is no room for fat in such a creation. The woman who wears this dress must be fit and flawless.

And yet when I look at myself I see only mistakes. I wear my sins as surely as a scarlet letter blazing across my chest. I hate the reflection staring back at me. This dress feels tight. This hair feels heavy. This makeup, thick enough to camouflage the angry, red scratch on my cheek, feels like it's caked all over my face, and I can't breathe. I can't do this.

I'm no goddess.

"Ready?" Stil enters the small room where I'm waiting at the Gansevoort Hotel. "I think every reporter in New York, including the *National Geographic* correspondent, squeezed into that ballroom."

"Not surprising." I turn to the side in the mirror, needlessly checking the dress for bulges and wrinkles. "The biggest freak show in this town is here."

"You're not a freak show, Sof."

"Tell that to the protesters outside carrying signs that say 'baby killer,'" I say quietly.

"Sof, I'm so sorry. Those are Manchester supporters picking at bones to make sure the support swings Kyle's way. You know that."

"They're picking at bones all right." I press my lips together. "Like buzzards hovering over my carcass."

"No one's paying them any attention."

"Oh, the reporters certainly are. You can best believe they're getting their B-roll ready for the six o'clock news."

"Sof, you know when you're ready to talk about..." Stil hesitates before going on. "About anything. I mean, you know."

I meet her eyes in the mirror, silently begging her not to ask me about the baby. She's known me too long and too well not to get the message. She lets a breath go, running her hand through the spiky hair.

"I'm good, but thanks." I turn to face her. "Is François going mad? He can't have imagined when he chose me as his inspiration that I'd come with all this baggage."

"Are you kidding me?" Stil snorts, twisting her matte red mouth into a grin. "He's practically jumping with glee. I think he's of the all-publicity-is-good-publicity school of thought."

Publicity? It seems that every news outlet in the world carried the same headline this morning.

"*I spit on you,* puta*!*"

And thanks to modern technology, camera phones all around captured the whole dreadful scene, giving anyone who'd like one a play-by-play of my awful confrontation with Seville.

"Well, I'm glad this publicity is working out for somebody." I retouch my lipstick, which doesn't need it.

"You seemed to be courting some attention yourself last night." Stil's eyes harden on my face. "I mean having dinner with Rip at Minnow. It was like gasoline on a kitchen fire. If they weren't talking about Seville, they were speculating about you and Rip getting back together."

"Mission accomplished then." I smooth my hair once more, turning to check for lipstick on my teeth.

"Is there a game plan here, Sof?" Stil stretches her arms out before dropping them to her sides. "We're supposed to be partners, and I'm in the dark about so many things right now. Like why you're cutting Trevor out and making the world think you're back with Rip."

"I don't care if the world thinks I'm back with Rip." I study the shoes pinching my feet. "As long as they don't think I'm with Trevor. That's all that matters."

"You think this is protecting him?" she asks incredulously. "From what? He's calling every hour, has been to the building several times asking to come up. You don't just throw a man like that away, Sof."

Thank God the door opens. If I have to hear any more about how much Trevor wants me, how he's fighting for me, I won't be able to hold out. I'll *walk* all the way to Brooklyn in these damn shoes and bang on his door until he takes me back.

"You are ready, *oui*?" François asks from the door. In his midsixties, François is still a handsome man, distinguished and always perfectly attired in a suit of his own design. His salt-and-pepper ponytail, a nod to his flamboyant younger days, is tamed into line down his neck.

"*Oui.*" I walk over to him, placing a kiss on his cheek. "How do I look?"

"*Magnifique, toujours, ma petite.*" He dangles my hand over my head and turns me to get a full look. "Just as I envisioned you. My Goddess. And the scent, so beautiful, yes?"

"Beautiful." I lean toward him so he can smell it on my neck. "I'm wearing it now."

"*Parfait. Parfait.*" He hooks my elbow through his and starts toward the door. "As we discussed, the curtain will drop to reveal the ad."

Just what I need today. Fifteen feet of my nearly naked body. It's all shoulders, knees, and face. No lady bits or tits, but still. Why couldn't I have posed in say...a habit? Sister Sofie has a nice ring to it. Maybe I should consider a convent once I'm done with modeling. This ridiculous banter running in my head is further evidence that I'm barely holding on, as if I needed proof. I may present a placid surface, may seem to be held together by steel bands and wooden bones, but it's all as fragile as porcelain. I know, *only I know*, that one more thing could shatter me. And I can't have that with half of New York waiting to see the Goddess.

As soon as we take the stage, the buzz in the room escalates to a fervent hum of speculation that has nothing to do with the perfume I'm wearing. I can't summon a smile, hard as I try, so I freeze my face into Ice Princess mode, hoping they'll take it for arrogance instead of numb terror that I'll fall apart in front of them all.

"Ladies and gentlemen," François begins, leaning into the mic to elevate his voice over the others in the room. "Esteemed members of the press, thank you for coming today. When I considered my new fragrance, I knew I wanted it to embody all that is beautiful about womanhood. I met Sofie Baston fifteen years ago when she was fresh out of high school, new to the runway. I was the first to call her the Goddess, you know."

He chuckles, offering me an affectionate smile I try my best to return.

"She was a goddess then, and she is a goddess now. Even more so."

The audience dutifully applauds. I look out for the first time. There are actually a lot of friendly, familiar faces. Mostly people from the industry I've worked with for years, mixed in with the story-seekers.

"Without further ado, I present to you my new scent, Goddess!"

François gestures to the wall behind us, and I hear the curtain drop. The crowd gasps, varying degrees of horror on their faces. Is it that bad? I'm afraid to look. Maybe something was Photoshopped badly, or is it a shadow of a nipple? What could it be?

I thought I was prepared for anything. Thought I could withstand whatever they threw at me, sure that I could duck before the next blow fell. But there was no ducking this. The word *WHORE* is spray-painted in bright red letters over François's perfume ad. They may as well have sliced open my veins and bled me out to scrawl it in my blood.

I've barely had time to absorb the initial shock, when my publicist, Geena, is right beside me, pulling my elbow to get me off the stage. I'm submitting, letting her drag me away, when Halima's words whisper to me again, as clearly as if she stands right beside me.

I tell my story every chance I get. Every time I do, I raise a fist against my oppressors.

"Stop." I jerk my arm from Geena's grip, digging my costly heels into the carpeted stage. "No, stop."

"Sof," Geena whispers urgently. "We need to get you out of here. This is not good."

I shake her free and walk back to the podium. François's sorrowful eyes meet mine, and I don't know if he feels worse for me or for his beautiful defaced ad. I press a quick kiss to his cheek and step to the mic.

"First, I want to apologize to my dear friend François," I say, my voice barely shaking. "This is such a special day for a very special man."

I look back at François, who blows me a kiss, eyes sad.

"I hate that all the drama surrounding me lately has intruded on his art, on this lovely scent I'm truly honored to represent."

I grip the sides of the podium, pressing my elbows against the wood to scaffold myself.

"This is all because I dared to speak out against a man who hurt me, a man I suspect has hurt other women the same way. He's a powerful man," I say. "And I'm not the first victim he's tried to silence and to intimidate. He's succeeded before."

I press my lips close enough to the mic to smear my lipstick.

"But I'm still here, Mr. Manchester, and my story remains the same. You may find people to call me a whore. You may find people who will call me a homewrecker. You may even send some to march out front and call me a murderer, but you will never, *ever* find anyone who can call me a coward, and I'm not backing down."

There're cameras everywhere. I find one to look directly into, narrowing my eyes with all the indignation and fury building in me with atomic force.

"Me, you won't silence," I tell Kyle. "Me, you can't make go away."

And with that, I allow Geena to pull me off the stage, to bundle me into a waiting car at the rear of the hotel. To smuggle me into my building, managing to avoid all the press out front. She herds me along, and I let her, but as soon as we reach my apartment, I stop her at the door. I stare her down, and just shake my head, closing the door in her face and locking it.

For a moment, I just stand there, unable to process any of it. Then the fortress I've built around my emotions starts crumbling. That thick skin that crusted over and is now as tough as an old scab covering an ancient wound cracks open. I wondered how it would feel when they found something sharp enough to cut through all the layers. I didn't know they'd come with an ice-tipped stiletto. I didn't know they would plunge it through my heart.

All the pain comes at once, like an avalanche I can't ward off. The old pain of what Kyle did to me, what he took from me. My parents' betrayal, a lifetime of their indifference. Losing my work with the foundation, the closest I've ever come to doing good. The violent ignominy of Seville's confrontation. All the insults and innuendos piled on my head and shoulders for the last few weeks. I feel it all and at once, and it is so much heavier, so much harder to bear than I thought it would be.

I stare at myself in the bathroom mirror. The Goddess looks back at me—perfect, composed, beautiful. She's such a lie. Such a shell, good for nothing but covering up pain. I hate her. I want this fucking signature color—*this green*—off my back. I claw at the neckline until it gives a satisfying rip, exposing my bra beneath. I peel the dress away, tossing it across the bathroom to land in my sunken tub. I kick off my shoes and strip away my underwear until I face myself naked.

And it's still not enough.

My hair swings down my back, the hair that so fascinated Esteban Ruiz. I'd wake up to him running his fingers through it every morning in Milan. I rummage through my bathroom drawer, searching for my shears. I've seen women do this in movies and wondered what's the point of cutting your hair when you hit rock bottom? Where is the *relief* in that? I can't speak for the many women who've gone before me into the cutting cliché, but for me it's the weight. The weight of other people's opinions, their judgments. It's the lie of my identity entwined with something that hangs around my shoulders, but is already dead.

At the first snip, I wait for the weight to lift. If I can just shed these trappings, this artifice, that lie about my pain, I'll feel lighter. I'll feel better. I snip again, lopping off a slivery chunk of hair and watching it waft to the marble floor.

Nothing. Still no lighter.

Tears boil in my throat, running over my cheeks like hot water as I snip and chop and clip until I'm standing in a silvery pool of my own making, the pile of hair silky against my bare feet and ankles. I catch a glimpse of myself in the mirror, and finally the Goddess is gone. In her place is a naked girl with butchered hair. Tears have washed her makeup away, and mascara streaks her face in sooty trails. A bright red scratch across her cheek stands out like an exclamation mark.

I sink to the cold floor, falling onto my side and pulling my knees to my chest, rolling myself up until I'm as small as an atom. With nothing left to cover me, I finally feel the pain, and it is awful, but it is real. It is true. I can't hide from it anymore.

I'm tired of trying.

CHAPTER THIRTY-THREE

Trevor

I've missed something.

Something vital, and it's bugging the hell out of me. I am, by nature and by necessity, a meticulous man. I don't mean that my socks all have their own cubby and all my shit is color sorted and alphabetized. I'm meticulous about the things that really *matter*. I'm meticulous about people. I observe them. I discern. I intuit. I'm rarely wrong. And if I'm not mistaken, Sofie Baston loves me. I saw it in her eyes our last morning together. It charged every touch, every kiss. I know it the same way I knew she hungered for significance.

Because I recognized it in myself first.

Henri can say we're not right for each other. Sofie can say it's too fast or she's not good enough. Everyone can tell me it will never work. Sinner, saint, whatever. I know my own heart. I always have. It told me I couldn't spend the rest of my life with Fleur, and it tells me with Sofie, I must. And she feels it, too. I'd bet my life on it.

So why am I reading a caption under a picture of my woman

having dinner with that damn quarterback? At Minnow last night? Why did she take me off her list? Why won't she return my calls? Or texts? Why is she boxing me out when all I want to do is protect her? Why didn't she tell me about the baby? About the abortion? It grates that she still doesn't trust me to accept her, flaws and all. I can't blame her. She's been rejected, exposed, and disdained in the past. For someone like that, unconditional love and acceptance is a foreign currency she doesn't know how to exchange. I experienced it from my family and closest friends all my life. I have to remember for Sofie, it's still a novelty.

But she could have told me.

I drop my head into my hands, elbows on my desk. I shove aside the documents ratifying the transparency measures I proposed for the Collective. I can't care about anything else right now. I'm no good.

"Long day?" Harold asks from the office door.

"Something like that." I lean back, composing my face and propping one elbow behind me on the chair.

"Still no word from Sofie?" Harold's eyes and voice hold caution. He rightfully ascertained that I'm a powder keg set to blow at the least provocation.

"No, and I don't get it." I shake my head, meeting my best friend's eyes. "I know she needs me, but she won't let me in. Believe me, I nearly got arrested trying."

"Did you see the latest development?" Harold takes the seat across from me.

"You mean dinner with Rip?" I grit my teeth but manage to speak. "Yeah, I saw. It's bullshit. There's an explanation for it."

"No, not that." Harold frowns. "You didn't hear?"

Dread creeps over me like a morning chill.

"What happened?"

"She had a press conference or something earlier today."

"Yeah, for her new scent, Goddess," I say quickly. "What about it?"

"Apparently some of Kyle's supporters, or maybe some protesters, defaced the ad. You can pull up the footage. It's everywhere."

I immediately search for the press conference on my laptop. The footage is awful, and Sofie is magnificent. Not just beautiful. It's what she says and how she stands. I don't see a woman's curves and the perfect hair and makeup. I see conviction. I see courage. I see a fighter, and she's my match. Let anyone try to tell me differently, even Sofie herself.

"She's pretty badass." Harold's eyes and words hold respect.

I glance up, pride in her making me smile, even though she won't even see me right now.

"Yeah, she is." I shake my head, but my thoughts don't settle. It still doesn't make sense. "I've been retracing my steps to see what went wrong. We were fine. We were fantastic, actually."

We made love that morning. It was perfect. I made omelets. We showered together. We laughed over things that only we would find funny.

"We left her place and came here," I say aloud, not seeing Harold, but seeing that morning. Seeing Sofie stretched out on my bed upstairs, smiling and tempting me to make love to her again. "She seemed quiet when we rode back to her place, but we were fine. And then when all hell broke loose at her apartment building, it's like a switch flipped. I don't know what she's doing or why she's doing this to us."

I lean forward, resting my elbows on my knees, hands hanging between them.

"To me," I add. "I don't know why she's doing this to me."

"Maybe I do," Henri says from the door.

I glance up to find her in the spot Harold occupied before he sat down.

"What do you mean?" I demand, tensing. "How would you know why Sofie's shutting me out?"

Henri walks fully into the office, sitting beside Harold, her expression tight. She takes off her glasses and cleans them on her shirt. It's her tell. She always does that before she apologizes. What does she have to be sorry for, and what does it have to do with Sofie?

"I'm waiting, Hen." I keep my voice even, but it's a struggle. "What do you know about it?"

"I, well, I…" She leaves it there for a few seconds, slipping her glasses back on and then peering back at me from behind the protection of the lenses. "She and I had a, um, conversation the other day."

Harold closes his eyes and shakes his head from side to side.

"Hen," he says. "We talked about this."

"What kind of conversation?" My teeth clamp off all the other questions I want to hurl at her. "What did you say to her?"

"Well, I just…I mentioned some of the concerns we had about—"

"We?" I slice in. "Who's we and what concerns?"

"I told her some members of the Collective expressed concerns about your relationship with her." Her head drops forward and she bites her lip briefly before going on. "And I told her that being with her could jeopardize everything you've worked for. Everything you want."

I shoot to my feet, leaning over the desk and jabbing my finger into the papers spread in front of me.

"How the hell do you presume to know what I want, Hen?"

"I d-don't." She stammers when people yell at her. "I…I j-just know how h-hard you've worked. She—"

"What else did you say?"

She presses her hand to her temple, like I'm giving her a headache.

"I, well, just that I…" She pulls a breath in from her chest and exhales slowly before looking back to me. "That if she cared about you she'd think about what will happen when she's done with you. I think, since things went so badly the other day, that maybe she's trying to protect you."

"Henrietta," Harold says sharply before I get the chance to respond. "Can't you see he loves her?"

I glance at Harold, surprised by his astuteness. Attracted to? Really into? Lusting after? He could have said any of those things, and been correct, but he said love. And I do love Sofie. I'm just surprised he knew.

"I thought she was a phase he was going through," Henrietta whispers, blinking back tears under Harold's rebuke. "I'm sorry."

I walk around the desk and perch on the edge.

"Hell, Hen." I reach down to grab her hand just as a tear splashes on it. "We've been through a lot. You know I love you like a sister, but Harold's right. I love Sofie. I know you don't get it. I know you don't approve—"

"No, now I get it." She looks up, blinking owlishly behind her glasses. "I saw that press conference earlier today. I get what you see in her."

The tight muscles across my shoulders relax just a little. A smile eases its way onto my face.

"Good, because you're going to see a lot more of her." I grimace. "If I can get her to see me at all."

My phone buzzes in my pocket, and when I see Stil's name flash across the screen, I take it as a sign that things might go my way.

"Stil, where is she?" I walk out of the office, already headed for the foyer and grabbing my coat from the hall closet.

"I…we're at her apartment." Her voice strains tears through the words. "I'm worried about her, Trevor. She's locked in the bathroom and—"

"Locked in the bathroom?" I stop on the sidewalk, raising my hand to hail a cab. "For how long?"

"Like the last couple of hours." Panic highlights her words. "Maybe I should have called maintenance or something to break the door down, or I could jimmy the lock. She…she just won't open up."

"I'm on my way." I slide into the backseat of the cab. "Do me a favor. Call downstairs and get the key. They'll do that for you. Make sure I can actually get in and up this time."

I can't free my voice from irritation that Sofie blocked me that way. At least now I think I understand why, but I won't feel much better until I'm sure. Until I can hear it from her for myself.

Once I'm inside the apartment and in Sofie's bedroom, right outside her bathroom door, I hesitate. What is on the other side? I know Sofie wouldn't let this lead her to hurt herself. She's too much of a fighter for that, but these last few days have cut deeply, have bruised and beaten her in ways she couldn't have been prepared for.

Stil stands right at my back, so close I can practically feel her breath. I turn to face her, placing my hands on her shoulders and bending down until our eyes are level.

"Hey, why don't you go get a drink or something?" I give her thin shoulders a reassuring squeeze. "Just give me a few minutes with her."

"I'm not leaving." Stil's eyes are hard as pebbles in her little heart-shaped face. "I've been with Sofie a long time, and I've never seen her like this."

She looks down at the floor, clearing her throat before looking back up at me, determination on her face.

"I'm not leaving."

Thank God Sofie has this woman. Her parents certainly offer no support. I pull Stil in for a quick hug and drop a kiss on her cheek.

"I'm not leaving either," I say. "So she's got both of us. Just trust me with her for a little while, okay?"

She looks like she's still not sure, glancing at the closed door for a few moments. She finally exhales a heavy breath and leaves the bedroom without a word.

I don't bother knocking. I use the key Stil got from maintenance, turning it until the bathroom door swings open. My heart plummets at my first sight of her. I know she's not dead, but she's so completely still in a small lifeless knot on the bathroom floor, wearing nothing at all. She doesn't even respond when the door opens. The beautiful hair she's known so well for surrounds her, severed and cast down into silvery heaps on the marble floor.

I take a few steps until I can see her face, and her eyes stare vacantly ahead, tears rolling silently down her cheeks, into her mouth, onto her neck. I want to squeeze the life out of something, to rage at everyone who hurt her and left her for dead. To choke

Kyle Manchester and everyone from his team. But I can't do any of that right now. I can only do this.

"Sofie," I say softly. "Sit up."

She doesn't speak, just shakes her head, eyes fixed on nothing and unblinking. I reach for her, startled by how cold her arm is.

"You're freezing, darlin'." Still no response.

I scoop her up and carry her into the bedroom. She doesn't protest when I pull the covers back and carefully place her under the sheet and comforter. Without thought, I kick off my shoes and crawl in behind her, pressing my body to her back, reaching for her hands and chafing them between mine.

I don't know how long we lie that way, the silence broken only by our breathing. Slowly, her back begins to relax into my chest, and I scoot as close as I can, tucking my chin into the cove between her neck and shoulder. I cross my arms over her waist, pulling her into me as tightly and gently as I can.

"I didn't abort my baby," she whispers.

I freeze. As much as the questions line up in my head, wait on my tongue, I hold them back. She has to do this, to tell her story in her own way. I squeeze her fingers between mine, silently encouraging her to say more.

"I...I was so young." Tears crack her voice, and she sniffs before going on. "I knew I was pregnant at the Paris show. I was scared. I didn't know what I was doing. I'd always thought I'd sow my wild oats and then settle down with Walsh, but he didn't seem much interested in a life with me. I had this amazing guy I thought loved me, and I started thinking maybe *he's* the one. Maybe *we'll* have a family."

Her laugh sounds harsh in the quiet darkness of the room.

"I was such a fool," she says. "I'm having this man's baby, and his wife shows up, confronting me, calling me names, making a fool of me in front of the whole world."

She shakes her head, the jagged pieces of hair brushing my chin.

"There was some foolish part of me that wanted that baby," she says. "Who did I have? Not my parents. I had no real friends, except Walsh, and he never wanted to be more than that. I thought, This is mine. I'm not giving this up. I wanted to believe Esteban when he told me their marriage was over. I was all set to tell him about the baby, but I needed reassurances, so I pressed about when he was getting the divorce."

She draws in a trembling breath.

"He finally laughed in my face and said, 'You actually think I would leave my wife for *you*, Sofie? This is all there is.'"

My jaw hurts from how tightly I'm clenching it to tamp down my anger. That little shit. I could crush his skull for doing that to her.

"So I didn't tell him," she continues. "I didn't tell anyone. I pretended it was just not there for a few weeks; like it would go away. I had shoots and shows. I was sick all the time, but not eating. I was so busy, and I...I guess I didn't take care of myself."

For a few moments, I know she's not with me. I know she's lost in a place she needs for herself at least a little longer. And then she invites me in with her words.

"I had a shoot in LA." Her voice is as soft and wistful as a sigh, barely there. "I had an early flight to catch. I woke up and I was...there was blood in my sheets. So much..."

I feel her muscles tightening as her story unfolds, and I rub her arms, hoping to soothe her.

"I had no one to call." I can hear in her voice that she's been transported back to that morning, to the fear and panic. It's there, woven into her words. "I...I hadn't seen a doctor. Only took a test. I called the closest thing I could think of. My therapist. She was a rape counselor, but she lived not too far away. She came and got me and took me to a hospital, but it was too late."

Sofie takes the corner of the sheet to wipe at her tears, sniffing quietly.

"I don't know how they found out. My medical records were private. They got it wrong. I did have a D&C, but it wasn't an abortion. It was a miscarriage."

She shivers despite the shared warmth of our bodies.

"And I wanted that baby. I wanted it for myself. I wasn't sure what I was going to do. Who knows what I would have done in the end, but when I lost it, I wanted it. I do know that."

She quakes with the cries wrenched from her. I feel every heave and every rough sob, not just the motion and sound of it vibrating through my muscle and bone, but I feel it in the places unseen. I feel it in my soul, and I know it's because Sofie and I are connected by something that goes beyond sex, beyond friendship. We are connected by love. I know I can't experience this hurt as deeply as she does, but I feel it with her. I'm attuned to every motion, every tear, every sigh. An intimacy that transcends flesh and blood tangles us together, so I know when she finally falls asleep. And I know it's not only because this day has left her spent, exhausted, but because here with me, sharing these hurts with me that she's never shared with anyone before, she found some measure of peace.

CHAPTER THIRTY-FOUR

Sofie

I jackknife to sit upright, confused by my surroundings. I dreamed of that night again. The night that severed me from the innocence of my mind and body. Sleep transported me back to my bedroom after the prom. I was wrapped in my fluffy robe, my spine, a pipeline for rivulets of water dripping from the hair hanging in tangled clumps around my neck. Icy water pooled at the small of my back. My fingertips puckered from the shower. My nails, broken from the fight, folded into my palms. My skin, scalded neon pink from all the scrubbing. But the scrubbing couldn't reach the shame. Nothing could.

But I'm not there anymore.

I'm not slumped on the floor in the bedroom where I hosted sleep-overs for the popular girls growing up. I'm in bed, and it's not the pink and white four-poster in my parent's Park Avenue house. The headboard is quilted and tufted at my back. I'm not in my fluffy robe. I'm naked, and a thickly muscled thigh brushes up against my hip.

The room's bulky shapes clarify as my eyes grow accustomed to the predawn light. A huge lump next to me rises and falls only slightly under the covers, the sound of breath drawn and expelled the only noise in the otherwise quiet room. My hand wanders a few experimental inches until I encounter the warm, hard slope of a naked shoulder. I slide my fingers into the hair at his nape, the strands cool and silky.

Bishop.

My relief is so deep and profound tears sting my eyes, and I have to catch a sob in my hand before it wakes him.

He's here. Oh, God, he's here. Thank God.

While I slept I was trapped in a montage of memories from that night fifteen years ago. I'm not sure how much of it was a fictional scene my subconscious cobbled together from scraps in my head, and how much of it was real. But the other part, the part where Trevor gathered me close—cold, naked, catatonic—and brought me to bed, that was real. The part where I unlocked the cell where guilt and shame held my past prisoner, and I told Trevor all the things no one else knows—that was real. The part where I fell asleep experiencing something I, by reason of my shitty week, had no reason to feel—peace—that was real. And everything real was because of the man asleep beside me.

I don't have the strength to push him away again. It nearly killed me the last time. I know Kerris said putting him first is love, but maybe I'm too broken for that kind of love. Maybe I'm too selfish to put what's best for him over the overwhelming need to have him in my life. To keep him. My heart aches that being with me might cost him his dream of running the Collective. I'm torn, but not perfectly, evenly in half. Most of me is too grateful to have him back, damn the repercussions.

"Sof?" Trevor asks, his voice gravelly with sleep. "You up, darlin'?"

I pass my hand over his brow, exploring the strong, high cheekbones and square chin. I'd know this face anywhere. Even in the dark, the angles, the planes, the curve of his mouth—they rivet me. He brings my hand to his lips, repositioning himself until his head and shoulders rest in my lap on top of the comforter. I slide my hand under his chin so my thumb can trace his mouth. This simple intimacy soothes the ache in my soul I thought beyond reach.

"Are you okay?" He pulls my hand down to his broad, bare chest, mingling our fingers.

"I'm better now that you're here." I pause, trying to swallow my guilt, but it doesn't go down easily. "I shouldn't have pushed you away and shut you out like that."

He tilts his head back, angling to see my face even in the dim light.

"No, you shouldn't have, and if you do it again there will be consequences."

"Like what?" I find a smile because I know this version of Trevor, and he always makes me smile.

"Like locking you in my house on Tybee Island and making you my sex toy."

My laugh is helpless and husky.

"You sure know how to punish a girl, Bishop."

"Don't do it again, Sof." The humor faded fast, and his sober tone behooves me to listen.

"I won't. I promise." I close my eyes, ashamed of the very public stunt I pulled. "Trevor, about Rip. Nothing happened between us the other night. I just...I wanted to throw the media off your trail."

He's quiet so long I wonder if he doesn't believe me. After a few moments he turns, grasping my hips and sliding me down until we're lying face-to-face, the brightening skyline revealing his watchful expression.

"Did you kiss him?" His voice pulls tight, braced for my answer. "Did he touch you?"

I reach up and push the hair, just now growing back, away from his forehead.

"No. I told him I'd finally agreed to see him face-to-face so he could have the closure he thought he needed." I shrug. "It was just an excuse, and had the added benefit of distracting the media from your involvement with me."

His hands at my hips spread over my bottom, his fingers warm through the sheet. He dips his head to my ear.

"How many times do I have to tell you that you're mine, Sofie Baston?"

My heart flips behind my sternum, his words sending a thrill through me. I fold my arms between us, elbows bent, fingers locked around his neck.

"And you are mine, Trevor Bishop."

"About damn time," he says, closing the space between us, pulling my lips between his, his mouth possessive, claiming me and yielding to me in the same breath. He pulls back after a few moments, pressing our foreheads together and running his hand over the choppy mess of my hair.

"Thank you for telling me about Rip," he says. "I needed to hear you say that, but in my heart, I knew nothing happened."

"How'd you know?" My hands press into the hard muscles of his back, run down to the taut waist.

"Because I trust you." He tilts my chin. "And because I figured you were trying to protect me. Henri told me what she said to you about the Collective."

I carefully pull my chin from between his fingers, lowering my head. I wouldn't blame him for choosing the Collective over me, but the same heart that flipped moments ago, hurts from that possibility.

"All I know is the woman who made a sacrifice like that for me, the woman I saw at that press conference yesterday," he says, taking my chin again and locking his eyes on mine. "That woman is worthy of my love. I just hope I'm worthy of hers."

If there is such a thing as time in this utopia we're in right now, then it stops while I try to make sense of what he just said.

"Love?" My voice lays limp between us, uncertain. "You...well, you—"

"Love you, yeah."

"Bishop, you don't have to say it." I shake my head. "If you—"

"Well, I need to hear *you* say it." He traces my eyebrows, his long fingers pushing back my hair. "Do you?"

There's no rationale to us. He's the saint. I'm the sinner. He's always known he wouldn't settle for anything other than an urgent love. I've only ever had phonies, sorry substitutes for this real emotion, this visceral connection we share. We shouldn't be here together, but we are. Our hearts defied those odds, and I can only be grateful.

"With everything," I whisper, tears on my cheeks. "I love you with everything I have."

He frames my face with those big hands, thumbs brushing at my tears, eyes melded with mine.

"Then you understand why I can't ever let you go, right?"

I laugh into the kiss he initiates, a mixture of mirth and emotion that has me mumbling against his lips.

"Oh, I'm counting on it."

CHAPTER THIRTY-FIVE

Trevor

The promise of a love like this, the possibility of it, led me to break my engagement with a woman who made perfect sense. This kind of love compelled my father to drive all night to be under the same roof as my mother. I refused to settle for anything less with no assurances that I would ever find it.

But I have, in the most unlikely place I could have imagined. On a billboard in a city where I never wanted to live. My dad used to say when he saw my mom, it was like a click in his head, the sound of his soul locking with hers. Is that what happened to me that day when I saw Sofie up on that billboard in Times Square? Who knows? Who cares? Click or no click, all that matters is that we're here now, and I haven't made love to her in two days.

Time to rectify that.

Except her phone keeps beeping with a text alert, and it's wrecking my moment.

"I should probably get that." Sofie traces circles on my shoulders with her nails. "It could be—"

"Doesn't matter who it is." I reach over to silence the alert, then lie back down to face her, grasping her waist and dragging her into me. "Whatever it is, whoever it is, they can wait."

"What if it's important?" Her smile tells me she couldn't care less about whoever is on the other end of that text.

"This"—I gesture between our two hearts—"is important. Everything else can wait."

She nods, eyes fixed on me as she takes my bottom lip between both of hers, coaxing my mouth open to her.

"Are you sure, Sof?" I frown, my hands pressing into the subtle curve between her back and her butt. As much as I want this, it was just last night she was weeping on the bathroom floor. Just last night she was unburdening things she'd carried around nearly half her life. "Yesterday was traumatic. I can wait if you need me to."

"I *can't* wait." She runs her tongue over the scruff of my jaw, dotting kisses over my chin, my neck, my shoulders. "You're right. Yesterday hurt."

She pauses, pulling back so I can see the shadow that passes over her face.

"But your love heals me, Bishop." She lowers her lashes, shaking her head. "I know it sounds silly, but—"

I take that excuse captive with my lips, swallowing any words she would have said. Gently, carefully, like she's fine crystal, I turn her to her back, positioning myself between her long legs, supporting my weight on my elbows. One hand pushes back her jagged, uneven bangs. My kisses traverse her face, her neck, the fragile bones of her shoulders. I'm steadily moving lower, pausing to suck her plump, tight nipples. Stopping to lick into the hollow of her belly button. Nibbling at her hips.

"God, Bishop, yes." Her breath catches every time I possess another part of her.

I hook an elbow under her knee, pulling it up. Pushing it back, feathering kisses across the silky skin of her inner thigh, licking and kissing until I reach her sweet center. I force myself to slow down, to take my time. I open her up, pulling the bud between my lips. Dipping my tongue inside. Her whimpers spur me on, making it harder to go slow. The taste of her hits my tongue, and all control slips through my fingers like loose reins. I grab her bottom roughly, pulling her into me, spreading her wider, eating voraciously, with hunger I can't check. One hand presses her knee back more, the other grazes her stomach on its way to her breast, to knead, to squeeze, to pinch, to roll. To love.

"Don't you dare stop." Her fingers plow into my hair as the rhythm of her hips matches the stroke of my tongue. "Please, don't stop. Don't…Bishop, don't—"

Her words dissolve into plaintive cries, her nails digging into my shoulders, her knees pressed into my head as she falls apart, syllables strangled in her throat. I live for this. I've waited for this all my life. To have the woman I love this way, an intimacy that comes only with knowing you are loved in the same way you love.

I rise up, propping myself on my elbows, aligning our bodies. I don't ask if she's ready. I know she is. Tremors still roll through her, and at the first thrust, I feel her quaking against me. She grips me tight, each time I pull out, her body reluctant to release me. She's not crystal. She's not glass, and as much as I wanted to be gentle, my body takes over, mercilessly slaking itself inside her. She anchors her heel behind my thigh, meeting every thrust.

"Yes. Just like that, Bishop. I love you," she whispers, meshing our fingers. "I love you so much."

Pleasure tips her head back into the pillow, eyes pinned to the ceiling above, mouth falling open with a silent sob, tears running down her cheeks. She clings to my shoulders, burying her head between my neck and my shoulder. "Don't ever leave me. God, Bishop, don't ever…"

"I love you, Sof." My throat is raw with emotion. My body slave to the want, the love, the unrelenting rhythm driving us both. "I won't go. Promise."

Love and lust crest between us, climbing and climbing until we crescendo. She splinters around me, her tears wetting my neck and shoulder. I drop my head into the pillow by her hair, cupping her head, twining our bodies so tightly it feels like she's drawing my breath and I'm drawing hers. Like her heart beats in my chest, and her heart beats in mine. I know in that moment, she's the fire burning in my chest, and I'd chase her down. I'd follow her anywhere.

CHAPTER THIRTY-SIX

Sofie

Trevor, we should get up." I lift up on one elbow, running my nail between his pecs. "It's late."

"Is it?" He groggily opens one eye. "That must be why I'm starving."

"Me, too. I wonder if there's any—"

A heavy knock on the door cuts me off. The wrinkle between my eyebrows matches the one between Trevor's.

"I hope you're decent," a muffled voice says testily through the door, "because I'm coming in."

Stil steps into the room, a hand shielding her eyes.

"I hate to interrupt this love fest, but—"

"You stayed here all night, Stil?" I pull the sheet up over my naked breasts and shoulders.

"Of course I stayed," Stil snaps, dropping the hand from her eyes. "Well, hello there."

I follow her eyes to Trevor's bare chest above the sheets. I yank the covers over him up to his chin while he just chuckles.

"Keep your eyes to yourself and off my boyfriend, hussy."

"Oh, so *now* you claim him." Stil's smile widens, eyes ping-ponging between Trevor and me.

"What's it look like to you?" I toss my head back, laughing like a lunatic because the happiness reaches into madness. Reaches into idiocy, it's so far beyond what I can contain. Trevor's eyes laugh back at me, and I think he's as happy as I am. I think that's how this works.

"Well, as delighted as I am for you both," Stil says, eyes sobering, "the world is waiting. You gotta get up, Sof."

"Waiting?" I slink down lower into the covers. "Get up for what?"

"Breakfast, for one." Trevor gestures to Stil. "Maybe you could get on with this so I can go cook us something."

"I want a Denver omelet," I whisper from beneath the sheet covering my mouth.

"Geena's been calling you all morning." Stil walks closer, phone in hand, carefully averting her eyes from any parts of Trevor uncovered. "I can't hold her off much longer."

"What's she want?" I mumble, hoping it isn't more fallout from the disastrous perfume release. "Is it about yesterday?"

"In a way." A hint of a smile touches Stil's lips. "Apparently, someone very important saw the press conference yesterday."

"Half the world did." I swallow the embarrassment working itself into my throat at the memory of the word "whore" scrawled behind me.

"This is a volunteer from Kyle's campaign." Stil gives a dramatic pause, lifting her penciled brows. "Who wonders if you meant it when you said you would stand with anyone who came forward against Kyle Manchester."

Trevor and I go still at the same time, our eyes finding each other's across the sheets.

"Is she saying—"

"She won't say any more than that to anyone but you." Stil extends her phone. "Thus Geena calling every five minutes to see if you're still in here fucking."

That makes twice in a week I've blushed, a record for my cheeks. Trevor just laughs, shaking his head and leaning back against the headboard, completely unabashed. If the media could see their "saint" now.

"Have her come here to the apartment." I need to shower. My hand flies up to my hair. "And wash my hair."

"*Wash* your hair?" Stil leans forward with her hands on her hips. "Just wash? Oh, it's a rescue mission, baby."

"It can't be that bad." I run my hand over the choppy strands.

"You look like the Bride of Chucky, and that's an insult to her." Stil narrows one eye, assessing the mess I made. "Lucky for you I graduated from the best cosmetology school in Jersey."

She heads toward the bathroom, signaling for me to follow.

"Jersey?!" I mouth to Trevor, eyes wide and panicked.

An hour later, I'm clean, and Stil has unbotched the botched haircut, turning my head to various angles so she can admire her handiwork.

"Much better. It'll do for now." Stil lays the shears on the marble counter. "You should have done this years ago."

"What?" Sarcasm twists my lips. "Had a nervous breakdown?"

"No, cut your hair." Stil nods decisively. "It's kinda Mia Farrow."

I have to agree. With all the blond hair gone, and the silvery cap of hair close and tight, longer in the front and dipping over one eye,

I look sophisticated in a completely different way. And somehow lighter.

"I can see it now." Stil frames her hands as if around a movie Mylar. "The haircut that everyone's asking for: the Sofie."

"Uh-huh, okay." I stand and brush excess hair from my shoulders. "We can discuss the cultural impact of my hair later. She'll be here any minute, right?"

"I think you'll have just enough time to eat whatever that man of yours has smelling so good." Stil glances at the text message from Geena. "They're about twenty minutes away."

I nod, smearing on a little lipstick and sliding studs into my earlobes.

"So he's the one, huh?" Stil asks softly, meeting my eyes in the mirror.

I can't stop the smile that splits my expression open. Even with this development, this possible breakthrough in the case against Kyle. Even with the memory of yesterday still lingering, nothing distracts me from the fact that Trevor loves me back.

"Yeah, he's the one."

Later, he sits beside me on the couch, holding my hand, eyes set on the young woman seated across from us. She can't be much older than I was when Kyle raped me. Twenty? Twenty-one? I squeeze Trevor's hand tighter, the memory of the broken girl I was after that night rising up to mock my confidence.

Geena's taking her turn grilling Tanya. Next will be my lawyer, Connor. Then I'm sure Karen will have questions of her own. Everyone wants to get this right, to not squander this chance that has dropped into our laps. The chance to bring Kyle Manchester down once and for all.

"So you volunteer with Manchester's campaign?" Geena probes from beside the young woman, Tanya.

"Yes," she says softly, not looking up from the flats on her feet. "I signed up about a month ago."

She gives her head a quick shake, running a nervous hand through her light brown hair.

"I believed in him. I thought he was...I thought he was the real deal, but he wasn't. He's not."

"What happened?" Geena flicks her eyes from Tanya to me.

"One night he asked me to stay back to help him with some demographic projections." Tanya swallows, closing her eyes. "I thought it would be the whole team, but it was just us in his office. He kept touching me and trying to kiss me. When I finally told him no and that I didn't think it was appropriate, he lost it."

She draws a ragged breath across her lips.

"He...he raped me."

"I hate to be indelicate," I speak for the first time since we greeted each other. "But he raped me, too. He raped Shaunti Miller, but neither of us has any proof. Do you have any...well, were you examined after the attack? Or do you have proof?"

"I wasn't examined," she says, making my heart sink. "But I did take pictures."

My head jerks up.

"You took pictures? You have proof?" I grip Trevor's hand probably to the point of breaking.

"I thought no one would believe me." She bites her bottom lip before glancing up at me. "I saw that they didn't believe you. Not only do I have pictures, but I have a check."

"A check?" Geena asks, voice eager and curious. "For what?"

"His campaign manager gave me hush money." The cynical laugh doesn't fit anything about Tanya. "He actually thought he could buy me off. I wasn't sure what to do, so I just let him think it was cool. That it would just go away."

She looks at me, her head tilted.

"Until yesterday, when I saw that press conference, Ms. Baston," she says. "Did you mean it when you said you'd stand with anyone who came forward?"

I can barely breathe. Finally a break in the clouds. A chance. Our best chance to discredit Kyle. My best chance to get my life back and move on with Trevor.

"I did mean it." I steel my voice against the tears that would make it waver. "And I'm ready when you are."

CHAPTER THIRTY-SEVEN

Trevor

I place the flat black jewelry box on Sofie's pillow. Then I move it to the center of the bed. Then to the foot. I'm just about to find some other conspicuous spot on the bed when she walks in, pulling up short when she sees the box in my hand. She walks over to me, hand outstretched, palm up.

"Mine, I presume?"

Her eager smile chases away some of her fatigue. The last few weeks have been tough, but worth it. When Tanya's allegations came out, she not only toppled Kyle's chance for a successful senatorial bid, but also Ernest's hopes of getting the Bennett board to vote against Walsh. The criminal charges filed against Kyle and his arrest have rendered him completely useless in Ernest's pursuit to lead Bennett. Without the political favors as a bargaining chip, board members fell in line with Martin's wishes and original intention to pass the reins to Walsh. I can finally taste my future with Sofie. So sweet.

"Yes, it's for you." I stretch my arm up over my head, putting it out of her reach. "But you have to sit down first. I have this whole thing worked out."

"You have a thing?" She sits on the edge of the bed, head tilted and eyes glued to the black box. "Well, do your thing, Mr. Bishop."

I squat down in front of her, placing the jewelry box on the floor and taking her hands in mine. My heart sprints in my chest. It feels like I have a plastic bag over my head every time I try to breathe. My fucking fingers are actually shaking a little. But I'm doing this.

She's the most beautiful girl I've ever seen. Sometimes she smiles, and my heart stops in my chest, awed by it. It seems to me that the more she learns about herself, about who she is beneath the beauty the world can't get past, the more beautiful she becomes. Her beauty isn't a flimsy thing, but it's girded by character and strength.

I've never wanted anything as badly as I want her for myself.

"Sofie, have you ever wondered what would have happened if we'd met at Princeton?"

Her eyes fly to my face, wide, somehow surprised.

"Um, yeah." She drops her eyes to the hands in her lap. "I've thought about it a few times. I wish we had."

"I'm kind of glad we didn't." I smile when she shoots me an uncertain glance. "What I mean is that I know it would have been wrong then. I needed all these years to become the man who could handle you. You needed that time to experience the hard things, the things that made you strong. Frankly, beautiful or not, I wouldn't have looked twice at you then. I was too young to see beyond my assumptions to your potential. We found each other when we were supposed to."

And I have no plans of ever letting go.

I pick up the jewelry box. She clasps her hands together, grinning and tugging at her bottom lip with her teeth. She takes the box and stares at it for a moment.

"What is it?"

"I think that's why people open gifts, Sof."

She rolls her eyes, mouth tilting to the side as she carefully lifts the lid, her eyes lighting up when she sees what's embedded in the plane of dark velvet.

It's a seed. It's been in my suitcase ever since I got back from my last trip. I wasn't sure when...or how...or why I wanted to give this to her, but now I know.

"Do you remember the Ugandan proverb?" I curve one palm around her face, tilting it up so I can see her eyes. "From my office?"

"Sow seeds." She caresses the small seed with one finger. "Wait and see what comes with the rain."

"The seed, everything you see on the outside, is a hard coat. A protective shell." I trail my finger over her hand holding the jewelry box. "The plant is under the shell and has to be awakened, and all of what we see on the outside has to fall away."

She nods, her eyes locked with mine. Her expression intent, absorbed.

"Over the last few weeks, I've gotten to see you in this process." I grab the hand resting in her lap, twisting my fingers around hers so she can't ever let go.

"You've discarded the trappings, the outside, and have awakened the part of you that is really alive. Germination is a kind of death, and it's painful." I pull her close enough to kiss her lips, but I don't allow myself that just yet. "You've experienced that pain, and you've had a lot of rain fall in your life. And now we see what has come after the rain."

I trace one high cheekbone with my thumb.

"I want you to know it's beautiful to me. Your passion, your courage and strength, all while being absolutely, unequivocally yourself. Flaws and all." I pause, staring at our clasped hands for a moment. "I don't know that we would have seen all of that without the pain. Without the rain."

Tears cling to her lashes, falling as she blinks.

"You've been with me through all the rain, Bishop." She raises her eyes to my face. "Most wouldn't have stood with me when there were no guarantees that I'd win against Kyle."

But she will. Now with her story, and the undeniable proof Tanya has provided, Kyle arrested and awaiting trial, she will. Even if that wasn't assured, I wouldn't want to wait.

"Sofie, I know there are still things that have to happen." Something that's half a grimace, half a grin shapes my mouth. "But let's not wait."

Sofie's brows knit over the confusion of her eyes.

"Wait for what? What do you mean?"

"You remember I told you how my father felt about my mom? That it was urgent?" I wait for her to nod before pressing forward. "That's how I feel about you. About us. I wanted to take everything slow, Sof, and we did, but I'm past slow. It's *urgent* to me that you know today what I want."

Her lashes lift, and I see the question forming in her eyes. Before it can make it to her lips, I carefully remove the seed from its velvet bed, and open her palm.

"I know it's unconventional." My voice almost fails me as those green eyes, clear as glass, blink back at me. "And I promise I'll get you an actual ring, but this felt right to me. Today. Right now. I have to ask you this."

"Bishop, what—"

"Will you marry me?"

All the air swooshes from her chest, through her mouth. Her eyes widen and her mouth falls open and then snaps closed.

"Bishop, I—"

"Say yes." I lean forward, caressing the skin behind her neck. "I don't want to wait for the smoke to clear or for everything to make sense. I have to know today that you'll be mine forever, Sof."

"This business with Kyle still has—"

"No bearing on whether or not you love me. On if we'll spend the rest of our lives together."

"There's still such a cloud hanging over me, though," she whispers.

I lift her chin, swiping my thumb over the tear streaking down her cheek.

"There's no cloud," I tell her, cupping her chin. "Not between you and me. The world can go to hell. Remember I told you once that you should follow the fire, find out what burns inside you and let it guide you?"

She lays her forehead against mine, nodding, one hand slipping behind my neck, fingers sliding in my hair.

"You, Sofie Baston, are my fire." My voice withers for a second, simply failing with the emotion of the truth. I swallow, determined to say these words. "What I feel for you guides me. Guided me right to you. To this moment. Forget the rest of the world."

I lean in to kiss her, melding our mouths, licking into her sweet heat.

"I've never seen anything more beautiful than you, Sofie." I punctuate the words with kisses. "Your strength, your courage, your conviction. Don't ever think you're not good enough for me. I only hope I can be good enough for *you* because you, darlin', are damn magnificent."

"Bishop, I—"

"Say yes," I mumble against her lips. "Baby, say yes."

She pulls back just enough to search my face, to probe my eyes, which I know reflect how absolutely sure I am about this. A smile starts in her eyes and works its way to her mouth. She closes her fingers over the seed tightly, protecting it in her palm. I hold my breath, waiting for her to give voice to what I see in her eyes. Waiting for her to seal what we feel right now into forever.

"Yes."

Epilogue

Sofie

Hey, Sofie! Could I get a picture?"

I turn in the direction of the request, shielding my eyes with one hand against the Hawaiian sun. It's not a reporter or a photographer. Just a woman approaching me, Kindle in one hand, phone in the other. Her kids build sand castles behind her, visors on their heads.

"Could I get a picture with you?" she repeats, smiling at me widely, genuinely. "I live on your site. Love all the Haven stuff."

I hesitate, shifting the weight of what I'm holding on my hip. I'm pretty wary of pictures these days. I've had enough of the limelight. Not that I'm completely out, but I haven't walked a runway in years. People don't stop me on the street as much. I still have a few endorsements, but I've deliberately shrunk the circle of light I stand in.

"This bathing suit is actually Haven," the woman continues, setting her Kindle on the sand.

I look a little more closely and recognize the suit from last season's Haven swimwear line.

"It looks great on you." I smile back, still not sure about the picture.

"Well, I do Jalene's videos on the site every morning," she says. "Even had the hubs install a barre in the basement."

"That's awesome. Well, I can tell it's paying off."

Her eyes catch something over my shoulder, admiration widening her smile even more.

"Isn't that your husband?"

I twist to look over my shoulder, my heart still leavening in my chest at the sight of Trevor after five years. Those damn butterflies are here to stay, apparently, because they still flap madly when he smiles at me like that, like I'm the appetizer, main course, and dessert all wrapped in one bite.

"Yep, that's him," I say absently, distracted by the cling of his wet suit molding the bulge of his arms, the muscles in his legs, the width of his chest.

He lopes toward us, water running from his hair and down his face. He reaches for the towel on the lounge chair where I've stowed our things.

"Hi, there," he says to the lady ogling him. I'm not sure if it's all the dripping wet, ginger-topped eye candy making her cheeks flame, or that hot, sticky-sweet Southern drawl of his. Both get me every time, so I can't blame her.

"Hi," she says a little breathily.

"Hey, baby," he says to me, tossing the towel down, palming my cheek and pressing his cold lips to mine. "I didn't know you were coming out."

"We wanted to see if you hit your target time."

His dark eyes light up and he relieves me of the weight on my hip.

"Gracie!" He lifts our daughter, Grace, up in the air and gives her a gentle shake. "Did you see Daddy in the water?"

Predictably, she giggles, compelling him to do it again, her green eyes bright in her chubby face under the bright red curls.

"Did you see Daddy in the water?" he asks again, pressing her a few inches higher in the air before bringing her down to kiss her little slobbery lips.

I glance from my husband back to the lady wearing the Haven swimsuit. I should offer to replace her ovaries since they probably just exploded. This big man so completely at the mercy of our daughter would explode my ovaries if I wasn't getting so much use out of them lately.

"You wanted a picture, you said?" I remind her wryly.

"Oh, yes." She blinks and smiles, shifting her eyes away from Trevor cooing to Grace.

"Go on, Sof," Trevor says, a touch of warning in his eyes when they meet mine. "I've got the baby."

His not-so-subtle way of making sure I'm not considering splattering our daughter all over Instagram. We turned down offers from *People* and several other magazines when both of the kids were born. They even offered to make a donation to one of our favorite charities in exchange for the pictures. Trevor wasn't having it. He's fiercely protective of Grace and our son, Carter. He's pretty protective of our privacy in general, but especially when it comes to the kids.

I wrap an arm around the woman's shoulder while she snaps a selfie and promises to tag me.

Gee, thanks.

Once she's walking off back toward her kids, still playing in the sand, I turn to face Trevor, who has—*have mercy*—peeled the top of his wet suit down so it flops over, baring the sculpted muscles of his chest and abs. With a house full of family, my libido is in overdrive because we aren't screwing nearly enough to satisfy me. I step close, sandwiching Grace between our hearts, reaching up to tangle my fingers in his wet hair.

"How was your swim?" I hope I'm working him up as much as he is me so we can have clandestine sex in a pantry or something later. "How're you doing on time?"

"Not bad for an old man." He chuckles, the subtle laugh lines at his eyes deepening. It *is* laughable to think of Trevor as an "old man," because at forty, my husband remains quite the specimen. Thus me hot and horny in the Hawaiian sun.

"You back on target?" I ask, knowing he's been trying to shave a minute off his swim time.

"I will be by the next race. I got a few months." Trevor shakes his head, sighing. "Things have been so busy it's thrown my training off."

"Busy, but going so well," I remind him, proud of all the global progress the Collective has made since Trevor sold Deutimus to Bennett and took the reins five years ago.

"Sorry I was on that call so late last night. I had no idea the issues were that complex."

"It's okay, but I *did* miss you. I like to fall asleep in your arms, if you hadn't noticed," I say huskily, leaning in to pull his bottom lip between mine.

The arm that's not holding Grace slips around my waist, dragging me closer.

"I love my family," he says against my lips. "But maybe we should have realized how little privacy we'd have bringing *all* of them to Maui with us."

"It's okay." My tongue darts between his lips for a quick taste of him. "Carter climbing in bed with us the last couple of nights is what's been the real cock blocker."

"I hated thunderstorms growing up, too." He squints up at the sky. "I think we should be fine tonight if the weather holds. Where *is* Carter?"

"Back at the house with your mom." I laugh. "It seems like all the girls are cooking something, and all the guys are watching ESPN."

"Sounds about right." His chuckle fades away, concern in the eyes assessing me.

"Are you still feeling up to the trip?" Trevor takes my hand and starts walking us back toward the rented beachside villa housing the whole Bishop clan while we're on vacation.

"Are you kidding me?" I laugh and tweak one of Grace's curls. "That trip to London is my best shot at getting laid."

"Truth. At this rate we might have to mile high it." He doesn't crack a smile, and I hope he's serious. Some of my favorite orgasms have been at thirty thousand feet. "And what about you? How's the morning sickness?"

"Not too bad."

I have to laugh when I think of that afternoon I spent with Kerris years ago, marveling at her having three kids in as many years. Here I am pregnant with my third in five years, and I can't even blame it on twins. Walsh and Kerris stopped at three, so far. The demands of running Bennett Enterprises have been greater than even Walsh could have anticipated, especially with my father's departure.

After more than thirty years as partners in corporate raiding,

Daddy and Martin Bennett parted ways. Daddy decided to leave rather than serve under Walsh. Last I heard he was consulting for some of the most powerful CEOs in the international business community. We Bastons always land on our feet.

Only I'm not a Baston anymore. I'm a Bishop. Trevor's huge family truly embraced me unreservedly, making me feel finally like I have a family, not just a lineage. His Sunday school–teaching mother never once made me feel like a sinner. She made me feel like the girl her son loves the way her husband loves her. Trevor's capacity to love in spite of flaws, to love without condemnation—I know where he got that now. It wasn't just red hair his mother passed on. She showed me a mother's love, something I realized I'd been missing my whole life, and it filled a lot of the holes my own mother left.

The public wasn't as easy to convince. Bets were laid about how long Trevor and I would last before I cheated on him, dumped him, humiliated him. Occasionally some reporter will still refer to my "wild days" or call me a "reformed bad girl." Trevor was right about those labels people slapped on my back. Ultimately, they don't matter. Thank God Trevor peeled back the persona to find the person underneath. Trevor has never cared what they say, and now neither do I.

I slow my steps to match his as we get closer to the house, both of us enjoying even this sliver of time alone without kids everywhere we turn. Much as we love his family, our time alone fuels us both. I can tell he misses the little quiet piece of the world we carve out for our young family as much as I do. After living out loud for so long, it feels good to live just above a whisper.

"Carter's loving the chance to hang with all his cousins." I stop a few yards shy of the villa entrance, taking in Trevor holding our one-year-old in his powerful arms.

"You still feel good about leaving him and Grace with my mom for a few days while we're in London?" Trevor searches my face, pushing back the hair I keep bobbed just above my shoulders.

"If there's anyone we can trust them with it's your mother, and all those sisters of yours." I shrug. "Besides it's just for a few days. We'll pop over for Halima's event and come right back. The kids won't even have time to miss us. Grace stopped feeding just in time."

I lean into my daughter, pressing my forehead to hers.

"Didn't you girl? Just in time for Mommy to go away. You're gonna be a good girl for Grammy, aren't you?"

She answers with a bubble and a tiny-toothed grin.

"Can you believe we're having another baby?" Trevor's mouth crooks with a satisfied smile.

I just roll my eyes and shake my head. Number three was not planned. I'm in the middle of launching the Haven Home line and planning a Paris fashion show to benefit all the charities Haven's proceeds support. I'd planned to wait until the dust settled some, but my body had other ideas.

I glance down at my brief shorts and tight tank top.

"I just got my body back, besides a few stretch marks, and now it's time to give it up again."

"You only get better and better." He tips my chin up, eyes growing warmer. "Inside and out."

I lean into him, pausing when the front door opens, his mother standing there holding Carter's hand. He runs out to us, throwing his arms around Trevor's knees.

"Someone's been asking for you, Daddy," Mama Bishop says, smiling before she slips back into the house, allowing us a few more minutes alone.

"Daddy," Carter whispers, dark eyes trained adoringly on his father, little arms stretched over his head. "Will you pick me up?"

Trevor holds Grace in one arm, Carter in the other. Carter immediately burrows into his father's neck.

How the two of us created a shy child, I'll never know, but Carter's personality is so completely different from either of ours. Besides Trevor's dark eyes, he's the spitting image of me at four years old, his hair Nordic blond. Sometimes I look at him and see my father's features so clearly, it makes my heart ache a little, though less and less as the years go on.

I try not to let it bother me that my parents still want so little to do with me. Even if they wanted more of a relationship with me, Trevor doesn't want them anywhere near our kids. Anywhere near our lives. I ran into my parents at a recent fund-raiser for one of Haven's charitable organizations. The air iced over between us, neither acknowledging me. For just a moment, I wanted to drop the social mores, ignore all the watching eyes and ask them if they ever loved me, if they ever believed in me. Or had even one proud moment? But I didn't because I'm afraid I already know the answer, and I can't let it matter to me anymore.

Trevor somehow manages to gather me into their little circle, pulling me close even with two children wriggling in his arms.

"Thank you for these little blessings." His eyes are suddenly serious, and I get it. I think about our life sometimes and am absolutely humbled by how good it is. Not the money or the things or the fame I still have despite my efforts to shake it, but each other. Our children. The chance to do good for the things we're passionate about. Mostly thankful for each other.

"I think we kinda made those blessings together," I say lightly, trying to lighten the moment. "This whole life we made together."

"And none of it works without you, Sof." His eyes burn on me, heating my cheeks in that way only he ever manages. "Nothing works without you. You're my fire. You know that, right?"

I can't speak for the tears clogging my throat as his words sink in. I absorb them, letting them water all the spots left dry by doubt and condemnation. All the places barren from years of shame and inadequacy. For a moment, I'm so grateful I finally proved that I'm good enough. Trevor stares at me so long, so hard, his love is unavoidable, a tangible thing that wraps around me as surely as his strong arms. I think, in some ways, he's seen me, he's loved me, almost from the beginning, and I never had anything to prove to him at all.

Maybe everything I had to prove was to myself.

Acknowledgments

I have to thank all the amazing authors who have been alongside me. Your wisdom, kindness and generosity have proven invaluable since I began my journey as a published author, and I don't see that changing any time soon. There are too many bloggers for me to name because I know I'll leave someone out, but for everyone who has been reading and reviewing and chatting and shouting, thank you. I can't imagine this path without you.

I have to thank my boys—my husband and son—who go without more home-cooked meals than they should, who watch dishes pile up around deadlines, and lose a huge chunk of me to my imagination when I'm writing. I love you so much. You're the center.

About the Author

A RITA and Audie Award winner, *USA Today* bestselling author **Kennedy Ryan** writes for women from all walks of life, empowering them and placing them firmly at the center of each story and in charge of their own destinies. Her heroes respect, cherish, and lose their minds for the women who capture their hearts. Kennedy and her writings have been featured in Chicken Soup for the Soul, *USA Today*, Entertainment Weekly, Glamour, *Cosmopolitan*, *Time*, *O Magazine*, and many others. She is a wife to her lifetime lover and mother to an extraordinary son.

You can learn more at:
kennedyryanwrites.com
TikTok: kennedyryanauthor
X: @kennedyrwrites
Instagram: @kennedyryan1
Facebook: facebook.com/KennedyRyanAuthor

GRAND CENTRAL

Your next great read is only a click away.

 GrandCentralPublishing.com

 Read-Forever.com

 TwelveBooks.com

 LegacyLitBooks.com

 GCP-Balance.com

A BOOK FOR EVERY READER.